Black Dogs

Part One : The House of Diamond

By Ursula Vernon

SOFAWOLF PRESS, INC.

SAINT PAUL, MN

Second trade paperback edition: January 2011

Third printing: July 2021

Published by: Sofawolf Press
                  PO Box 11868
                  Saint Paul MN 55111-0868
                  www.sofawolf.com

ISBN: 978-1-936689-02-6

Printed in the United States of America

Contents

THE AUTHOR APOLOGIZES

The book you have in front of you is one half of a very, very long novel I wrote many years ago. It was my first novel, and as such, I am both very proud of it and desperately embarrassed by it.

I'm told this is normal.

Since writing *Black Dogs*, I have gone on to write a fair number of other books—at last count, including comic collections, I have either written or am under contract to write fourteen books by the end of 2012 or so—and I have done it often enough that I am starting to get over the urge to apologize whenever I see anyone with a copy of one of my books in their hands. But I still feel a twinge about *Black Dogs*.

It's not that I think it's a bad book. Actually, it's better than it has any right to be, granted that I started it when I was sixteen and knew about as much about life as a small, sheltered turnip. My younger self was surprisingly clear-eyed and unsentimental about some things, and I am grateful for that, because it made my job as adult re-writer much easier, and she fearlessly tackled a number of things that adult me would probably know better than to try.

But nevertheless, I wrote it when I was very young, and it was the book that taught me all the ways that you can fail to do justice to a book you're writing—all the chunks that you thought you'd fit in, that cool image, that one clever subplot, but you didn't find a place for them, and suddenly you're at the end of the book and you realize you'll never find a place to put it, and now you have to go back and rip out the foreshadowing, assuming you remember where you put it.

This is a hard lesson for a writer to learn, but the alternative is to put out meandering 900-page doorstops that take ten years to write.

This was also the book where I learned how important an editor is. Sadrao's eye-color changed no less than seven times in the first draft, a fact which I blush to recall. And when it came time to edit Book Two, nearly a decade after I wrote it, I did an initial read-through and wanted to track down my younger self and scream "You cannot plug a plot-hole with adjectives!"

Sigh.

So I still feel the urge to apologize for this book. And I'm going to try and get it out of my system right now. Here goes—

I'm sorry, god, I'm sorry, are you sure you wouldn't like to put this down and read something else? (Preferably from the same publisher, so they won't lose money on the deal.)

Black Dogs

Part One : The House of Diamond

When he comes to the river, he waits until nightfall, then swims across.

Prologue

The dog-soldier is hunting.

He has been walking for a long time now, alone in the woods, and the trappings of civilization, one by one, have begun to fall away. He still wears the clothing of men, still carries the heavy curved sword across his back, but the niceties of conscious thought have faded far back into his mind and instinct rules his actions. His last meal he ate raw, barely bothering to clean it.

The dog-soldier is traveling.

He came across the plains to the south, a broad rolling sward. They are not the desert savannah he grew up on, but they are enough alike to bring back old memories. The scent of the first spring rush of grass, crushed beneath his clawed feet, is as heady as a drug.

He crosses into the forest, avoiding other travelers. He is not ready, yet, to rejoin the haunts of men, to take up the responsibilities he knows await him among humankind. He is looking for something, and though he does not frame the thought so clearly, he trusts that he will know it when he finds it.

The dog-soldier is searching.

When he comes to the river and the human settlements around it, he waits until nightfall, then swims across. The water is cold from snow-melt far up in the mountains, and the spring air still holds a chill of winter. The dog-soldier shakes water from his fur. Although he is cold, he does not think of building a fire.

Instead, he continues walking. The wind leads him east, and he follows.

Chapter One

The world was green and grey, balanced on a serrated knife of pine and madrone, stretching as far as the eye could see. The sky above lay gingerly across the sharp-edged trees, like a woman on a bed of nails. The forest below dripped with moisture, the wet green of spring standing out against the darkness of the conifers. On the other side of the hill black smoke faded slowly as the rain put out its source.

Under the sodden canopy, a girl limped downhill.

She was neither particularly tall nor particularly short, her body slender and unmuscular, a thin smoothing of baby fat gentling the hard lines of bone. She was somewhere between sixteen and twenty, wrapped in stained wool and stiffened leather. Her hair, matted down with dried blood, shone dull red-brown across her shoulders, stiff and stained against her scalp. A bandage was wrapped around her left forearm, and blood had blossomed through it in a long brown line.

There were pain lines etched around her eyes that had not been there a day ago. Her lips were thin, and eyes that might have been green or grey were dark holes in her face. Pale skin, slicked with sweat, drew tight across high cheekbones and stubborn chin.

She stank of soot and blood and fear. A hunting dog could have trailed her for miles. She had tried, at first, to leave no trail, but had long since given up and now crashed through the brush like an injured deer.

Take a step. One foot in front of the other. Bodies were an amazing thing, really, to walk with such assurance when the mind was incapable of direction. *Take another step.* The long knife at her belt banged awkwardly against her thigh. Wet leaves, half-decayed from last season, slid under the soles of her boots. Her body adjusted automatically, balancing on the other foot, taking another step. She would have found that fascinating, if she had had the energy to spare.

A rock loomed ahead of her, a massive outcropping crusted in orange and green. She half-leaned, half-fell against it. *Breathe. Slow. Deep. In. Out. In.* She closed her eyes. She could hear the drip of water through the pine needles. The ground was drinking the rain with thirsty rustling sounds. A crow cawed from somewhere nearby, the sound harsh and almost tangible in the quiet.

When she opened her eyes again, her shoulder had begun to ache with the cold of the wet stone and her arm throbbed. She pushed away. The forest swam before her eyes for a moment. She felt faint. Blood loss, or hunger, or exhaustion. She went on. She had no choice.

One foot in front of the other.

Lyra. My name is Lyra. I am the daughter of the House of Volfrieds.

She found the stream almost by accident, certainly not through any conscious direction. She had been angling away from the river on the other side of the hill—and, not coincidentally, the main roads that followed it. A tributary of the river snaked down this valley and curved around the hill to the south before joining up to the main waterway. She'd forgotten about the stream.

It was too small to have a formal name and probably wasn't on most maps. As a child, Lyra and her cousins had called it simply "the rill," and spent long summer afternoons falling, or being pushed, into it. Even an unathletic young woman could have crossed without getting wet above the knee. Two days ago she would have waded in without hesitation.

Now, the chill of the water made her shiver uncontrollably. She stared at it with dull eyes. Her feet couldn't get much colder, but still...

She wrapped her good arm around herself, nose wrinkling at the stench of wet, sweat-soaked wool. Her injured arm hung stiffly at her side. Still shivering, she knelt and drank a little, shuddering with cold. The water made a ball of ice in her stomach, but she felt a little stronger.

Lyra. My name is Lyra.

A rock loomed ahead of her. She half-leaned, half-fell against it.

Great, she thought bitterly, *I'll be sure to tell the bandits that. Perhaps they'll write it on my gravestone.*

She rose, swinging her arms and stamping her feet. She would cross in the morning. Tonight she needed a fire.

Lyra opened the pouch at her belt. In it was a flint firestarter, a ring, and a half-handful of coins. No food. The raiders were thorough, but not quite thorough enough. They had overlooked a linen closet, and its lone, terrified occupant.

She shoved the memory back before it could wake the prickle of tears. She had no time. It was already growing dark.

Starting a fire with wet wood was brutally hard. Her head throbbed, and twilight was already pooling under the trees as she scrounged for kindling. She was shivering in the cold, hard enough to make her hands unsteady, so she generally had to reach for a stick two or three times before her fingers actually closed on it.

Her firestarter was a simple enough device of Slothan make, a case holding a small wheel of pyrite that, when flicked, struck a piece of flint and caused a spark to jump. She was terrified that it might break—they were notoriously fragile—and she had to flick it a half-dozen times before a spark finally flashed onto a piece of tinder and took hold.

Breaking the branches into chunks small enough to burn nearly defeated her. Her sole other possession was her knife. It was sixteen inches long, forged iron, the blade a long curving river of lines left from folding the metal in the fire. It was the honor knife of her family. It was more than five centuries old, and she rather doubted that in that five centuries it had ever been used to chop wood, but it served.

Lyra breathed an apology to the spirit of the blade. She had never believed particularly strongly in the honor of her clan—her father had sired far too many bastards, and she'd seen the underhanded dealings in the account books—but it never hurt to be certain.

"Poor thing," Lyra muttered, more for the sound of her own voice that anything else. "We've both come down in the world." She braced the wood between her knee and a large rock, her left arm hanging limp and useless at her side. The wood splintered rottenly as she chopped at it.

She hacked apart the last chunk of wood and examined the blade anxiously. It seemed unmarked, and she let out a sigh of relief she hadn't known she was holding.

Her camp, such as it was, was half under a fallen tree. The forest giant had fallen sideways into its neighbor, forming a small hollow underneath the trunk. She huddled in the cave-like space, cloak pulled tight around her shoulders, while the tiny fire smoked and crackled and slowly grew warm. The rotted wood around her was damp and punky, and fell away in chips under her back. Dank scents of decay and the acrid, smoking fire stung the lining of her nose and left her eyes red and watering. Mousetail ferns draped long threads over the decayed trunk, tickling at her back. She ignored them. She tried not to think about termites, or crawly things with too many legs.

She was cold and hungry, but she was alive.

Before exhaustion-mazed eyes the fire swam, became the flicker of torchlight in the great hall. Lyra stood at one of the side doors, pushed it open with one hand, the grey stone expanse of the hall before her. She had been planning an excuse for being late to dinner. The torches danced and flickered in the draft of the opening door.

She had just finished Asylyn's *History of Western Clans* and was wondering if she could wrangle another book out of her father so soon. Being late to dinner was not a particularly good start, but if she said she had been reading—rather than daydreaming— she might stand a better chance. Through the gap in the door she could see the head of the table—her father wasn't there, for some reason, perhaps he was late too—

The sound of metal clanging together came from farther down the hall. One of the servants had probably dropped a platter. The sound of voices and rowdy diners was even louder than usual today, a riot of shouting and thumping of feet.

There was something on the floor a few feet away from where she stood in the doorway. It was moving along the floor with a liquid motion, and finding a crack in the flagstones it spread out in crimson threads.

She did not realize that it was blood until a human hand, outflung, landed in it, the fingers spasming in the last throes of death.

Moving automatically, unthinking, she shoved the door open and leaned out, into hell.

There was blood everywhere, enough to prove that the minstrel songs of fields awash in blood were no mere exaggeration, and rough-clad men in leather were butchering the unarmed diners of the hall. Her eyes skittered about the room and fixed in fascinated horror on the sight of a man, a foot of steel emerging from his back, his murderer's hand on his shoulder as the blade pulled loose—

She noticed, with absurd clarity, that the blood was almost exactly the same shade as the red silk shirt he was wearing, turning darker where the cloth adhered to his body.

Then he fell, half-turning toward her, and she saw it was her father, lord of the house, and the man standing over him, wiping blood from his face, sword dripping, her half-brother Jasen—

No.

Surely not.

She didn't stay to find out. Instead, animal instinct took her, cowardice working where courage had failed, and she ran like a rabbit down the corridor, from the hall. A man loomed before her, tall and dark in leather armor, silhouetted against the flicker of firelight from the kitchen behind him. Terror fired through her nerves in an icy prickle and she lunged to one side. Her mind was blank with the pureness of terror.

He roared something at her. She could no more understand his words than she could have flown. She ran, practically under his arms, and down the hall.

His sword flashed at her. She threw up an arm in pure reflex.

Something hit her forearm with a shock of impact. Her arm went numb to the elbow. It didn't hurt at all. Lyra lifted her eyes in stark terror to the man's face. His teeth were bared like an animal's. She pulled away.

For one sickening moment, she felt metal dragging through her flesh. It still didn't hurt. She bolted. Walls and doorways loomed in front of her and slewed away as she ran through the corridors. She didn't look back. If the brigand had given chase, she lost him in the corridors.

Unerring instinct drew her from the kitchens and habitable areas to the storage rooms, to a linen closet where one might lie if one were small and pulled one's knees tight against one's chest and tried not to breathe. She flung the door open, arm tight against her body. It still didn't hurt, but there was a queasy throbbing beginning, not at all what she would have expected. She bundled her arm under her shirt. Blood welled hot and sticky against her breasts.

It was a tight fit. Her legs cramped under her almost at once, and her arm was beginning to throb in earnest. She clenched her teeth to keep from whimpering. It hurt. Her body lost any sense of distinction and became a seamless ache from head to toe. Her bladder was full.

The only thing to retain any sense of individuality was the slash on her arm. It pounded in time to her heartbeat, a bright throb of pain wedged between her knees and chest. Lyra ripped her undershift free with her good hand and tried to wrap her arm. The pain was incredible. She kept having to stop and press her forehead against the cool wooden panels of the linen closet.

Oh god it hurts, ithurtsithurtsithurts.

She concentrated on breathing through her mouth, soundlessly, on not weeping.

Twice she heard the raiders, once in the very room. She closed her eyes and bit her lip. Footsteps thumped, furniture crashed to the floor. If they opened the door, they would kill her at once and she would die with her eyes closed, cowering. She was ashamed of her fear. It was no way for a daughter of a noble house to die, but still, she kept her eyes closed.

Please, goddess, don't let me have bled on the floor, something they can track. Oh, please, don't let them find me.

Oh, god, please...

Chapter Two

The dog-soldier is tracking.

He has been following a scent since midday, the scent of an injured human, the iron tang of blood and the oozing sweat of fear. His ancestors could track a wounded deer across half a continent, through jungle and savannah, tireless as death. His senses are not so acute as those ancient brindled hunting dogs, but it is a fresh scent and he follows it with ease. Occasionally he pauses to put his nose to the ground, dropping to his hands and knees and breathing deeply.

The dog-soldier remembers.

The smell of a wounded human awakes old instincts in him, desires to protect those in need. He was bred to be the ultimate guardian, protector and defender, loyal beyond price. He is all of that and more, but sometimes, divorced from civilization, the old ways come back, and he sinks into the old animal dream again. He has been walking for hours now, as he has been walking for days before this, the words of human speech distant to him. When the trail he follows crosses another one, the scent of other humans mixed with leather and steel, he goes down to one knee and studies it for a time.

Then he stands and begins to run.

⸙

They did not find her.

A day after she stumbled into the linen closet, weak and shaking, Lyra shoved the door open and half-crawled, half-fell into the room. Her muscles were so cramped that she couldn't walk. She crawled on hands and knees, sobs catching in her throat, making a painful "uhhn, uhhn" sound under her breath.

There was a bucket of water in the kitchen. She dunked her whole face in it, laved water onto her arm, washing it tentatively. She knew that she should clean out the dark, crusting blood at the heart of the wound, but the touch brought pain, and sluggish blood. The bleeding had stopped.

I should clean it. Dress it. Dressing a wound was something they always mentioned in books, but she had never read any with exact instructions. How did you dress it? What did you dress it with?

She had a brief, absurd image of her arm wearing one of those little pink doll dresses that her late Aunt Marrow had given her every year since she was five. Hysteria caught her by the throat and she began giggling uncontrollably.

When she came to herself, she was crouching on the cool tiles, head between her knees, weeping. She stopped. Her throat was swollen and tight.

Okay, I have no idea how to take care of this. I should probably clean it, but it hurts so bad...

She wrapped it, instead, in torn strips of her shift. Her underclothes were better material, but she had not been able to hold her bladder for an entire day. Despite the nausea the pain and smell evoked, her stomach growled.

The raiders had gotten most of the food, but she found a half-loaf of crusty black bread forgotten in one of the back cupboards. She tore into it ravenously.

It was stale and hard enough to cut her gums. She had to go back to the water bucket and soak the crust, but she ate it all.

Lyra tried to crawl to her feet then. Leaning on the wall, she stood, swaying, light-headed. There were bodies in the doorway, mouths and eyes open, crawling with black, bloated flies. She left them. She could never bury or burn them all. She had to get away.

She made her way, slow and shaky, to the Great Hall. A single step through the door and the stench struck her like a blow. Her father lay in a pool of flies and dark, tacky blood.

Lyra went down to her knees and retched, weakly. Her hasty meal came back up. She vomited until there was nothing in her stomach, but the taste of bile flooded her mouth and she shuddered convulsively at the stickiness of the flagstones under her fingers.

She averted her eyes, gritted her teeth, and removed the knife from her father's belt. Jasen had not taken it. No. She shook her head again. It could not have been Jasen. She had been mistaken. Shaking, lips coated in acid, she looked for the signet ring set in dark malachite that should have been on her father's swollen finger. It was gone. Of course. It was too obviously valuable for a raider to leave it. She rose, weaving an unsteady course to the relatively cleaner air of the corridor, and leaned against the wall, breathing in great, ragged gasps that turned to sobs, and then to fear, then to dry heaves again.

Her father was dead. She crawled away from the hall, sobbing. He would not buy her any more books, then hide them and surprise her with one at dinner. He was dead.

They were all dead.

She found herself in the kitchen again, a long time later, her eyes red and sore with weeping. She finished the last inch of water in the bucket and stared dry-eyed at the floor.

They might come back. Jasen would come back (but surely it had not been Jasen?) to the house. She had to get away.

She went to her room.

They had butchered her maid, Giselle. Fifteen years old, more beautiful than Lyra would ever be, her fine-boned features gone slack in death. Lyra stepped over the pitiful body in the hallway, took two mechanical steps more, and fetched up against the wall. She put her cheek against the cool plaster and shuddered for a moment.

I have to go. I have to get out of here.

She shoved it all down, fear and pain and nausea alike, swallowed it back like bile. *I don't have time for this. I have to go.*

There were clean breeches on the dresser. She put them on. There would be a clean shirt in the closet in the next room. Lyra turned and strode toward the open doorway.

On the threshold, she stopped as suddenly as if she had struck an iron bar.

The light through the window was filtered by the whispering lilac outside, but it spilled dappled sunlight across her bed. Flies rose up lazily from the black stain across the sheets.

Ah, gods, no.

Her other handmaiden, Lisette, whom Lyra had always suspected of being one of her father's by-blows, was splayed across the bed like a gutted deer. Her legs were spread, her head turned to one side. Blood had spread out from between her thighs, and from the ruin of her throat.

Lyra backed away from the room, turned, and ran blindly for the hall.

She left the house, creeping like a mouse through the courtyard. Her pockets were light, with only a firestarter, a handful of coins, and a cloak from a closet in one of the guest rooms. She avoided the river, going instead away from it, behind the house, to the steep rise of the Tanglelore Hills. She plodded up it, stopping often to rest.

When she was halfway up the hillside, she turned and looked back and saw the little town, the trade village built around the dock, in charred ruin, black smoke rising in lazy billows. It choked her. She was the last of the Volfrieds. The simple traders and fishermen that looked to her family for protection had burned while she crouched in the linen closet.

Sorry, she thought. Her lips were too dry to speak. *I can't even help myself.*

She turned away.

The memory of smoke gave way to the blur of her smoky fire. Lyra found herself with knees drawn up, sobbing into her arms, unable to stop. *Dead, all dead, ah, gods...*

A branch snapped.

Old pain vanished under the need for present survival. Lyra choked down sobs, cursing the catch in her throat that left her unable to listen. It had not been her fire crackling. It had come from farther away, to her right, the direction that she had come.

Someone on her trail. Lyra had no hope of hiding the fire. She shrank back under her log, the knife in her hands. Had the brigands followed her?

There was a long moment of silence. The woods were terrible dark, the shadows dancing around her fire. The exposed roots of her tree looked like groping claws. Lyra's heart pounded in her ears, and the knife trembled in her hand. She waited, mind calling up threat after threat. Brigands...wild animals...trolls...

To the right of her campfire, the bushes parted.

Lyra gasped. Knife clutched before her, she scrambled backward, wedging herself even farther under the log. Rotten, punky wood powdered under her scrabbling feet.

Eyes.

Gold eyes.

And under them, bared in a carnivore's smile, the firelight gleamed red on inch-long, razor-sharp fangs.

⊰⊰⊰

The dog-soldier is running.

He covers ground with the tireless, mile-eating lope of his people, the path a blur beneath his clawed feet. Twilight falls around him, and he runs on, slowing only slightly, his bronze eyes straining in the gloom, his large ears catching every sound. Still the scent of blood teases his nostrils, draws him forward, and then through the trees he sees a stirring of firelight.

The dog-soldier awakens.

He stops in the darkened forest. He breathes deeply, his hand on the hilt of his curved sword, and remembers. Little things like words, manners, politenesses. Large things, like loyalty, the need to defend, the way to go gently and not frighten one already hurt and scared.

The human is only a few yards away, oblivious to his presence. He could walk straight up to the guttering fire without being noticed, but he does not wish to startle the wounded one.

He reaches out, finds a branch in the dark, and breaks it loudly over his knee, the sound like a crack of thunder in the night forest. He hears a sharp intake of breath, and he steps forward into the circle of firelight.

Chapter Three

"Stay away," hissed Lyra in a voice she barely recognized as her own. "I'm warning you." The hand not holding the knife snaked out and caught a branch from the fire, flame blossoming at its tip. If it was an animal, fire might keep it at bay.

It stepped forward. Lyra's jaw sagged.

It was no animal. It resembled nothing so much as a hound that had mastered the art of walking upright.

Taller than a human, over six feet, with large, upstanding ears that added another foot to its height, it wore a cloak and thigh-length tunic of patterned black, clasped with worked gold. A skirt of armored leather strips hung down to his knees, and intricate bracers covered both forearms. The hilt of a sword protruded over one shoulder. Lyra swallowed, hard.

It—he—smiled at her, tongue lolling between sharp lower teeth, lips drawing down to cover the massive upper canines. He lifted his hands—paws?—in a universal gesture of peace. His fingers were blunt-clawed, furred in the same mottled red-brown and black that covered the rest of his body.

"Peace, child," he said. His voice was deep and calm, rough at the edges. Lyra clutched her knife more tightly, untrusting. He was easily twice her size, bare arms corded with the heavy muscle of the swordsman. She licked dry lips.

"I mean you no harm," he said, tilting his head. Not quite a human voice, the "R" edged with a growl.

"I—" Her voice caught hoarsely and she stopped. Started again. "Are you a—?"

"Dog-soldier, yes." He smiled at her again, took another step forward, hands still spread peacefully.

"From *Kamir*?" she asked, amazed, wonder and old books and old knowledge rising to the surface.

Peace, child. I mean you no harm.

"Khamir," he corrected gently, his grin spreading. "You are educated!" As if they had settled any question of territory, he dropped into a neat crouch on the far side of the fire.

Lyra had read about dog-soldiers, of course, and heard stories, but she had never actually met one. They usually preferred warmer climates, hailing from the far southern deserts, and there could be no more than a handful on this side of the Blue Havens.

They were a courteous, dangerous, but honorable people by all accounts. More than one author had implied that, unique among the races of the earth, they had been made, not born, created out of magic untold years ago.

Certainly the one across the fire from her looked more like one of her father's great brindled hounds than any being Lyra had ever seen. A black patch over one eye reminded her of a deerhound puppy she'd had as a child, but the large yellow eyes held an unmistakable intelligence.

"Forgive me," said the dog-soldier gently. "My name is Sadrao Majiid."

Her deerhound puppy had been named Amanderxes, after the scholar who invented the modern woodcut technique of printing books.

Lyra, already regretting having spoken at all, said nothing. Simply because he was a dog-soldier—and unlikely to mean her any harm—did not mean he meant her any good, either.

The image of Lisette, raped and murdered on Lyra's own bed, came back to her, and Lyra flinched. The world was a dreadfully cruel place. She could not afford to forget that.

The dog-soldier's face was quintessentially canine, with sharp teeth and black-nosed muzzle. His skull rose higher and broader than a true dog, with large, furred ears that flicked from side to side to catch every sound. A line of gold rings glittered in one, gleaming against the fringe of white hairs inside the ear. Between his ears a bristling crest rose several inches, whorled with black and red.

He didn't seem aware of her rudeness, but instead reached over to her small pile of wood. She pressed herself backwards, away. She thought he was pretending not to notice, though large gold eyes did flick briefly to her face. He picked up a few of the thicker branches and rebuilt the fire. She had made it sloppily, and it was already beginning to die, but under Sadrao's quick, efficient movements it flared back to life and settled into a hungry blaze.

"See," he said cheerfully, "you stack the wood so, and the fire burns inward instead of out, hai?"

She craned her neck, then yelped as the burning branch in her hand, forgotten, seared her fingertips. She dropped it into the fire, where it kicked up a few sparks, and sucked on her finger.

Sadrao had the grace not to laugh, but the long feathery tail curled around his haunches stirred. Lyra felt her cheeks burn and tightened her grip on the knife.

"Well," said Sadrao, reaching over his shoulder and unslinging a pack, "you've been kind enough to share your fire with me, so the least I can do is share food with you." He rummaged for a moment, then took out a flat, round loaf of bread and a few strips of dried meat.

Food. Lyra hadn't eaten for two days, except for the bread, which she had lost immediately afterwards. She felt herself salivating but reminded herself firmly that this could be a trap to coax her from under the log. He could hardly come at her through the fire without being burned or stabbed, but if she came out she would be easy prey.

The dog-soldier bent his head over the food, murmuring something in a soft, growling language, then broke the bread into exactly even halves. He placed half the meat on top of it, then leaned far over, around the side of the fire, and set the food gravely down within her reach. Then he leaned back, moving so that the fire was firmly between them, and began to eat.

She watched him warily for a moment, appreciating what he had done. She could grab the food with her free hand without moving from under the log, but he would have to reach through the fire to get her—or rise and move, which would give her plenty of time to move back under the log. Keeping an eye on him, she leaned forward and caught the bread with her left hand. It was not heavy, but her wound twinged warningly. She ignored it, pulling the food closer.

Sadrao did not move during this procedure except to bring food to his lips. Lyra tore a chunk of bread off with her teeth and chewed. It was tough and sour and utterly delicious. She had to force herself to keep the knife ready in one hand, rather than dropping it and tearing into the food.

Sadrao finished a little before she did and pulled a tooled leather flask from his pack. He took several swallows, then stoppered it and rose to his knees. Lyra froze.

The dog-soldier lifted his hands and, with exaggerated slowness, moved around the fire until he could lean over, at full extension, and set the flask down. Then he backed away to his side of the fire again.

"A few swallows only," he suggested. "It's very potent."

Lyra eyed him warily, then slowly leaned over and caught the flask. She unstoppered it and sipped cautiously.

Warmth exploded against her tongue, then burned down her throat and lit fire in her stomach. She choked, re-stoppered it with eyes tearing, and coughed, hard. A moment or two later she finally fell back against the log, gasping for air and pounding herself on the chest with her free hand.

Somewhere during the procedure she had dropped the knife, but the dog-soldier was not moving.

Sadrao gave her a long-toothed grin. Lyra gave him a dirty look in return, then opened the flask again and took another, deeper sip. Brandy. Very good brandy. It warmed her belly, soothed the ache of abused muscles. She closed it and, after another look at Sadrao, leaned out of her shelter and set it down.

He waited until she had moved back under the log before moving to reclaim the bottle. Lyra was beginning to feel boorish. He was so obviously working to put her at ease—a bandit would hardly take so much trouble with someone who had nothing worth stealing.

"Thank you," she said, finally, amazed at how hoarse her own voice sounded.

"You're welcome," said Sadrao promptly, holding his hands out to the fire. "Ahh. It gets cold here at night, does it not?"

"Mmmm." The hollow where her body lay was warming, but the side away from the fire was still cool. She drew up her knees and folded her arms over her chest, favoring her left forearm.

"So tell me," said Sadrao, removing a small knife from his belt. Lyra tensed, but he started cleaning neatly under his claws. "How does a human child come to learn of Khamir and dog-soldiers?"

"A book," she said, looking up eagerly. "Forsyth's *On the Southern Lands*. He talked about Khamir, and then the dog-soldiers, and the Amir of Sarappa—"

"Forsyth," said Sadrao definitively, "is perfectly correct in several places and wildly inaccurate in others. *Southern Lands* isn't bad, compared to his other works, I've heard, but I confess my knowledge there is limited." He leveled a claw at her. "The section on dog-soldiers isn't bad—we were bred by the Amir to be guardians. One of his more successful creations—we flatter ourselves that we are the most successful." (Lyra heard herself chuckle, and wondered at that.) "That much is fairly accurate, but we are not immortal, our blood is red, and we most certainly are not all male."

Lyra laughed aloud at that. "I doubted that part when I read it. He said in *An Eastern Bestiary* that bear cubs are born from stones their mothers swallow, and I *know* that's not true."

She paused, hearing her voice echo cheerfully from the trees. It rang in her ears like an accusation. Her family barely a day dead, and she was discussing books with a chance-met stranger. She turned her face away, sobered.

Sensing her shift in mood, Sadrao poked pensively at the fire with a stick, his eyes occasionally flicking up to hers. Finally, he seemed to come to some decision. He set the stick down.

"Forgive my meddling," he said, his ears flattening ingratiatingly, "but you—ah—seem to be having some difficulty." He gestured with one hand to her bandaged forearm. "It hasn't been dressed properly. Did you do it yourself?"

She nodded, feeling shamed at her lack of knowledge. She knew many things, book-lore, the origins of those commonly called dog-soldiers, but not how to build a fire or tend a wound.

Sadrao nodded. "Nothing to be ashamed of. It's hard to do with one hand, especially if one doesn't have the materials."

"I didn't know how," she said quietly, drooping.

"Well, here, then. I'll show you." Sadrao rummaged around more in his pack and emerged with some bandages and a jar. "Ginger poultice," he said, with a wink. "Old Majiid-clan recipe. Draws out infection."

"Infection!" she said. Of course, wounds got infected. She hadn't thought that far. To be honest, she hadn't really expected to survive the night. She bit her lip. If it was infected, and she was unable to reach a healer, she might lose the arm, or her life.

Sadrao balanced the strips of cloth and the jar, looked at her, and frowned. "Here," he said. He rose and, moving slowly, set them down within her reach before backing away. "I'm going to go get you some water. It will need to be cleaned again."

He pulled a small iron pot from his pack—evidently the bandages and jar had been packed within it—and moved into the darkness. Lyra picked up the supplies, and then rolled her sleeve back to the elbow. Teeth gritted, she began to unwrap her arm.

The blood had dried, sticking the fabric to the wound. She took a deep breath. Closed her eyes. Jerked it free.

The pain flared explosively. Her breath hissed between her teeth. She opened her eyes and saw fresh blood welling brightly through the blackened crust.

Sadrao loomed in the firelight. His nose came up, nostrils flared, and he wrinkled his muzzle. "Smell blood. But no infection yet," he added cheerfully. He sat down cross-legged and passed her the pot of water. "I will sit here, yes? You stay there, I will instruct you."

She nodded. He was close enough that he could probably jump her, particularly since she would have to set down her knife, but she rather doubted he would.

"First, clean the wound," he instructed. She dabbed at it gingerly, wincing. "Here," he offered, passing her a soft cloth. "Try this."

The cloth helped somewhat. Dried blood flaked off, revealing raw skin underneath. Sadrao leaned over farther, and she turned it toward him.

"Hmmmm. Looks more scraped than cut. Sword?"

Lyra nodded. Sadrao looked at her seriously. "You were lucky. Very lucky. Against a good swordsman, you will not be so lucky. Best thing, try to dodge the sword next time, instead of blocking with a bare arm, hai?"

Lyra shuddered. "I hope the situation never arises," she said ruefully.

Sadrao laughed. It was half a bark, and his tail thumped the ground companionably. "Probably best. Still, the world is an unpredictable place. Now, put a little of this on the wound—only a little. Take another drink first. This will sting."

She took the offered brandy, swallowed a little, then poured a bit over her arm. The pain made her yelp. "Ah—*ahh*—gods—that stings!"

Sadrao rescued the flask before she dropped it. Lyra realized suddenly that he had inched within arm's length without her notice. She slid a glance to the knife at her boot.

He certainly didn't appear threatening. Instead he held out a hand, and after a moment she placed her arm in it. His palms were tough black pads, but his fur was soft. His claws were blunt and black like a dog's and fitted in a neat curve over the ends on his fingers.

He studied her arm carefully, head bowed. "Hmmm. A scrape, really. Looks uglier than it is, hurts a lot, but not deep. It's going to scar," he added, almost apologetically.

Lyra shrugged. "As long as I keep the arm."

"Oh, no doubt of that." Sadrao glanced up and grinned at her. "Here, let me show you how to do this." He smeared some of the contents of the jar delicately over her arm. She winced at the pressure. The salve was warm, and after a moment or two the throbbing pain seemed to lessen, fading to a dull ache. Sadrao took out the bandages and showed her how to wrap them. "Not too tight, else the blood gets cut off, and the whole limb can die. Like so, hai?"

Lyra nodded. Sadrao patted her shoulder and then moved back to his side of the campfire. She settled more comfortably under her log. He had not taken advantage of her lapse, but he might be waiting for her to expose her back, or for reinforcements to arrive. She bit her lower lip. She wanted to trust him, but gods! Her family dead little more than a day. A chance-met stranger would hardly aid another not even of his species, without some kind of agenda.

Though, to be honest, she had never heard that the dog-soldiers of Khamir were anything but honorable.

"Dawn will be coming early," said Sadrao from the other side of the fire. She looked up, met amused gold eyes. "I am for sleeping, I think." He leaned forward and began banking the fire. She watched closely—another thing books had not taught her.

Perhaps sensing her scrutiny, he made his movement slow and deliberate. She developed some notion of the process of leaving the embers to smolder through the night, though she dreaded trying it herself.

"Pleasant dreaming," said Sadrao, spreading out his long cloak and bundling into it. Lyra, at a loss, shifted under her log.

"Aren't—I'm sorry—should we—set watch?" She felt silly. By herself she could never have stayed awake, and he might be as likely to harm her as beasts of the woods, but setting watches was something they always mentioned in the books.

Firelight gleamed on Sadrao's smile. "Ah, but you camp with a dog-soldier tonight! Never fear, child. If anything approaches, I will waken in time." He chuckled deep in his chest. "And I am a much larger meal than most beasts will try to swallow. On the morrow, child." The shine of firelight off his reflective eyes vanished as he closed them.

Lyra shifted, several times, in an effort to find a comfortable position. She didn't dare sleep. Unthreatening as he had seemed, her best course of action was to wait until Sadrao slept, then leave quietly. Sleep was totally out of the question.

Having decided that, she closed her eyes and fell immediately into a deep and dreamless sleep.

⁂

She woke.

Her surroundings were totally unfamiliar, and she sat up, confused. Where was her bedroom, or the tangled lilac bush outside her window? She was in the woods. Had she gone camping? She never went camping. Her father would have had kittens if she'd even suggested it. Virgin daughter out alone in dangerous woods—it didn't bear contemplating. She looked from the merry blaze of campfire, up, to Sadrao's angular-muzzled face.

"Good morning," he said, handing her a tin cup full of hot liquid. Dazed from sleep, she sipped. She was warm, wonderfully warm, but very stiff. And hungry.

The tea tasted of herbs, strong, very bracing. It was when she looked down at the cup between her fingers that she saw the fall of black cloth across her forearms and realized that she was wearing Sadrao's cloak, and that she was no longer under the log.

Her knife. She looked around for it, frantically, fingers white-knuckled around the tea.

"Here." Sadrao held the sixteen-inch blade. It looked tiny in his hands. With a practiced flip he reversed it and offered her the hilt across the back of his arm. The edge of one sharp canine showed in a slight, knowing smile.

Lyra took it, feeling suddenly foolish, like a child clutching at a favorite toy. In the grey light of morning Sadrao was no longer the indistinct monster in the firelight but a typical dog-soldier—if any member of that race could be called typical—a head taller than Lyra, minus the great upstanding ears, his fur rather more reddish in the daylight than Lyra had thought. The black patch went over one eye like a mask, bleeding into brown down his muzzle. His stiff crest stood up several inches on his scalp, turning into a kind of mane that ran down his neck and over his shoulders, braided in several places with small beads. The way his crest came forward reminded Lyra of the manes of certain shaggy, feral horses, or the stiff topknot of a bluejay.

"Forgive me for moving you," he said, apologetically. "You were thrashing about in your sleep, and I was afraid you might roll into the fire."

"No—I—thank you." Lyra took another drink of tea, feeling guilty. The fire was crackling cheerfully. Sadrao had probably saved her from a death of exposure, or at least a near-fatal brush with it. "I'm sorry. I don't have any way to repay you..."

"You could start by telling me your name," said Sadrao. He raked two leaf-wrapped packages from the edge of the fire.

"Lyra," said Lyra. "Lyra of House Volfried."

"Volfried..." Sadrao pulled two thin metal plates from his pack—she was beginning to think that he was prepared for any eventuality, no matter how unlikely—and unwrapped the little packages. "One of the human houses, hai? A major shipper along the River Tanglelore."

Lyra was ashamed at the burning behind her eyes. She dropped her head and pretended it was smoke. She would not cry. Again.

Sadrao gave her an ears-back look, nose wrinkling slightly as if to catch a scent, and turned his attention back to the food. The packages cracked open to reveal flaky white fish. "Fresh caught this morning," he said cheerfully, dropping one onto a plate and passing it to Lyra.

It was very hot, and she had never liked fish anyway, and she burned both tongue and fingers and didn't care in the slightest. It was glorious. When she finished, she sat back, eyes closed, savoring the feeling of fullness and the subtle flavors of her second cup of tea.

Sadrao did not disturb her. She heard the soft rustlings of his movements, the leathery creak of packing. She opened her eyes again.

"So," said Sadrao, tying up the opening of his pack, "not meaning to pry, but where are you headed, Lyra-of-House-Volfried?"

Reality reared its ugly head. Lyra's vague, transparent contentment vanished, leaving only exhaustion, and she huddled closer to the fire. "I don't know. I guess...Jeppeth." It was the nearest city. Her father's trading partners had an office there. They might help her. Then again, they might not. Regardless, she could not subsist on leaves and dirt, once the dog-soldier had gone.

"Well," Sadrao said, folding blunt-fingered hands together, "by a happy coincidence, I'm headed in that direction myself. Shall we travel together?"

"But—I—why? What do you want?" Lyra's eyes narrowed. There were a number of questions swirling behind her eyes, and when she opened her mouth, the bluntest one came out. "Why are you helping me?"

Sadrao met her eyes with his own frank gold ones. "You've never met a dog-soldier."

"No. What does that—"

"If you had," he interrupted, "you would know." He sighed, tapping the claws of his index fingers together. "We were created as guardians. Soldiers. Protectors. And a human child loose in the woods, with no supplies, no trust, and not the faintest idea of how to survive—well, such a one needs protecting." He slid a glance to her bandaged arm. "A child bearing sword wounds, and the honor-dagger of her House...it does not take a scholar to put two and two together."

To her horror, Lyra felt tears spilling down her cheeks. "They killed them all," she whispered. "All of them. My father—"

She choked. Sadrao, ears flattening with obvious distress at her pain, splashed more tea into a cup and pressed it into her fingers.

She drank. The warm liquid steadied her, allowed her to fight down the tears. Sadrao looked away, his ears flicking absently from side to side. Birds called from the trees around them.

"Have you no family elsewhere?" he asked, finally.

She thought about it, tea clasped in both hands. "No. My mother's family, perhaps, but she died when I was young, and I don't know where they would be, or if they even exist." She laughed humorlessly. "Or, for that matter, what they were called."

"None of your father's kin?"

"No...a few bastard children, here and there, but I wouldn't know them if I met them. Except—"

She stopped, biting her lip.

"Except?" prodded Sadrao.

"Jasen," she said dully. Jasen was still alive. He—no, surely she had been mistaken. "My half-brother. But he—I think—I'm afraid—"

Sadrao waited patiently.

"I think he killed them," she said in a small voice. The forest seemed terribly quiet, as if in horror. "I thought I saw him. I could have been wrong."

"Could you have?" asked Sadrao, patient, inexorable.

Lyra drew a deep breath. She was seventeen years old, far too old to hide from reality like a child. She felt at least a hundred. "No. It was him. I'm sure." She took another drink of tea. Tears were spilling down her cheeks. She ignored them. "He always resented that Father would not take him as a legitimate heir. He could have led the brigands—got them through the gates—"

Sadrao leaned back with a sigh that seemed to come from his toes. "Such things are not unheard of," he offered. "How did you escape?"

"Base cowardice," she said dryly, and told him about the closet. "I don't know," she said, after she finished and the silence had grown oppressive. "Perhaps—my father's trading partners might take me in. Or, if not—in a city, I might find work as a scribe—"

Sadrao leaned forward, fixing her with a direct, searching gaze, his nostrils wide and working. She tried to meet his eyes, and finally, uncomfortably, looked away, scrubbing at her raw cheeks with her sleeve. Her soul felt scraped. She had just woken up, and already she felt tired.

"Hmm," said Sadrao, almost to himself. "I wonder—"

And then he stopped. He was an old dog-soldier, though Lyra did not know it, and there were many things he could have said, but it was not the time for any of them. He stood up, instead, and patted her shoulder with a blunt-clawed paw, and went to wash the dishes.

Chapter Four

"We'll make for Jeppeth, then," said Sadrao thoughtfully. "And once we're there, perhaps we can find word of these bandits. It's the only large city hereabouts, and the bandits have to trade with them. More, if they've been together more than a year they have to winter in Jeppeth, and someone may know something."

Lyra nodded distractedly. Sadrao's reasoning was something she would not have thought of herself, but she was content with his logic.

Already, in a few hours of walking, she had learned the names for a dozen trees and edible plants, and a few others that, while not strictly edible, had various medicinal purposes. "Sorrel," Sadrao would say, plucking a heart-shaped leaf and munching it, passing her a leaf. The taste was tangy and sour. Or "Cattail—peeled, the roots are edible, but cook them for a long time—"

And so on. They walked in a meandering path around the foot of the rolling Tanglelore Hills, following the stream south-west in the knowledge that it would eventually flow into the River Tanglelore and then west to Jeppeth. Lyra had managed to put the one of the largest of the foothills between herself and her ruined home the first night. Sadrao added several more hills to that distance, their path making a broad loop that curved back toward the river.

The trade road that flanked the river was by far the easiest way to travel. Unfortunately, they did not dare use it, not until they were several days farther out from the site of the massacre, so they were reduced to picking—and occasionally hacking—their way through the tangled forest. Every now and again Sadrao would go down on one knee and breathe deeply, his face inches from the leaf-mulched ground, seeking a scent. Lyra was reminded of the deerhounds on the hunt, and told him so.

"Their noses are better than mine," said Sadrao honestly, rising, "but I can tell a human from a deer well enough...I haven't smelled any humans, not for several days." He looked thoughtfully up their backtrail.

They were still too close to the site of the massacre for Lyra's comfort, and she told him that, too.

He nodded gravely. He did not say anything to indicate that her fears were foolish, and Lyra was absurdly grateful at how seriously he took her dread. She did not think she would ever be far enough from the house, and the hall full of dead men, but she didn't say that either.

Perhaps, thought Lyra tiredly, *what we are not saying is more important than what we are saying,* and she thought, almost wryly, that Sadrao, leading the way with his broad ears cocked, might have thought so too.

⁂

They angled back around the curve of hill, turning uphill to avoid any travelers on the road below. Sadrao suggested they halt while there were still several hours of daylight. They made camp under a large, jutting stone, within sight of a small, pleasantly riling brook. Sadrao set her to gathering firewood. When she returned with several armloads, he had what looked like half of a dead tree laid across a stone brace. She set down her sticks, wondering if he would use the large, curved sword laid across his back to cut it.

He did not. Instead, he gave her a brief canine grin, lips pulled politely over his upper teeth, and set one leg against the lower half, wrapping his hands around the upper section. Heavy, furred biceps flexed once, and the wood, as thick as Lyra's neck, snapped. He broke it further, into two-foot lengths, and then began laying the foundations for a fire. She crouched to watch.

Once the fire was burning and the camp set he stood and, in a smoothly practiced motion, slid his sword from his sheath. Lyra took an involuntary step backwards.

He lifted an eyebrow and brought the sword up over his head, then down in a clean, precisely controlled cut, stopping the strike with a snap of the wrists. He took a step forward, swung the sword up to block an imaginary blow, then struck again, a welter of powerful movements that left Lyra wide-eyed. She could almost see an invisible opponent going down under the blade.

Her lips twisted in wry self-mockery. *Yeah, I was gonna hold him off with my honor knife and a burning branch, mighty warrior that I am.*

Sadrao reversed the sword and offered her the hilt.

"His name is Mohenja." Again that soft, growling tongue. "You would say, perhaps, 'East Wind'. Here, take him."

Lyra took it gingerly. The blade was long and elegantly curved, heavy in her hand. She tried for a better grip, but her wrist sagged immediately.

"You've never held a sword," remarked Sadrao dryly.

"Is it that obvious?" She tried to swing it, and had to grab with her other hand to steady it. A two-handed grip seemed a little better. Sadrao prudently moved out of range.

Lyra had read several bad books on swordsmanship, and one very good one by the Tchang author Mozan Ku-Rai. She was quite certain, however, that swordplay was not an art you could pick up by reading about it. Her wrists were beginning to shake.

"Mmmph." Sadrao advanced, hands held up, and backed around her, placing his hands over hers on the hilt. "Like so. And so. Hold your arms looser."

He let go. Her wrists immediately began to shake again. Sadrao planted one hand on her spine, the other on her shoulder, and pushed in opposite directions. "Put your shoulders back. More. It feels strange at first, but try to keep your shoulders and your hips and your feet lined up."

Lyra, her shoulders far back (and consequently, her breasts much more obvious than usual) and her feet planted wide, felt somewhat indecent. She could practically hear Aunt Marrow clucking her tongue and saying, "Well, she's no better than she should be." Her father would've taken one look at her and banished her to her rooms for a fortnight.

Sadrao rescued Mohenja and eyed it, then her arms. "Hrrrrm. You are, perhaps, not too old to learn the sword." He laid his forearm next to hers—it was almost twice as large around. "Perhaps with a lighter blade..."

He sheathed his sword across his back in a casual motion that would have gutted Lyra had she tried it. Then he began sorting through the firewood until he located a branch as long as Lyra's arm, and relatively straight. "Here. Let us try this."

"Why?" asked Lyra, rubbing her palms on her pantlegs. "I mean—not that I mind, but—why?"

"Come, now, you have read more books in the last year than I have in a decade. Surely one of your authors has said that no knowledge is wasted?"

"In a lot of variations, yes. But—Sadrao, I'm no kind of warrior."

"Because you have never been taught!"

He handed the stick to her, then stripped off his cloak and spread his arms. "Here. Come at me."

Lyra eyed him dubiously and made a tentative thrust. Sadrao lifted the two feathery patches of tan fur that served him as eyebrows. "You can do better than that. Here." He tapped his chest. "Try it. Cut me. Don't worry about hurting me."

Lyra took a deep breath. Then lunged, putting most of her weight behind it.

"Alright, freeze." Sadrao had caught her "sword" with one rough-palmed hand. She froze, at full extension, wobbling uncertainly on one foot.

"First of all," said Sadrao pleasantly, "that was a thrust, not a cut. Not a bad idea, but what were you aiming for?"

"Your heart?" asked Lyra, uncertainly.

"Also not a bad idea, in theory. In practice, not so good. You were aiming too high. You have to come in under the sternum and aim up. You want to just nick the bottom of the heart."

"Lovely," said Lyra dryly. Then, "Can't you just go straight through the chest, like the saga with Lord Saxworth and the ogre?"

"First of all, nobody fights ogres with a sword," said Sadrao, a lecturing note coming into his voice. "Crossbows, nets and boar spears, and even then you're throwing dice with demons. Secondly, Lord Saxworth notwithstanding, you can try to go through the sternum. You might even succeed. You will then have a dead man permanently affixed to the point of your sword, while his sixteen maternal cousins make their extreme displeasure known by cutting you into little bits, hai?"

Lyra giggled, then covered her mouth with her hand, shocked at the sound, or at the knowledge that she could laugh.

"Either way," Sadrao continued, "it will be a long time before you're up to hacking through sternums." He strolled casually around her. "Balance. Your worst problem is balance. We'll work on that." Without warning, he kicked her supporting leg.

Lyra yelped. It didn't hurt, but it knocked the foot out from under her, and she toppled to the leaf-covered ground. She didn't think anybody had ever knocked her down in her life. She blinked up at Sadrao, who was grinning with his lips pulled down over his teeth. He leaned down and offered her a hand, and pulled her upright. "You see my point."

"Vividly," said Lyra, rubbing at her rump, and decided to be amused, because being offended at Sadrao seemed both useless and potentially dangerous.

Sadrao eyed her thoughtfully, twisting a braided lock of mane between his fingers. "Hmmmmm. No, I think I was right to begin with. The sword is not a weapon for you yet. Too much precision, too little defense. Perhaps in time, but for now..." He paused, worrying at a red glass bead in the braid. "Yes, I think so. Wait here."

He turned and strode into the trees, tail wagging briskly behind him. Lyra watched him go, bemused, then busied herself hauling water in from the river.

Sadrao reappeared just as she had run out of useful things that she knew how to do. He was carrying a length of wood a little taller than she was and as thick around as her wrist.

"Staff," he said, by way of explanation, thumping the end on the ground. "I think this might be more your style, until you become more comfortable with a blade." He passed it to her. Lyra took it in both hands and hefted it experimentally. It felt more comfortable than the sword had, balancing between both hands. She gave it a practice swing.

"Whoa!" Sadrao avoided decapitation with expert reflexes, dropping into a roll that brought him up, out of her range, into a crouch. "Father of jackals! Yes, I think this is definitely more to your style." He approached, grinning, as she flushed beet red. "No, really, the staff is not as glamorous as the sword, but I think it will keep you alive better for now. Most opponents will have a greater reach—" he demonstrated, his arms almost a foot longer than hers, "—and the staff will correct that. It is a good weapon for keeping people away from you. Also," he flicked his ears apologetically, "a human woman with a sword tends to attract unwanted attention. But a woman with a walking stick?" He shrugged.

Lyra grimaced at the truth of his words.

"Now, then," said Sadrao, rubbing his hands together, "we will practice staffwork later. Balance." He took up a stance in front of her and spread his hands apart at shoulder height, gesturing that she should mirror him. She did so. His shoulders, and hence his hands, were significantly higher than hers.

Mozan Ku-Rai's book had indicated that being shorter than your opponent was frequently an advantage. Eye-level with Sadrao's furry, but impressively muscled chest, she wasn't quite sure how that was supposed to work.

She did notice that he had three sets of nipples, and possibly another set vanishing under his armor, but she didn't think that was particularly relevant. One on the lower left side had a gold ring piercing it.

"Don't worry about the height," said Sadrao, as if reading her mind. "Most of any fighting art is getting underneath your opponent's center of balance." He held his hands up, palms out. "The rules are simple. Don't move your feet, don't use anything but your hands, and try to knock me off balance."

Lyra looked at him dubiously.

One of his hands snaked out and shoved her lightly on the shoulder. She swayed backwards.

"Don't lean," he advised. "Turn your hips, keep your shoulders loose, and bend your knees. Just absorb it, don't fight it." He poked at her again, and she let the touch turn her shoulders, keeping her feet still. "Good. Now you try."

She poked him. Sadrao lifted the furry tan patches that made up his eyebrows. "You can do better than that."

Lyra gritted her teeth and shoved.

Sadrao simply dropped his knees slightly, and didn't move an inch.

She tried again, putting her weight behind it. This time, he let his torso turn with the force. Expecting more resistance, she lost *her* balance and had to take a step to catch herself.

"The key," said Sadrao, his tail making a half-wag of amusement, "is to stay centered all the time. Keep your weight in your hips, and your balance on the backs of the balls of your feet." He straightened. "Again."

After three or four attempts, Lyra got sneaky and feinted with one hand, then shoved quickly with the other. Sadrao rocked on his feet, but didn't go down. He smiled at her. "Good. Again."

"Again."

"Again."

⤛⤛⤛

Lyra rolled over in her sleep, ground a rock under her shoulderblade, and came awake.

She lay with her eyes open but unfocused for a moment, seeing an unfamiliar pattern of light and dark above her. Her face was cold. She tried to burrow deeper into her blankets and discovered that there were no blankets, that she was laying on hard and uncomfortable ground.

The light and dark above her resolved into leaves and moonlight filtering through their black, jagged-edged shapes. They swayed in the slight breeze, whispering, a colder, wilder sound than the rustle of lilac leaves outside her window at home.

I'm not at home.

Lyra rolled over. She had been sleeping wrapped in Sadrao's cloak, his pack making a lumpy pillow. The embroidery on the collar of the cloak was scratchy on her face as she pulled it over her head.

I'm not at home. I don't have a home anymore.

Her throat closed. She tried to muffle her tears into the cloak, but they spilled out anyway. She bit her lower lip.

Sadrao, however kind he might be, was not human. Lyra knew that she was a burden, and could hardly believe that he viewed her as anything but a weak, furless, spineless creature. The books she had read said that dog-soldiers were utterly loyal guardians, but Lyra knew perfectly well that the authors of those books might not have ever even met a dog-soldier. She felt helpless in the face of his calm competence, and she knew full well that he could have traveled twice the distance they had gone yesterday. She was sore and aching from unaccustomed exertion, and she feared that Sadrao might leave her as suddenly as he had arrived, if she proved too much of a hindrance.

She did not want to give in to the weakness of tears.

She scrubbed at her damp cheeks with the back of her hand, swallowing, feeling her breath catch in her chest.

There was movement on the other side of the dying fire.

Without saying anything, a warm body curled up next to her in a neat ball, one long, furred flank against her back. Lyra snuffled, turning over. She hid her face in the cloak and tried to stop the welling tears.

The dog-soldier reached over and gathered her up in his arms.

The gesture undid her completely. She buried her face in his shaggy ruff, as she might have one of the huge, patient elkhounds in her father's hall, and cried.

Sadrao patted her shoulder, growling soft, tuneless lullabies in his native tongue, and held her as no one had since her mother died.

⁂

The next day they turned south, in a path that would eventually intersect the river and the road. Lyra, still wrapped in Sadrao's cloak, was mostly silent. Sadrao, too, said little, great ears sweeping from side to side to catch every sound.

It was as they splashed across a tiny brook, barely as wide as the length of Lyra's arm, that Sadrao's hand closed over her shoulder.

She looked up, into his face, and saw the gold eyes fixed forward. Following his gaze, she stiffened.

Two men stood in a half-clearing before them. The larger of the two had a face pocked with scars, as if from some childhood disease. They were clad in ill-fitting leather and wool. Both carried swords slung at their hips. Sadrao was bowstring-taut beside her.

Three more men materialized out of the woods behind the first two. Sadrao gave no sign of surprise — perhaps he had known they were there.

"Well," said the scarred man, "what have we here?"

"Travelers," said Sadrao evenly. "Seeking no trouble, and offering none."

"No trouble t'all," said the second man, grinning. Several of his teeth were missing. "Just give us the girl, and any money you might have, doggy, and we'll see you on your way."

Lyra felt, obscurely, shame for the way that members of her species were acting, especially in the face of Sadrao's calm dignity.

Sadrao, in a smooth motion, pulled Mohenja from his sheath and stepped a little before Lyra. "I suggest you reconsider," he said, calmly, but there was a growl rumbling in his chest.

All five had swords out. Lyra had a terrible sinking feeling in the pit of her stomach. She gripped her staff more tightly.

The scarred man stepped forward, almost close enough to strike. "There's five of us, and one of you. Put the sword up, or we'll cut you down where you stand."

Sadrao moved. There was one heart-stopping instant when everything blurred around him, and then, with a kind of surprised grunt, the pocked man was sliding off the end of Sadrao's sword.

"Four," said Sadrao, not quite under his breath, and smiled into the shocked face of the second man. The dog-soldier's teeth were long and sharp and very white, particularly compared to the yellowed stumps of his opponent.

It occurred to Lyra in passing that there was a significant difference between Sadrao's polite smile, lips pulled down over the top fangs, and this deadly ivory grin.

The second man, ignorant of the implications of the dog-soldier's smile, charged Sadrao with a roar, sword swinging. Sadrao caught the blade on his own and bound it, hilts sliding together with a clatter. Lyra, several feet behind Sadrao, didn't hear any words exchanged as dog-soldier and human brigand came together, faces only inches apart. What she saw was Sadrao turn his muzzle slightly to one side, jaws opening. He darted his head forward with the speed of a striking snake. Massive neck muscles pulsed, and the brigand fell backwards, his face a red ruin. Blood stained Sadrao's teeth and ran down his fur.

Lyra suffered one wrenching moment of horror—her protector had *bitten* this man's *face* off—and then, with hoarse shouts, the other three descended on Sadrao.

The dog-soldier fended them off with broad sweeps of Mohenja, shooting a quick glance over his shoulder at Lyra. The gesture cost him, one of the brigands scoring a shallow cut along his ribs. One of the others made as if to break away, looking in Lyra's direction. Sadrao engaged him at once.

He was doing his best to keep her safe, still. Lyra's horror ebbed at once, replaced with shame, and then renewed fear. Sadrao was holding his own—one brigand's arm hung limp and useless, another favored his side, but there was blood mottling the dog-soldier's fur as well.

Lyra bit her lip, hefting the staff. She wanted to help, but she feared getting in Sadrao's way. She had no illusions about her skill.

The trio moved, finally doing what they should have done in the first place and encircling Sadrao. He spun, weaving a cage of steel around himself, but there were three. One, his back to Lyra, moved to strike.

Lyra leapt forward, terror constricting her throat, and brought the heavy end of the staff down with all her strength on the back of the brigand's head.

He staggered, sword sagging in his hand, then spun. Lyra's eyes went wide and she backpedaled furiously.

Maddened by pain, he pursued, leaving his companions to finish off the dog soldier. Steel chimed behind them, and a human screamed. Her attacker ignored it. He might not have heard. Blood was beginning to pump from the cut in his scalp. He lunged for her.

Lyra leapt backwards again, into the tiny stream. A rock turned under her foot and she fell. Her staff went flying.

In a tiny, distracted voice in the back of her head she thought, *That wouldn't have happened if I kept my weight centered like Sadrao told me to.*

Pity he won't get a chance to yell at me about it.

She had time enough to look up, note that her attacker's eyes were muddy brown, and say goodbye to life. A sword rose above her. Reflex lifted a hand over her head, as if it might really stop a roundhouse slash of the blade.

A blunt-clawed hand clamped down on the man's shoulder, and a foot of steel slid out of his chest. Brown eyes rolled back in his head, and he fell to one side, blood washing away in the stream.

Lyra realized that she was saying "Ohgodohgodohgod—" in a tiny, keening voice, and stopped at once.

"Well," said Sadrao, wiping blood from Mohenja, "that was invigorating."

She might have had a reply, but her gorge rose and she turned to one side and was noisily, messily sick.

Sadrao, with cool, matter-of-fact compassion, picked her up out of the cold water and set her, on hands and knees, on the bank. Tough-skinned fingers gathered her hair back into a loose knot at the base of her skull.

"Feeling better?" asked Sadrao gently, after the wracking spasms had passed.

"Uhn-huh." Lyra wiped her lips and sat up. "Th-that was— oh, *goddess*—"

"You did great," said Sadrao cheerfully, pulling her to her feet and pressing the staff into her hand. "Absolutely. Much better than I did the first time I got in a fight."

"You lie," muttered Lyra, leaning on the staff.

"Well, a little." Sadrao gave her a broad grin. "But you didn't freeze, and if you hadn't acted when you had, you might be pulling a sword out of my guts right now, and think what a mess that would be."

The mere thought made Lyra shudder. She wiped her forehead. "We should get out of here."

"Oh, yes, definitely." Sadrao rolled one of the bodies over with his foot. "Hmmm..." He glanced up their backtrail. "I would say—probably from your House, going toward Jeppeth. Though I do not think they were looking for you specifically—I suspect they might have been going for supplies. We should make haste, ourselves." He paused, ears flicking backwards. "And hope that these five will not be missed too quickly."

Chapter Five

It took them a week to reach Jeppeth, traveling sometimes by night, sleeping on the ground and bathing in icy mountain streams one step removed from snow melt. Sadrao kept them from the main roads for some days, deftly avoiding bandit patrols that Lyra would have blundered into. They had narrowly missed a half-dozen more run-ins with Jasen's men. She had gotten used to being frightened, to lying quietly in the bushes, and to obeying Sadrao without question.

"Are they following us?" she asked the dog-soldier one afternoon, as they crouched in a thicket of madrone and ten-leaf, watching a trio of brigands several hundred feet down the slope. Sadrao's mottled red-and-black fur blended with the pattern of slick red madrone bark and leafshadow like a forest spirit. Her lips were so close to Sadrao's left ear she could see the fine white hairs stir under her breath.

"They're following me," answered Sadrao, just as quietly, "or rather, whoever killed those five men. I doubt that your brother is much concerned with finding you. You're a loose end, and not one likely to survive."

Lyra nodded, freezing as one of the men glanced up the slope. "He might not even have noticed I'm not one of the bodies," she agreed, as the patrol moved off again.

"Either way," Sadrao said, rising and pulling her to her feet, "he could hardly anticipate you falling in with a dog-soldier."

Lyra followed him down the slope, pushing aside tangles of vegetation with the shaft of her staff. She thought, ruefully, that she could scarcely have anticipated it either.

When she remembered her family, it still hurt with a desperate ache, but she had far more pressing concerns, like hiding quiet as a rabbit in the woods while Sadrao spied out their path. When

They crouched, watching a trio of brigands several hundred feet down the slope.

she thought of them, her fingers groped for the hilt of her honor-knife, but Sadrao was carrying it in his pack. Jasen might not be looking for her, but there was no point in chancing that a brigand might recognize the significance of such a blade.

She woke sometimes, missing the lilac-covered window of her bedroom, but she began to have difficulty remembering her father's face.

The few times that grief took her too strongly to ignore, Sadrao let her cry and rumbled soothing nonsense in the growling dog-soldier tongue. He did not let her feel ashamed afterwards, either.

If he had not had such a solid, earthy presence, if he had not been so totally here-and-now, she might have doubted that he was real.

She asked him a few times why he was here. His answer was not evasive, but not terribly satisfying—he had some information for friends of his, in Jeppeth, that they would find useful. When she asked about what, he said "Brandy corks," and flicked his ears at some secret joke, and changed the subject.

Three days outside of Jeppeth, they had left the area around House Volfrieds behind and descended back to the main road. Sadrao relaxed and began to laugh more, telling her stories about exotic Khamir. In the evenings, he would build larger fires and they would practice staffwork. At least she thought they were practicing staffwork. They spent quite a while, morning and evening, standing toe to toe, trying to knock each other off balance. Compared to that—and his tendency to turn on her in mid-hike and shove her to see if she was staying centered—the amount of time she spent with the staff in her hands was actually quite minimal. Still, Lyra began to enjoy the journey a little, even if her legs still ached at the end of a day's march. In three days' walk from her home she had seen things she'd never seen before—wild animals, strange plants, a traveling group of troubadours that shared a fire with them one night and sang hysterically funny murder ballads while Lyra giggled and Sadrao attempted to sing along. (Sadrao had an incredible howling range and told Lyra proudly that he was considered quite an excellent singer in Khamir. Lyra didn't have the heart to tell him that the wailing arias of dog-soldier songs were quite intolerable to human ears.)

One afternoon, they even startled a giant porcupine in a clearing just off the road. The massive rodent was larger than Sadrao and turned a placid eye on them before waddling around to present his needled back. They gave him a wide berth. The longest spines were as large as javelins.

"Don't go near it," said Sadrao, unnecessarily.

"I know that," said Lyra, a bit testily. "They don't throw their quills, though, no matter what de Matthias says in *Monsters of the Forest*."

"No," said Sadrao, "but you won't believe how easily the quills jump. You'd swear you weren't within a foot of him, but you're picking spines out for hours." He chuckled softly. "I had a friend who made a cuirass out of porcupine hide. Curing it was the very devil, but you didn't want to be his enemy in battle." He paused thoughtfully. "Or guarding his back too closely, for that matter."

Lyra chuckled.

When they approached Jeppeth, they joined a thickening stream of farmers and tradesman on the road. Tributaries of people joined from the cultivated lands to the right of them, and occasionally from small docks or fishing houses on the Tanglelore, to their left. Everyone gave Sadrao a respectful berth.

The road separated from the river a mile before Jeppeth and turned toward the city walls, through pens and stables built outside of the population center, until it approached the city proper. The stream of people poured through the gates of the walled city, breaking into a dozen rivulets that went down each street, while the main bulk flowed into a series of open courtyards that housed the central bazaars.

Jeppeth was a city-state built on trade, and it showed in the brightly colored, eclectic market. It was early evening and most of the merchants had closed for the day, but to Lyra's eyes it was still bustling with people. She clung to Sadrao's side as he meandered through the marketplace, chatting with merchants in a dozen foreign languages. Lyra could only understand two or three, but he evidently heard something that interested him. The next moment, they were making a bee-line for an inn near the stockyards. Lyra shrank from the smoke and the noise, but Sadrao was insistent.

The Hanged Dog tavern (Sadrao flicked his ears back briefly at the name) was filled with smoke—tobacco and sweet hashish, enough to make Lyra dizzy. Sadrao's sensitive black nose twitched repeatedly, but there was a gleam in his eyes, almost like that of combat.

"Come, come," said the dog-soldier, his hand on her shoulder, guarding her back with the sheer wall of his presence. Holding her protectively before him, he threaded a way through the tavern, past tables full of tough brown men with the look of professional fighters. A table full of wiry, gaudily-clothed men and women fell silent as they passed. To Lyra's eyes, the men wore as much gold as the slim, dangerous-eyed women. They watched as the dog-soldier and his charge moved past their table, then began speaking again in low voices.

Tavern wenches flounced by, painted within an inch of their lives, lost in the sea of smoke and voices. Sadrao steered Lyra toward a back table, his ears sweeping constantly from side to side to catch hints of conversation.

Lyra looked across the tavern's far wall, seeing an entire table of white bodies—four lithe, weasel-like Ferran and two humans with skin as white as chalk. One of the humans glanced up and met her eyes with palest pink ones, rock-hard despite their watery color.

"Sit," said Sadrao brusquely, pulling out a chair with unthinking chivalry. "And stop looking," he added, taking a seat himself. Lyra was wedged into the corner of the tavern, with Sadrao between her and the rest of the world. Sadrao himself was turned so that his back was to the wall. The implication was obvious—anyone seeking to harm the young woman would have to go through him first.

"But—"

"Trouble," said Sadrao, with the same curt authority he used during their erratic weapons practices. His ears kept easing back against his skull, until he consciously brought them erect. "House of Diamond trouble. And not our trouble either, so don't borrow any." He said something else, not quite under his breath, in his own tongue. Lyra looked down and became very interested in the scarred wood of the tabletop.

A shadow fell across the warped wood. She looked up, startled, into the flushed face of an extremely large, extremely drunk man.

Sadrao, who had twisted his neck around to eye the increasingly rowdy table of mercenaries, turned back immediately, his nose wrinkling in obvious distaste. Lyra could see, or rather smell, why, even with her weak human nose. The man's gravy-and-beer stained tunic had obviously not been washed in weeks, which seemed to coincide with the last time he himself had probably bathed.

The man slurred something at her. It was timed with a roar from the mercs' table, and it took Lyra a moment to decipher what he said.

"No," she said, sure that her face was burning red, "I am *not* interested in leaving my pet so you can show me a good time."

He looked blankly at her. He was past his prime, stubbly hair bracketing a growing baldness. His frame was large, and had obviously been muscular once, but had run to fat.

It occurred to Lyra suddenly that she ought to be frightened. His neck was thicker than her waist, even if most of it was fat. She looked over at Sadrao.

The dog-soldier had risen to his full, impressive height. His ears were flat back across his skull. He dropped a clawed hand on the man's shoulder.

The man put his hands on the table and leaned forward. His breath reeked of ale. "C'mon," he began. "Don'sh be a cowld bitch—"

At that moment, he seemed to finally notice the iron grip on his arm and turned around, into Sadrao's teeth-bared grin. His eyes grew round as saucers.

"I suggest you leave," said Sadrao, through locked fangs.

A brief ripple of silence spread around them as other diners turned to watch the drama unfolding.

"Now," added Sadrao, and put a thunderous growl in for good measure.

The man left, muttering something that (fortunately) was lost in another shout from the mercs' table. Lyra looked up, saw the table of albinos watching them with sly smiles (at least on the humans—it was impossible to tell what the four slender weasels were doing at this distance) and looked immediately back down at the table.

When it became obvious that there wasn't going to be an altercation, conversation resumed around them, settling back to the dull roar. Sadrao smiled faintly at her, his upper fangs covered, and she returned it, careful to keep her lips over her teeth.

By the time their food—a somewhat dubious pair of steaks—arrived, she had gotten up the nerve to steal another look across the tavern. The albinos were gone, the table taken by a half-dozen disreputable-looking men with the bright red-orange hair and freckled skin of the lands south of Hurricane Way. She hadn't seen the pale men and Ferran leave, but Sadrao seemed a good deal more relaxed, his ears forward.

The steak was tough enough that even Sadrao was forced to abandon his usually flawless table manners and simply shear through the meat with massive canines. Lyra suspected that, while it probably came from a hoofed mammal, it was one more likely to be pulling carts than giving milk. She wondered with the absent economy of a merchant's daughter how much the knackers charged for a prime cut of horse, compared to beef.

"Sadrao," said Lyra plaintively, using her belt-knife to saw at her steak, "why are we here?"

"Not for the cuisine, certainly," said the dog-soldier dryly. He took a longish swallow of ale and gazed thoughtfully around the tavern before leaning closer. "I am supposed to meet friends in Jeppeth. But I do not know quite where they are. So I am being very visible and waiting, and hoping that they will follow the story of a dog-soldier to me." He grinned at her abruptly. "Forgive me, I don't mean to be mysterious. But we'll know soon enough."

The meal demolished, Sadrao sat back with Lyra's untouched ale. Lyra slouched back in her chair, picking her teeth with a splinter from the table. She hoped that she looked hardened and dangerous, but rather doubted it. The way Sadrao's ears eased back in amusement every time he looked at her wasn't helping.

She wondered what Sadrao's friends were like. She wondered what information he had for them.

A disturbance across the bar caught her eye. She lifted her head, aware that Sadrao was also intent upon the scene.

Two women, both elven, were threading their way across the tavern. Lyra raised her eyebrows at that. Elves weren't common in this area, or anywhere, outside the elven homeland of Anu'tintavel.

The elven nation, Lyra had read, was one of the few regions on the northern part of the continent that could really be called a nation. Unlike the loose patchwork of city-states and feudal lords that made up most of the human lands, Anu'tintavel boasted a centralized ruling council consisting of members from every elven clan and region, a standing army organized at the militia level, and a border controlled to the point of polite xenophobia.

As the daughter of a merchant house, Lyra knew that the elves were a largely self-sufficient group, importing only those foods that could not grow in the temperate woodlands of Anu'tintavel. They exported beautiful fabrics and art objects, many in the complicated style of elven knotwork, medicines and herbal potions, but no timber, few foods, and absolutely no labor. If Lyra's father's trading partners were to be believed, the elven nation was disdainful of the easy raveling and unraveling of alliances between human houses, city-states, and feudal lords, and distrustful of the lawless areas between such alliances, where bandits could descend upon the unwary with no fear of repercussions. "Lookin' down their damn ahri-stoh-cra-tik noses at us," had been her father's senior partner's exact words. "The skinny little blonde bastards. Think their people are gonna get killed the minute they step out've Anoo-tin-tah-vull. Hell with 'em."

Privately, Lyra thought that if the human lands (which, to be accurate, were also home to a large number of Ferran and other non-human races) had been a bit more centrally controlled, the sort of massacre perpetrated on her house would not have been so depressingly easy. She didn't blame the elves for not wanting to risk their artisans on the alternating stretches of law and anarchy outside Anu'tinavel's borders.

Two elves then, a week's travel from the borders of their nation, while not unusual per se, were not something one would expect to see in a bar like this.

The shorter of the two had the delicate beauty common to elvenkind, high cheekbones set off by magnificent turquoise eyes and blond hair like a waterfall of gold. More than one catcall followed in her wake. She ignored them.

The other woman was as different from her as day from night. She was tall and wiry where her younger companion was rounded and soft, her ash-white hair cropped close against her skull. There was a sword strapped across her back, in the same shoulder harness arrangement as Sadrao's. Black leathers encased her lean, athletic form, like a scabbard fitted to a sword.

"Aha!" said Sadrao.

Something about the taller woman's stance toward her companion reminded Lyra of Sadrao's own protective hovering. When one particularly rude comment rang out, the smaller elf ignored it. Her guardian, however, tilted a cool grey gaze in his direction.

"Whatsamatta, girl," slurred the drunk—one of the table of mercenaries near the door. "Youse afraid your li'l bird gonna leave you fra real man?" His companions sniggered.

The ash-haired elf said something in a low, melodious voice, like a mourning dove calling. Lyra couldn't hear it, but it made Sadrao wince—and chuckle. The two elves had moved past the mercenary's table before whatever it was penetrated the drunk's sodden brain.

"You—damn—bitch!" he snarled, standing up abruptly. His chair went over with a crash. "I'll teach you—!"

Conversation died in concentric circles around the confrontation. Into that quiet, like a stone dropped in a still pond, the tall elf said, very clearly, "You and what army, dog?"

"That's torn it," said Sadrao regretfully, rising. He pulled Lyra to her feet with one hand. "Stay close. Keep your head down. Watch your footing—once the beer spills, it's going to be slick."

"Wha—?" began Lyra intelligently.

Across the tavern, the drunk lunged at the grey-eyed elf with a roar of drunken fury. The woman sidestepped neatly, sending the drunk careening into the table of gypsies. The table went over. Indignant shouts rang out as the gypsies leapt to their feet, steel flashing in their hands.

The other three mercs, realizing that their companion had just started something, stood up. Several of them went for swords.

The smaller elf, with a strength that belied her size, hooked her hands under the edge of the mercenaries' table and shoved.

The remains of a meal and a dozen mugs of ale showered the men and they jumped backwards. Nearby diners, some receiving the benefits of the elf-woman's largesse, others getting bumped by the trio of mercs, also rose. Weapons were appearing like some kind of conjuring trick.

Sadrao drew Mohenja with a cold hiss of steel. One hand planted in the middle of Lyra's back, he shoved her toward the door. Unfortunately, this led through the heart of what was rapidly turning into a brawl.

Finding her eating knife in her hand, Lyra stumbled forward, wishing desperately that she had her staff. A week of Sadrao's rough-and-tumble training had left her feeling naked without it in hand, even if it was more of a security blanket than a serious threat. Sadrao had made her leave it in her room, saying that a nervous-looking young woman with an obviously homemade staff was going to attract more attention than he was ready to deal with before dinner.

She was consoled by the fact that she wouldn't have had room to use it in these quarters anyway.

The tall elf woman had a sword out now, swinging it in easy arcs, trying to keep a space between herself and the mercenaries. The gypsies had risen. Two of them were rolling the drunkard off the remains of their table, cursing in an exotic tongue, while the other four were viciously defending their neutrality in the conflict by the expedient of stabbing anyone who came within five feet of them.

The smaller elf started to move out from behind her guardian, but the grey-eyed woman snapped a command in the liquid elven tongue, and the other subsided with obvious ill-grace.

"Duck!" said Sadrao, almost cheerfully, and shoved Lyra down before she could do so under her own power. Her left knee landed in a puddle of ale and was immediately soaked. Mohenja swung in a gleaming arc over her head, biting into the leather armor of one of the mercenaries. The man recoiled. Sadrao scooped Lyra up in one arm and half-dragged, half-carried her toward the elven warrior.

The strategy became clear to Lyra as Sadrao plowed through the fray. Neither he nor the elven woman actually engaged anyone—they simply created a cocoon of spinning blades that kept any opponents at arm's length, while backing slowly toward the door. If anyone managed to get inside their guard, they were rapidly dispatched.

"Coming through, Sinai!" roared Sadrao over the general cacophony. He lifted Lyra over a knot of bodies, picking his footing carefully on the beer-slick floor. Behind him, the brawl closed in a sea of pandemonium as people, in the wrong place at the wrong time, sought to take it out on their fellow diners.

The tall elf looked up at what must have been her name. A wild grin split her face suddenly, transforming the elegant, icy, older warrior into a mad-eyed girl. She whooped aloud and brought the hilt of her slim sword down on the head of a man who had been crawling toward her. He crumpled in a spreading pool of spilled ale, spilled food, and spilled blood.

Sadrao threw his head back and howled in response. Lyra squawked in most unheroic counterpoint as the dog-soldier flung her over his shoulder. "Hang on," he advised. "Need both hands."

"Oh goddess," said Lyra, throwing her arms around Sadrao's neck and wrapping her legs around his muscled back as if she was climbing a tree.

Sadrao spun around on the pads of his feet, Mohenja in his hand, looking for opponents. His back was now to the door, the elves behind him. The gypsies, off to his left, were swarming a pair of red-haired sellswords. The original trio of mercs had vanished—one of them was facedown, practically under Sadrao's feet. Lyra saw, with a queasy horror, that he was missing one arm below the elbow, blood mixing with beer across the floor. The fight was getting increasingly ugly. The waitstaff had retreated to the safety of the bar. The barkeeper had a cudgel out, and the wenches were alternating between drinking the now-undeliverable beers and cracking the unwary across the skull with their trays.

Lyra had no illusions about how she would fare in this madhouse if she lost Sadrao.

As the dog-soldier danced backwards, one of his feet landed on the injured merc's arm. It turned under his heel. Sadrao lost his footing on the slick floorboards and went to one knee.

He was up again almost at once, but the motion completely unseated Lyra. The young woman knew, with that gut-wrenching, absolute certainty of terror, that she was going to fall. She shoved an arm through Sadrao's sword harness and clung with the strength of panic.

Two mercenaries had come up with swords and were advancing. Sadrao backed slowly, Lyra clinging to his neck, covering the elves' retreat with broad sweeps of Mohenja.

Lyra, face smashed into Sadrao's shoulderblades, was conscious of the dog-soldier's musky scent and her own sweat. She lifted her head, seeing a blur of faces over Sadrao's heavily muscled shoulder, then yelped as the dog-soldier engaged one of the men in a flurry of swordsmanship. Steel rang out.

The bunching of Sadrao's muscles and the lurch of motion did her no good. Lyra felt herself slipping and scrabbled at Sadrao's sword harness for a handhold. Sweaty palms skidded on the slick leather. One leg came loose and flailed.

Sadrao dispatched the final mercenary with a magnificent slash-and-kick combination that took the man's feet out from under him and left him semi-conscious on the floor. The dog-soldier's shift of balance proved too much for Lyra's burning arm muscles. She shrieked, lost her grip, and fell off. The floorboards came up to meet her.

It was a measure of how unpleasant the floor had gotten that Lyra actually slid across it, like someone falling on ice, for a good yard before slamming into someone's boots.

A sword gleamed over her head and she lifted her hands in futile defense.

She thought, tiredly, *I have got to stop trying to stop swords with my hands.*

A pair of grey eyes looked down and the sword point flicked away from her throat. The elven woman reached down and hauled her to her feet with one hand.

"Time to go," she said, turning and shoving Lyra out the door. Lyra stumbled on the curb as she was propelled out into the street, narrowly avoiding the blue-clad form of the smaller elf.

"You must be Sadrao's protégé," said the elf cheerfully, as if she got in barroom brawls every day. "I'm Jacyl."

"Lyra," said Lyra automatically, too confused to frame the terrified questions wandering through her head. "I—what— Sadrao—!" She started to turn back.

"Inside," said Jacyl, patting her arm reassuringly. "—or not," she added, as the dog-soldier flung himself out the tavern door, teeth gleaming in the light of the lanterns. The grey-eyed elf was hard on his heels, her grin as feral as Sadrao's.

"The watch will be here any minute," panted Sadrao, tongue lolling between his teeth. "Which way?"

"Here," barked the tall elf, catching Jacyl's arm and shoving her toward an alley across the street.

"I love it when they do that," said Jacyl wryly, trading a glance with Lyra as Sadrao manhandled her into the darkened street. "Always feel like a bloody snail."

Lyra liked her immediately.

Hoofbeats sounded up the street. Sadrao sheathed Mohenja and broke into a fast trot, urging the three women on ahead of him. With the tall elf leading, they plunged through the streets too quickly for Lyra to keep track of turnings. She was well and thoroughly lost by the time Sadrao called a halt.

They leaned against the wall, panting. Their breath steamed in the cool air. It was moving toward mid-spring, the danger of late frosts almost past, but the nights were still cold. The streets were nearly deserted of people, now that they had left the main rows of taverns behind.

Sadrao rolled his head to one side, looking down at the grey-eyed elf.

"You and what army, dog," he said flatly. "Couldn't come up with a more original line." He rolled his yellow eyes, white still showing around the edges. "You and what army, dog. Sinai, I'm ashamed of you."

"Given the audience, I thought I'd keep it simple."

"Mmmph. Yes." His tail thumped twice against the brick with amusement. "Missed you, Sinai," he said. "Glad you're still alive."

"You too, old wolf," said Sinai. She appeared barely winded. Lyra was obscurely grateful that Jacyl was also leaning against the wall, blowing like an exhausted horse.

"Lyra," said Sadrao, looking away from the elf's grey eyes, "two of the finest people to ever come out of Anu'tintavel—Sinai and Jacyl."

"We met," said Jacyl, shoving sweaty blond hair from her eyes, "while you two were disrupting the peace." She drove a small fist at Sinai, who blocked it carelessly. "Sinai. Dear Sinai. *Friend* Sinai." Her voice dripped with mock sincerity. "It is not necessary to answer every insult to my virtue from every drunken lout in every bar we enter—"

Sadrao gave a barking laugh. "Haven't changed, I see."

Lyra, who was looking at Jacyl, was caught by a fleeting look of pain that crossed the elven woman's face.

Sinai's lips, however, curved slightly at the dog-soldier's words. Already, the laughing hoyden had been replaced by the cool, elegant warrior. Lyra put Sinai's age somewhere between thirty and fifty. It was hard to tell with elves once they passed puberty. A woman in her prime, certainly, long-lived as elves were. Jacyl looked somewhat younger, late twenties to mid-thirties, her face unlined.

"You haven't changed either, old wolf." Sinai looked at Lyra, thoughtfully, eyes grey as stormclouds, missing nothing. Lyra saw that there was a small gold ring in one ear, etched with a tiny flower, identical to one of Sadrao's.

Lyra, feeling self-conscious under the elf's thoughtful eyes, sketched a bow and said, "*Ano daro tu kurimano.*" Her accent was probably atrocious.

Both elves and Sadrao stared at her.

"Be careful, Sadrao!" said Jacyl, with a laugh like the trill of a songbird. "This one is more than she appears to be!"

"*Gozu daro,*" Sinai said, the correct reply. "And where," she added in trade-tongue, something almost like a smile touching her lips, "does a human child learn formal—and archaic—elven greetings?"

"I read it in a book once," said Lyra, and blushed.

The mouth of the alley where they stood was a few inches higher than the street. Brown water trickled by through the gutters, splashed with pale lamplight. A puddle at their feet reflected three pale ovals of the women's faces and the bright citron glimmer of Sadrao's eyes.

"I trust you had no trouble finding me," said Sadrao, as the group picked their way onto the street. Sinai nodded.

"Your people aren't so common here that one's not an event. Although I did not realize you were traveling with a companion. That...changes matters."

"Oh?"

"I had...a request to make." She frowned, looking up the street.

"Had?" inquired Sadrao mildly. "No longer?"

"You have a protégé," said Sinai, her eyes flicking to Lyra and back again. "I had hoped you would escort a charge to Knaxos."

"Knaxos!" Sadrao turned to look at her, his nostrils flaring as if tracking an elusive scent. "The Isle of Books?" He paused, his voice dropping. "The House of Diamond?"

Sinai made a sharp, silencing gesture. "Yes. Jacyl and I would travel with you overland as far as the mouth of the Tanglelore, and from there it's only two weeks by boat."

"Faster to go up to Frieze, perhaps," said Sadrao mildly, as they crossed a side street and splashed through another puddle. "Four more days overland, and it's only another three by boat.

"Frieze is dangerous of late," put in Jacyl, drawing her cloak tighter around herself. "More boats, but more priests too, and the Church has been preaching against non-humans lately. They've extended it to include elves." She made a gesture that took in pointed ears and tilted, cat-like eyes. "I can almost pass, if I keep my head down, but Sinai might as well have burned their Sacrificed God herself."

Elves and humans were, technically speaking, the same race, in the same way that bulldogs and greyhounds were both dogs, but neither the elves nor the Church were particularly proud of the connection. When Lyra considered that the other intelligent races of the world were mostly fur-bearing and closer kin to Sadrao than humanity, both sides seemed a little silly, but she was not going to say that to someone as elegantly self-possessed—and dangerous—as Sinai.

"Have they said anything against dog-soldiers?" inquired Sadrao with silky menace, the last "R" turning into a soft growl.

Jacyl made a rude noise. "No. Not specifically. The dog-soldiers are too rare, and too consistently above reproach. You're not *welcome* in Frieze, of course, but even they wouldn't dare claim you were out to undermine humanity."

Sadrao permitted himself a humorless smile. "So. You wish me to accompany this person to Knaxos. Who?"

"My cousin-son," said Sinai, her grey eyes bleak. "A half-breed elf, twenty-three years old. My cousin—"

"I did not know you had a cousin," said the dog-soldier mildly.

Jacyl made a sound, choked off so quickly that Lyra could not identify it.

"My cousin Lythara was raped," said Sinai, still staring into Sadrao's eyes. There was a hairline fracture in the timbre of her voice. "Kidnapped and drugged and raped, until she got with child. A sorcerer's get, a son. By the time she escaped, it was too late to lose the child, so she bore it. And loved it," she added bitterly. "Lythara always had more heart than brains." The twist of her lips indicated that this was not a malady Sinai herself suffered from.

"He should have died. He should never have been born. We thought—we knew that we could not rear a half-human child. *Should* not. Not there—not so close—so Lythara raised him among humans, elf-friends, close to Anu'tintavel. We thought his father dead, or ignorant. We were wrong."

"When Trent was nine," said Jacyl, taking up the thread of the tale, her voice curiously dispassionate, "his father came for him. The sorcerer. Lythara was killed defending her son. His father took him to his keep. To Ironspine."

Sadrao's breath hissed inward in disbelief. "*Ironspine*..."

"Vade," said Sinai, her voice low and cold as an owl's cry. "Kingbreaker. The sorcerer of Ironspine. We thought him dead. Janna Skinstrong brought his fortress down around him an elven lifetime ago. But he lives."

A rumbling growl rose in Sadrao's throat. Without speaking, he reached up to touch Mohenja's hilt, as if to reassure himself it was still there.

Lyra hugged herself, chilled, although from the night air or Sadrao's obvious disquiet she couldn't say.

"Trent escaped last year," said Jacyl, when it seemed that Sinai would say no more. "Or was set free. We don't know. He came to Anu'tintavel, but they would not let him within the Elvenlands.

There is a darkness in him, places that none of us can reach. I sense no evil in him—I think the darkness could be pain, and fear—"

"Or something placed by Vade himself," said Sinai coldly. "I don't know. We could not take the chance. We needed to know why Vade bred himself a son of elven blood. And why he trained him in the lesser sorceries, for the boy is trained. He would be an incredible weapon against Vade, but we dare not trust him yet. We needed resources, archives, and better mind-mages than elvenkind—"

"So you send him to Knaxos," said Sadrao. "To the greatest library in the world, and the House of Diamond."

"Indeed. When you sent word that you had information, that you needed to meet us—it was a godsend."

"Why me?" Sadrao looked from one to the other.

"Because it's your sort of task," said Jacyl, laughing painfully, her voice like broken bells. "Because you're the best. Because you aided me once, like you're leading this girl now, and you gave Sinai and I each other." The blond elf slipped under Sinai's arm and pressed close to the taller woman.

Sinai, whose gaze had never left Sadrao's eyes, looked down suddenly into her companion's face. Lyra was surprised to see Sinai's hard grey eyes soften. The tall elf cupped Jacyl's face with her scarred hands, in a tender, unselfconscious gesture.

Lyra felt somewhat embarrassed, wondering if the elven woman had forgotten that she stood in the presence of a stranger.

"Exactly," murmured Sinai, still looking into Jacyl's turquoise eyes. "You brought my heart and soul to me, Sadrao," she said quietly, not looking around. "I will not ask you to leave your charge—and any path with the boy will be fraught with danger. You were my best hope."

"Why not—" Lyra's voice cracked and she started again, "why not take him to Knaxos yourself?"

Sinai looked up, finally, seeking Lyra's face. There was no self-consciousness in her eyes.

She didn't forget I was here. She just doesn't care. Either Sadrao vouching for me is good enough, or she doesn't care what anyone thinks about her and Jacyl.

"We are needed elsewhere," said Sinai, in answer to her question. "Needed badly. Jacyl and I have talents that are...unique. We will go as far as we can, but we are needed elsewhere."

"We're spies," put in Jacyl. She tried to force a smile, and even Lyra could tell it was a show.

"Vade is moving against Anu'tintavel," said Sinai quietly, killing the false smile on Jacyl's face. "The raids—well, there have been raids for the last few decades. But these are more than raids. Once it was a raid or two a season, his creatures slipping across the border and killing and slipping away again. Now there are several a fortnight. We lose a little ground each time, an inch at a time. And the pattern has changed. He is not merely harrying us— he is seeking to gain a foothold, and—" She paused and looked at Sadrao. Her voice came lower than before. "—and he has help from somewhere inside. We simply do not have time and luxury to go all the way to Knaxos. I can ill spare the time to go as far as Delta, but I will not allow my cousin-son within Anu'tintavel, either."

The dog-soldier muttered something in his own tongue and sighed heavily. "And that," he said, "is why I wished to see you. The help inside—I have news—"

He paused and looked around with a faint, self-deprecating smile. "And some news is better shared somewhere other than standing in the middle of the street, yes?"

"Of course," said Sinai. "We are staying at the Inn of the Red Bull. This way."

Chapter Six

The Inn of the Red Bull was nominally full—at least until Sadrao glowered at the landlord, whereupon a pair of adjoining rooms suddenly opened up and the price of meals mysteriously plummeted. The dog-soldier laid down a sizeable deposit, then ducked out to retrieve their gear from the much inferior inn where they had left it. Lyra dropped her backpack—and its meager contents—next to the bed. The room was small, only a bed, a nightstand, and basin, but a narrow window overlooked the courtyard and let in the cool night air.

A knock at the door admitted Jacyl. "There's a bath down the hall," she said, "water's cheap but towels are outrageous, so use this one." A fluffy towel, neatly folded, landed on the bed.

"Oh...thank you," said Lyra, a little faint at the notion of a real bath. With hot water, instead of splashing in an icy stream. "I haven't seen a real bath in ages."

"I know how it is." Jacyl grinned at her. "Sadrao and Sinai are two of a kind—they can go for months washing in streams and ponds. But *I* can't, and I don't expect you can either." She paused, her eyes traveling over Lyra's worn clothing, much the worse for wear after the fight and not in exactly good condition before that. "Ah—don't take this the wrong way, Lyra, but—do you have any other clothes?"

Lyra flushed. "No," she stammered. She was acutely conscious that her back and knees were soaked with ale and blood and bits of food, sticking to her body like a disgusting second skin. Her left trouser leg was split up the knee. "I—ah—didn't—my home—"

To her utter horror, her eyes filled with tears.

"Oh, my dear," said Jacyl, putting her arms around the younger girl. "I thought it might be something like that."

Lyra fought down the lump in her throat and dashed her tears with her wrist. "I've been trying not cry about it anymore. It's stupid—it's been just a week, but it feels like so much longer. It's all been so crazy. I go all day, and I hardly even think about them because I'm hiding in the woods, or Sadrao's trying to teach me something, or I'm too worried about staying alive myself! Gods, that's horrible, isn't it?"

"I think it's perfectly normal," said Jacyl quietly.

Lyra plunged onward. "But then something silly comes up— like only having one pair of clothes to my name, and I realize that it's all gone, everything I grew up with—" She stopped and took a steadying breath.

Jacyl put a hand on her arm, saving a moment that was rapidly turning awkward. "Well. Never fear—I've got something you can borrow for tonight, and tomorrow we'll go to the market. We won't leave here for a few days, at any rate, and we'll get you outfitted like a proper adventurer." She winked at Lyra.

"Thank you," said Lyra faintly. "I don't have much money—"

"Pfagh." The elf waved a hand carelessly, leading the way down the hall to the bathing room. "Anu'tintavel can foot the bill. If you go to Knaxos, consider it payment—and if you don't, consider it a kindness from one of Sadrao's former charges to the current one."

"Oh! So that's what he meant by aiding you once…?"

"Fifteen years ago," said Jacyl with a laugh. "I was in a similar strait to yourself—no family, no one to turn to. Sadrao found me—saved my life. And introduced me to his friend, a *very* serious young scout named Sinai." She smiled at the memory, leaning against the doorframe. "I don't think even he knew how we would take to each other." Jacyl's smile faded uncertainly.

"It doesn't bother you, does it?" she asked abruptly. "Sinai, and me?"

Lyra rather doubted that anyone cared what she thought, but recognized that Jacyl was trying to find out her opinion. "Umm, no…" she said, awkwardly. "I mean, I've read, uh, about people like that. You. Um." And had been shocked senseless the first time she adequately comprehended what the words were describing, but she wasn't going to tell Jacyl that. "It's none of my business. I mean, you seem like nice people."

She stared at the floor and felt her cheeks burn.

"*I* am nice people," said Jacyl archly. "Sinai is not at all nice, but she has other virtues. Good. I've never known Sadrao to make mistakes with his charges, but sometimes people are very sheltered. I wanted to avoid any misunderstandings."

Lyra didn't know what to say to that, but ventured a smile. Jacyl grinned back and pushed the door open. "I'll leave the clothes outside the door. Have fun!"

The bath was heaven. Wood-heated in the next room (Lyra could smell the smoke through the slightly ajar window), it entered the bathing room in an ingenious, and undoubtedly expensive, set of copper tubs bolted to the ceiling. Either the hot or cold water (also in an enormous copper tub) could be accessed by throwing two small ivory handles connected to a very simple sluice gate.

Lyra, who was used to breaking ice over the privies in midwinter, sank back in the water and reflected that they didn't have *anything* like this at home.

She scrubbed her skin until it was raw and attacked her ragged red hair mercilessly. Jacyl had thoughtfully left her a hairbrush, and Lyra pulled great tangles loose from her smarting scalp. When she was thoroughly clean, free of even the memory of dirt, she sank into the final tub of hot water with a groan of purely hedonistic pleasure.

Her wounded arm was healing much more cleanly than it had any right to. She had washed it carefully every day, as Sadrao instructed. It had faded to a long red stripe, still tender, but no longer in danger of re-opening every time she moved.

It was not until the water had cooled to lukewarm that she could bear to drag herself out. She reached for her towel, dried herself off, and wrapped it around herself long enough to pull the clothes Jacyl had left her into the bathroom.

Blue leggings and a loose silk shirt, in a shade of grey that seemed familiar. Lyra chewed her lower lip in thought, then placed it suddenly as the exact color of Sinai's eyes. Jacyl must have chosen it with her lover in mind—now *there* was a pair. The notion of his daughter traveling with two such women—her father would simply have died. And elves to boot. Bones of the Goddess, but these were strange times she had fallen upon. Lyra dropped the towel and reached for the leggings.

And stopped.

A full length mirror stood against one wall, proving once again that this was not an inexpensive inn. Lyra stared at herself in it.

The red-haired, green-eyed stranger staring back at her looked older than seventeen, older and harder than Lyra felt. She straightened her back and squared her shoulders.

A week of hard physical exertion and iron rations had left her sore most nights, but, she now saw, it had begun to melt away the baby fat that clung stubbornly to her frame—or perhaps the strain had left her face thinner and more drawn. Her muscles still lacked the hard definition of Sinai's, or even Jacyl's, but given time... Her hand crept down to her breasts—not large, just more than enough to fill her cupped hand. She turned slightly, following the long curve over ribcage, in at the waist, over hip and down the long elegant sweep of thigh.

Her skin was tanned where the sun touched it, almost translucently pale elsewhere. Her face was more defined than it had been, the softness under her chin almost gone. There were lines around her eyes that hadn't been there a week ago. She was half surprised she hadn't gone completely grey.

It was with something akin to a shock that she realized she was attractive. Not pretty exactly, hardly beautiful, but pleasing to the eye. Something that a man might look twice at.

Seventeen, and a virgin, Lyra realized with a shock where her thoughts were tending. She moved hurriedly, putting on Jacyl's spare clothes, her fingers clumsy on the buttons of the cloud-grey shirt. Her father had never taught her about men, and her mother little enough. She had learned fascinating things from her maid Lisette—and the final, terrible thing, too.

The stab of grief that she expected came, but it was curiously blunted. Lisette was dead. Her father was dead. She mourned him, still, but her life had changed so much in a week that she did not miss him—or rather, she missed him the way she missed the lilac bush outside her window. She remembered them fondly, but they seemed to belong to a different life, a different person. There was no hole in her new life where he had been, as there had been a hole in her old one left by the death of her mother. When she thought of him, her chest grew tight, but she did not often find herself thinking of him.

Nothing like running for your life and traveling with a dog-soldier to make you forget your grief.

In her mind's eye, her father was set aside with her mother, who had died when she was a child. Her life had changed, utterly and dramatically, and her old home had no part of this new world. But with that change came...possibilities.

Goddess, am I so cold?

She was no longer being saved for any marriage alliance. No one would look down their noses at her—certainly not Sinai and Jacyl, unwed and, the Church would claim, unnatural. Their good opinion, she realized, was already important to her. And Sadrao—what would Sadrao think?

She tried to imagine him safeguarding her virtue like a nun, and laughed out loud at the thought.

So she took the time to smooth the clothing out, over slender hips, and brush her hair back. She left the bathing chamber feeling far better than she had since she had first woken, wrapped in Sadrao's cloak, in the forest under the hills.

Jacyl had said that they would be down in the common room. Lyra trotted down the steps and into the main room. It was a long, low room, with fireplaces on either end, the floors polished oak, the tables muffled with cloth hangings. It was quiet, at least compared to the Hanged Dog, the clientele restrained. She made her way to the table where her companions sat.

Sadrao hooked a chair with a furry ankle and pulled it out for her. She sat down, and the serving girl brought over another bowl of stew and a mug of cider.

"Lyra," said Sadrao gravely, "allow me to introduce Trent." His eyes flicked across the table, then back.

Trent sat with his back to the wall, between Sadrao and Jacyl. Lyra looked him over, aware that he was returning the same thoughtful scrutiny.

He was tall—even slouching a little he was as tall as Sinai, not quite as tall as Sadrao, a hair over six feet. He was gawky, as if his flesh had not yet caught up to his frame. Behind thick glasses, his eyes were large and grey, a warmer shade than Sinai's, but recognizably similar. They were mild, singularly gentle eyes, those, Lyra imagined, of a scholar or healer, and yet they seemed a little sad.

His elven heritage might have been responsible for his height and the color of his eyes, but there it seemed to end. His ears were only slightly pointed, almost within human norms. Instead of angular beauty, his long face was only angular, with too-high cheekbones and a pointed, stubborn chin. His mouth was broad and generous, but there were lines etched at the corners—there, and at his eyes. Not the lines a person got from smiling, and yet, despite the lines, his face looked curiously unlived in, as if he had learned long ago not to let anything show. He was not handsome, but not ill-favored either. The gentle grey eyes saved him from that.

He looks like that saint in the back of the Church canon, the one preaching to swallows and bears out in the forest. Saint, uh, Kernos. The one that everyone thought was mad, until he talked that pair of dragons into sparing some town. Except that Kernos had a tonsure, of course.

Trent's hair must have been entirely from his father, for instead of elven fairness it was a dusty brown. Far from being cut in a tonsure, it was an unruly mane, only held back with a string of incongruously delicate crystal. It reminded Lyra of Sadrao's own tangled mane.

"Charmed," said Trent, with a wry smile. His voice was mild, surprisingly deep, but not unpleasant.

"Likewise," said Lyra, feeling self-conscious about feeling self-conscious. She knotted her hands in her lap.

"So," said Sinai, with controlled impatience. "Now that we have all the pleasantries out of the way—"

The dog-soldier sighed. "Indeed. I had found something peculiar in my travels south, and—oh, it might have been nothing. But it made my clawtips itch. I wished to inform you, just in case. And having heard your news, now I see that I was right."

Sadrao reached to his belt, opened a pouch, and withdrew something. He held his clawed hand over the table, eyes locked on Sinai, and opened his fingers one by one.

A handful of corks, their tops sealed in wax and stamped with an elaborate elven pictogram, bounced to the table and rolled.

Jacyl, Sinai, and Trent each took one and examined it. Lyra did so as well, although it looked like any other cork to her.

"The Wineroot Clan sigil," said Jacyl quietly, and Sinai cut across her with: "Where did you get these?"

"The hold of a slave ship," said Sadrao quietly. "They had sold their cargo, and this was part of the payment they received."

Trent made a choking noise.

"There were crates stacked to the ceiling," said Sadrao, never taking his eyes from Sinai. "This was not a few stolen bottles of brandy. This was a shipment, and not the first. At least three ships' worth have come into the southern ports, and possibly more."

"The slavers?"

"Dead."

Sinai made a frustrated noise. Lyra looked from one to the other in bafflement, and then across to Trent, who met her baffled gaze with sympathetic eyes.

"Before they died, however," said Sadrao, leaning back, "one told me a name you might recognize." He tapped a claw on the table. "Ironspine."

Sinai's fist came down on the table with a clatter of cutlery, and Lyra yelped.

"It could be a coincidence," said Jacyl, slowly. "It could be—"

"It isn't," said Sinai flatly. "They've been paying a tribute to Ironspine, and he's trading it for slaves. We knew all along. We just needed proof that we could take to take the council."

"You have the word of a dog-soldier," said Sadrao mildly.

"On that word, the council might move," said Jacyl tiredly. "If the Wineroot Clan didn't sit on it. And if there weren't others, which there might be. We knew Wineroot was up to something, but some of the others might be as well. We just don't know."

"The scouts will follow you," said Sadrao, looking at Sinai.

Sinai looked away. "Not like they used to. I am...not in the favor I once was."

Silence reigned for a while.

"They were the ones who wanted to send Trent to Anu'tintavel," said Sinai, spearing her cousin with a look like a blade. "Some of the others, too, but Wineroot led the argument on the council. I wonder what they know that we don't."

Trent looked at the floor.

"It is more imperative than ever that you go to Knaxos," she said to Sadrao. "*Please*. I will beg you if I must."

"Enough, Sinai. Tomorrow."

Sinai started to say something, but Sadrao turned away, his ears pointedly swiveling in Lyra's direction.

"Assuming we go, Jacyl and Sinai would be coming with us as far as Delta—that's the town on the mouth of the Tanglelore," said Sadrao. "It's three weeks on horseback, if we don't want to kill the horses, so tomorrow Jacyl—" he nodded to her, "—has offered to take you to get outfitted, while Sinai and I find us mounts." He drained his ale and motioned to the serving girl for another. "We'll leave three days from now. *If* we decide to go."

"I had hoped to leave the day after tomorrow," said Sinai, over her wine. Her voice had the soft, dirge-like quality of an owl calling after prey.

Sadrao shook his head. "You come to me, and we'll do it my way. Lyra and I have been sleeping on the ground for a week, and I'm not eager to return to it so soon. There's few enough inns on the way to Delta—assuming I agree."

Trent smiled into his glass, saying nothing. Lyra would not have caught it, had she not been looking.

They finished the meal in relative silence, then leaned back, almost in unison, and relaxed. Lyra felt weariness crash down on her and stifled a jaw-cracking yawn behind one hand.

"Well," said Jacyl, rising, "I know you two can ride—or hike—all day, and then get in barfights, and still stay up all night swapping lies, but some of us need our sleep. Come on, Lyra." She helped the young woman to her feet, then looked over to the other member of their group. "Trent?"

"I concur." He rose as well—proving that he was actually taller than Sinai. His head came almost level with the top of Sadrao's skull, although the dog soldier's enormous ears and stiff, upstanding mane made him appear taller. Trent ducked under the top of the doorframe with the ease of long practice.

"See you in the morning," said Jacyl as they left Lyra at her door. "If you need anything—well, if I know those two, they'll be up all night, trying to prove who can drink more, but I'm just down the hall. G'night."

"Goodnight, Jacyl—Trent—" said Lyra. Trent's deep-voiced "goodnight" rumbled down the hallway. Lyra stepped into her room and closed the door.

Moonlight streamed through the window, so she ignored the unlit candle and undressed in the dark. The touch of cool sheet against her skin—and, the gods be praised, a mattress—was so magnificent after a week on the ground that she fell at once into a deep and dreamless sleep.

For the first time since her home had been destroyed, she did not miss the rustle of lilacs outside her window.

⚜

She woke, confused, in darkness, with someone shaking her. "Sadrao?!"

"Yes—half a moment—" A candle flared and gleamed off fangs. Lyra was too tired to think of how, in barely a week, that had come to be a comforting sight.

"Forgive me, Lyra," said the dog-soldier, crouching on the floor next to her, "but we must talk, briefly. Sinai wants an answer in the morning."

"Nghhh?" Lyra sat up, pulling the sheets around her.

He tapped his front claws together. "This mission of Sinai's. Whether or not I take it depends on you."

Lyra blinked muzzily at him.

He sighed. "I must confess to you that I did not plan to leave you here. I have little enough faith in merchants to care for the child of a partner, and even if they did, I suspect it will be some time before it is entirely safe for you so near your House. If your half-brother is indeed there, and if he trades in Jeppeth as I suspect—well, I believe it could be dangerous for you."

She nodded soberly, sleep fleeing. She had not thought of it, but now that he explained, it seemed obvious. If Jasen heard of her—well, it would be ugly.

And you don't want to throw yourself on the charity of strangers anyway, admit it. You want to stay with Sadrao.

It was true. He was her friend. She'd cried into his fur. He taught her things. She had lost her father and her home—she had not even considered that finding her father's business partners would mean losing Sadrao.

"I had actually thought we might travel up the coast a ways and see what presents itself…" he continued, and then stopped to pat her hand on the sheet, while she scrubbed with the other one at her suddenly watering eyes. "It's okay, Lyra. You're my charge now. I won't leave you alone in some strange city."

"Why?" she asked hoarsely, hearing the lump in her throat and forcing it back with pride that she had only recently remembered.

He shrugged. "It's what we do. The sky is blue, birds fly, dog-soldiers don't leave their friends to uncertain fates."

The lump in her throat changed. Sadrao was her friend. The darkness seemed warmed and less threatening.

"But now—well. Shall we take Trent with us? Will you travel to Knaxos?"

He's being kind. It will be months—years, maybe—before you'll be able to hire warriors to deal with Jasen. And you know the merchants won't do anything. It would be best to leave the Tanglelore Hills entirely until you can come back and settle with Jasen. Her throat tightened at the thought. She was not sure when it had occurred to her that she *could* settle with Jasen, that he was a man, and men could die, that what one group of warriors could do, another group could undo. She thought perhaps she had simply woken up one morning and found the thought there. *So long… But—Knaxos! The greatest libraries in the world!*

"Yes. Of course. See the libraries! I mean—it's not like we're going anywhere in particular—is it?"

Sadrao smiled. "I thought perhaps you'd say that."

❧

The dog-soldier is waiting.

Her fur was the color of sunlight on ice, and her eyes were the milky blue of a blind cat's, but she walked with the assurance of one who can see perfectly well in the dim light of the library. She passed across the broad central plaza of the room, and the sunlight, allowed in only here, away from the delicate books, flared up around her.

The dog-soldier remembers.

The sunlight here was not like the harsh, glorious sunlight of her homeland. The light of Khamir was tawny and abrasive, like bleached bone. This northern light was cold and watery, and even lancing down from the skylights to wake brilliance in her fur, it could not warm her.

The dog-soldier is watched.

To most observers, the scene would be almost blinding, over-exposed—white dog-soldier in white robes, crossing white tiled floor, the hard glittering sun painting chiaroscuros of light across her fur. But the man who watched her has spent six decades in the House of Diamond, and his eyes are used to brightness.

"Iyara," he said, from the balcony.

The white dog-soldier's ears flicked back, and she turned her head. "Your Eminence?"

Her voice was calm, as her voice was always calm. The man watching her felt his lip curl, almost involuntarily. There was something about her stoicism that rattled his nerves after a while and made him want to do something terrible and unexpected, merely to see those still, blue eyes flicker.

He did not act on these urges. He told himself that Iyara was too valuable, loyal with the unquestioning loyalty of dog-soldiers to their pack leader, and only a fool would waste it—and he was, in any event, not an evil man. Under that, somewhere, was a fear, never quite articulated, that the worst he could dream up would be met with that empty blue calm.

"Come up here."

She nodded, like a human would, her ears pricking forward, and walked to the stairs. She was not moving slowly, but neither did she appear to hurry, white fur drifting in white sunlight. He looked away and rubbed his eyes, feeling irrational anger, knowing it was irrational, and sighed. Iyara did not deserve his temper for merely being herself.

"I would like you to take a message to Frieze," he said, handing her a wooden tube, sealed with wax. "It is for Cardinal Jacobin, at the cathedral."

She crossed the broad central plaza, and the sunlight flared up around her.

"The Church of Frieze does not care for dog-soldiers," she said. It was not a question. It was certainly not defiance. It was an observation—the sky is blue, the sea is green, the church does not like dog-soldiers.

He nodded. "It will do them good to be made uncomfortable. They assume too much." They would also not try to bribe Iyara. Even if they had someone capable of overcoming their distaste for non-humans, she would have looked at them evenly for a while, and they would have gone away, feeling embarrassed. While there were a number of non-humans in the House of Diamond, including Ralthas, Ferran captain of the guard, Iyara was the only one whose loyalty he could take for granted.

Iyara inclined her head, bowed, and turned away.

The Archmage of the House of Diamond watched her go, and sighed.

⋘⋙

"Rise and shine, sleepyhead!" said Jacyl cheerfully.

Lyra opened her eyes and winced. Sunlight flooded the room. The rust-colored blur at the end of her bed resolved itself into Jacyl, in an autumn tunic and black leggings.

"Graggh..." said Lyra, rolling out of bed and onto the floor. A real bed had been too much for her, and, by the angle of the sunlight, it was nearly noon.

"Cold breakfast downstairs," said Jacyl, not without sympathy. "Sinai and Sadrao left a few hours ago, but I decided to let you and Trent sleep late. You looked like you needed it. I'll be waiting."

"Gnnnrrf," said Lyra, on her hands and knees on the floor. The blanket covered her nudity, but hindered her mobility. She groped for her clothes, her head pounding the way it always did when she overslept. Sadrao was zealous about rising with the dawn, and she'd fallen out of the habit of sleeping in.

"Mmfph-gark," she said to Jacyl, who appeared to be waiting for some kind of acknowledgement.

The elf woman gave a bird-trill laugh and left Lyra to her waking.

She was most of the way down to the common room before she realized that she had not woken wondering why she was not at home.

Breakfast—and more importantly, very hot tea—revitalized her. By the end of her second cup she was feeling positively human again. The common room was empty, cool and dim, with cold bacon and trencher bread laid out on the hearths for straggling guests. Sunlight came through the small, glazed windows (glass was expensive, even for inns of this quality) and shone on the polished floorboards, but most of the tables were alcoved in shadow. Lyra selected one close enough to a window to get a light breeze, but out of the line of light.

Trent came downstairs after she did and took a chair at the same table. He, too, made for a cup of black *sah* tea and sank into it. They exchanged a single, understanding glance, but did not attempt conversation. Lyra was grateful for the silence.

"Well," said Jacyl, strolling in from the front of the building, "I'm ready." She jingled a purse in one hand. Coins clinked inside. "One nice thing about this job—it pays damn well."

"You really don't have to—" began Lyra, feeling embarrassed.

"Think nothing of it," said the elven woman. "I can hardly spend as much as I make, and since Sinai can live in one pair of clothes for a year—" she rolled her eyes at this inexplicable behavior, "—I get to spend her share as well. Please. Allow me the pleasure."

Lyra blushed and mumbled something. A minute later, she and Trent were propelled out of the shady common room, into the bright glare of the morning.

"First order of business," said Jacyl, leading them down the maze of streets to the bazaar. "You need new boots. They'll take a while, so we'll have them fitted first."

Lyra was amazed at the bazaar. She had been expecting something on the order of the farmer's market at her village, a bit larger perhaps, but this! More people than she had ever seen in her life, all shouting and haggling and hawking their wares. Men in brightly colored turbans, dark-skinned women hung with gold and silk. Even a few non-humans—lithe-bodied Ferran, like giant, five-foot tall otters, clad mostly in their fur, and in belts and harnesses that were more decoration and storage than clothing. She was reminded of Sadrao's thigh-length black leather, armor rather than modesty. And far off across the square, making his way toward a distant archway, a Slothan, one of the shaggy-pelted giants from Hurricane Way, over seven feet tall and weighing at least half a ton. He stood head and shoulders above the crowd, like an armor-clad wall. His black cloak could have made a respectable ship's sail.

As Lyra was looking about, marveling at exotic foods and clothing and people, a flock of vendors, obviously spotting a naïve mark, descended on her. The press of people was frightening, a dozen voices shouting at her to come look at this, buy this, sample this. She backed up a step and bumped into Trent.

"Country girl, huh?" he said, sympathetically. "I was the same way, when I—"

He broke off abruptly, and instead steered her toward the waiting Jacyl without actually touching her, hands hovering a few inches from her arms. Lyra was glad to enter the cobbler's shop looming before them and escape the mad press of people.

"The dove grey leather," ordered Jacyl. "And a pair of the brown, too—you never have a spare pair when you need one. And there's nothing worse than badly fitted boots."

The cobbler, a stocky Ferran with badger stripes running down his face, grunted agreement and took careful measurements of Lyra's feet. "Hmm. Six silver apiece. Come back an hour before sundown."

"Leave a space for a knife," commanded Jacyl, almost as an afterthought.

The badger-faced Ferran looked offended, as if she had stated something particularly obvious. "Well, of course."

"Won't that, uh, chafe?" asked Lyra plaintively as they left the store.

"You have no idea," said Trent dryly.

Shopping for clothes took them well into lunchtime. Jacyl seemed to enjoy it as much or more than Lyra did, although after she stopped worrying about the cost Lyra began to enjoy being fitted. Now and again, unable to decide, they would ask Trent's advice. The half-elf seemed amused by the whole affair, but offered his opinion willingly.

The clothing had to be durable and easily packed. Silk and leather were the easiest, with a wool cloak thrown in. Lyra eventually wound up with three silk shirts that fit into a surprisingly small space, a pair of sturdy black leather pants, and a grey doeskin tunic. "Soft," said Jacyl thoughtfully, "and it won't stop a sword, but it binds a knife surprisingly well." Lyra blanched a little at the thought, then squared her shoulders.

Lunch was a type of flatbread with meat and cheese cooked inside from a vender wearing an extravagant orange turban. They sat on the edge of the central fountain, munching their food.

"Trent," said Jacyl, with a thoughtful glance at Lyra, "go buy us some of those funnel cakes, will you?"

He stood, with an ironic glance that let them know that he knew full well they wanted to speak alone. Jacyl grinned at that, then leaned over toward Lyra. "He'll give us plenty of time. Tell me, Lyra, you're—hmm, seventeen?"

She nodded mutely.

"So you've had your courses for, what—four years? Five?"

Lyra's jaw dropped. Of all the possible questions, that was not what she expected.

Jacyl, with a wicked gleam in her eyes, appeared to be waiting for an answer.

"Five," whispered Lyra, finally.

"And a virgin, too, hmm?"

Lyra turned scarlet and managed a bare nod. Her father had to be rolling in his grave.

Jacyl laughed like a bird singing. "I've embarrassed you. Lovely. Well, better me than Sadrao. He was all set to give you the talk, you know."

The thought of Sadrao, earnest, matter-of-fact Sadrao, *male* Sadrao—

"I'd've died," she muttered, sure that she was blushing to the roots of her hair.

"No doubt," agreed Jacyl. "I remember when he gave me that little talk. I was probably even more sheltered than you were… My, your face is a study. Well, I wanted to make sure you had everything you needed for…hmm…hygiene along the road."

"I could use something, I guess," Lyra agreed, not having given the matter any real thought. "It hasn't exactly come up yet."

"Believe me, it will. You'd be amazed the things that the smell of blood will attract, even if that thing about bears is an old wives' tale...We'll pick you up something then," said Jacyl cheerfully, as if she was discussing shoe leather. "Which brings us to the second matter. Do you have any kind of contraception?"

"I believe the Church frowns on it," Lyra mumbled, blushing more. Her father was probably wrenching himself from the ground and preparing to track her down in a display of undead parental outrage.

"Oh, probably. Look. It's simple enough—I'll get you some pills. You can get them at any apothecary, so it shouldn't be a problem. Just take one the next day after you—ah—well, you know." She took mercy on the scarlet-faced girl. "I thought someone ought to tell you, and better me than Sadrao. He'll fend off most of the rabble, but if you meet a nice young man, there's absolutely no reason why you should deprive yourself. And here's our dessert," she added, as Trent returned with the funnel cakes.

"I trust by the color of Lyra's face that you've finished your little chat," he said dryly. Lyra muttered something into her funnel cake about pointed-eared meddlers and there being no decency left in the whole misbegotten world. Jacyl only laughed.

They did visit an apothecary, and Jacyl bought her a small tin with a dozen small pills in it, as well as some absorbent, washable sponges for her menstrual flow. Lyra thought the dozen pills was probably excessive, since she'd never had the opportunity to use even one. These items joined a small pile of handy travel equipment—a tiny brazier, firestarters, a canteen and several packages of iron rations. Lyra almost protested the coil of rope, and the sleeping roll, but Jacyl pointed out that they would be on horseback, and there was no reason to deprive oneself of a pillow. "When you're back on foot, then you can strip down to the bare essentials. As it is, we're traveling light."

"One more visit," said Trent as they left the store. Lyra looked at him, puzzled.

"We've got everything I can think of—"

"He's right," said Jacyl. For once, there was no trace of humor in her voice. "As it is, you're practically walking around naked."

"Huh?" said Lyra articulately.

"This," said Trent, leading her to a table covered in knives. He picked one up, flipped it expertly, the hilt landing in his hand with a solid slap. She noticed for the first time dozens of small nicks and cuts on his hands.

He picked out two matched stilettos for her new boots and a longer one for her belt. The honor-knife was still in Sadrao's pack, away from prying eyes.

Jacyl handed her a sword, then snorted and took it away from her. Trent rolled his eyes and began digging through the swords like a dog searching for a bone.

"Sadrao was right," Jacyl said. "A staff is best—or perhaps—" A speculative light entered her eyes, but she said nothing more, leading Lyra to a carpet covered in spears and polearms, like bristling stalks of wheat.

A tall spear fitted her hand well, but she recoiled from the open threat of the naked blade. "I don't know," she said, "it's awful...militant looking. And if I'm going to advertise, I'd rather know how to use it."

Jacyl frowned, but Trent agreed. "Something more subtle," he advised. "Like—hmm—" He picked up a long staff, the end capped with iron, leather wrapped around the middle. The head, almost as tall as Lyra, was carved in the likeness of a mare's head.

It fit easily in Lyra's hand, and more than that, it felt right. She smiled at Trent, swinging the staff cautiously. "I think this is it."

"This, too," said the half-elf. He measured a slender sword against the length of her forearm. She could lift it without her wrists trembling, but was wary of trying to swing it for fear of accidentally gutting her companions.

"You'll never be a master swordsman," he said, inching around her and removing the blade from her hands. "But if Sadrao and Sinai can't at least make you competent, then I'll eat that sword."

"My incompetence will surprise you," predicted Lyra.

Jacyl, however, only nodded pensively and turned to the armorer. Like the cobbler, he was a Ferran, but taller and slimmer, his face masked like a ferret.

He baldly quoted a sum to make Lyra blanch and try to put the sword back down. Trent stopped her.

Jacyl slapped six coins down on the counter. They were the white-gold of Anu'tintavel, the color slightly dulled from handling, but unmistakable. Lyra, who had learned, grudgingly, to balance some of the books of her merchant house, knew that the white-gold coins were good virtually anywhere on the continent.

"Jacyl," she said, slightly horrified, "I can't let you—"

"Yes, you can," said Jacyl pleasantly.

"No—"

"Yes," said Trent, "you can." He smiled down at her. "Really, Lyra. If you're going to escort a dangerous criminal halfway across the continent for the elves, the least they can do is see that you're equipped..."

Jacyl winced. "You're not a criminal," she told him, sounding more irritable than Lyra had yet heard her, "but other than that, he's right. Sadrao will be paid quite handsomely for his services, and outfitting you is part of that. Trent, make yourself useful and carry that sword."

They stopped to pick up the boots—which fit as well as anything Lyra had ever owned—and walked back to the inn before sunset.

The common room was full tonight. Lyra stowed her purchases and changed into her own clothes—*her own clothes!*—the silk soft against her skin, then went back downstairs to dinner.

"A word in your ear," said Sadrao, catching her by the shoulder as she left her room.

Lyra bit back a yelp of surprise. The last few days had begun to seem almost normal, but some part of her was still lying in the bushes and shivering with dread, and that person was still quite easily startled.

"Sorry," said Sadrao contritely. "But I wanted to talk to you out of sight of the others."

Lyra nodded.

"I've been scrounging for rumors of your House for most of the day, just to see if anything had changed. It's more extraordinary for what I haven't heard." He held up a blunt-clawed finger, as if the argument balanced on its tip. "One. The bandits around here are not organized and have no central leader. There's a group from the north that preys on trade from Mews, but this stretch of the Tanglelore simply isn't wealthy enough to support an organized group of brigands. Two—" he held up a second claw, "There aren't even any rumors that someone has set himself up as a bandit lord." Ring finger. "Three. Trade from your House has gone missing, but—I'm sorry, Lyra—two other merchant houses have stepped in to fill the gap."

"Beryl Long's clan," said Lyra automatically, "and probably the Scorpion River trade coalition."

Sadrao blinked. "Exactly right."

"Beryl would sell admission to the gates of hell," said Lyra dryly, "and the Scorpion River traders have been trying to edge out Volfrieds' market share for as long as I've been alive."

"Indeed. And I fear that your father's partners have signed with them, as well."

Lyra nodded glumly. "I can't blame them," she said. She did anyway, but practically speaking, it made sense. The two powerful trade houses would snap up the trade arrangements immediately, now that Volfrieds was gone. Her father's former partners would have had to sign, or be edged from the market.

"Well, despite that, I haven't heard anyone suggest that either house was behind the destruction of yours—"

"Of course not!" said Lyra, shocked. "It's just—not—you don't *do* that!" And under Sadrao's ironic eyebrow, "Well, not along the Tanglelore you don't. Maybe in Delta, or one of the big cities."

Sadrao ran his tongue over his teeth, his eyes fixed on the ceiling, and said, "Well, in any event, that doesn't seem to be the case here. Four—" he held up his little finger, "A caravan coming west along the river road, past your house, is currently five days late." Thumb, and final point, "Lastly, a number of rather shady characters are noticeable in town by their absence. Some of my informants said that they actually felt safe walking down the street at night." Work finished, the hand dropped.

"Meaning?" said Lyra.

"Meaning," said Sadrao heavily. "Meaning that your brother did not hire a local bandit lord to do his work, but probably collected the men himself, from Jeppeth and surrounding areas, presumably with the intent of leading them. That means that they probably don't work particularly well together, yet, which would explain why their patrols were less than efficient. They're continuing to prey on local trade—i.e., the missing caravan—and have no intention of setting up as merchants themselves."

"Jasen would've been a lousy merchant," said Lyra.

"He won't be a good bandit, either," said Sadrao. "Most of the trade here comes down the river, so unless he sets himself up as a river pirate, he'll find slim pickings. It would take a minor miracle to last through the winter, with the number of men he's trying to support."

"Hunh." Lyra looked up at Sadrao. "So what does it mean?"

"You have two options," said Sadrao. "You can stay here and attempt to raise some kind of local effort to drive them out. Some of the local merchants might back you, since they'll be losing their overland trade. The disadvantage is that the bandits are entrenched in their position, and right now they'll be alert to attack."

"Or?"

"Wait. Go to Knaxos, like we planned." Sadrao sighed. "By mid-autumn, they'll be starting to feel the pinch, and by next spring they'll be easy prey. A handful of men could clean out their nest. Since we are doing a service for Anu'tintavel, and I'm well enough known there, we could do worse than to return here, with or without Trent, and may be able to pick up a few people there who will help us. Elves get crazy in mid-winter, particularly the young ones. They start spoiling for a fight."

Lyra licked her lips. It was not, after all, so difficult a decision to make. Hadn't Mozan Ku-Rai written that you should always let your enemy do the work for you? "Knaxos," she said. "We'll let him starve in my father's house for a while."

Sadrao nodded. "It's what I would do in your place," he said. "And speaking of starving, I think I smell dinner…and it's *not* horse."

Actually, it was stew, and the meat was probably mutton, but it was definitely good. Sinai and Sadrao spent most of dinner arguing over whether or not Sadrao had gotten a good bargain on the horses, with the good-natured viciousness of old friends.

Lyra hoped, silently, that Sadrao had gotten a quiet horse for her. She was no master equestrian, not by a long shot, even if being (nominally) a member of the nobility meant that she was no stranger to horseback. It would be a humiliating experience to fall off a horse in front of the elves. She was already feeling slightly odd as the only rounded-eared member of the group, despite Jacyl's warm camaraderie.

She stared dubiously down at her mug of ale, took a swallow, and grimaced.

Sadrao grinned at her across the table, carefully not exposing his fangs, and ruffled her hair with a furry hand. She smiled back, keeping her own teeth covered, and took another drink of ale.

Chapter Seven

Two days later, sitting on the back of a nearly comatose trail horse, she realized she need not have worried. The woolly-coated dun was separated from a mattress only by the presence of ears and a tail and followed Sadrao's massive draft horse with a stolid lack of imagination.

She'd been surprised at Sadrao's choice for his own mount—a heavy-bodied animal more suited to plowing than battle. Sadrao had shrugged. "I'm not a knight," he said dryly, tightening the cinch around the horse's middle. "I'm heavy, but I'd rather fight on foot if I can." Lyra nodded, remembering Sadrao's performance in the tavern—as much kicking and biting as swordplay. Given Sadrao's impressive natural armaments, it made sense. "But in case I do need to fight on horseback," the dog-soldier added, ducking around the front of the horse and patting it absently on the neck, "I need an animal solid enough not to panic if I start swinging a sword around. And I'm certainly not going to fork over a king's ransom on a war horse." He grinned abruptly. "The horses are Sinai's back-handed way of paying me. She thinks I don't realize it, but I'm still not going to spend that much of Anu'tintavel's money."

The elven steeds were impressive.

Jacyl's horse was the white of starlight and seafoam, a tall, magnificently delicate stallion with narrow, wedge-shaped head and feathered heels. It was said that elves bred their horses out of hippogriffs, and Lyra almost believed it. (Not quite. Hippogriffs were notoriously unstable and exceedingly carnivorous.) Jacyl rode him with dark blue tack that made a remarkably beautiful picture. Lyra, having already learned that Jacyl's prevailing flaw was vanity, was certain that she'd chosen him for his looks and the amazing pair they made.

This was borne out by the fact that the stallion, though elven trained and good-natured, was also dumber than a rock and forever rolling in the dirt.

The other horse was a tall grey mare, the color of twilight, more obviously muscular than the white stallion, less ethereal, but with clean, strong lines, and a dark, intelligent eye. She was Sinai's. "At least, she tolerates me," said Sinai cryptically, saddling the mare with the air of a woman who throws dice with demons. "I don't delude myself that I'm her master, but Jegger travels with me until she finds someone else she likes better."

Trent was riding an unextraordinary black gelding who had never quite realized he was gelded and kept trying to induce Jegger to mate. It was hard to tell who was more offended by the process—Sinai or her mare.

The scenery outside of Jeppeth was mostly rolling fields, the road broad enough for three to ride abreast. Fieldhands in dusty clothing worked alongside the road. The travelers passed the occasional farmer driving the first of the earliest spring harvest to market, but most of the spring crops were still midway through the growing season. Whenever they passed another traveler, however, or one of the workers straightened and looked toward the road, Sadrao, and to a lesser extent the elves, became the subject of incredulous stares.

After the third oxcart nearly edged her off the road, the farmer staring open-mouthed at an amused dog-soldier and the two sardonic-faced elves, Lyra reflected that she could have stood up on the equine mattress's back and recited epic poetry, and no one would have spared her a glance.

She didn't mind. She was content, the first day, to remember what shreds she knew about riding and to revel in *not* having to walk.

Not that riding was easy. It was work, particularly after three or four hours in the saddle, using muscles that Lyra hadn't had occasion to practice in a long time. But there was none of the ducking and scrambling that she'd been doing on the trail with Sadrao, and the scenery went by a good deal faster.

Trent proved to be an entertaining companion. While quiet and not forthcoming about himself, he was also, if anything, better read than Lyra. Whatever kind of mage his father was—Lyra had never heard of Vade, and only fragments about the mountain fortress of Ironspine—he evidently possessed an incredible library.

There was only so long that you can talk about books, however, even with a pleasant, mild-mannered half-elf who is as desperate for conversation as you are.

By the second day she was saddle-sore and bored stiff.

"You smell bored," said Sadrao, dropping back beside her.

Lyra cocked a jaundiced eye at him. *Can he really smell—? No.* He was grinning at her, tail swishing good-naturedly. "Really. If you sigh one more time, I may weep."

"I'm sorry," Lyra said contritely. "But all these fields just start to look the same, and there's not much to do."

"And we've exhausted most of the conversational possibilities in books we've both read," added Trent, pulling up on the other side of Sadrao. "At least until we know each other well enough to get in a knock-down-drag-out philosophical debate, and Sinai will throw me in a mud puddle if I try to discuss magic with her one more time."

Sadrao rolled his eyes hard enough to show a white rim around the gold and choked down a barking laugh. "Well," he said, the edge of a smile in his voice, turning to rummage in his saddlebags, "perhaps I have something to keep you amused. Close your eyes."

Lyra closed her eyes obediently.

A clink of metal reached her ears. Trent laughed aloud. Lyra's eyes flipped open, and she said "Hey—"

With a lightning movement, the dog-soldier clapped a length of chain around her wrist, threw a loop over the saddlehorn, and yanked it taut. Lyra yelped. "Hey, now, what the hell are you—?!"

Sadrao flipped a massive, slightly rusty padlock open against his palm, shoved it through the chain, and closed it with a disturbingly final *click.*

Lyra stared at the chain on her left hand, then at Sadrao, then back down at the chain. Her jaw was dangling open.

Sadrao produced a short length of metal, half as wide as Lyra's finger, bent at one end, and handed it to her. Trent's shoulders were shaking as he tried to suppress his laughter.

"This," said Sadrao cheerfully, "is a lockpick. That is a lock."

"You have *got* to be kidding," said Lyra.

Trent kicked his gelding forward several lengths, leaned forward over the horse's neck and guffawed. Lyra was amazed that his glasses didn't fall off.

"Oh, well," said Lyra philosophically, "at least he didn't laugh in my face...Sadrao, what in the name of the Lady of Lights do you expect me to do with this?"

"Pick it," said Sadrao cheerfully. "We make camp in—oh, six hours or so. That ought to be plenty of time."

"Great," muttered Lyra. She poked the lockpick into the keyhole and began wiggling it experimentally. Had she ever read a book on picking locks? No. Gradenius's *Secrets of the Underworld*—cheap sensationalism, nothing useful. She'd seen her maid pick a jewelry box lock with a hairpin once. How hard could it be?

Two hours later, her wrist starting to chafe, she was still working at it.

"...lousy, arrogant, miserable, condescending, patronizing... chain *me* to a damn saddle will he..."

Trent leaned over, sunlight glinting off the thick lenses of his glasses. "Any thoughts?" she asked ruefully. There was a raw patch developing under one particular link. She wriggled the chain, wincing.

"I've never picked a lock in my life," he confessed.

"Can you magic it?" she asked, curious, looking over into his angular face while still twisting the lockpick idly in the tumblers.

"I could." He shoved his glasses higher up on his nose. "I would, I suppose, if I had to. No, actually I'd just break the chain—it's cruder, and it would take more energy, but it's a lot easier. Unless I didn't want anyone to sense me using magic. Then I'd probably have to work the lock."

"Other mages can sense you working magic?" she asked curiously.

He nodded so vigorously that his hair fell in his eyes. "Yes. Definitely. Sinai—" he glanced forward to the elven woman's back, "—says she'll kill me if I do any magic. She thinks Vade will sense it." His face grew pensive, lines forming at the edges of his eyes. "I don't blame her. He could do it."

Lyra felt uncomfortable. She looked back down at her hands, then back up at the half-elf. "I'm sorry. Uh. Is it hard…not using magic?"

"Not really. Sinai's very persuasive." He grinned ruefully. "A lot like Sadrao, I think—that's something she'd do." He tapped the padlock. "Sometimes—there are things that you can do with magic you can't do any other way. Then it's hard. Most of the rest of the time, it'd be easier to do it any other way than magic."

Lyra, half-convinced that she'd go mad if she had to devote any more attention to the padlock, grasped at conversational straws. "So…how does another mage sense magic?"

Trent smiled, cleaning his glasses on the edge of his shirt. "I wish to the gods that I knew. You just…do. If you're looking. You kind of pick up anything in the area. I could probably feel if someone did a spell within a few miles right now. It's harder in cities, all the minds drown it out. People are sort of a little magic themselves, you know." He put his glasses back on. "I'm sorry, I'm lecturing."

"No, I'm interested. How could, um, Vade sense you? If he's miles away?"

"Scrying." He gestured absently with one hand. "Crystals. Pools. Fire." His face did not precisely fall, but his expression slackened as if he were retreating from the flesh and what memories it might have held. "Fire—and stone—are Vade's gifts. He builds incredible lenses out of molten metal. He could see the entire world if he took the time to look."

Lyra struggled to find something sympathetic to say, still twisting the lockpick absently in the tumblers. She heard a click.

Sadrao's ears flicked back, and he tilted a grin at Sinai and Jacyl, as on the road behind them, Lyra's whoop of triumph accompanied the clatter of the chain being unwound. "Two hours," he said to no one in particular. "Well, they can't all be natural born thieves…"

Jacyl laughed at that. "I think she's sweet, Sadrao."

"This would be great," they heard her say to Trent in wry tones, "if I could just remember what the hell I did…" The half-elf's incongruously deep laughter joined hers.

"Be careful," said Sinai to the dog-soldier, abruptly, her low voice unsettling in its intensity. She slid her cool grey gaze to

Sadrao's bronze one, and it was as if the day had grown colder despite the sun.

"She's a girl, Sinai," said Sadrao uncomfortably. "Not the strongest I've ever trained. One of the brightest, perhaps, but not dangerous."

"Yet." Sinai's pupils were dilated as if she saw visions, or only darkness. "Go softly, old wolf. Be wary. I think this one may surprise you."

⁂

They stopped at an inn that evening. The weathered sign over the door claimed it as the "Frog and Turnip Inn," complete with a peeling painting of a grinning frog clutching an indeterminate root vegetable.

"Frog and Turnip?" asked Lyra of no one in particular.

Trent leaned over in her direction and said, "Let's hope that's not the house specialty."

A stableboy came out of the low stable and caught the reins of Sadrao's plowhorse under the animal's chin. "Two copper apiece," he recited in bored tones, "three 'fya want oats instead of..."

He stopped. He had come around the side of the horse and face to face with its rider, who was sliding out of the saddle. Lyra could actually see the boy's brain working furiously as his eyes went from Sadrao's muscled midriff (on an eye level with the young stablehand) up the column of throat to the drop-jawed smile and bright gold eyes.

"Uh," he said. "Uh, uh, y'r horse, sair—"

Sadrao took pity on him, handed him a half-handful of copper and said "Extra oats for all of them."

"Uh. Uh, uh. Yes, sair! Uh—of course!" He backed away, leading the plowhorse, and caught the reins on Lyra's and Trent's mounts.

Sinai swung down from Jegger's back and gathered up the reins on both the elven horses. Jacyl pulled a pack free from each steed as she dismounted. When the stableboy returned, Sinai set both pairs of reins in his hands, looked Jegger in the eye, and muttered, "Follow." The mare rolled a deceptively mild eye at her and followed obediently.

They stepped through the door into a mostly empty common room. What little conversation there was died immediately as three peasant farmers stopped with ale tankards frozen halfway to their lips.

The barkeeper looked up from the counter. His gaze went from elves to half-elf to dog-soldier to Lyra and back to the dog-soldier. He reached out to the bar, took a pinch of blueweed leaf from a box on counter, and tucked it into a larger wad in his cheek.

"Dog-soldier, eh," he said. His teeth were stained blue from the leaf. "Don't see many of your kind here, sair. Nor too many of your kind either, ladies, beggin' your pardon." He nodded to the elves.

Sinai inclined her head a measured fraction. Jacyl smiled charmingly.

Sadrao nodded pleasantly, and gave the man a tooth-covered grin. "I trust you can find lodgings for us all?"

"Eh. Got two rooms. Three silver. There's a meal and breakfast in that apiece, too." He shifted the wad of blueleaf to the other cheek. "Dinner's shepherd's pie."

The mostly-empty room seemed to hang on the dog-soldier's next words. Sadrao smiled winningly. "That will do nicely."

The barkeep returned the smile with his own blue-stained one. Tension visibly drained from the air. The farmers started their conversation up again and continued drinking their ale.

"Ain't never seen a dog-soldier before," Lyra heard one remark laconically.

"Cousin met one down in Delta, once," one of the others replied. "Said he was a nice fellow. Fair, Silas said."

"Your cousin Silas wouldn't know fair if he found it a-growing in his melon patch," claimed the third.

"Ahuh, now, that's as may be..."

Lyra did not catch the rest of the conversation about the dubious virtue of Cousin Silas as she followed Jacyl up the steps to their rooms.

The two elven women took one room. Trent and Sadrao took the other, which left Lyra standing in the middle of the hallway, wondering if she should go sleep in the stable with the horses.

Sadrao held the door open and gestured to her. "Come on," he said. When she brushed by him, he leaned down and murmured

"I think Jacyl and Sinai need a bit of time alone together, and there won't be many more inns on the way to Delta."

"Oh—oh, right." Lyra nodded, feeling a flush creep up her face.

Trent nodded politely to her and slipped past them. "I'll go get my bedroll," he said, which neatly solved the problem of who was taking the bed.

The shepherd's pie was good. Not fantastic, but a welcome change from Sadrao's rough cooking. The bread was fresh, and delicious. Lyra and Trent demolished most of a loaf between them. "I'd forgotten how much I missed fresh bread," Lyra said, around a mouthful.

"Ummmh-hmm," said Trent, buttering the heel and going after it like a starving man.

Sadrao was talking to one of the farmers about the quality of the road and the likelihood of encountering bandits, a conversation consisting mostly of Sadrao's polite, gravelly voice, a long pause, and then a slow reply begin with "Ahuh, ahuh, Ah know what your-ah askin'..."

Eventually, nearly falling asleep in the pie, Lyra rose and made her good-nights. Trent rose as well, with a jaw-cracking yawn.

Sinai and Jacyl had their arms around each other's waists, Jacyl's head on Sinai's shoulder. No one was giving them any odd looks. Lyra wondered if the farmers simply didn't care, or if the elves were beyond the standards of normal behavior, by virtue of being elves.

Lyra yawned, and nearly stumbled as she went up the stairs. Trent steadied her with a hand against her back. "Sorry," she mumbled.

"No problem," he replied. The hallway was unlit, and grew black as pitch once they left the stairs. Lyra put out her hand to grope through the dark.

"Here," said Trent. He slid past her and walked sure-footedly through the dark. She heard him open the door without having to feel around for the knob. A moment later, one of his hands took her lightly by the sleeve and he led her to the doorway.

"They must not get many travelers," she muttered, as the half-elf guided her to the edge of the bed.

"Not this early in the spring," said Trent. She could hear him moving in the dark, with none of the fumbling she would have demonstrated, proving that elven vision must be significantly better than hers.

"Yeah," said Lyra, remembering the patterns of shipping for a merchant house, "most of the trade around here is along the river, anyway. Farm traffic picks up in summer and fall, but this is a pretty dead season."

"Ahuh, ahuh, Ah know what your-ah sayin'..." Trent drawled, in a wickedly accurate imitation of Sadrao's farmer.

Lyra snorted with laughter, as light flared up between the half-elf's hands. He turned back, the flame of the small lamp lighting twin reflections on the lenses of his glasses.

"Do you get the feeling that these gentlemen," he jerked his chin in the direction of the common room, "will be talking about Sadrao for years to come?"

"Ah saw a dog-soldier once," said Lyra, trying to match the accent with some success, "on tha road to Delta. Nice, he was. Fair, ahuh?"

Trent made a muffled whooping noise, rather more than the joke warranted, and that set Lyra off into giggles. She couldn't have said why it was so funny, but whenever she looked at Trent she started laughing again, and then he'd laugh, and eventually both of them were clutching at their sides, making choked noises. Trent slid partway down the wall, still chuckling weakly.

Lyra finally got herself under control, tried to say something, and lost it in a jaw-cracking yawn. Trent succumbed to yawns as well. Lyra fell backwards on the mattress.

"It'll (yawn) be so nice not to wake up covered in dew," she said, trying to kick her boots off and discovering that the hilt of the bootknife was leaving a chafed spot on her ankle, not to mention a hole in her sock.

"Ahuh," said Trent, which set them both off again.

When they recovered from the second bout of laughter, Lyra managed to get her socks and tunic off. She briefly debated stripping down to her underwear, which was what she had normally been sleeping in, decided that Trent was in just a little too close proximity, and left her pants on.

The half-elf waited until she had slid between the rough-spun blankets before he blew out the lamp and padded to his bedroll.

From the hallway came the sound of floorboards creaking, and of Jacyl's trilling laugh. The door across the hall opened and shut. Lyra was glad that Sadrao had settled the sleeping arrangements the way he had. Sinai and Jacyl deserved a little privacy— and given Sinai's total disregard for what *anyone* thought of Jacyl and herself, sharing the same room could easily have gotten very awkward, very quickly.

That her father would have given birth to a litter of live water oxen at the thought of Lyra sharing a room with a young man, even in this chivalrously chaste manner—well, life was strange sometimes, and Lyra wasn't going to worry about it. She supposed they could have split the bed and slept with an unsheathed sword between them, like in the sagas, but that had always struck her as overly melodramatic. In fact, given her tendency to thrash around in her sleep, it would have been downright dangerous.

She wondered briefly what sharing a bed with Trent, *sans* sword, would have been like. His hands, the few times he had touched her, were warm and very strong, which knowledge translated into exactly nothing practical for Lyra, but was a detail they always mentioned in the sagas.

You've only known this man for five days.

Yeah, and you're going to be traveling with him for at least another month.

A lot can happen in a month. Hell, look at the last two weeks!

On that bittersweet thought, she gave up the internal argument and allowed sleep to claim her.

It took Lyra less than half an hour to pick the lock on her hands after they left the inn the next morning. Sadrao grinned at her. "Good. Very good! Now, do it again." He looped both her hands in chain, less than an inch of slack between them, and trotted his horse away. Lyra stared dubiously at the padlock and the lockpick in her hands.

"Great," she muttered to herself, or her horse, digging the metal into the keyhole with rapidly cramping fingers.

The horse, which she had formally dubbed "Mattress," rolled an eye back at her and snorted.

Trent rode up and inspected her work. "What do you think," she asked, "will he blindfold me next or just hang me upside down from the saddle?"

"Both, I'd say," he said judiciously. "At a gallop. In the rain."

"Great," she muttered, working at the lock. It was an awkward angle, but the same rhythm—first tumbler and around and second and *twist*—

The padlock fell off. She cursed and dove after it, forgetting that one of her hands was still chained to the saddle. Mattress chose that moment to sidestep, and Lyra had to lock her legs around the horse's barrel to keep from a magnificent face-plant in the dirt.

Trent's arm snapped out with speed better suited to a preying mantis's strike and *caught* the lock.

"Misbegotten son of a plowhorse," said Lyra in a conversational tone to her mount. Trent reached out a steadying hand to hold her in the saddle and handed her the padlock with the other.

For someone as raw-boned and mild-looking as Trent, he was incredibly fast. She had already seen several demonstrations of remarkable strength. Lyra brushed herself off, eyeing the dozens of small scars up and down the half-elf's forearms. She had not spent a great deal of time among men in her life, and their greater strength—completely out of proportion, she thought, to the marginal size difference—always took her by surprise.

On the other hand, remembering the ease with which Sinai handled her sword and casually tossed mercenaries around taverns, Lyra thought perhaps his being a half-elf had as much to do with it as being male.

"Knives," said Trent.

"Hmm? What?" She looked up at him, unwinding the chain from her bruised wrist.

"The scars. Knives." He tugged a sleeve down self-consciously. Lyra realized she'd been staring.

"I'm sorry, I was just woolgathering..."

He smiled. It seemed forced. "Don't be. It's nothing."

"Ah." Lyra wound the chain neatly around the saddlehorn. "Um. Knife...fighting?" And then, mentally, *Oh, really smooth. He's certainly been forthcoming on the issue.*

"No," he said, while she cursed her curiosity. "Ritual." He held out his hands, flipped them over. The backs and palms were mostly unmarred, except for a few short white marks across the heel of the hand and ball of the thumb. "Knife fighters usually have cuts on the backs of their hands—same with wild animal attacks, or people who fight with chains." He tapped a fingernail on her chain with a subdued clink. "Comes from trying to hold weapons off with your hands. Fewer scars on the forearms."

Lyra could sense a lecture in the making and was hard-put to repress a smile. Even if she *was* interested, his light, dry tone was still amusing.

"Ritual bloodletting," he continued, his voice dropping, deepening, "and those types who cut themselves up for pleasure—which, by the way, I am *not*—cut across the arms. More blood, fewer nerves. Less likely to damage the tendons."

"If the situation ever arises," Lyra promised, "I'll keep that in mind." *May the gods keep me from ever using that knowledge,* she added silently.

Trent grinned at her abruptly, something like a flush creeping up his face. "Sorry," he mumbled. "I tend to lecture at the drop of a hat. Usually on things you don't want to talk about during dinner."

She would have said something else, but she was staring, in fascinated horror, at the underside of his arms. A long river of scar tissue flowed from the base of the wrist and vanished under his sleeves.

"Furthermore," said Trent, with a grim continuation of his earlier speech, "if you're going to slit your wrists, do it up the entire forearm."

"Good god," said Lyra, shocked. "How—why—?"

"Because sometimes it's all you can think of to do," said Trent flatly. "And even then, it doesn't always work. Particularly in the house of a sorcerer."

She was groping for a follow-up when Sadrao dropped back on his horse, examined her freed hands with a "hmmmph" sound, and locked up her right hand again.

"This time, no lockpick. For variety."

"What the hell am I supposed to use, then?" she asked testily, rubbing a raw patch of skin on her wrist.

"Good question." He flicked his ears at her, then reached out and tapped her nose with a black claw. "If you're ever locked up, do you think they'll provide you with a lockpick?"

"It'd be nice," she groused, but she leaned over the lock thoughtfully anyway.

She took several runs at it with her eating-knife, but the blade was too wide. Her earrings were far too small. She wasn't wearing hairpins.

"If this is a subtle way of telling me that I should carry something lockpick-like, your point is made." She sat back, running her free hand through her hair. "Okay, I admit defeat. You want I should unlock it with my tongue?"

Sadrao's lips twitched. "That'd be impressive," he allowed.

Trent cleared his throat. Lyra looked over at the half-elf. With a sidelong glance at Sadrao, he reached down and scratched one calf ostentatiously. Under the boot.

"That's cheating," said the dog-soldier mildly, but he smiled as Lyra slapped her forehead, then reached down and worked a stiletto loose from the side of her boot. She still wasn't used to carrying knives in her footwear.

It took her a few minutes to work the padlock with the point of the knife, but eventually it gave. Sadrao reclaimed his lock.

"Next village," he promised, "I'll get a few new ones."

"Good skill to have," said Trent laconically, and then was staring in dismay at his own hands as Sadrao slapped chain and padlock over the half-elf's wrists.

"Sadrao," said Sinai, dropping back to ride beside them, "are you chaining my cousin-son to the saddle?"

"Only temporarily," he replied.

"Novel solution." The humor in her eyes grew cold, and she ignored the sudden hunch of Trent's shoulders. "Should have thought of that myself..."

⸎

"Your Eminence."

The Archmage looked up and saw white—white fur, white robes, white walls, white light. "Iyara."

She bowed, moved into the study, and set a message tube down on his desk with a precise click. Her nails were clear, slightly yellow, the quicks a pink half moon.

"Ah. Word from Frieze." He opened the tube while she watched, scanned the message, and harrumphed deep in his throat. "Well. They have their fingers in many pies, it would seem."

He tossed the sheets down on his white oak desk and turned away to stare fixedly up at the ceiling. "Frieze is making demands. They want something, or they close the ports to the House of Diamond."

"They would lose commerce as well," said Iyara calmly. "Many who come to the House of Diamond stop at Frieze. If they cannot continue here, they will go to Delta instead."

"True," said the Archmage glumly, "but they would lose a small amount of commerce, and we would lose nearly half of ours. They can afford it, and we cannot."

Iyara made the slightest twitch of her fur, nothing as graceless or as energetic as a shrug.

"And yet if we accede to their demands," he continued, "then they learn that we can be pressured." He stared up at the ceiling again.

Iyara said nothing.

The Archmage sighed. "Fortunately, in this case, what they want is something that I also want, for other reasons. But I do not like the precedent. We are a small island, and while we cannot be invaded, we can easily be starved."

"Is there some other demand that they have made, that you can refuse, then? To present the appearance that one will accede, but not capitulate? Or can you make a demand of your own?"

The Archmage lifted an eyebrow. Talking to Iyara was often like talking to the sky, but the mind behind her eyes was extremely sharp. It was easy to forget, sometimes.

"Not a bad idea...if I make a demand for lower tariffs, in return, perhaps we can continue to pretend that we are engaged in trade, rather than blackmail."

Iyara inclined her head.

A few hours later, before the salt of the sea air had even dried on her fur, Iyara was again boarding a boat, returning to the mainland to carry the Archmage's message.

She was not resentful. She had no right to be resentful. Her own work in the archives, on hold now for a week, was of interest only to her, and perhaps to a few scholars of ancient manuscripts. (Lyra, nearly six hundred miles away and at that moment picking stones out of Mattress's hooves, would have found it fascinating.) Her pack leader had made a request, and though she would undoubtedly spend at least another week in Frieze, being delayed by the cardinals simply to prove that they had power in the situation and she did not, she was honored to do what was asked of her.

The white dog-soldier stood at the prow of the boat, looking up, her eyes as blue and empty of emotion as the sea.

Chapter Eight

Trent had worked himself loose of the chains—if not of Sinai's derision—by the time they called an early halt. Sadrao picked a spot next to a cheerfully gurgling stream and baited a line with a shiny piece of metal while the others made camp.

When the fire was going and the horses tended, Sinai moved a little way off, into a clear patch of grass and horsetails, and shrugged out of all but a sleeveless tunic and her leggings. Lyra watched her thoughtfully.

Every evening, the elf woman stepped aside from camp and began a series of movements that was unlike anything Lyra had seen before, and yet strangely compelling. It was like reading a much-loved poem in a different language—the vocabulary was totally unknown, but the cadence and rhythm were familiar.

"Sinai?" she asked, finally, when the tall blond woman had finished and was standing still, knee-deep in horsetails and clover. Sunlight streamed down around her, filtered through the trees and illuminating elven-pale skin like a statue carved of alabaster. "What is...that? That dance?"

Sinai bowed deeply to the sunlit forest, then turned to Lyra. "It is not a dance," she said, her voice less mournful than usual—a dove's cry instead of an owl's. "Or—it is not a dance any more than it is anything else. It is the Kytha."

"Kytha..." Lyra's Elvish had improved in the last three days from nonexistent to merely very poor, but she did not know the word. And yet, she would not have sworn that she had not heard it before—there was something about it that rang inside her ears, beat inside her blood, whispered magic into her brain.

"The blood-magic," said Sinai, still standing, looking for the moment as fey and alien as the Church claimed elves to be. "A force within the body—within bone and breath and heart. The Kytha is our name for that force—and for the movements that channel it." She made half a turn, as if in illustration. "I am what we call Kythar."

It might have been a trick of the streaming sunlight, but Lyra could have sworn that a trail of light followed Sinai's hands for a moment, half-visible, like a crow's call in still air. She looked from the barely-present glow to the elf-woman's face, framed by the short cloud of ash-blond hair.

Sinai's stormcloud eyes locked with her own for a moment. Lyra felt as if she was being tested for something, but she did not know what for, or how to pass the test.

Abruptly, Sinai sighed and one corner of her mouth crooked up. She ran a hand through her hair, leaving a dirt smudge across her forehead, and looked suddenly much more human.

"Here," she said, beckoning with one hand. "I will show you."

The sound of Trent's head snapping up was not exactly audible, but Lyra saw the abruptness of his movement from the corner of her eye, and felt that it deserved some kind of loud *crack* in accompaniment.

She could feel his eyes on them as she rose awkwardly and joined the elf in the horsetail meadow.

"Stand," Sinai said, demonstrating. "Feet apart. Bend your knees. No, loosen your shoulders." Trent was watching them with the kind of patient, reserved, yet desperate intensity that Lyra associated with the eyes of forest-jackals, seen from the little window over the stairs, as they waited for the cooks to throw offal on the refuse-heap.

"Here," said Sinai. She stepped around behind Lyra and moved close to her back, laying her arms along the underside of Lyra's own. The elf was tall enough that Lyra felt the flat curve of belly against her spine and small breasts pressed against her shoulderblades. She could smell the spicy, faintly acrid scent of elven sweat.

"Step forward," Sinai said, pressing her right leg into the back of Lyra's, "and move your arms forward. Turn. Keep your wrists loose."

They continued. Lyra took her cues from the elven woman's movements. Sinai fell quiet after a few moments, continuing to

She became nothing but skin laid over movement.

direct her in silence. Trent's eyes were boring holes in the two of them. Jacyl, too, was watching, her face unreadable.

After a few minutes, Lyra no longer noticed. She stopped thinking about what the next move would be. Her mind felt empty of anything but sunlight and horsetail fern, and the absent twittering of birds. And motion.

The movements were more than familiar now. There was something comfortable about them, so that she almost knew each one before Sinai led her to it. Each one was purely itself, and led naturally into the next, laying a path before it that she had only to follow. When she breathed in, the sunlight seemed to flow liquidly into her lungs and out again. Her eyes were dazzled, watching the trails her hands made in the air, until it seemed she was walking through a hundred versions of herself, all caught in different stages of the Kytha. She closed her eyes and gave herself up to the slow, building heat in her veins, as she had never given herself wholly to anything. As she had never known she could. She became nothing but skin laid over movement.

She danced beyond pain, beyond all the small aches and agonies of the body. She danced beyond thought. She danced beyond existence.

When she opened her eyes again, she realized two things simultaneously—first that it was twilight when a moment ago it had been merely late afternoon, and secondly that Sinai was no longer holding her, and had not been for some time.

She stumbled on the last step of the movement and felt the power that had flowed through her wash out of her in a rush, pouring into the ground like water into a pool. It left her feeling drained, but exhilarated. She propped her hands on her knees and swayed on her feet.

Sinai was sitting on a fallen log, her chin in her hand. Lyra wanted to ask her how long she'd been sitting there—and how long she'd been stepping the Kytha alone.

Instead she asked, "What—what happened?"

The elven woman sighed and stood up. She put an arm over Lyra's shoulders and led her to the campfire, where Sadrao was baking the fish and watching them with cryptic golden eyes.

"What happened," said Sinai, handing her a tin cup of tea, "is that some people are more sensitive to the Kytha than others, or perhaps it is stronger in them. They can learn to let it direct their actions. It becomes—a dance, a martial art, other things. It can have many uses. We call those people Kythar. I am one." She sighed again, more deeply. Trent was watching her face with an almost frightening intensity.

"You, it seems, are another."

Lyra stared at her. "Me? But—but I'm not—"

What she had no words to say—what she would not have known how to say—was that she had lived her entire life in her mind. She was a scholar, not a warrior—she danced badly and could hardly stay on a horse. She hadn't even tried to climb a tree in years. She could not imagine a less likely candidate for a physical magic as the Kytha seemed to be.

"You have it or you don't," said Trent, unexpectedly, from the far side of the fire. "It can be learned, to a degree, with difficulty, but Kythar...know."

Sinai inclined her head grudgingly.

"So...so I can do that? Again? Just like that?" Lyra heard her own voice, higher and thinner than usual. She took a largish swallow of tea.

Sinai shook her head. "No. Not quite. You were riding on my Kytha, to an extent—I provided a spark from which to light the fire. The movements are ritual...they can provide a way to light your fires. You can learn to call it." The shadows in her face deepened. "Sometimes, it won't be there when you need it. And sometimes, it comes on its own."

Lyra licked her lips, then took another drink of tea. She took a deep breath. "Can you teach me?"

Sinai sighed. Jacyl stirred next to her. She laid a hand on her lover's wrist. She spoke a phrase in Elvish, her voice rising on the last syllable in a question.

"Wise or not," Sinai answered in trade-tongue, "it is done. I will teach you, Lyra."

Trent lifted his head. When he spoke, it was also in liquid Elvish, obviously addressed to Sinai, but his eyes never left Lyra's face.

Sinai's reply was harsh, and it went on for a while. When Lyra looked away from Trent to the elven woman, she saw Sinai looking older than she ever had before, the lines in her face etched with anger. The elegant elven vowels were brittle on her tongue.

Obviously excluded from the conversation, but catching the words "Kythar" and "Vade," Lyra dropped her eyes and stared at her hands resentfully.

They don't have to talk about me as if I'm not here.

She looked up quickly at the sound of someone rising. Trent had stood up. He bowed curtly to Sinai, then turned on his heel and stalked into the dark.

"Well, Sinai," said Sadrao tightly, "perhaps you'd like to explain to those of us who don't speak that dialect of Elvish what the hell just happened?"

Sinai poked the fire with a stick. "It is a private matter."

Sadrao folded his arms and stared at her.

Gold and grey eyes locked for a moment, and surprisingly, it was Sinai who looked away. "I swear that it has no bearing on you or Lyra."

"I'm not certain I believe you," said Sadrao.

"It's nothing. Truly," said Sinai.

"Trent wanted to learn the Kytha," said Jacyl, when it became obvious that neither Sinai nor Sadrao was going to give way. Sinai gave her lover a sharp look, which Jacyl ignored. "Sinai refused to teach him."

Sadrao's ears went back, then came forward again. "Is that possible?"

"He is a sorcerer," said Sinai coolly, "and of my blood, and he could probably learn, but I will not teach him."

"But you'll teach me?" asked Lyra, in disbelief.

"Yes."

"Will learning the Kytha put Lyra in danger?" asked the dog-soldier, laying a protective hand on Lyra's shoulder.

"No." The elven woman paused, looking at Lyra. "Not much."

Sadrao's ears eased backwards just slightly. "Not much?"

"Maybe I shouldn't learn it, then," said Lyra, glumly, all her unexpected joy in the Kytha stolen by the argument and the elves' behavior.

"You don't have a choice," said Jacyl, unexpectedly. The fire painted dark shadows over her blue eyes. "The Kytha won't let you alone. Kythar learn to use it, or they are used by it—even I know that much." She reached out and took her lover's arm. "She's woken it, Lyra, for good or ill."

"My own Kytha demanded it," replied Sinai, unruffled, meshing her fingers with Jacyl's. The Kythar looked up to the bronze eyes of the dog-soldier. "I make no excuses, Sadrao. She will have to learn to use it, or she will be in more danger than if she did not. But I will teach her. The Kythar has saved my life many times. It is no better or worse a thing to learn than swordplay."

Sadrao held her eyes for a long moment, inhaling slowly. "I do not smell deception on you," he said finally. "And we have known each other for a long time, Sinai." His gaze lingered on the dark where Trent had vanished, but he said nothing more.

"Does it always happen this way?" asked Lyra the next morning, stepping through the last of a dozen forms that Sinai had shown her. The Kytha was a pleasant buzz in the back of her muscles, new and yet already become familiar. "Someone else wakes it up in you?"

Birds sang from the trees, the twittering chatter of larks and robins occasionally underscored by the mournful cooing of wood doves. A bold copper jay, feathers bright as a new penny, scolded at them from the branches of an evergreen.

Sinai rested her hands on her knees and stared at the leafy ground. "Not always," she said thoughtfully. "You came to it quite late in life. Were you ever a sleepwalker?"

Lyra blinked at the apparent change of subject. "When I was younger. Nine or ten, I think."

"Probably when you were nervous, or unhappy," said Sinai confidently. "Most Kythars manifest at puberty, but it starts becoming obvious a bit earlier. Sleepwalking is common. So are poltergeist fits. The Kytha seeks to defend you from a perceived threat, but can't quite move through you yet. There are others. The child's parents will usually drop a quiet word in the ear of a local Kythar. Then around menarche for girls, a bit later for boys, they receive training from an older Kythar." She gave Lyra a rueful smile. "I'm not a particularly good teacher, if truth be known.

If we were in Anu'tintavel, I'd take you to my old Kythar master. As it is, you're only seeing the Kytha that a scout or a warrior would use. I'll try to remember some of the other forms."

"Was that how it happened for you?" Lyra wanted to know. "It just started coming on at puberty?"

Sinai arched an eyebrow at her.

"Um," Lyra said, suddenly self-conscious, "not that it's any of my business—"

"No, no," said Sinai, with a surprisingly mellow chuckle. "You have a right to know what sort of teacher you've acquired." She straightened. "I was quite young, actually. Seven, I think. We lived near the *Jehandarill*—that's the, um, horse-spirit-river. River of Ghost Horses? Anyway, the Jehandarill is one of the smaller rivers in Anu'tintavel. Not like that," she jerked her pointed chin at the break in the trees, where the broad, lazy Tanglelore was glittering in the early sunlight. "Faster, and colder. There are rapids to the south, but we lived by a relatively gentle stretch. I used to play in it.

"The Jehandarill is haunted," continued Sinai quite seriously. "The name is quite accurate. The water is home to pookhas, river horses. Water spirits that take the form of elves, or horses, or something else."

"Like kelpies?" hazarded Lyra. "I thought they were myths."

"That might be what they're called in your tongue," said Sinai. "To be honest, I thought they were myths, too. No one I knew had ever seen them—or her, to be more precise. The Jehandarill pookha is seen up and down its length, so no one knows if there are a dozen, or a hundred, or only one. They all claim to be the soul of the river."

"But what *are* they?"

Sinai shrugged. "They're demons, I suppose, though I've never heard of a sorcerer who could control a pookha. A few have gone mad trying. They're not really malicious, but they're totally amoral, and they simply don't understand that the rest of us object to drowning. It's quite a foreign concept to them. At least, that's what I felt when the Jehandarill drowned *me.*"

"You?"

"Yes. Seven years old, as I said, and playing near the banks of the river, which I was strictly forbidden to do."

"And the pookha pulled you in?" asked Lyra, wide-eyed.

"No," said Sinai, "I fell in quite legitimately. I was not a particularly well-coordinated child. Most Kythar aren't. I fell in, and the current got hold of me and swept me under."

"I've always said," rumbled Sadrao from where he was cooking breakfast, "that humans should stay out of the water. They haven't the faintest idea of proper swimming."

"And I've always said," replied Sinai, "that your hearing is far too good for an honest creature, old wolf. At any rate, I was swept into some rocks, and I tried to catch hold of them. I got quite bruised and banged up, and when I screamed, water rushed into my lungs. I remember thinking, very clearly for a child, that my mother was going to be quite furious with me for drowning."

Sadrao snorted audibly, over the sound of frying bacon.

"Well, I was grabbing for the rocks again, and catching nothing but water, when the water—this is hard to explain—the water became solid. Not like ice, but like flesh. Something rose up out of the water, and I was holding it, or held by it."

"The pookha..." breathed Lyra.

"The pookha, yes. Like a giant horse, except that it was made out of water, and instead of riding it, I was inside of its body. I didn't know it was even a horse, at the time—all I saw was light streaming through its flanks like a prism, and the river banks distorted by the water around me." She scratched at the back of her neck. "To this day, I don't know why I didn't drown. My lungs were full of water, but the pookha was talking to me. Not in words. I can't remember most of what she said, except that she asked me *why* I wanted to live, when the life ahead of me would be so hard." The elven woman sighed. "She was right, too, but I didn't know that. I didn't want to die. I told her I had to live. I got the impression she wasn't really one being. She kept arguing with herself, and she kept shifting, and I was drowning inside the pookha's body." She shook her head ruefully. "I don't think she understood that I was drowning. When I tried to explain that I couldn't breathe, she said 'There's plenty of air in the water.'"

She fell silent, obviously thinking about the pookha's cryptic words. Lyra prompted her. "And then?"

"And then she let me go," said Sinai. "Not very dramatic, is it? She kicked me out onto the bank, and I looked up, choking, with my lungs full of water and saw this horse, bigger than a warhorse, made out of glass, standing over me. I started coughing, vomiting up water, and it whirled and ran to the river. It left hoofprints full of water."

She shrugged again. "A friend of my parents saw the whole thing and managed to pump most of the water out of me. I looked like a half-drowned rat, I'm sure. He told me that he'd seen me in the river-horse's body, but he hadn't heard anything she said. The Kytha came on soon after that." The elven woman sighed. "Spectacularly, I'm afraid. And there were wet hoofprints around my house, most nights. The two were definitely related—there's been little enough Kytha in my family's blood before now. My parents got frightened, and who can blame them? So we moved away from the Jehandarill."

"That's an incredible story," said Lyra, in awe.

Sinai shrugged, looking almost uncomfortable. "I'd rather have had poltergeist fits. But now you know why I am not the best of teachers—my own Kytha is strange by most standards. I am sorry. You should have better lessons."

"Come and have some of this bacon," suggested Sadrao, and they spoke no more of pookhas.

Chapter Nine

"Jacyl?" asked Lyra, two days later, her muscles still aching pleasantly from the morning's Kytha practice.

"Uh-huh?"

"Can you tell me about the Kytha?"

Jacyl cast a mild blue gaze down at her. Lyra's horse's withers barely came up to the white horse's shoulder, and the elf's stallion took one stride for Mattress's every two.

"Sinai would be the one to ask," said Jacyl after a moment. "I'm not a Kythar."

Lyra shifted uncomfortably in the saddle. "Sinai's hard to talk to," she confessed. "She does seem really mellow in the mornings, but I'm afraid I'll offend her, because I don't know enough not to."

And mornings, practicing the Kytha with her, are so peaceful, I don't want to spoil it. It's a side of her I wouldn't have expected, but I feel like I'm finally getting to see what Sinai's like when she isn't scared, or mad, or reacting to something.

Jacyl, as if tracking Lyra's thoughts, sighed. She looked up the road to her lover's charcoal-grey-clad back.

Sinai and Sadrao had stopped a farmer coming from the opposite direction with a heavily laden oxcart. They were talking to him—or rather, Sadrao was talking, and Sinai was eyeing the man like a large grey hawk circling over a rabbit too small to eat.

"Fair enough," said Jacyl heavily. "I know that Sinai can be difficult. Though about the Kytha, I think you could ask. She won't hold ignorance against you, and she does care for you, Lyra. She doesn't mean to be so harsh; it's just the way she is."

Lyra wasn't sure what to say about that, so she ventured a smile. Jacyl returned it warmly.

"On the other hand," the elven woman continued, "I have lived with a Kythar for many years now, and perhaps I can offer you some insight." She picked at a worn spot on the sky-blue leather of the reins.

Lyra sidled Mattress closer to Jacyl's stallion and waited expectantly.

"First of all," said Jacyl, "I can't tell you what the Kytha is. You really will have to ask Sinai about that, and even she might not be able to tell you what it means for you. But I can tell you that my people, the elves, respect the Kythars immensely. Revere them, even. Being a Kythar forgives a great deal. I think it's because we understand that sometimes the Kytha moves you, and you have no choice but to follow."

"That's kind of scary," admitted Lyra.

"Sometimes, yes. To those that love you, no less than yourself." Jacyl was staring fixedly between her horse's ears, and Lyra knew who she was thinking of.

Sadrao and Sinai finished their conversation with the farmer, and the oxcart rumbled by in a cloud of dust. Jacyl shook herself and gave Lyra a rueful smile.

"Sorry," she said. "I don't mean to scare you. Many of our scouts have some touch of the Kytha, if not as strong as Sinai. Mostly it does what you want it to, just sometimes you do what it wants you to." She shrugged. "Not all the Kythar are warriors, either. There are healers, shamans, artists...I have a friend, Kevran, who's an artist and a healer Kythar. Sinai will teach you the warrior's path, because that's what she knows, but you needn't follow it."

"Yes, I do," said Lyra, thinking of Jasen, and feeling the anger laying like red lead, far down in her mind. Some days, the world was so strange and new that she almost forgot about it. Not today.

Jacyl braided two strands of white mane between her fingers. "That's a decision you have to make for yourself."

Sadrao dropped back to ride quietly alongside, his huge ears pricked in Jacyl's direction. The elven woman nodded to him. "I was just telling Lyra about the Kythars," she said.

The dog-soldier nodded. "Go on," he urged. "I know a little about it, but I'm curious, too."

"Yes. Well, as I was saying, there are different kinds of Kythar. I don't know if that means there are different kinds of Kytha, or if it's the same, and everyone just experiences it differently. I'm not a philosopher. The Kytha—the motions, I mean—were developed to harness the power and direct it. Almost all Kythar use them to some degree. But, oh, Sinai and most of the others scouts are warriors, and some people are healers, or shapeshifters, or, or, well, there's lots of different kinds."

"Shapeshifters?" Lyra lifted her eyebrows. "Will I be able to do that?"

"Probably not," said Jacyl. "There's just not enough quicksilver in your soul, my dear. Many of the Kythar have connections with certain animals, but true shapeshifters are very rare, and among the most powerful of the Kythar. Sinai can't do it."

"Damn," said Lyra. "That would've been *incredible*."

Jacyl laughed. "There used to be more shapeshifters, but Janna Skinstrong was one of the last. There's a certain amount of overlap between talents, though, as I said. One or two of the Kythar I've met can actually shift a little bit. And the stronger Kythar usually have some of the healing gift. Most Kythar can at least heal themselves—you'll do it instinctively, dear, before you start bombarding me with questions. I'd venture to guess that's why you didn't bleed to death in that closet." She nodded to the long red scar on Lyra's arm.

Lyra's mouth hung open, and worked briefly, but no sound came out.

Jacyl trilled a laugh, before continuing. "A few of them, like my friend Kevran, can heal others, too. You'd like him. You know how I said that Kythar have connections with certain animals? He can see that. He does very beautiful tattoos of them...makes me wish I wasn't afraid of needles."

"Does Sinai have one?" asked Lyra.

"No, she doesn't, for some reason."

"Wolf," opined Sadrao.

"Maybe," said Jacyl, "but Kevran won't look unless someone asks, and she won't ask. If it is Wolf, they're not particularly demonstrative. I knew this one Kythar who couldn't step foot outside her house without having magpies land on her. And in the old days, of course, there are stories of Kythar calling up whole armies of wild beasts. That was a long time ago, though."

"Not really," rumbled Sadrao unexpectedly. "Janna Skinstrong supposedly called an army of wargs to attack Ironspine, and that was only a few decades before I was born."

Jacyl shrugged. "Well, that's as may be. According to our scholars, supposedly there were lots more Kythar back then than there are now, and they were stronger. I don't know about that. It runs mostly through elves, although every now and then you'll get a human Kythar, like Lyra here." She grinned.

"Great," muttered Lyra, "I'm a mutant."

"Well, 'anomaly' might be a better phrase." Jacyl trilled her bird-like laugh. "You're unusual, certainly. The Kytha's been getting rarer, according to our historians. Unlike sorcerers, which have been appearing under every bush lately."

"What's the difference between Kytha and sorcery?" Lyra wanted to know.

"Don't ask Sinai that," warned Jacyl, "unless you really do want your head bitten off. The love of my life is a bit irrational about sorcery. So far as *I* can tell, the main difference is that sorcery is learned, and the Kytha is instinctive, except that you do need some kind of basic talent, however small, to make sorcery work. On the other hand, the Kytha can only draw on your own reserves, and what you can do is mostly a function of how strong your gift is. A sorcerer, if he knows what he's doing, only needs a very little talent and can find other ways of gaining power."

"Sacrifice," rumbled Sadrao.

"Exactly. Bloodletting is the most powerful one, which is why most sorcerers are *not* nice people. Some sorcerers, Vade among them, also use demons, although I don't know very much about that. Fortunately, most sorcerers are working with a little natural talent and a few shreds of knowledge gleaned from old grimoires, so they're no match for even a weak Kythar. Or even a completely physical warrior." She grinned over at Sadrao. "I've taken down a few in my time, which might give you some idea."

"You do yourself too little credit," said Sadrao mildly. "After all, I trained you."

"Hmmph. True. I'm a better spy than a warrior, though, no offense to your training. I doubt I'd provide Lyra much of a challenge in a few more months."

Lyra opened her mouth to deny any such thing, but Jacyl laughed at her.

"Anyway," the elven woman said, "there's not a great deal more I can tell you. The important thing to remember, Lyra, is that the Kytha's part of you. It won't turn you into a monster, if that's what you're worried about. It won't do anything you wouldn't do—it just sometimes does it without asking first."

"Great," muttered Lyra. "Just great. Like I didn't get into enough trouble on my own merit."

Jacyl laughed, and the conversation turned to other things, but Lyra did not stop thinking about the matter.

⭇⭇⭇

Gradually, they settled into a pattern. In the mornings, Lyra woke a half-hour before dawn and performed the ritual movements of the Kytha with Sinai. It no longer flowed with quite the impossible ease of the first time, but there was something stirring in her blood that roused to the motions. It was like being angry, or excited, or grief-stricken—a feeling contained more in the body than the mind, quite apart from conscious thought.

Sinai was a very good teacher, whatever she claimed, but there was almost nothing to be taught. The elf woman freely admitted that what worked best for her might not work as well for Lyra, so it was more as if they were dancing together, instead of teacher instructing student. Sinai would show her a particular sequence, and they would practice it in companionable silence, until Sadrao called them to breakfast.

Some of the things Sinai taught her woke immediately in her blood, like the way to use the Hare Kytha to slip through the undergrowth, moving quick, quick, quiet, trusting the power to set her feet down in a kind of twisting, awkward dance that somehow failed to disturb leaf or twig or crackling brush. Sinai could do it so well that Sadrao himself couldn't hear her coming until she was close enough for her breathing to give her away. And she was *fast*, too, moving at a light jog, without breaking so much as a twig.

Lyra could do it, slowly, for about ten yards, on her toes, going from rock to stump to bare patch of ground, running lightly along a half-rotted tree, then getting pulled sideways by the not-quite-instinctive draw of the Kytha before the bark gave way under her feet. Then two more steps on the ground, leaves barely sighing in her wake, then back up on another rock, crossing to a ridge of mossy, half-decayed wood...

Then she'd start thinking about what she was doing, her feet would go in two opposite directions, and she'd fall over with a crash.

But other things Sinai taught her didn't make any sense on examination—like the half-dozen Snake Kythas, which Sinai said were good for slowing bleeding, or the Cat Kythas, which she said were good for seeing in the dark. But how? Lyra couldn't see any connection between a graceful (at least, when Sinai did it) dance, and actually changing the way her eyes saw. And she couldn't see how one could even *do* the Snake Kythas, particularly the spine-destroying Serpent-in-the-Oleanders, if you were in danger of bleeding to death.

"It doesn't matter," said the Kythar when she asked. "It's all in the mind. Dance the Kytha in your mind, and the body follows." Whatever that meant.

At first Lyra was self-conscious about practicing in front of Trent, knowing that the half-elf had wanted to learn the Kytha, and been refused. But after the first time, Trent simply ignored them, helping Sadrao with breakfast and sitting with his back to their practice ground.

When they finally did mount after the morning rituals, they would ride for most of the morning, then stop for a midday break. Then on again, walk and trot and occasional canter. The body was busy, but the mind grew restless.

Lyra thought, often enough, about her family. Her father, really—her assorted bastard siblings had never had much to do with her. Sometimes the memory left her hanging her head, feeling the tightness of suppressed tears at her temples. But his face had gotten dim over the last two weeks, and until now she had been far too busy to dwell on her sorrow. She still missed the lilac bush outside her window, but when she thought of her father, it was with a kind of exasperated grief.

Gods, maybe I am some kind of monster, she would say to herself, and then Trent would jog up on his shaggy gelding and she would think no more about it.

They would travel for most of the day and halt at late afternoon. Then Sinai or Sadrao would spar with her—or more likely, slap her with the flat of the sword and shout until she stopped hyperextending, or clutching her sword too tightly, or whatever sin she was guilty of today. However kind she was as a Kythar, Sinai was a harsh teacher of the sword. Sadrao was less so, but even dog-soldier love-taps left bruises.

She would have resented it, but she knew perfectly well that a real opponent wouldn't have been as kind.

Her teachers were so adept at matching their skill to hers that she did not realize at first that she was getting better. It was not until one day, when she actually worked her way under Sadrao's guard with an entirely unorthodox dive-and-slash that would have hamstrung him, that she realized how she had improved.

Lyra was so shocked by the slap of wood on furry flesh that she failed to land the roll correctly. Her shoulder smacked into the ground, her feet went over her head, and she landed stretched out on her back with her wooden sword tangled up in her legs. Her head rang.

"Are you quite through?" asked Sadrao, his head appearing in her field of vision and looking down at her.

"Quite," said Lyra, and began giggling.

"That was very good, except for the end," said the dog-soldier. "I'll make a swordsman of you yet." He tapped his practice sword against his calf. "For today, however, we are going to work on rolls."

Every now and then, Trent would spar with her. He was a great deal better than she was, but she doubted he would have given Sinai or Sadrao more than a few minutes of competition. He never yelled at her like the elf woman, and she suspected he was pulling his blows more than was entirely warranted. Lyra comforted herself that he had to be increasingly quick to fend her off, even if she would never match his strength.

Sinai was harsh to him to the point of cruelty.

"Why is she like that?" Lyra asked Trent one day, when Sinai had delivered a scathing critique of the half-elf's sword technique, personality, and scatological habits, then turned on her heel and stalked away. "You didn't deserve that."

"Not for my parries, no," he said sadly, setting down his practice sword.

"Then what?" she demanded. "Why?"

He reached out a hand and squeezed her shoulder.

"Nothing you can change." The half-elf sighed. "It is a war. A private war."

"You didn't start it. It isn't your fault."

"No," he said softly, turning away, "but it doesn't matter. Vade and Sinai drew the battlelines before I was ever born."

"What—er, Sinai, forgive me, but can I ask you something?" Lyra had to dig her heels into the sleepy Mattress to bring her up alongside the elven mare.

"Ask."

"What—who—is Vade?"

Sinai looked sharply at her, then away. A week ago, Lyra would have quailed under the steel-grey gaze, but she had learned, from the elf-woman's instruction in the Kytha, to stand her ground.

"He is a sorcerer," said Sinai finally, the elegant arch of her ears drawing down slightly as her jaw muscles tightened. "He inhabits a mountain fortress called Ironspine, south and east of Anu'tintavel." She glanced down at the smaller woman on the short, shaggy horse. "We call him Kingbreaker in our tongue. He brought down the last house of elven kings a hundred years ago, and we have had only a council since."

"Ah," said Lyra, feeling foolish but not knowing any other comment to make.

"Shortly afterwards," Sinai continued, her owl's voice roughened with some private emotion, "an elven Kythar, one of the last of the old blood, a shapeshifter named Janna Skinstrong, breached Ironspine and destroyed Vade's stronghold. We thought—we hoped—she had destroyed Vade as well."

Lyra opened her mouth to make some inane comment like "Damn, that's rough," and squelched it again.

"Twenty-four years ago," said Sinai, her voice as precise and chill as a blade cut from ice, "we learned that he was still alive."

That must have been when Sinai's cousin, Lythara, was kidnapped, thought Lyra, and she felt a pang of sympathy for Sinai's pain and for an elven woman she had never met. It was the opposite, in a way, of what she had experienced—instead of her family torn from her, Sinai's cousin had been torn from her family—and yet Lyra could imagine all too easily how it must have felt. At least she had had Sadrao, and Lythara had had no one at all.

Sinai said nothing more. Jacyl's showy, stupid elven stallion jogged up beside them. Finally, Lyra bit her lower lip and said, "So—I'm sorry, Sinai, but what exactly do evil sorcerers *do?*"

"Whatever they can get away with," said Jacyl, her laughter sharp as a jay's.

Sinai looked over at her lover and the hard planes of her face softened slightly. "Come, now, Lyra," she said, a little more lightly, "you've read every book within a hundred miles of here. You must have heard stories about sorcerers."

"Well, the usual stories, but how accurate they are..."

"Bathing in blood," said Jacyl sarcastically, "eating babies for breakfast and the brains of elves for dessert—"

"Using Ferran-skin napkins," chimed in Lyra, "kicking puppies and engaging in malicious wildflower destruction—"

Sinai, despite herself, snorted with laughter. "Very funny, you two."

"Not to mention the sheer crime against good taste," continued Jacyl with a theatrical shudder. "The *clothes.* D'ya remember that one, two years ago—the one who wore nothing but peacock feathers and green lizard skin? She had those two hlizza-hounds with the matched emerald harnesses."

"Lyra could have taken her with one hand," said Sinai dryly, and then, fingering an old ridge of scar tissue, "but those hounds left something to remember themselves by." Her half-smile faded abruptly, and she spurred Jegger forward with hand and reins. "I'd rather fight a hundred peacock mages than come within a mile of Vade."

Jacyl said nothing.

"He does not bother with theatrics," said Sinai to Lyra finally, her gaze fixed on her favorite spot in the air between Jegger's ears.

"He does not need to. His creatures are elegantly efficient, constructed without a single wasted sinew. He does not waste time with elaborate costumes and he does not make raids merely to increase the terror of his name. He would not expend a captive elf on something as trivial as dining on her brain, and I doubt he razes fields of wildflowers." Her words were black and humorless, delivered with the voice of a woman who has seen her own death and is merely killing time until it comes. "I do not doubt that he has committed acts that would make the stories seem like bedtime tales for children."

Lyra twisted in the saddle to look back at Trent. The half-elf was looking off into the woods, smiling faintly at the birdsong, or at nothing at all.

He looked incredibly normal for someone who had grown up under such a yoke, who had become an intimate acquaintance of atrocity. Or perhaps he had not seen it at all. It was easier to think that he had been sheltered from the worst of Vade's acts, that such mild grey eyes could not mask memories as Sinai hinted.

"Vipers look innocent, too," said Sinai coldly, obviously able to track the direction of her thoughts. "And the young of land-eels can rip a man's hand off minutes after they are born." She looked down at the younger woman, her steel-grey eyes pinning Lyra in the saddle. "Do not delude yourself."

Jacyl made a sound almost of pain and kicked her stallion protectively in between Jegger and Mattress. Sinai gave way without speaking. Jacyl reached out and laid a sympathetic hand on Lyra's shoulder.

"But what does Vade want with Anu'tintavel? I mean, it's not as if you wake up one morning and say 'Hey, let's go invade the elven nation!' do you?"

Sinai said nothing, loudly. Lyra's words hung there, surrounding them, like the dust from the horses' hooves. Lyra could feel a hot wash beginning in her cheeks that inched upwards in the silence.

Don't joke about it, crud, why did I try to joke about it, Sinai does not like jokes about Vade—

Jacyl sighed. "That much, at least, we learned from Trent—"

"If he can be trusted at all," growled Sinai.

"Yes. Well. There had always been lords of Ironspine, I should explain, but in centuries past they had been—not good neighbors, exactly, but quiet ones. They did not turn their eyes on the elven lands, and we did not turn our eyes toward theirs. And Ironspine controls a small enough territory, and so long as we did nothing to interrupt the caravans going to and from the mountain, there was peace enough between us."

"But that changed? With Vade?"

"Yes. What the council was able to get from Trent, and piece together, is that Ironspine itself is the greater part of the power of the sorcerer lords who live there. The mountain itself has power. The sacrifices, the blood magic—that's to provide the power to harness the mountain, not the source of the power itself. It's why Ironspine's sorcerers are so much greater than any of the little sorcerers you find from time to time."

"They've been practicing blood magic for centuries," Sinai cut in. "And we did nothing to stop them. We reap what our ancestors sow, in the end."

There was a little silence after that, too, as the bitterness in her voice stained the air like smoke.

"But what's Ironspine got?" asked Lyra. "I mean, how does a mountain have magic?"

"As far as we can tell, there's some kind of hot spot under it," said Jacyl with a shrug. "Like a hot spring, say. It's an old volcano, that may have something to do with it. And as long as Ironspine was over the hot spot there wasn't much problem. But evidently the hot spot moved somehow—or rather, it stayed put, but the land moved on top of it, the way that land can shift in an earthquake. So, gradually this hot spot had slipped south and west, out from under Ironspine. It took centuries, of course—probably millennia. But finally—"

"—the hot spot wandered into Anu'tintavel," finished Lyra. "So what—Vade wants it back?"

"He wants control of it again," said Sinai. "Make no mistake, there is still great power in Ironspine. But it has faded from a thousand years ago. They had become hermits instead of kings. Vade himself—I do not know. He is a genius. There is no weakness in him." Her voice had gone flat again, not the respectful voice of a warrior for a worthy foe, but the dead voice of a survivor for the experience that had broken her. "The previous lords were content enough with the power they had, but when Kingbreaker took Ironspine from his father, everything changed. He wants to reclaim the power that Ironspine had once, and he killed the last elven kings and butchered our great armies like cattle to do it."

Her voice fell, almost faltered, and the words emerged on a thin sigh. "We get only what we deserve, but we will fight back even so."

She looked ahead, down the road, but Lyra could see that her eyes were fixed on nothing at all, and so she could not have seen the look on Jacyl's face. Lyra looked away. She could see too much, too clearly in the elven woman's face, and she found that there were some things she did not want to know about other people.

It was on the tip of Lyra's tongue to ask how Sinai's cousin had fit into all of it, what Vade could have wanted with her, but she did not. They rode in silence instead, marred only by the sound of the horses' hooves and the thin, high notes of Trent whistling.

⚜

Iyara spent a week and a half in Frieze, waiting. There were no amusements for a non-human in the xenophobic city, and while a dog-soldier was not spat on the way another race would be, neither was she treated with anything but veiled contempt. Iyara met it all with unfailing, bland courtesy. She did not get angry. Even a dog-soldier might have bridled at the treatment, but Iyara had been gone from her home for many years, and the door to her temper was locked and tightly barred.

One night, following a day which had been particularly trying, she went out to the edge of the city, took off her robes, folded them neatly, and slipped into the somewhat murky marsh-forest surrounding Frieze. Her white fur made her stand out like a rogue star, and she had been a librarian, not a warrior, for many years, so it took her several hours before she caught and killed a small deer, snarling savagely and tearing at the flesh. She tore the carcass apart with her bare hands, ate messily, and then searched for another hour to find a clean bit of water, clear of mud and duckweed.

She cleaned her fur neatly, found her clothes, and walked back into Frieze, as cool and elegant and controlled as ever. The next day, yet another of a series of faceless theocratic flunkies informed her that what she asked was impossible, she could not be given an audience any time soon, so sorry, so much delay. She looked at him and imagined the deer. Perhaps something flickered in her eyes, because he went oddly pale and went away, and two days later, having tired of exercising petty power, the cardinals gave her their reply and sent her home.

Iyara met with the Archmage and gave him the message.

"Wait—" he said, as she turned to leave. She turned back, and waited. He read the message, slowly, at length, his nostrils flaring. For a moment, Iyara saw the deer again, and something like shock went though her, but the Archmage did not notice.

I have been among humans too long, she thought, with a trace of bitterness. *Too many human faces. I forget what it is to be a dog-soldier, to be loyal.* She bowed her head, and when the Archmage ordered her to carry yet another message, she felt a brief, unsurprising flare of annoyance, and then something like despair.

Lyra woke in the middle of the night.

It was the twelfth day since they had left Jeppeth—the eighth since Sinai had begun instructing her in the Kytha. The landscape had gone from the gently rolling fields around the city to a more heavily wooded area. There was still land cleared for farming, bordered by low stone fences, but when they camped at night it was usually in lightly forested copses.

Spring had achieved a tighter hold on the land as they traveled, the leaves darkening from chartreuse to a more sedate green. Lyra lay quietly in her bedroll, smelling the rich scent of growing things and looking up at the canopy of leaves and blazing stars.

Her bladder was full, which was probably what had woken her. Lyra wriggled into her outer tunic and trousers and rose.

The fire had died down to a dull burn of red, crosshatched with orange embers. As usual, Jacyl and Sinai were sharing a bedroll several yards outside the circle of firelight. Sadrao was sleeping a few feet from Lyra's head, curled in a neat ball. Trent had rolled over, blankets tangled around him, one outflung arm practically in the fire. As Lyra slid her feet into her boots, sans socks, he rolled over, rescuing his hand from the heat, and snored into his elbow.

She grinned and padded into the dark. Twigs and pine needles crunched under her feet, releasing the tangy scent of evergreen. She found a clear patch of slope to tend to nature. *First law of wilderness survival,* Lyra thought wryly, *always face uphill and keep your feet out of the way. Goddess, I envy men.*

Important business concluded, she rose and turned back to camp. *Let me see, did I come through by the sumac, or by the big teapot-shaped rock?* She picked the latter of the two, slithered quietly through the undergrowth, realized immediately that she had gone the wrong way, and stopped. *Umm. If I angle to the right, I should come out at camp.*

A few seconds later, she caught a gleam of orange and made toward it. She entered the copse from the opposite side that she had left it, took one quiet step around a tree trunk, and froze. The deeply furrowed pine bark bit into her fingers as she caught at it.

The moon had risen high enough to break through the leaves and illuminate the sleepers. Lyra's eyes, dilated for the darkness, were riveted on Jacyl and Sinai.

She had come in at Jacyl's back, and a little up from their position. The embankment around the pine's roots lifted her several feet above the level of the ground.

The elves were sleeping curled up together in the bedroll, the top blanket sashed modestly across their waists. Lean, wiry Sinai lay on her side, with Jacyl's face tucked in the hollow of her collarbone, one arm stretched out to pillow her lover's head. She held one of Jacyl's hands in hers, cradled between small breasts. The tanned skin of their hands and faces seemed very dark next to the almost blue-white where sunlight rarely touched.

While Lyra had read about women and...other women...she had to confess to herself that she had never quite figured out the mechanics of it. She still had no idea, but she realized, hiding in the shadows the tree, that Sinai and Jacyl were beautiful, and she thought she understood a little of why they felt as they did.

As she watched, Jacyl stirred, making a sleepy noise, and snuggled deeper against Sinai. Her hand slipped free of the other woman's, moved across Sinai's breast and ribs, then down over her hip.

Sinai smiled in her sleep and drew her lover close, her free hand trailing up the smaller woman's spine. Jacyl kissed the neck in front of her, her hand sliding beneath the blankets.

I should go. I shouldn't be watching this. Lyra didn't move.

Sinai opened her eyes. Lyra shrank farther into the shadows, feeling her face heat, but she need not have worried. Sinai had eyes only for Jacyl. As Lyra watched, the Kythar leaned over and cradled Jacyl's face between both hands. She kissed her, tenderly, but with great passion.

Jacyl caught her lover around the waist and pulled the other woman on top of her. Sinai chuckled deep in her throat, a sound so warm and earthy that Lyra could scarcely reconcile it with the cool alabaster warrior she had come to know. Sinai pushed herself up on her hands and knelt over Jacyl, back to Lyra.

Jacyl slid a hand up between her lover's thighs and Lyra ducked back behind the tree, biting back a gasp.

While she suddenly had a very good idea of the mechanics of the process, that wasn't what left her staring wide-eyed into the dark. Sex was quite suddenly the farthest thing from her mind.

Sinai's back, which had been turned toward her, was burned into her mind's eye.

A network of scars, layered and labyrinthine as elven knot-work, striped the Kythar from slim shoulders to the base of her spine. Lyra had seen similar scars on the lowest kind of slaves, on dying carthorses. Whip scars.

Someone had *beaten* Sinai, within an inch of her life, probably within the past year. The scars were healed, but still red and shiny. When Jacyl touched her, blood pulsed in the pale scars and turned them freshly crimson.

Lyra could not imagine any situation where Sinai—cool, elegant Sinai, vicious warrior Sinai—would have taken that kind of punishment.

A sound came from behind her, unmistakably of pleasure. Lyra leaned against the pine, feeling sap adhere unpleasantly to the backs of her arms. Her mind whirled with unaskable questions.

She drew away from the pine tree, slipped quietly through the woods a few paces, then turned around. Then she began walking through the forest, back toward the campsite, making no attempt at silence.

By the time she arrived at the camp, the two elven women were modestly covered by blankets, wrapped deeply in shadow. Lyra didn't glance in their direction, but picked her way to her bedroll and slid into it. Under the blankets, she stripped out of her tunic and trousers and dropped them by her boots.

There was the sound of soft breathing and blankets moving. Lyra rolled over, the fire warm at her back.

Strange, she thought wryly, *sex between those two doesn't shock me, but the thought that someone beat Sinai has me absolutely floored.*

And then, unbidden, *Though I wouldn't have believed that Sinai had such emotion in her.*

She was ashamed to admit that despite knowing Sinai and Jacyl, some part of her had still cleaved to the beliefs, taught to her since childhood, that labeled them unnatural, until tonight.

She realized, staring into the forest shadows, that she would give a great deal to have someone touch her with such tenderness—man or woman, elf or human, anyone who would love her the way that Sinai and Jacyl loved each other. Despite the scars, visible and invisible that they both bore.

Her last thought, before she sank down into sleep, was to wonder if anyone ever would.

The next day, Lyra waited until Sinai and Jacyl were riding up ahead, and Trent trailing absently behind, to broach the question to Sadrao.

"Sadrao?"

"Yes?"

"Can I ask you a question that's probably none of my business?"

Sadrao threw his head back and gave a barking laugh. "Something tells me I probably shouldn't agree to anything...but go ahead."

Lyra met the dog-soldier's good-natured golden eyes. "How did Sinai get her scars?"

Sadrao looked puzzled. "Scars? The same way I got mine, and you got yours." He nodded to the pale slash across Lyra's left forearm. "Obviously somebody tried to kill her."

"No," said Lyra, "I meant the *other* scars. The fresh ones. On her back."

Sadrao's eyes narrowed, the good-humor fading. "Tell me," he ordered curtly.

"The whip scars," said Lyra faintly. She was used to Sinai's harshness, and no longer took it personally, but Sadrao's sudden intensity was a little alarming.

"Whip scars," echoed Sadrao. He cast a sharp look up the road at the elven woman, then back down at Lyra. "Bad?"

"The worst I've ever seen on anyone still alive," said Lyra honestly.

Sadrao said something obscene in his own tongue. "I *thought* she'd gotten more body-shy," he muttered, "and she was never one to care before." He looked down at Lyra. "I don't know what they are," he said, "but we're about to find out."

"Uh—" said Lyra, not at all wanting to explain to Sinai how she'd seen the woman's bare back.

"Don't worry," said Sadrao, "I don't intend to ask her." He kicked his plowhorse forward into a trot, calling, "Jacyl? Hey, Jacyl! You got any thread?"

Up ahead, the elven woman turned in the saddle, then slowed her white stallion. Dust had stained his hocks the color of mud. Sinai's mare continued at her usual even pace, carrying her rider farther up and out of earshot. Sinai was not a fan of sewing.

"Thread?" asked Jacyl cheerfully, as Sadrao and Lyra flanked her. "Sure. What color?" She reached into her saddlebags. "I've got black, white, grey, red, blue—"

Sadrao's furry hand closed over her wrist. "I'm not really interested in thread, but we're going to pretend we're really interested in mending something, in case anybody looks back here, alright?"

Jacyl looked from him to Lyra, then back to the dog-soldier, a line forming between her eyebrows. "What?"

"We need to talk," said Sadrao, "about Sinai." He dropped her hand. Up ahead, Sinai turned and glanced backwards down the road at them. Seeing nothing out of the ordinary, she turned back.

Jacyl eyed him warily. "What about Sinai?"

Sadrao jerked his muzzle in the direction of the elven warrior. "Why does she have whip marks on her back?"

"Why don't you ask her?" asked Jacyl evasively.

"Because I'm not a fool," he replied tightly, "and I want a straight answer. Look me in the eye, Jacyl Larkheart. Sinai's been acting strange since we met up with you, and I want to know what's happening."

"Don't call me that," Jacyl mumbled, staring fixedly at her hands and the ridiculous sky blue reins. "It's not my name anymore."

Sadrao's ears flicked back at that, but he said, "Don't change the subject, Jacyl."

"It was a bloody-damned mission," said Jacyl, with sudden, unexpected heat, "for the bloody-damned council. She went into a slave caravan because they needed a damned Kythar and none of the other scouts would do it. They all thought it was a suicide mission." Her normally musical voice was tight and ugly with anger. "The damned cowards."

"Why?" asked Sadrao.

Jacyl still refused to meet his eyes. "The council had to find out who was running the caravan. They knew that it was going to Ironspine, and that Vade had been buying slaves for years." Her voice grew flat and tired with the recitation. "They thought that a certain group—the Wineroot Clan—might be sending elven slaves as some kind of tithe to Ironspine, and they needed someone who could get in and talk to the slaves, find out where they'd been captured, and stand some chance of getting out again."

Sadrao whistled.

"We thought it was them, but we didn't have enough proof. None of your corks, just rumors, and rumors are hardly enough for the council—which reminds me, if they ask, you didn't hear any of this from me." She glanced over to Lyra. "That goes for you, too."

Lyra hoped fervently that she'd never be talking about this in front of the elven council, but said, "I promise."

"Well," said Jacyl, "she got in as a slave easily enough. I actually sold her to them." The elven woman laughed bitterly at that. "Fifteen gold for an elven body slave, excellent condition, but took a blow to the head last year and hasn't been quite right since then. Has fits, you know, starts twitching and foaming. *Most* unattractive." She laid a delicate hand across her collarbone in a remarkable imitation of a spoiled noblewoman, then dropped it. "Goddess, but I hate being a spy."

Lyra didn't know whether to say something or not. She felt slightly sick.

"Go on," rumbled Sadrao.

"Anyway," Jacyl continued, "she got in and found out quickly enough that the Wineroot Clan is indeed paying Vade's blood money—mostly in gold and spices, but there were two other elves in the caravan from their region...notably ones who were protesting paying tribute to Ironspine in the first place. At least, that's the gist of what she got—one of them had his tongue cut out, and the one who could talk really did have fits. There was also the usual assortment of criminals and unfortunates you find in any slave caravan, and a shuttered wagon with a pair of women who had been kidnapped from one of the Plains tribes, not that Sinai knew that at the time."

"And the whip marks?" asked Sadrao.

"Come on," said Jacyl angrily, "have you ever known Sinai to stand by and let well enough alone? You know how slaves are usually treated, particularly the women, and she couldn't watch that without trying to stop it. She made so much trouble that the slave trader probably would have cut her throat if he hadn't paid such an outrageous price for her. As it was, by the time she escaped, the Kytha was the only thing keeping her on her feet."

"But she did escape, obviously," mused Sadrao.

"Oh, yes," said Jacyl, meeting his gaze with a strange, pained pride. "Strangled the trader with her own chains and escaped with half the caravan. Got them into Anu'tintavel, snuck them through the Wineroot lands at night—she didn't dare trust the clans there—and was half-dead of wound fever by the time I caught up to them. Her back had festered so badly we could barely keep her alive, let alone do anything about the scars." Her voice tightened with frustration. "The Wineroots denied everything, of course, and the council doesn't dare offend them. They control too much land, and too many troops."

"But now—now maybe we've got a chance. Your wine corks, and your word. At the very least, it may spook the Wineroots into miscalculating, into admitting something. And it will support what Sinai has been saying all along."

Sadrao sighed. They were all silent for a while.

"No wonder Sinai's so abrupt," said the dog-soldier finally. "Though it doesn't sound as if she's really changed a great deal." He looked over at Lyra, in an obvious effort to lighten the mood. "When I first met her, Sinai wasn't much older than you are, Lyra, in elven terms. Proud, prickly, stubborn young woman. Even then she was taking all the jobs that no one else was brave enough, or stupid enough, to take, because she wouldn't admit anything was beyond her. And most of the time she succeeded, too. They called her the Winter Wolf." He smiled at the memory. "There's something to be said for the elven way of naming."

"That was a long time ago, Sadrao," said Jacyl softly. Something in her voice made both Lyra and the dog-soldier look over at her.

"Vade's been harassing Anu'tintavel for years now," said Jacyl, still in a low voice, almost like Sinai's own. "For the last few, though, it's been more than the occasional skirmish. They've been fighting a war and the council won't admit it, for fear all the clans will split apart over what to do. And Sinai is still taking all the missions that no one else will do—" Jacyl stopped and drew a deep breath, "—and they're getting worse and worse. When Trent showed up in Anu'tintavel, though, she changed. They had to admit it was Vade then, but it didn't help." She glanced back down the road, to where the half-elf was absently braiding his hair back behind his ears. "You're not wrong, Sadrao. She started taking the hardest, trickiest missions, the ones that other scouts had died on. I keep trying to s-stop her, but she won't listen to me at all. They say—they say—she's looking to d-die herself—"

Her voice broke. There were tears in her blue eyes.

Sadrao and Lyra both reached out and touched her, but there was little real comfort they could give. They exchanged pained looks over her head.

"I think the council was glad of the excuse to send her away from Anu'tintavel," said Jacyl dully, when the tears had stopped. She knuckled her reddened eyes. "Because you're right. She has changed."

"Jacyl—" began Sadrao.

"They call her the Dead Wolf now," Jacyl said, her voice quietly undercutting him. "*Mourneloupe.*"

Lyra saw the muscles in Sadrao's jaw tense, but the dog-soldier's voice remained calm. "I see." He gathered up the reins of his horse, looking up the road at Sinai's back. "And they don't call you Larkheart anymore..."

He trailed off. Despite his composure, Lyra could see a shadow of the protective love he still held for his old charge. "Jacyl?"

"*Mourneloupe-daro*, they call me," said Jacyl dully. "The Dead Wolf's Shadow."

⊱ *Interlude* ⊰

When Sinai was sixteen years old, she went to a party held by her cousin Lythara.

It's a stereotype that elves are a somewhat bloodless race, more fond of light wines and aged cheeses than a good beer and a good fight. The truism goes that for a pleasant evening with tasteful flower arrangements and music heavy on the pan pipes, you go to the elves. To get hammered and party, hang out with the humans or the icebears—or for the truly adventurous, a pack of dog-soldiers with a few pints in them.

Like all stereotypes, there's an element of truth to this one, but elves are people too. Some of them want nothing more than a white wine and a good book, and some of them like spicy food and strong ale and causing immense amounts of property damage.

Sinai, at sixteen, belonged firmly to the latter camp. Fortunately, in a slightly more decorous fashion, so did Lythara.

The young Sinai worshipped Lythara, her beautiful older cousin. She was herself a leaner, colorless version of the older woman, her hair white-blonde instead of gold, her skin pale instead of rose. They were both tall and wore their hair in long braids down the back, both fond of fast horses and rough hunts. They had the same angular faces and cheekbones you could sharpen a sword on.

The similarity ended there, however.

Lythara was bright and sunny of disposition. Even at sixteen, the Kytha already burning hot and wild in her veins, Sinai was colder and had a fey streak of inner darkness. Lythara attracted men like a flower attracted bees. Sinai had yet to find a man who had that nebulous *something* she was seeking, and was beginning to cool on the entire breed.

Lythara threw parties. Sinai mostly went to them and got drunk.

She had only recently been made a full scout—one of the youngest in the history of Anu'tintavel. She was proud and a little embarrassed to be wearing the silver sun-badge on her right shoulder. The other scouts mostly hung out together in small knots of black and grey leather. Whenever they nodded to her, and gave the little half-salute to an equal, she wanted to turn around and look for who they were acknowledging.

With half a dozen scouts in attendance, and thirty or forty others of less militant character, they should really have had some warning.

Vade struck at early twilight, just when the revelers had begun to relax, and dusk had spread under the trees. They were very near the borders of Anu'tintavel, and there was no excuse for not posting guards, but it was early summer, the weather was glorious, and even a scout's paranoia had eased a little.

One minute, Sinai was waving across the clearing to Lythara and thinking that her cousin had never looked more lovely. She was wearing a white cotton shirt with slashed sleeves, and simple grey leggings. Sinai, as always, was wearing black hunting leathers.

The next minute, there were warriors everywhere—lean-bodied creatures with ropy sinews and arched backs. Chitinous armor slid in plates over the joints, studded with backward-curving spines. They had the elegant efficiency of insects, designed by a master artisan with an aesthetic based on function over all.

They cut an appalling swath through the elves. Most of the scouts had swords, but the rest were unarmed. The insect-warriors did not waste a great deal of time on the noncombatants,

There were warriors everywhere. They had the elegant efficiency of insects.

smashing them out of the way with casual blows from spiked forearms. They focused instead on the few scouts, the only ones putting up an organized resistance.

Much later, Sinai thought that it must have been her youth and relative delicacy that kept the chitinous warriors from turning on her. More than one huge, beetle-shelled monster passed by her without a second glance.

Three of the scouts, including one of Sinai's weapons-masters, threw themselves onto one of the insect-soldiers. Sinai, groping for her sword, froze, transfixed by the scene. Her weapons-master would have yelled at her, but he was straddling the creature's neck and sliding his sword in between the armored plates at the base of its skull.

The soldier went down. Sinai drew in her breath to whoop with glee. It came out as a shriek of horror instead.

A second warrior swung a spined arm like a scythe. The bone hooks punched through the weapons-master's chest and knocked him forward into the grass. He looked down at the blood streaming down his chest, his expression filled with nothing so much as *surprise,* and crumpled.

Sinai yanked her sword out. The Kytha was waking hot and hungry in her blood.

The remaining scouts pulled back into a knot with Lythara and a few others in the middle. Sinai staggered forward, intending to join them, when another figure entered the clearing.

He was perhaps six feet tall—rangy for a human, with chiseled features and hair just barely turning grey at the temples. He had a faint smile on his face.

He paused at the edge of the clearing with his arms folded. Two of the soldiers flanked him, a taller, more heavily carapaced breed than the others.

He was looking at the other elves, who were fighting back to back, retreating toward the trees. The insect warriors were surrounding them, pressing them backwards. Whenever one of the elves advanced too close to the edges of the circle, a spiked arm turned, chitinous swords angling inward, and swung.

If they were quick, the elf dodged back. If they were not, they joined the ranks of the stunned and dying.

Crouching in the shadow of the trees, her black leather blending with the spreading darkness, Sinai had gone unnoticed. She lowered her sword, rising onto her toes and the fingers of one hand. If she could just take him by surprise...

Their attacker had turned to face the elves. He took a step forward, then another.

"I am Vade. The one you so quaintly call 'Kingbreaker.' I have a proposal for you," he said. His voice was deep and thoughtful, the voice of a sage or a philosopher. It was polite, genteel, considered. It was a voice so trustworthy that Sinai mistrusted it at once.

"We will not deal with you!" snarled a voice from the crowd. Cries of agreement echoed him.

Vade made an economical gesture with one hand. The insects closed the circle another few feet, sending the elves crowding back.

"Let us be reasonable," he said.

An arrow came out of nowhere. One of the scouts evidently had stashed a bow somewhere. Sinai leaned forward eagerly.

It streaked crisply toward Vade's left eye. The scouts of Anu'tintavel were nothing if not crack shots.

There was nothing so dramatic as a flare of light. Only a brief sputter of static, and the arrow rebounded a few feet and struck the ground. The milk-white fletching shone like a star against the dark grass.

He had a mage-shield.

Arrows, and most warriors, would never penetrate. She was not most warriors. On a good day, when the Kytha was willing, Sinai could slip through shielding magic. She gritted her teeth, dug deep. Somewhere just below her heart there was power waiting, somewhere just...about...*there.*

The power hit her like a fist, like diving into icy water, a shock that left her gasping. It might be enough. It might not be.

An older, more experienced scout would not have tried it—not alone. They would have sunk back into the trees and run for reinforcements, run with the Kythar's unbreakable, ground-eating stride. By the time help arrived, however, Lythara might already be dead.

She was sixteen. She was appallingly young and appallingly arrogant, and only the fact that she was also appallingly strong had kept her alive this long.

In later years, she thought about that, often with a bitter smile. But at this moment, spurred on by mad courage and the whip of the Kytha, she thought only, *This man must die.*

She lunged.

The guards didn't notice her until she had broken cover and was less than three strides from Vade. They turned with insectile grace, closing behind their master, but they were not going to be fast enough.

The Kytha was absolutely wild inside her, as unstoppable as a thunderstorm. If only she could breach the shields…

The gods were with her today. Vade's shield parted like hot butter in front of her sword.

She ducked under a swipe from one of his guards and drove the sword at his chest. The Kytha was burning patterns in the air for her, her muscles screaming in ecstasy at the use. She had only to follow the path it laid for her, the blade twisting down and forward, the point aiming for his heart…

He made a simple, sweeping gesture with his arm, almost contemptuously smooth. The blade of his hand stroked across the inside of her wrist with the weight of magic behind it.

Pain exploded in her arm, nausea overwhelming her. The Kytha fell out of her like water from a broken cup. She looked down in horror.

White ends of bone were protruding from the inside of her wrist, the arm snapped backward at an unnatural angle. Her sword dropped from nerveless fingers.

What?!

She looked up at his face, her skin gone ashen. She could not believe that this was happening.

He smiled down at her and wrapped his hands around her throat.

A sound came from the assembled elves, a sighing noise of dismay.

This can't be happening!

He pulled her back against him and lifted his eyes to the knot of scouts and Lythara.

"I have a proposal for you," he said, practically purring. "In fact—a simple trade. Mine for one of yours."

One of the female scouts, a woman named Ysla Serpentwife, stepped forward, her sword held low at her side. "Let the girl go," she said warily.

"No, no," said Vade. "Not you. Her." He jerked his chin to the center of the knot of elves, to Lythara.

"No!" gurgled Sinai through the bruising grip on her throat.

"No deal," grated one of the elves—one of Lythara's suitors, not one of the scouts. Ysla gave him a look that could have melted stone. So did Lythara.

Lythara took a step forward, her skin pale as milk. Sinai tried to say something and choked.

Vade took his hands from her throat, put his lips next to Sinai's ear, and said "Tell her how frightened you are."

"Go to hell," said Sinai, and slammed her head backwards into his face.

He jerked his head back—*what kind of impossible reflexes had sorcery given him?*—and slid his hand down her arm. His fingers curled around her broken wrist and squeezed, once. Not even particularly hard, but precisely.

Pain rolled over her in black waves, drowning her in a savage nausea. She had thought she knew pain, but this was something else again, something with magic behind it, something that made mere pain look like a lover's caress. When she came back to herself she was on her hands and knees, throwing up on his boots.

If she had hoped that he would recoil in disgust, she was disappointed. Unlike every other sorcerer in existence, Vade Kingbreaker did not appear particularly concerned with the state of his clothes. He locked her good arm behind her, the wrist pressed between her shoulderblades. She heaved until there was nothing left in her stomach, her arm throbbing like a shattered star.

His grip was not hard or cruel, merely firm. He patted her shoulder absently with his free hand, as if she were a hound choking on a piece of gristle.

She had just enough presence of mind, through the pain, to be utterly humiliated.

I don't even exist in this man's mind.

I'm going to kill him.

He was saying something, but the sound of her own retching drowned most of it out. Quite a lengthy conversation went on over her head while she fought to stop vomiting.

She had never felt pain like that in her wrist. There was magic laced into the pain, like some kind of bitter anti-Kytha, rousing the nerve-endings to agony.

All she caught of Vade and Lythara talking, in a brief space while shock began to stroke chemical fingers up her spine, was her cousin saying "How do I know you won't kill me?"

To which Vade replied, almost gently, "You don't."

There were blood vessels breaking in her eyes, or she was so furious the world had gone red. It was hard to tell.

Shaking, lips coated in bile, she staggered upright when he tugged on her arm. She lifted her head with an involuntary moan.

Lythara was standing there, just outside the mage-shield. Her skin was deathly pale, but her face was resolute.

"Lythara, no!" Sinai's throat was raw and torn, but she croaked a denial through it. "Don't!"

"There's no choice," said her cousin.

Vade nodded and shoved Sinai forward.

The young Kythar fell out of the mage-shield, tried to roll on her intact arm, and came up in a crouch that immediately listed sideways. She tried to reach for Lythara, to catch her back.

The ground came up to meet her, hard.

I can't fail! Dammit, Sinai, youstupididiotbitchselfGETUP!

Her fingers just missed Lythara's heel as the insect warriors reached out. Spines rattled along their arms as they plucked Lythara neatly from the ground and turned away.

Vade, without a wasted word, without stopping to gloat, turned and left the clearing. The jointed warriors waited a few moments, then followed.

Silence reigned in the clearing. Ysla Serpentwife picked her way over Sinai.

The young scout looked up at her with blind grey eyes. "Lythara—we have to stop her—"

"Sinai, child," said Ysla with rough sympathy, "she's gone."

"NO!" shrieked Sinai, and tried to clench her fist.

The pain of abused tendons went practically unnoticed, but when she slammed her fists into the ground, the impossible agony cut through her grief and, mercifully, she lost consciousness.

⊱

They sewed her up, and she healed. But they could do nothing for her heart, or her guilt, or her injured pride. She had changed, hardened, saddened. Some things could not be healed.

When Lythara limped back into Anu'tintavel, a year and a half later, bearing Vade's child, Sinai was away on a scouting mission. Her cousin's return freed her of some of the weight she had been carrying, but could not excise the darkness entirely. She was never comfortable around Lythara's son. She spent a great deal of time on scouting missions—tricky, dangerous work that earned her the name of the "Winter Wolf."

When her dear friend Sadrao introduced her to his protégé, an earnest young elven woman named Jacyl, some of what Sinai had been seeking was found at last.

The year she met Jacyl was the only unadulterated happiness that the elven Kythar could remember. She was twenty-six years old and loved the younger woman with a passion so intense it bordered on pain. That someone so beautiful and bright of spirit returned her feelings was a miracle that never failed to take her breath away.

A year later, when the pair was staying with Lythara just outside Anu'tintavel, Vade returned to claim his son.

In the fighting that ensued, Sinai single-handedly slaughtered half a dozen of the insect warriors. The Kytha had only grown stronger with age. But she was one woman—too little, too late, and Trent was taken and Lythara killed.

All she remembered, truly, was standing in a pile of chitinous bodies, her white hair and skin striped with ichor and her own blood, like fool's motley. She remembered putting a hand to her throat, wondering why it felt so raw, and only then realizing that she was screaming.

It was only Jacyl's love that kept her alive after that.

Still, there was a strength to Sinai. A few years passed and old scars began to fade, old wounds to heal. She and Jacyl took missions outside of Anu'tintavel, where there were no old memories to plague them.

She dreamed often, in the later days, of rushing water and streams as clear as diamonds, of water demons with the faces of women. There was something prophetic to them, but she barely knew what.

Always, there was Jacyl. Even when Vade's aggressions began to assume the shape of a war, even when the council sat paralyzed with indecision, Sinai could look at her companion and take comfort in her presence.

And then Trent returned, and all the old wounds were ripped open and bleeding again, and this time there was no healing it.

She was forty. The years lay lightly on her, physically. As an elf, she might have gone on for many years yet, but when she had looked into her cousin-son's half-elven eyes, she felt something break.

She became wilder, more reckless. She took missions that would have killed anyone else. In her heart of hearts, she might have been trying to die. It was only Jacyl's beloved presence that kept her from taking a more active approach, from turning Jegger toward Ironspine and riding at Vade until he killed her.

The other scouts began to call her the Dead Wolf, and to avoid her. Scouts that worked with her died. For several months, she grew colder and wilder, until the council finished with Trent.

In the end, she took him from Anu'tintavel, Jacyl at her side, and sought out her old friend Sadrao. There was no chance of her healing anymore, but for the sake of Lythara's memory, and the desperate love she still bore Jacyl, she would keep on living until she was given a chance to strike a last blow at Vade's heart.

It was all she had left.

It was enough.

Chapter Ten

"I don't understand elven names," said Lyra to Trent the next day, as they trotted toward the distant foothills.

"Mmmm?"

"The last names," she clarified. "I've read about plenty of elves, and Sinai's mentioned a few. Janna Skinstrong and Adali Icequeen. And all the elves in—um, you know, the one by Xyth Treefriend, the one with the green binding—"

"*The Forest Lords,*" said Trent promptly. "Sentimental drivel. Though his history of Anu'tintavel isn't bad, even if he dwells on the civilizing effect of elves on human nomadic tribes in the area—um, sorry. You were saying?"

"Right. Well, how come all the elves I've heard of have those bizarre last names? And Sinai and Jacyl—"

She stopped abruptly, unsure if Trent knew about the elven women's strangely tragic titles. Normally, she would have asked Jacyl about anything involving elven culture, but names were obviously a tender subject with the older woman just now.

"The Dead Wolf and her Shadow, yes," said Trent quietly.

Neither of them said anything for a moment.

"But how do they get those names?" asked Lyra, finally. "Who would dare call Sinai something like that?"

Trent shrugged, shoving his glasses higher up on his nose. "I doubt Sinai cares much about her name. Although I'd like to see *anyone* call Jacyl '*Mourneloupe-daro*' in Sinai's presence."

"Or in mine," rumbled Sadrao, the heavy hooves of his draft horse clopping on the road as he edged the animal up beside Lyra.

"Of course," said Trent, bowing slightly in the saddle.

"I was just asking Trent about elven names," said Lyra, abashed. "I didn't mean to—"

"No, of course not." Sadrao smiled at her, his tail brushing absently along the horse's flanks. "You're curious. Naturally." His smile broadened. "I'm surprised you haven't read any books on it."

"My father wasn't too fond of elves," said Lyra. "I only had one or two books on them, and they were more general histories than anything else."

"Well…" Sadrao cracked his knuckles in a remarkably human gesture. "Elves traditionally only use a set number of first names—"

"Two-hundred-twelve," Trent interjected, "after the first founders of Anu'tintavel."

"—Thank you, yes. They use descriptive last names to distinguish themselves. In Elvish, of course—most of these are just trade-tongue translations." Sadrao rubbed the back of his neck. "Whereas dog-soldier last names reflect the lineage of their sponsor into the pack—'Majiid' indicates that I was sponsored by Majiid Vayloor, the Dog-With-His-Back-To-The-Desert."

"Elven names can change over the course of their lifetimes," Trent continued, taking up the thread. "Even after death. Adali Icequeen was Adali the Icetiger while she was still alive, but it got changed posthumously."

"So you're what? Trent, ah…?" She paused, struck by the sudden blankness of his expression. "If I may ask?"

"Trent *Ashtuk*," said Trent. Sadrao winced. "Trent the Bastard is probably the best translation."

Lyra bit her lip.

"When I was in Anu'tintavel last," said Sadrao, in an obvious effort to change the subject, "some of the scouts named me *Koraloupe*—the Old Wolf. Not," he added archly, "that I am old."

"How old are you, anyway?" asked Lyra curiously.

"Seventy-nine," said the dog-soldier easily.

Lyra's jaw dropped. "Seventy. Nine. Years. Old."

Trent, his good-humor evidently restored, reached over and used a fingertip to push her chin up. "You're going to catch flies that way," he observed gently.

"Come now," chided Sadrao, "you don't think the Amir of Sarappa would have gone to the trouble of designing us, and then given us a mere sixty or seventy years, do you?"

"How long *do* you live?" asked Trent. "As long as elves?"

"Not quite so long," said Sadrao. "One-hundred fifty, perhaps. I am middle-aged, for a dog-soldier. Sinai's forty now, and she should outlive me by a good many years."

"Barring accidents," said Trent. Sadrao looked at him sharply, but the half-elf only returned the dog-soldier's gaze with his mild grey eyes.

Lyra was running through her limited grasp of Elvish in her head. "So Anu'tintavel means what?"

"Heart of the World," said Sadrao.

"From *ano*, meaning 'heart' and *tintavos*, 'all the world'," added Trent. "Not particularly modest of them."

"Then, *Ano daro tu kurimano*," Lyra quoted the elven greeting. "Um, 'your heart unshadowed'?"

"Very close," said Trent. "'May your heart never cast a shadow.' The reply is abbreviated to '*Gozu daro*,' but it means 'Your light creates no shadows.'"

"Ah," said Lyra, "and '*gozu*' is...?"

"Casts, which is odd, because it translates as 'casts shadows', even though it means exactly the opposite. Did you ever read *A Theory of Languages* by that linguist from the Blue Havens? The one who studied the evolution of certain phrases over time?"

"Thesson Rael," said Lyra. "Yeah, he did that fascinating chapter on the influence of Slothan formalities on the dialects around the Blue Havens..."

Sadrao, who liked to keep his feet dry, but his conversations less so, kicked his plowhorse forward and left them to their discussion.

Her body still aching from Sinai's latest lesson, Lyra cleaned her sword with cinnamon-scented oil, and what felt like the last dregs of strength, then staggered down to the nearby pond.

She had one arm out of her tunic when Trent cleared his throat apologetically.

"Sonuvabitch," muttered Lyra, hastily straightening her clothes. Trent started to laugh and turned it into a polite cough.

"I'm sorry," he said contritely. "I'll go in a moment, but—look over there."

"Hmm?" She joined him on a convenient log and followed his hand. "What—sweet goddess...!"

Deathwatch herons stand some twelve feet tall at the crown, a deep rusty crimson with black crests and lantern-yellow eyes. They are less common than smaller herons and egrets, often hunted for their plumage, and were a rare, shy sight. One was picking its slow, elegant way across the pond sixty feet away, each step breaking the surface into rings of mirrored water.

Lyra inhaled sharply, then let it out slowly. "Oh, my..."

It was beautiful. Lyra had seen one once before, near her father's keep. His men had hunted it with nets and spears, but it had killed one with its massive beak and escaped in a flurry of savage red wings.

The sword-like beak was currently digging through the mud for snails.

"Are—are they dangerous?" she asked quietly.

"Everything's dangerous," said Trent absently, still watching the heron. He glanced over at her and smiled briefly. "No. Not if you don't provoke them, usually. I wouldn't make a great deal of noise."

"My father tried to hunt one once," she mused. "Not the brightest idea he ever had." She smiled, half a grimace, at the memory. "Like his idea to stock the fishpond with sturgeon."

Trent lifted an eyebrow at that. "You're kidding."

"No. He's always doing thi—"

She stopped. "Was. Was doing."

Homesickness seized her by the throat so suddenly and unexpectedly that she choked. Her temples ached with the tight, burning sensation of unshed tears.

Trent patted her awkwardly on the shoulder.

"Sorry," she said, when she could speak again. "I'm sorry. I don't—don't usually get homesick."

"A home is a hard thing to lose," offered Trent.

"It's not really the place," said Lyra, staring at her hands. "It wasn't much. But I don't have a home at all. We'll leave this place, and go on tomorrow, and the next day, and there's no place that I think *someday I'll come home here.* I don't have anywhere to go except to wander." She laughed weakly. "And if it wasn't for Sadrao, and now Sinai, I wouldn't even have a direction to wander in."

Trent sighed and tossed a pebble at the water. "I know how you feel. Or I would like to know how it feels. I am only pulled in one direction and another, on Vade's leash, or Sinai's. Sometimes I would like a few moments only to rest." He looked over at the heron, which was standing like a statue of scarlet marble. "But I do not miss Ironspine. It was never a home."

Lyra licked her lips, then asked a question she had been wanting to ask for several weeks. "How *did* you escape?"

Trent gave a short barking laugh, making the heron start up and ruffle its feathers. "A trick so clever it nearly killed me. Vade has a scrying lens, you see, poured of molten copper. It was bound with my blood to follow me at all times." He took his glasses off and cleaned them on the edge of his shirt. "To break a link like that, you must do one of two things. Either enter a place so wrapped around with wards that scrying cannot penetrate; or change. Become other than what you are, something so different that you are no longer what the pool watches, and break its link to you."

"I don't understand," Lyra confessed.

"I turned myself into a deer," said Trent.

"You *what?!*"

"A deer," he confirmed, nodding ruefully. "The most nondescript, shit-brown buck I could come up with. Then I ran like hell."

"I didn't know that was possible!"

"It's not," said Trent, shoving his glasses back up his nose. "Most mages wouldn't even have been able to do it, and most of the rest would have been smart enough not to try. Only a fool or someone as desperate as I was would have—and I don't think I could do it again."

"Why not? I mean, there are shapeshifters—Janna Skinstrong was one, wasn't she?"

Trent nodded. "It's a gift that some have. Not magic, exactly—more like the Kythar. To do something like that without such a gift takes immense amounts of power, and it's a trap. Because a shapechanger knows it's a shapechanger, and some part of it remains a shapechanger—the essence doesn't change." He laughed softly. "The irony is that if I *had* been a shapechanger, I could not have escaped that way—the pool would have known my essence and tracked it. As it was, I very nearly spent the rest of my days grazing and scraping velvet off my antlers."

"Why?" asked Lyra, digesting this.

"Because my essence did change. I *became* a deer, not merely a mage in deer's clothing—and a mage might be able to change into a deer, but what deer could become a mage? Or would want to if it could?"

"So you ran," said Lyra, turning to face him, "as a deer?"

"I ran," he confirmed, tossing another pebble at the lake. "I remembered that much, that I wanted to get away. And the scrying pool must have lost me—I was just one more deer in the forest. The pool was tracking Trent the man, not Trent the deer. I guess—I hope – that the pool simply went dark, as it does when your subject dies. Two months later—there's a lot of thick forest around Ironspine, since no one settles there, and I wasn't moving in a straight line by any stretch—I crossed into Anu'tintavel."

"What was it like as a deer?" she wanted to know.

He thought about that for a while. Twilight spread across the pond and left the far side of the lake, and the heron, in darkness.

"It was very peaceful," he said finally. "And frightening, too. Deer live on the edge of death all the time, but they don't fear it. They run, but they don't—they don't *know* that they're going to die. They live in their senses. They don't remember one day from the next." He tossed another few rocks into the pond and let the silence stretch out around them.

"Mostly, I remember the sounds. And running."

"And—the elves found you?" prompted Lyra.

Trent laughed aloud at that. "You might say. That's the last day I remember as a deer. I wandered into a hunting party. I was picking my way through the woods, and arrows started flying around me."

"Good god," said Lyra.

"I remember the sound they made when they hit the trees," said Trent, almost dreamily. "The buzzing sound. I was running before I knew what it was. I leapt right over an elf standing in the bushes—I don't know which of us was more surprised." He stood up, suddenly, as if the memory demanded activity, and began pacing restlessly along the edge of the pond. "I saw his face looking up at me, and I thought, "Elves! Why are elves shooting at me?" It was the first thought I'd had in months—since I turned into a deer."

"What happened then?" asked Lyra, on the edge of the log.

He stopped pacing and grinned ruefully at her. "They shot me." He unlaced his tunic and showed her a puckered scar across his chest. "There's another one on what was a haunch at the time, but I won't show you that one. It didn't hurt at all, at first, but suddenly the ground wasn't flying under me and I was sliding through the brush on my shoulders, screaming like a rabbit."

"I'm guessing they spared your life," she said dryly. "Some kind of magic? Spiritual aversion? Dumb luck?"

"They didn't want to kill a deer wearing glasses," said Trent, smothering a grin.

"*Glasses?*"

"Yeah," he said sheepishly. "It's a spell. It keeps them unbroken and on my nose and I forgot about it. It was just a thing glued to my muzzle—it was so far down that I couldn't see it as a deer, not with my eyes on the sides of my head the way they were, and after a while I stopped trying to scrape them off."

"So they saw the glasses," said Lyra, through tears of laughter, "and knew something had to be afoot—"

"And took me to a very talented elven shaman named Syla Redeyes," Trent finished. "Who pulled the arrows out and brought me back to myself. I wanted to come back—it wasn't as hard as it could have been. It might have been harder if I hadn't been scared to death and in pain." He snorted loudly, turned, and skipped a rock across the water. "It was probably the most peace I've had in my life, being a deer, and I don't think I'll ever be able to do it again. I enjoyed it too much at first, and then I got lost in it. I couldn't sleep indoors for days, even after Redeyes changed me back." He made a half-defensive shrug of one shoulder. "Of course, that wasn't much of a problem. As soon as they realized who I was, they took me out of Anu'tintavel, before I even regained consciousness. My only memory of the elvenlands is a blur of trees going by over the top of a wagon and Sinai yelling at the drovers to hurry it up."

They didn't want to kill a deer wearing glasses.

"How very strange," said Lyra, shaking her head. "That's got to be the most bizarre story I've ever heard."

"You should hear about how Sinai found m—*aaaaaigh!*"

Afterwards, Lyra was never able to say how she moved so quickly. It was not something she would have thought herself capable of. Perhaps it was the Kytha, pulling her along in its path. It was easier for her to think of it that way.

What happened was that Trent's back had been to the water. Either their voices had been too loud, or Trent's careless rock had disturbed it, but the incredibly tall form of the deathwatch heron was suddenly looming out of the darkness. The beak was as long as Sadrao's sword and capable of shearing through flesh and bone as easily as a snail shell. Its head swept back to strike at the oblivious Trent, and Lyra lunged at him.

She took his legs out with a sweep and felt him fall heavily across her ankles. The blow, instead of impaling him, tore a shallow wound across his back, and the heron pulled back for another strike.

Lyra was on the ground, looking up at the impossible height of the heron as it danced like an enraged scarecrow, all thin gangly limbs and flying feathers. The eeriest thing about it was the silence. Deathwatch herons have no voice, and there was only the splash of its scaly feet in the lake mud to signal its intent.

Struggling to pull her feet free, Lyra heard her own voice shouting, like an idiot might shout at a dog.

"Go away! Go home! Go home! Get out of here!" She waved her arms at it—not even a rock or a stick or her sword, just her own stupid voice—"Go home! Get out of here!"

It leapt back, wings waving out. Each primary feather was longer Lyra was tall. Trent rolled to one side, hissing in pain. The move freed Lyra's feet and she rolled up to a crouch. She could barely see in the dark, her eyes dazzled with adrenaline—it was as if she knew exactly where everything was, but was utterly blind. She knew that she had to fling herself to one side, away from Trent, and she did, landing half in the water with a terrific splash. The beak sheared down and struck the mud next to her.

It occurred to her much later that drawing the heron away from Trent would have been a great—not to mention noble—idea. She rather wished that she had been thinking of it, but at the time she was not even thinking at all—she was simply reacting, and the bird was following the moving target away from a prone Trent.

The next strike actually buried itself in Lyra's hair. She looked up into inscrutable avian eyes and screamed something wordless in rage and terror. It jerked its beak out of the mud, ripping long red hair loose, and Lyra knew with desperate certainty that she was not going to move in time.

The roar of a dog-soldier filled the air. The heron drew back, and something struck its legs with a much higher-pitched shriek.

It was Trent. Lyra sat up, gasping, as the injured half-elf tackled the bird's legs with suicidal bravery.

The bird whirled, stabbing down at Trent as if he were a snail. It was an awkward angle, but Trent screamed again as the beak slashed open his right arm. It drew back for a better strike, and Sadrao hit it full force, baying savagely.

The dog-soldier was too much for the heron. It struck the water, twisted, and buffeted him with massive wings as it struggled free. Sadrao, his fur dripping water and duckweed, stood over a cursing Trent as the heron launched itself into the air.

"Oh," Lyra heard herself say, "oh—oh—*oh god*—" She crawled to her knees, her teeth chattering with adrenaline. "Oh, god—oh, ohmygod—"

"Lyra," said Sadrao calmly, "get out of the water."

She obeyed. She could not stop shaking. Sadrao said something else to her, but she didn't hear it at all.

There was a brief, jarring shock, and a bright flash across her vision. It didn't hurt, but it brought her back to herself. She looked up at Sadrao, who had just slapped her across the face. Cold air was starting to sting in her cheek.

"Lyra," he said, very calmly, "there's blood all over your head. You are absolutely forbidden to go into shock. Now, again, are you hurt badly?"

"No," she said, sitting up. "No. I don't think so." She touched her head, felt warm stickiness. "I can't tell, Sadrao, I'm sorry—"

Trent's breath was hissing between his teeth. Blood leaked between his fingers as he clutched his injured bicep.

"It's all right," said Sadrao, still in that too-calm voice. "It's a head wound, and they bleed a great deal. Sinai will look at it. Now, what happened?" he asked, sheathing his sword and crouching to pick up Trent.

"I don't know," she said, staring at the blood on her fingers. "We must have made it mad. We couldn't even see it after it got dark."

"Trent," said Sadrao, evidently dismissing questions of heron behavior until later, "your back's hurt. Can you move your legs?"

"Yes," grated Trent.

"Good," said the dog-soldier, scooping him up and turning. "Where the hell is Sinai?" he growled.

"Here," said the elf-woman, coming out of the dark. Her hair was flying in an ash-blonde cloud. She took the situation in with one long look and crouched to slide an arm under Lyra's shoulders.

Half-walking, half-dragged by Sinai, Lyra made it into camp. She was exhausted in ways that she could hardly believe.

Jacyl, with many concerned clucking noises, began bandaging Trent's back while Sadrao, still growling softly, cleaned Lyra's scalp wound. It was neither deep, nor serious, but he dumped the alcoholic contents of the leather flask over it anyway. Lyra yelped.

"You did very well," he told her quietly, bandaging the stinging cut. "That could have been deadly. You have come very far in these last few weeks."

"You were rolling like an acrobat," said Trent dryly. "Or a Kythar."

"I didn't do anything," Lyra said numbly. "I wasn't thinking anything at all. I just moved."

"Little fool," said Sinai sharply, "what do you think a Kythar does? It is all 'just moving'. The movement summons the skill, pulls you along with it. When it works."

"If it works," added Jacyl. "It's a fickle gift."

Sinai grunted an agreement. "The Kytha was moving you, no doubt of it. It usually works, if it thinks your life is in danger. Other times you have to summon it, with the forms—the Snake Kytha, the Hawk Kytha, the others...and sometimes it doesn't come at all."

"I don't understand," Lyra said.

"Nobody really understands the Kytha," said Sinai acidly. Lyra took no offense. Sinai had been frightened for her, and Sinai grew harsh when she was frightened. They all had their ways of whistling in the dark.

"It's a summoning magic," said Trent hoarsely, then hissed through his teeth as Jacyl applied a stinging poultice to his back.

"What?" Sinai glared at him, but he ignored it.

"It's—ah!—a summoning. Truly. Like shapeshifting, a little. You call—aah!—on the spirit you need with the form." He twisted in response to Jacyl's prodding. "Why do you think they're named after animals—plants—totems? You use the Snake Kytha to take the strengths of the snake into yourself: slow blood, cool body, quiet mind. The Cat Kythas give you eyes in the dark, softness of foot. And the Kythas of combat are the same—you call on that fighting spirit that inhabits every warrior."

"How do *you* know that?" asked Sinai rudely. Jacyl shot her a quelling look as she bandaged Trent's arm.

"I'm a sorcerer's bastard, after all," said Trent, with bitterness to match her own. Grey eyes met like steel on steel. "I've summoned demons, Sinai—yes, and I told the Council so, too. It's different in form, but the essence is the same."

"It is *nothing* like that," rasped Sinai.

"To summon a demon you call it up, define its essence, and then pour that essence through your magic," countered Trent. "To summon the Kytha, you call up the power, define the form you seek, and take that essence into your own. It is the same, Sinai. Whether you call it into yourself, or into the circle to keep it contained. It *feels* the same."

Sinai rose and stood looking down at him, her whole body tense as wire. Sadrao looked up at her mildly, but Lyra was very aware of the dog-soldier's hand closing protectively over her shoulder.

Trent did not rise to meet her, but looked up. Adrenaline and relief were making him foolhardy, but he did not seem to care. "Explain how so many of the Kythars could summon animals in times of need. Adali the Icetiger, you remember—the great white cat that saved her? How Uri Skytalon called the army of eagles to fight the Denathi hordes? He died doing it—that kind of power will unbalance any mind—but they won the war. Or your mighty Janna Skinstrong—"

"Enough," growled Sinai.

Trent ignored her. "She was a Kythar among Kythar, the last of the old blood, and when she called the spirits, she could make them manifest in her own flesh. That's what shapeshifting is, if you have that kind of gift. She had all that and more, to pull Ironspine down around my sire's ears. She would have been an incredible sorcerer. Wild beasts would come and lick her hands—"

"I said enough!"

The *crack* of Sinai's hand across Trent's face made Lyra jump. Sadrao's grip tightened on her shoulder.

Jacyl spoke a sharp elven word. Sinai's head snapped up.

Her lover's face was drawn in hard lines, her cheekbones triangles leading to a grim slash of mouth. There was ice in her blue eyes.

Sinai took a deep breath, let it out, then nodded coolly and stalked away from the fire.

"I didn't ask for this," said Lyra plaintively, turning into Sadrao's furry shoulder. "I didn't want the power!"

Jacyl's face softened. "Of course you didn't, child," she said, as Sadrao stroked Lyra's hair. His claws combed absently through the coppery strands.

"She isn't angry at you," Jacyl continued. "But she's frightened by Trent's power, and by her own." She looked down at Trent and frowned. "You don't help it much."

"It's true," said Trent mildly, turning to look at her. "For every great power, a Kytha to summon it, harness it to a Kythar's will. I do not doubt that there is a Kytha to summon demons." He looked thoughtfully at Lyra. "That would be an interesting test. Demons are well worth seeing...on the other side of the circle."

"Stop it," said Jacyl coldly, "or *I'll* slap you."

"That's what frightens Sinai, you know," said Trent softly, ignoring her. "The thought that the Kythar and the sorcerers call upon the same forces. She uses motion to capture it. Vade uses blood. But they are truly not so different, or else the Kythar could not hope to stand against them..."

"It is instinct, with us," said Sinai hoarsely, from the shadows. They all turned to look at her, a dark form barely touched by the firelight. "Instinct. The Kytha moves you, and you follow. It is a natural thing, a natural force. We do not try to control it, like the sorcerers. We do not step beyond what nature had intended. We create no monsters!"

She turned and vanished into the darkness.

Lyra realized that she was burrowed into Sadrao like a child with a huge stuffed toy and she released him. His whiskers brushed against her forehead when he spoke.

"They say the old Kythars did control the magic," said the dog-soldier slowly. "Not with words and mind, like the sorcerers, but control it they did. Uri Skytalon, as you said—he controlled it well enough to call up an army of birds of prey."

"And it killed him," said Jacyl. "The Kytha was stronger in those days, Sadrao, and the Kythar strong enough to bend it to their will." She looked worriedly after Sinai. "Even then, powerful Kythar rarely lived to an old age. Janna Skinstrong called up her beasts, and she died in the ruins of Ironspine with her wolf's teeth at Vade's throat."

"He still has the scars," said Trent quietly. And then, "Sinai could summon beasts if she chose. She is strong enough. Wolves, perhaps. Or demons."

A little silence fell.

It was too much for Lyra. Exhausted, hurt, frightened by a power she barely understood, she turned back to Sadrao with a muffled sob and buried her face in his ruff.

The dog-soldier gathered her up in his arms. "Shh," he murmured, "shhh." And to Trent, more sharply, "You're scaring her."

"Good," said Trent, looking very like his aunt for a moment. "Better that she should be afraid. This is not a power to be taken lightly."

"On that, at least," said Jacyl softly, "we are agreed."

Chapter Eleven

The town of Six-Mile was the last stop on this side of the mountains. It stood at the crossing of the major river road and a road that wound in from the mountains to the west.

The Tanglelore River made a broad, meandering curve south at this point. The river road continued to chase it, eventually bending north again, up to Delta. Most trade took the river, or the river road, keeping to the low wooded hills and avoiding the main body of the mountains.

For those to whom speed was essential, however, there was a shortcut. The mountain road led from Six-Mile into the hills, spawning dozens of trails that ran up to logging camps. There, timber was cut and hauled down the road to Six-Mile, where it was loaded onto boats and shipped along the river. The farther up the road one went, the fewer logging roads split off from it, until finally it narrowed to a rough track that snaked up into the mountains and through them to the other side. Crossing the mountains cut weeks off the journey to Delta, but it had its drawbacks.

The road was rough and claimed by no lord or city-state. Bandits roamed it during the trading season, hoping to catch merchants more concerned with speed than safety. The weather was harsh and unpredictable. It took a certain amount of desperation to take the mountain road, particularly in mid-spring, when storms were more common than not.

Of course, Lyra reflected ruefully, *there was never any doubt that Sinai would have us taking the mountain road. I better buy an extra blanket while we're in town.*

They rode into Six-Mile at mid-morning, just as the market was beginning to hit full swing. Jacyl crowed with delight and slid off her stallion's shoulder, throwing her reins to Sinai. The Kythar sighed and pressed her lips together.

There was never any question that we'd take the mountain road... but there was also never any question whether Jacyl would pass up a chance to go shopping. She'll make us stop here for the bazaar, and a night in an inn. With real beds.

"Jacyl," she said to the blonde woman, dropping off Mattress and joining her in front of a stall, "I'm putting you up for sainthood."

"Saint Jacyl...hmm, I like the sound of that. Patron saint of marketplaces, do you think?" She balanced a brooch carved in the likeness of a blue lizard on her palm. The color was almost the exact shade of her horse's tack. "Now this is lovely..."

"Sinai and I are going to find an inn," said Sadrao, catching Mattress's reins. "We'll come back in an hour."

Trent joined Jacyl and Lyra on foot. He looked from the dog-soldier to Jacyl, then back to Sadrao again. "An hour?"

Sadrao watched the elven woman digging through her pack for coins. "Never mind," he said, grinning. "I'll come back and tell you where we're staying. Take your time." And when Sinai sighed loudly enough to cut through the babble of the market-place, "Give it up, my dear, we're not going on tonight. We need to get more supplies anyway."

Sinai looked over at Jacyl's rapidly dwindling form, and her gaze softened. "Ah, well," she said, "one night more or less..." She gave Lyra an unexpected smile. "Do try to keep her from buying more than the horses can carry."

"No promises," said Lyra, "but I'll see what I can do."

The market wasn't as large as Jeppeth's bazaars, but it did have a fairly broad selection. The locals were evidently used to an assortment of travelers, because no one gave them more than a brief scrutiny, pointed ears and weapons notwithstanding. Lyra had recently taken to wearing her sword instead of carrying her staff, preferring to have her hands free on horseback. While she was probably the youngest person going armed in the market-place, she certainly didn't stand out.

Jacyl was loading Trent up like a pack mule with wrapped bundles, which surprisingly enough did include a few practical supplies. Lyra, who hadn't watched her father for years without picking up a few tricks, jumped in occasionally on the haggling.

"He's cheating you!" she protested at a flour merchant's stall. "Not more than eight copper!"

"For such coarse meal, I should hope not," said Jacyl indignantly. "Look at this grind!"

"Ladies, I implore you..." The Ferran merchant held up his hands in protest. "You'll beggar me. I have a litter of eight small children! Look at this flour, the finest in the city, I swear it..."

Trent was looking at the heavy sacks of flour and obviously envisioning himself having to drag one across the bazaar. "Let's try some other place," he suggested. "We haven't even been on that side of the market yet."

"No flour over there," said the merchant, twitching his whiskers disdainfully, "all frills and silks and fripperies—"

He trailed off in dismay as Jacyl bolted in that direction with a gleam in her eye. Trent and Lyra exchanged tolerant looks and followed in her wake.

There really was some lovely jewelry, Lyra observed, trailing her hand over a necklace of twisted gold links. She passed it by, though, and left Jacyl to haggle delightedly. She wondered if they had anything a dog-soldier would like, then remembered that she didn't have any money anyway.

She found Trent standing by a stall covered in remarkable ironwork. While there was the usual assortment of pots and ironmongery, there was also an array of incredibly delicate wrought iron adornment. The woman behind the stall, an older human with the flat, sinewy muscles of a blacksmith, smiled up at her and nodded to the table. "Try one on," she suggested.

Lyra picked up something like a cross between a bracelet and a vambrace, a delicate black wrist piece in elaborate curling knots. The curves suggested the unfolding tendrils of a fern stalk. She slipped her arm into it.

"Here." The ironworker took it, and bent the ends between her powerful fingers. "There, and...there. Now try it."

It fitted like it had been designed for her, making a slender black filigree across her left forearm. The long red stripe of scar tissue nearly vanished under the iron. She twisted her arm. The inside edges had been filed smooth.

"It's lovely," Lyra said, "but I really can't." She took it off and made as if to return it to the table.

Trent stopped her. "How much?"

"Six silver. It won't turn a good blade, but it should keep anything from cutting your arm off. And it looks lovely on your young lady." The blacksmith nodded to Lyra with a knowing smile.

"I'm not his young lady," protested Lyra. "Trent, you can't—"

"Yes, I can," said Trent firmly, paying the smith over Lyra's protests. "You saved my life from that heron." He turned, met her eyes, and smiled warmly, sliding the iron bracelet over her arm. "It's nothing compared to that. Let me do something to thank you."

"Um." He was standing awfully close to her. He was still holding the inside of her arm. His hand was warm and the metal was cool, making alternating bands of heat and cold against her skin. "Okay."

"Trent!" Jacyl called from across market. "Trent, come carry this!"

Trent dropped Lyra's arm and rolled his eyes. "Coming..."

Lyra looked down at her arm. She seemed to be having difficulty catching her breath.

Don't be silly. He's just trying to find a way to thank you, like he said.

"I'm really not his young lady," she said plaintively to the blacksmith.

"Uh-huh," the woman said, running a hand through her salt-and-pepper hair. "I've got two daughters, dear. I know it when I see it." She grinned. "You enjoy that bracelet, now."

Lyra nodded absently, running her fingers over the metal. Seeing Sadrao enter the market square, she waved to him and went to go find out where they were staying.

In deference to Sinai's desire to make up lost time, they rode out almost at dawn the next morning. The fields around Six-Mile gave way quickly to wooded hills, and then into the rugged escarpments of mountains. A tributary of the Tanglelore River cut a gurgling canyon through the mountains. They traveled beside it, losing it occasionally as the path wound narrowly through the peaks, finding it again, always farther and farther down the stone cliffs. Lyra could look over the edge and see clouds and birds, and then far down, the muddy snake of river.

On the third day in the mountains it rained and it was horrible.

They were already traveling single file—Sadrao first, Sinai last, Jacyl, Lyra, and Trent sandwiched between them—along a narrow ledge more suited to mountain goats than horses. There was no place to stop, no place to turn around. The rain began with a few delicate drops, dappling Lyra's sleeves and making tiny circles in the dust. It picked up to a light drizzle while they dug in packs for oiled cloaks. Then, within the space of a minute, it became a savage torrent. The horses were soaked through, saddle blankets squishing with every movement. Wet reins burned hands gone red with cold. Lyra could barely breathe—it was like standing under a waterfall.

Trent was shouting something. She twisted on her horse, her clothes sticking to her in the heavy, unpleasant fashion of wet wool. The half-elf had crowded his horse over so that Jegger could pull up next to him and was shouting something to Sinai, gesturing frantically.

"...It's not a natural storm!" she heard him say, then lost the next few words. Then, "Vade's creatures may be out—we have to find cover!"

Sinai said something back, in Elvish, but the tone came through just fine. Sinai was not pleased with this development. She worked Jegger past Trent, then past Lyra's stolid horse, close enough to shout at Sadrao to "get moving! Mage-creatures and wizard weather—" and then a few elegant Elvish obscenities that sounded like a set of wind chimes being strangled.

Sadrao's draft horse was the biggest and clumsiest. If it could pass the rocky path, any of the other mounts ought to be able to. The dog-soldier urged it forward, letting it pick its own path over the uneven stone.

They went at a walk, the whole way, five small creatures clinging to the face of the rock while the wind and rain pounded them. A brief shower of hail—most of it tiny, or else they might have died right there—buffeted their shoulders and the horses' flanks. Lyra stared at the backs of her hands, red and chapped with cold, bleeding where tiny shards of hail had cut into her skin. The rain washed it away almost at once.

The path got narrower and narrower. The rain got harder and harder.

Thunder cracked somewhere above, and a shower of mud slithered off a precipice and splattered across Lyra's head and Mattress's sodden flanks. Ahead of her, Sadrao's plowhorse took a step, slid, and righted itself with a snort. Trent's gelding missed the same step and staggered, and Trent cursed wearily and slid off the animal's back, practically falling in the mud himself.

And then the rain stopped. It did not merely lessen and drift away. Instead, it cut off with an almost mechanical precision. Sinai snarled like a wolf.

Trent stood up. His clothes were soaked, the hems black with mud. He ignored Sinai, inching wearily around his horse and picking up the reins to lead it on foot, his head bowed. Lyra could see that he was, very deliberately, not looking up.

There were still stormclouds all around them, and rain on every horizon—it was like standing in the eye of a hurricane that, for whatever reason, did not spin. But the sky above them was clear, and a hesitant sunlight touched Lyra's face and caught rainbows off the slopes.

Sadrao led his horse onward. Sinai stood, still glaring balefully over Lyra's head at the sky, until Jacyl called up and asked if she planned to stand there the entire damn day.

The elven Kythar's eyes were like flint chips, but she turned without another word and continued.

Two things happened almost simultaneously—the precipice to the right softened to a merely very steep slope, wooded halfway down with stunted pines, the path turning from stone to packed earth—and the distant thunder all around them stopped completely.

"I don't like this at all," said Trent into the sudden silence.

Lyra was wondering if non-spinning hurricanes were still technically hurricanes—it wasn't anything like a tornado, maybe some kind of circular storm? There was something about giant whirlwinds in Agatheria's *Meteorologica*, but you couldn't trust Agatheria—he claimed the wind was made by giant beetles beating their wings in the center of the earth.

Something dropped out of the hole in the clouds. Lyra stopped thinking about weather.

They had a very good view of the creatures as they descended. They must have been flying over the level of the clouds and chosen—or created—the break in which to attack. Trent groaned, throwing the reins over his gelding's neck. He drew his sword.

There were four of them. The creatures had five or six foot wingspans with broad, black-feathered wings and hooked vulturine beaks on naked grey heads. There the resemblance to vultures ended—the heads were broader than a bird's, wedge-shaped, and almost equine in the flat slabs of jaw muscle. The eyes were ovoid and set far forward. They had long, streaming tails and two hooked, heavy talons on the forefront of each wing. The hind legs were almost hooved, the middle toes fused together in a heavy shaft of bone flanked by two delicately clawed toes.

"Nightshrikes," said Trent glumly. "Gods, he must have emptied the whole eyrie. And they're so rare as it is..." He trailed off, lowering his sword.

"Trent," said Sinai very calmly, "what the hell are you muttering about?" The elf woman, still on Jegger, had her sword out. Sadrao had slid off the massive-muscled draft horse and was loosening Mohenja from its sheath.

"They're nightshrikes," Trent called. "They caused the storm." He paused for a moment. Lyra saw a line form between his eyebrows.

She'd read about nightshrikes. In, ah—Skulton's *Bestiary Exotique*, that was it, the one with the bizarre illustrations of cockatrices and elephants. The real thing didn't look anything like the illuminated manuscript, but Skulton's wolves were breathing fire and his dog-soldiers had more teeth than crocodiles, so she wasn't really surprised.

Lyra could hear their calls now, a strangely musical wail at odds with their vicious appearance, high and haunting. It echoed from the stone walls of the canyon.

The sound seemed to affect Trent. He straightened, the line between his eyes smoothing itself out, and sheathed his sword.

"It's no good fighting them," he called. "If they get a scratch in with their claws—and they will—you'll be dead in minutes. They

They're nightshrikes. They caused the storm.

must have been looking for me for days, and once they spotted me, they opened the storm." He drew his knife.

"I'll kill him," said Sinai, half to herself. She slid off Jegger. Jacyl, blocking her way, was looking up at the oncoming nightshrikes.

"It's okay," said Trent. He made a sort of choking laugh. "With that storm, there's no way he'll spot this." The half-elf pushed up a sodden sleeve and made another quick, sharp stroke across the top of his forearm, one more mark in a field of dozens, with the unflinching ease of long practice. Lyra could see skeins of blood across his hands from the last cut.

"More magic. *Blood* magic," growled Sinai, trying to muscle her way past Jacyl. The ledge still wasn't large enough.

"All magic is blood magic," Trent shot back. "Even your precious Kytha." There was blood welling between his fingers. He touched his throat, leaving a carmine smear across his skin, and held up his wrist like a falconer.

Then he called.

It was a sound that shouldn't have been able to emerge from a human throat, a watery, wavering sound, a high wailing call like the cry of the nightshrikes themselves.

The birds responded at once. Three of them pulled out of their stoop and circled overhead. There was a certain grace to the sweep of their broad wings.

The fourth bird continued its dive, then pulled up in an elegant aerial maneuver that brought it directly over Trent's head. It hovered for an instant, the downward sweep of its wings blowing the half-elf's hair wildly, then set neatly down on the proffered wrist. It was at least as large as a small eagle. He brought his wrist down at once—it must have been sheer agony to support the weight. Lyra expected to see blood from the bird's massive talons, but the nightshrike had settled with surprising delicacy.

Sinai stopped trying to get past Jacyl.

Trent, for his part, merely drew a fingertip down the heavy hook of beak and murmured something in a language that Lyra didn't recognize. It was a harsh, sibilant tongue, but Trent's tone was gentle. He offered the nightshrike a finger stained with red, and the bird set its beak around it like a tame parrot, touching its tongue to his skin.

Sinai was turning Jegger with the look of a woman preparing to charge her horse in what is almost certainly a suicidal gesture.

Trent said something else to the nightshrike, then cast his arm up like a falconer releasing a hawk. The bird gave another musical, mournful cry, then caught an updraft and spiraled into the clouds, followed by its fellows.

"Damn," said Lyra. "That was *amazing*."

Trent would probably have said something clever, but his skin had gone ashen and he was leaning up against his gelding, clutching his aching wrist. White, bloodless bands of skin bloomed suddenly red as blood rushed back into them, already starting to purple with bruises. "Oh gods," he muttered. "That hurt."

"Not as badly as I'm going to hurt you," said Sinai tightly, from Jegger's back.

"Vade will guess that I unbound them, but he'll have a hard time telling where. The storm will muddle any scrying he may do."

"Not good enough," growled Sinai.

"Would you rather have killed them? Or be killed by them?" he added, almost as an afterthought.

"Your magic is unclean," said the elven woman, in a high voice. "Do not use it again, or I *will* stop you."

"Sinai—" Jacyl began.

The taller woman made a curt gesture with one hand and turned Jegger to continue down the path.

There was a brief, awkward silence. Jacyl's lips were pressed tightly together, her blue eyes the hard, metallic color of polished steel.

The rain started again, all at once, and broke the moment. Lyra moaned. She could hear Sadrao growling his disgust from the front of the cavalcade. Trent was still leaning against his horse, looking drained.

Lyra's mild-mannered dun took a step forward and stopped. Its hooves squelched through the mud that the path had become. Lyra felt something shift, more than just the motion of the horse. She looked over to her right just as Trent shouted a warning.

Mud was oozing slowly over the edge of the path down the slope. It was the most innocent looking thing in the world. A clot cracked and showed streaks of red and yellow clay crumbling over the edge.

Aha! I bet that's what a mudslide looks like.

The path groaned under the horse's hooves. Mattress neighed nervously, something he never did, and shifted from foot to foot.

"Oh. Shit." Lyra said, enunciating very clearly. *How fitting,* the back of her mind quipped, *my last words. Perhaps they'll carve that on my tombstone.*

The entire hillside calved off in a mudslide, and horse and rider went down. Lyra lost her seat on the horse and saw, through rain and panic, the rapidly sliding mud coming up to meet her. There was a mad, rapid roll when up was down and down was up and the sky was full of mud and broken trees.

She had no memory of hitting the ground.

⁂

Lyra must have been out for no more than a few seconds, because when she came to the ground was still moving under her—albeit much more slowly—and she was just rolling to a halt against the base of a fir tree.

Luck and the gods—and the fact that she had been at the top, rather than the bottom of the very short mudslide—were with her. No broken bones. Plenty of bruises. She was covered in thick, grainy brown mud. She sat up. Her head swam.

It took her nearly a minute to spit the mud out of her mouth, and longer to crawl out from under the battered fir tree.

The rain sluiced the mud off her instantly, chilling her to bone. She held her temples together, aware that she should move in case any more of the path came down, but unable to stand up just yet.

Even if I don't have any broken bones, I'm not going to be able to climb up that *mess to the path.*

When she finally did stand up, she couldn't see the path anyway through the fallen net of trees. The mudslide looked to have brought half the forest down. She turned in the direction of something that wasn't covered in mud—a rocky outcropping just visible through the jumbled treeline—and started slogging toward it.

She found Trent, and her horse, simultaneously.

Mattress was quite dead. He was half-buried under the mud, his neck broken. Trent was digging half-heartedly in the area around the saddle, a grim expression on his face. He, too, was a combination of wet and clean and wet and muddy, depending on how the rain was falling.

"Hey," she said, feeling mostly dead herself.

He looked up, then jumped to his feet. Relief spread across his features. Somehow—and this was entirely beyond the realm of natural possibility—his glasses were still on his nose.

"Lyra! Thank the gods—I thought I saw you fall off the horse, but it was all just mud and branches—"

"Yeah. I think I got knocked out for a second." She rubbed the back of her neck. "You go down, too?"

He nodded. "My horse must not have, or he would have crushed me. And I haven't seen a sign of the others."

"Hopefully they were a little luckier," said Lyra, wiping wet, stringy hair out of her eyes with the back of her hand. "Poor Mattress." She blinked back tears, but it was too wet, and she ached too badly.

"Yeah," said Trent.

Lyra pointed through the trees to the rocks. "I thought we could look under there for a cave, or a nook, or something. Get out of this rain."

Trent nodded again, as if speaking was too much effort. They began slipping and sliding across the muddy ground, boots squelching. Lyra was somewhat surprised to find that she was the one having the easiest time, knock on the head and all. Trent looked like hell, and was already lagging behind.

"You look terrible," she said.

"You look fantastic," he said, mustering the attempt at humor. "Muck is definitely your color."

"Was that magic? What you did with the nightshrike?"

"Yes." He seemed disinclined to offer more.

Lyra would have pressed the issue, but they had reached the rocks, heavy granite encrusted with lichen, and glory of glories, there was a sort of cave.

It was really more of a hole under a large rock, with a slanting ceiling of stone on two sides and a bramble bush on the third. It was damp and shallow, but it was considerably drier than standing around in the rain. The floor sloped down to the entrance, keeping water from puddling inside.

They were both starting to shiver with the aftermath of adrenaline and exposure. Lyra wedged herself inside. Trent followed.

They huddled together, watching the rain pour down outside the tiny cave, absolutely drained. Lyra wrung what water she could from her cloak and offered him half, huddling together under the wet wool.

"Do you think they'll find us soon?" he asked, because someone had to.

"I'm sure, once the rain lets up," she answered, again, because someone had to say it. The rain came down so hard that it looked more like a river. She was grateful that they were under a rock, and not in an earthen cave that might collapse. "They'll find my horse, anyway, and we're not that far. I hope they made it okay."

"Sinai's tough as old leather," Trent said, rousing somewhat, "and Sadrao could walk through the last circle of hell and crack jokes. How's your head?"

She grunted. "Doesn't really hurt. I don't think it's concussed, anyway—my vision's fine."

"Well, that's something." By mutual consent, they wedged a little closer to the back of the cave, eventually settling practically in each other's laps. Even under Lyra's cloak they were shivering with cold. Body heat helped a little, but the cold rock was sucking warmth out of them. "I'd suggest we get up and move around," said Trent, dryly, "but there's nowhere to move." He wrapped his arms around Lyra and drew his knees up to his chest, wiggling his toes to keep them alive.

She crouched more or less across his lap and leaned her head on his shoulder—a surprising intimacy, but the only possible position that kept them dry and didn't result in one or the other losing blood to a limb.

"Trent?"

"Ya-huh?"

"If you use magic to keep your glasses on—"

"Probably the first spell I ever got to set permanently. There's one to keep them from being broken, too."

"—Why can't you fix your eyes, instead?" she finished.

"Congenital defect." Trent tapped his temple with one long finger. "Healing's one thing—the body *knows* what it's like to be whole. You just provide it with the power to do so. But as far as my body's concerned, this is the natural way of things. I'd be mucking around with things I don't understand and probably go blind."

"Mmmm."

"I thought about it, you know," he offered. "Dissected I don't know how many sheep eyes." *And a few human, too, but you don't need to know about that.* "All those damn lenses and nerves convinced me that glasses were an easier solution."

They were quiet for a while. The rain pounded on unabated.

"I've read about nightshrikes, you know," mused Lyra. Trent stiffened beside her.

"Why does that not surprise me?" he muttered, half to himself.

"They're very rare, especially this far west," she continued, watching him closely, "and they're vicious in a fight. I don't think that one person in a hundred has even heard of one. I've found a few references in bestiaries. But I've never heard that they were poisonous."

"They aren't." Trent leaned his head back against the stone and closed his eyes. "They're perfectly harmless if you don't irritate them—unlike deathwatch herons!—and they're almost extinct, even in the east." He sighed. "Those four are the adults from the only breeding eyrie on this half of the continent. Which happens to be on a mountain adjacent to Ironspine."

"So Vade did send them."

He opened his eyes and looked over at her. "Yes. Of course. Beasts are easy to control, unlike intelligent species. People—of any species—are nearly impossible. Too many layers of motivations. But beasts, you just tamper with their natural instincts, convince them that this person, no matter how far away, is a threat to their nest, or something, and they'll do your bidding. If you're careful."

"So how did you stop them?"

He ran a hand through dusty brown hair streaked with mud. "If you tie up an animal," he said, holding his hands in front of him as if to encompass imaginary bonds, "you need to tie it tightly.

Bind its beak and its claws and its wings and feet. Hood it, blind it, muzzle it, whatever. You need materials, and time, and skill. But to free them—" he made a slicing gesture with his hands, "—all you need is a sharp knife."

"And it's the same with magic?"

"Essentially. At least, I can't explain it any clearer." Trent sat back with a sigh. "It still would have been a near thing, but I used to spend time watching the nightshrikes. Fed them, watched their nest. There's all kinds of things around Ironspine, since nobody settles near the mountain and hasn't for centuries. Nightshrikes are one of them. I was fairly sure that I could control them with just a light compulsion. And I couldn't bear to kill them."

"They're too rare."

"Yes." He shook his head, staring up at the stone ceiling. "It would have pleased him to make me kill them to stay alive. He will have a hard time controlling them now—I am mage enough for that."

"It seemed—ah, not to disparage you—but it seemed awfully easy for you. I mean, for fighting something controlled by someone who's supposed to be such a psychotic-brilliant hundred year old sorcerer," Lyra scratched the back of her neck absently.

"It was easy," said Trent. "And we can both hope that Sinai didn't think so, or else I may spend the rest of our journey in chains. He didn't plan to kill us, with either the storm or the nightshrikes. He just wants to let me know he could have."

There was silence between them. It was starting to get warmer—only a little, but the stone was no longer ice cold. The light outside was grey and growing darker.

"Trent, can I ask you something else?"

"Ask."

"What did Sinai say to you, that first night she showed me the Kytha?"

His sigh stirred the wet strings of her hair. "It was an Elvish dialect, used within Sinai's clan...of which, to her eternal disgust, I am a part."

He was silent for a minute, then continued. "She said that if I was truly my father's son, I had best not think to entrap a pet Kythar of my own. And that she would not allow you to suffer Lythara's fate."

"Lythara—her cousin? Your mother? But—"

He looked away from her, as if ashamed.

"That's awful!" she cried, in righteous indignation, sitting up. Trent hissed in pain and gestured frantically until she stopped digging a hipbone into his gut. "Sorry," she added, settling back into her old position. "But what does Lythara have to do with anything?"

Trent became very busy cleaning his glasses. "My sire kidnapped an elven woman, that he might get a son of elven blood. He kept her drugged, and raped her until she got with child. That was his goal. There was no more emotion to it than a stallion paying stud service to a mare. Not," he added bitterly, "that he probably didn't enjoy it—my mother was a beautiful woman. It would have been to his liking."

"Sinai had mentioned that. It's terrible," said Lyra. She swallowed, all too aware of how little words like "terrible" really expressed, then continued, a little more timidly, "but I still don't get it."

Trent chose his words carefully, seeking refuge in euphemism. "My sire wanted an elven child. Me."

Lyra looked blank. Trent abandoned any hope of hinting around the subject.

"A child with the Kytha flowing through them, and elven blood—would be a great sorcerer. A great tool. And to get such a child, Sinai fears that Vade—or his son—would breed a Kythar until she got with child. Willingly or not."

He was carefully not meeting her eyes. "In some ways, Vade was a fool," he said, seeking words to fill the silence. "Sinai would have been a far better choice to bear his son—elven and Kythar. He had a chance to take her—she was with Lythara when he kidnapped her—but he chose the more beautiful one instead, the more tractable."

"I can't imagine Sinai—" Lyra struggled for the least hurtful words she could find, and in the end, took refuge in euphemism also, "—keeping the child of such a union."

"No," said Trent quietly. "Probably not."

She asked him no more questions.

An hour or so later, the rain continuing unabated, Lyra dozed off with her head pillowed on Trent's shoulder. She was curled up in his lap, her cloak pulled up to her chin.

Trent studied her face in silence, the stubborn jaw and faint frown eased by sleep, the lines of her face softened. This close, he did not need his glasses to see her face. She looked terribly young, almost childlike. Terribly fragile.

Fragile enough to fend off a deathwatch heron while you lay on your back in the mud! Fragile enough to take Sinai's love taps and get up and come back for more, which is more than you can manage half the time.

Fragile as a wolverine, or Sadrao would've left her at the first town he had friends in. Naïve, maybe, but don't underestimate her.

She *was* young, though. When he was her age—

A bitter memory curled his lips. At seventeen he had summoned demons into carefully drawn pentagrams and cut the throats of half-dead victims to drain their life away. It was the only kind of mercy available to him. Vade's figure loomed always, in the background, ready to strike with brutal magical force if he faltered. Master. Tormentor. Father.

God, he felt a thousand years old.

Lyra made a soft sound in her sleep and burrowed tighter against him. Trent snapped out of memory and looked down at her again. Vade had not touched her. Out of everything Trent had known, Lyra remained untainted. The innocence that exasperated him at times was a fragile, fleeting thing. If Vade once had her in his hands—

Trent bared his teeth silently at the thought. He would die before letting that happen—No. About this, he had no illusions. Vade would never allow him to die. The long river of scar tissue on the underside of his wrists would testify to that. He would kill Lyra first, and give her the mercy of a quick death.

Carefully, he thought, guilt seizing him like a fist under the ribs. *Oh, go carefully. It was to grant quick deaths that you first picked up the hiltless knife, and once it starts, it never stops.*

Hesitantly, he ran a finger over her cheek, feeling the texture of her skin. He half expected to leave a stain behind, like the old cliché, as if the blood Vade had forced on his hands had left a tangible mark.

He had no right to touch her. Another woman, perhaps it would not have mattered. He had never made love to a woman, he realized, that he could not have ordered killed in the next moment. The knowledge made a cold knot in his stomach. But she looked terribly innocent of such things. He was certain that she had never known a man, perhaps never even been in love. Never taken a life in cold blood, or hot.

He felt like some kind of vicious predator.

His hand wandered, of its own accord, up her jaw and through her damp hair. He wished that he dared kiss her, but that would be too irrevocable. If she woke now, it would be only a friend, offering comfort. It could not be more than that. He would not let it be more than that.

If she had been drugged and in a circle of runes, the black glass knife would have carved a sign of power across her forehead — three quick strokes and a long, fishhook mark. Her blood would have been starkly red against her skin. Then down across the collarbone, and a second rune, this one a circle cut in half by chevrons. Trent caught his fingers following that pattern and pulled away.

The first one had been an unextraordinary woman, with black hair and brown eyes. She had screamed a man's name the entire time — her husband, perhaps. The fourth had been blonde with hazel eyes and surprisingly broad shoulders. She had wept, mostly. The twelfth had salt-and-pepper hair, and by then he had gathered courage to insist they be drugged into semi-consciousness. And there is no way to explain that you are as trapped as they are, and that if yours is the hand that holds the knife the pain will only last a few minutes, and then there will be a bright flash across the throat, and peace. That if you are the instrument of their death you can insist that they be drugged, can put the agony at a remove. That if you weaken, if you lock yourself away, if you refuse to hold the knife, their pain will last for long dying hours in the dark, because the lord of Ironspine has no thought of mercy and will not waste the energy to kill them.

There is no way to explain, while you are killing someone, that when you are done and they have died, you envy them. You nod to the cold-faced man that fathered you, and stagger back to your rooms, shaking and sick. And you curl up in a ball, and wonder how you go on, how many years it will last. Trying to kill yourself doesn't work, and it means more people die to heal you. You just go on and on and hope that eventually your sire will lose his temper too far and kill you.

He knew perfectly well, even at the time, that this tangled web of rationalizations was only Vade's plan. That if he could not trap you with sadism, he would trap you with mercy, until you were committing unholy acts to stave off even worse ones. He had known that at fifteen, when he first picked up the obsidian knife, because he could not bear to see another person dying by inches while Vade's pets gnawed at them in the dark. He knew it when Vade praised a particularly deft stroke of the knife, and he felt a son's pride, even as his stomach churned. He knew it the entire time, and eventually it didn't matter any more. You just kept putting one foot in front of the other, and hoping that death would come for you eventually. If there was a hell, you were already living in it.

Trent's hand lay across the column of Lyra's throat. Her pulse beat, strong and steady, under his fingers. If he closed his hand, he could have killed her. The thought made him want to weep. He closed his eyes.

When he opened them again, some hours later, the rain had stopped. Lyra still lay curled against him, and he had fallen asleep with his cheek against her hair.

Sadrao was watching him from the entrance to the cave. Trent lifted his head, quickly, as if he had committed some impropriety. The sudden movement woke Lyra.

Before she could begin to be embarrassed, Sadrao had reached in and was hauling them both outside. "Ancestors!" said the dog-soldier with forced heartiness. "You're soaked to the bone. Jacyl's got a fire going—we've already stripped the horse. I was pretty sure we'd find you nearby—you've got more sense than to go far."

"Thanks," said Lyra, stretching cramped muscles and wincing. "I feel like—"

"Like you got soaking wet, caught in a mudslide, fell off your horse by the greatest stroke of luck, and spent the rest of the night huddled in a cave that could barely accommodate one, let along two?" offered Trent. "That's just a guess, you understand," he added. Then ducked, as she took a mock swing at him.

"Through the tree-break," said Sadrao to Lyra, pointing. "We'll be there in a second."

As soon as she was out of earshot, the dog-soldier's hand closed like a vise on Trent's arm. Trent knew better than to fight it.

"This is simple enough," said Sadrao, quietly. "If you are all that you appear to be, then I have no quarrel with you. You seem an honorable young man." He emphasized the word *seem*. "But if you are other than that—" and the hint of a growl in his voice suddenly blossomed to the full thing, "—and this is some kind of deep game you play, then I will kill you." His teeth were a mesh of ivory, barely an inch from Trent's ear. "I like you, Trent. And I will not tell you not to hurt Lyra, because she is young and in love and pain is always the other side of that coin. But I will be watching you, and if need be I will repay that hurt ten—no, a hundredfold. Do I make myself clear?"

"If—if I—" said Trent hoarsely, and stopped. It took a moment to find his voice again through the lump in his throat. "Nothing you can do to me could matter. It goes no farther than this, Sadrao." He took off his glasses and cleaned them. His hands were shaking. "I am not fit for anyone. After the things I've done—"

Grief and guilt and self-loathing choked him. He put his glasses back on without saying more. Sadrao watched him with wide eyes. He'd managed to startle the dog-soldier. *Amazing.*

Sadrao, turned from threats to comfort in a moment, squeezed his shoulder. "It can't be that bad—"

"Do you know how many women I've tortured?" Trent asked in a conversational tone, aware that tears were pouring down his face.

Sadrao's hackles lifted, his ears flattening. He stepped back sharply, baring his teeth and licking his lips as if he had picked up a piece of meat and seen the white squirm of maggots in it. It was easy to forget, Trent thought distantly, that Sadrao, for all his charm and elegant manners, was closer related to a hound than a human. Until, like now, you had pushed him too far.

"Sixteen," Trent continued, determined, for once, to get the whole sordid mess out. "Two a year from the time I was fifteen. For rituals. I cut the runes of power into their bodies with obsidian knives. Then I killed them. I still remember every one of their faces." He took off his glasses again and scrubbed at his face with a sleeve. "Because I had to. Because the alternative was watching him carve them up the same way, and leaving them alive, for hours, dying of shock, while the things that live in the dark chewed on them. So I did it, because I would cut their throats at the end of the rite and give them a quick death." He made a sound that might have been a sob.

"Gods of the *pack*," said Sadrao hoarsely.

"I told myself it was mercy. It pleased him a great deal."

The dog-soldier was staring at him with his ears tight back against his skull. It made him look more like a weasel than a wolf. Trent plowed doggedly onward.

"I envied them their deaths. Because they escaped. I just went on and on, digging deeper and deeper, committing worse and worse crimes to stop him from even worse ones. Atrocities on top of atrocities." He could taste bile at the back of his throat from the memory.

"You were a child, afraid—" offered Sadrao hesitantly.

"Afraid? Yes. Of course. But it was more than that." Trent's laugh tore a hole in the air between them. "I loved him, Sadrao. The elves didn't understand that. Sinai does, and hates me for it. But it wasn't like loving a person. The priests of the Sacrificed God say that you should love and fear their god. That's what it was like. That's just exactly what it was like."

He did not look at Sadrao. He could not stand the same expression of pity, and loathing, that the mages of Anu'tintavel had worn. Gods only knew how much they had told Sinai and Jacyl. Everything, probably. But Sadrao probably hadn't known the full, sordid extent of his crimes. Well, he did now.

The silence stretched out unbearably. Trent couldn't bear it any longer. "For the love of the gods, say something," he snapped. Not expecting anything but condemnation. Certainly not understanding.

Sadrao—faithful, gallant Sadrao—amazed him.

"What crimes you committed were not entirely your own. Sometimes there are no good choices, only evil ones," said the dog-soldier gently. Sadrao reached out a furred arm and embraced him, almost cautiously, giving him every chance to pull away.

It was an offer of solace, of forgiveness. Trent leaned against that strength, so much greater than his own, and sighed. There were too many tears left in him. If he began, he would never stop, and it might kill him in the process. He pulled away, finally, grateful for the acceptance that Sadrao gave him, had always given him.

"If it is any comfort," said the dog-soldier as they picked their way toward camp, "I don't believe that you're an evil man."

"Perhaps I'm fooling us both," Trent said quietly. Lyra twisted from her perch beside the fire, wrapped in dry blankets. The line of her neck, falling to her collarbone, then lost in grey wool, was fragile as a bird's keelbone. He sat on the other side of the fire, Sadrao's guardian presence between them.

They did not go any farther that day. Lyra slept again, shortly, exhausted. He stared at nothing, his hands clenched tight around a cup of untouched tea, the knuckles white.

Jacyl laid a sympathetic hand on his shoulder. Sinai was silent, as always, moving through the steps of the Kytha with slow, precise grace. She did not speak to him about magic or nightshrikes. Sadrao had vanished some time back to hunt some small game. Trent wondered if the dog-soldier had talked to her. He wouldn't want to have seen that fight. It might explain the lines around Jacyl's eyes.

Finally, inactivity driving him mad, he rose. Taking the small hand axe, he began chopping a downed tree into short lengths. His fury wore itself out, eventually, and left him drained. He said little that night and sought his bedroll almost as soon as dinner was finished.

His sleep was deep and troubled. He could see Lyra speaking to him, but there was an invisible wall between them, and he could not hear her voice nor understand the message she sought to convey.

The sagas had it that wizards communicated through dark, curtain-hung portals, or magic mirrors, or direct thoughts flung across vast distances.

The sagas were mostly wrong, except for the bit about magic mirrors, which had a certain basis in reality. Some mages did like mirrors for scrying, although Trent was not among them, and neither was Vade. As for the rest—well, portals were possible but so exhaustively power-intensive as to be utterly impractical…and telepathy was another gift entirely, and usually not coupled with magecraft.

The simplest method of communication was a sort of mutual scrying, each watching the other party. Unfortunately, this required that both parties have some kind of link by which to attune to the other, like blood or hair or semen, and that required a mutual trust unlikely among powerful mages.

Which left the entirely more prosaic, but much more destructive process of possession.

A skilled mage could, at a great distance, imbue a proxy with a certain mental spark. They lacked a great deal—their intelligence was low, and they did not respond well to unexpected events—but such a proxy could play brief host to a sort of shadow, a mental imprint of the personality of a mage. The possessor could not cast spells through the proxy, or speak directly through it, but the proxy could deliver specific messages, and even, to a limited extent, extemporize, conversing as the mage would. With clever scrying the mage could watch his proxy ask the questions that he would ask, even conduct brief interrogations. The more intelligent the host, the longer the possession would last…but never more than a few minutes, and never without completely destroying the mind of the proxy.

The Archmage winced at the thought.

There was no help for it. If he continued using Frieze as a go-between they would choke the House of Diamond until they starved. If he was to keep them alive—all the knowledge, all the librarians that depended on him—he had to negotiate directly with…well, with the important party.

There was no other choice.

And that meant that he needed a victim.

The Archmage was not, by many measures, an evil man. The notion of killing someone for this sat badly with him, and yet… and yet…what other choice did he have?

He summoned Iyara.

The white dog-soldier appeared, bowed, and looked at him. He wondered if this time, this request, the façade would crack. He hoped not. This was hard enough already.

"I need you to go to Frieze," he said, "and bring me someone who deserves to die."

Iyara's ears flicked, almost imperceptibly. "I beg your pardon, Archmage?"

He sighed.

"I need a life for this magic," he said. "I have tried everything else that can be tried, and there are no other options. This magic takes a life."

"I will volunteer," she said remotely.

He blinked at her. He had not expected that. "No. This is a waste, a waste of a life, and the only thing I can think of is to find someone who deserves killing. Go to Frieze, and find me some-one—a murderer, a rapist, a slaver of children, someone!"

"This is not right," said Iyara. Her voice was as distant as ever, but far down in the depths of those empty blue eyes, he saw a flicker of reproach.

Judgment, at last. It was what he had wanted and, irrationally, it made him angry.

"Don't you think I know that? Do you think I like the idea of murder? This is terrible, but it is all I can think of!"

The fine hairs at the edge of her ears trembled almost imper-ceptibly. "Is there no one else you can send?"

"No one *moral*," he said, taking a kind of savage pleasure when she flinched visibly. "You are a dog-soldier. Your ethics are legendary. If I send Ralthas, the gods know what I will get, but if you go, you will find someone who truly deserves death."

Iyara was a swift, if not original, thinker. She saw the trap, felt it snap shut around her, and bowed her head. Her pack leader had given her orders. She would do this thing so that it would be done correctly. She knew that it was not the right thing, and she knew as well that she would do it anyway.

"I will do as you ask," said Iyara tonelessly, and turned to go.

Chapter Twelve

It is night, and Lyra is dreaming.

She knows she is dreaming because the time sense behind her eyes that separates one moment from the next is gone. There is neither past nor future, only a seamless Now.

She also knows that she is dreaming because she can still, faintly, feel the warmth of the bedroll pulled around her and the pressure of her closed eyelids over her eyes.

At the same time, she can hear the voices arguing.

There are three of them. The voices are familiar, by turns angry or soothing or dismayed.

Lyra knows that Trent is lying just on the other side of the fire, and that the three voices would not argue within his hearing.

So she must be dreaming, because she can still hear them.

"It's inevitable," says the first voice, a resigned birdsong. Jacyl. She sounds a little amused. "They're both young, and traveling in close quarters together, into danger. They're both intelligent. They've read the same books."

A second voice, low and savage, like an angry owl: "*I don't like it!*"

Sinai, of course.

"You're being paranoid," rumbles the third voice. Lyra smiles in her sleep at Sadrao's protective baritone.

"I'm not being paranoid. Are you both blind? He looks at her like a starving man—"

"He looks at her like a young man looks at a young woman," says Jacyl, a bit testily.

"Trent?" Sinai barks a humorless laugh. "He was never young. He was murdering innocents when he was younger than Lyra."

Sadrao's voice has an uncertain growl in it. "Sinai—I don't think he is entirely to blame. Vade had a great deal to do with it."

"Vade had *everything* to do with it," Jacyl agrees.

"It has nothing to do with blame," says Sinai raggedly, unable to believe their naïveté. "It's a line. A line you don't cross."

"I realize that Lythara was dear to you," says Sadrao gently, "but you have no right to hate the boy so."

The low voice makes a noise of frustration. "The gods damn you, Sadrao, *listen* to me! Look—do you remember when you first killed a man? Do you, Jacyl?"

There is a long silence. Sinai continues.

"Do you remember how everything changed? How from that moment on, whenever you looked at another person, some tiny part of you assessed if you *could* kill them if you had to, and how you'd go about it? Just for a second? Don't say you don't, Sadrao. I do it. Jacyl does it. That wide-eyed apprentice of yours will do it, when she finally kills someone with those assassin's tricks you're hammering into her."

The voices are silent for a moment.

Then the baritone says, "Just because we do that doesn't make us monsters."

"No," says Sinai forcefully, "but it *does* bring us closer to them."

"In any case," says Jacyl, "as you said, we *all* do it. Just because Trent does too—"

"He doesn't do it." The owl-like voice grows chill. "He isn't just a killer. He's a sorcerer's get, a torturer's apprentice. He's carved human flesh up like marble. When he looks at me, he doesn't see if he could kill me, he sees how long he could keep me alive, what kind of demons he could call up in my blood."

"Now you're *really* being paranoid," Jacyl growls, in a tone more suited to Sadrao than her own bird-like voice.

"No. I'm not. I'm really not. And when he looks at Lyra—and she looks back at him, like a damn little bird in front of a viper—it's going to be like Lythara all over again. Except she's walking into it with open arms." Sinai's voice is shaking terribly. Lyra has never heard her so upset, and it troubles her dreams so that she tosses restlessly in the blankets.

"If we had more time!" the elven woman says, her low voice lower than usual. "If we could keep them apart until Knaxos, even."

"Don't look at me," says the dog-soldier. "You're the one whose species is in heat all the time."

There isn't much any of them can say to that.

Lyra is drifting into deeper sleep when Sinai's voice disturbs her again.

"He's playing some kind of game, I know it."

"Maybe he's exactly what he seems," says Sadrao mildly.

"Maybe? *Maybe?!* Yes, *maybe,* and maybe Vade will come back and say 'oh, terribly sorry, don't know what I was thinking, here, have your territory back,' and *maybe* fish will learn to sing madrigals so we can have music with dinner!"

"I think he's just a boy," says Jacyl stiffly. "And if you weren't so paranoid that he was more than that, we could have taken him into Anu'tintavel and found out one way or the other."

"Gah! I will not have this argument with you *again!*" The frustration in Sinai's normally level voice is enough to make Lyra twist herself up in the blankets and burrow under the pillow.

None of the voices say anything for a while.

"Well," says Sadrao finally, "I'm not a fool enough to come in between young love. Or lust. It only makes it worse."

"That's true."

"If it's even as innocent as lust. I'm afraid for her, Sadrao. When she began practicing the Kytha...young men don't look so hungry. And yes, I do remember what they look like, Jacyl, so stop rolling your eyes."

The voices fade away in the distance after that, as if they are moving away. Lyra sinks deeper into dreaming, fragments of the day mixing in with stray archetypes and shreds of virginal erotica.

In the morning, she does not remember the dream at all.

"Sadrao?" asked Lyra from horseback, looking up to the dog-soldier.

"Yes?"

"Have you ever been in love?"

They were five days past the mudslide. The road was still narrow, studded with loose plates of shale from the cliffs rising around them, but they were over the high point of the crest, the slope beginning to angle downwards. Two could ride abreast on the road now, but they saw no other travelers. Lyra and Sadrao were ahead of the others. Since losing her horse Lyra had been riding on Sinai's mare, Jegger, while Sinai rode double with Jacyl on her big white stallion. Lyra was a bit bemused by the arrangement, but Sinai had told her bluntly that if it came down to fighting she would only be a hindrance to a rider on horseback. "You may do well enough on foot with the Kytha to back you, but I won't bet your life on it. Best you're out of the way and on a mount that will keep you ahorse and out of danger...and Jegger is the only one I trust to do that."

The twilight grey mare had gaits like silk, was patient and reasonable, and after almost a week Lyra still couldn't shake the feeling that Jegger found her awkward rider amusing.

She was secretly glad that she was not riding double with Sinai. The elven woman had been pricklier than usual lately. The only time she seemed less than remote was during their quiet morning dance of the Kytha.

Lyra could have ridden next to Trent—and probably enjoyed it, too—but the notion made her peculiarly uncomfortable.

"Love?" rumbled Sadrao. He looked down at her, amused. "Of course."

"What's it like?"

Sadrao rolled his eyes and scratched at his ruff. "Goddess, child. What a question." He thought for a moment. "It's like—like being—like—oh, hell, Lyra, I don't know. It's different for everyone, and it's different when you're young, and I don't doubt it's different if you're a man or a woman or a human or a dog-soldier." He sighed.

"Sorry," said Lyra contritely.

"No, no, I'm glad you asked. I suppose it's not that different at the heart of it. Hmm. Ask Jacyl sometime, she might be able to tell you better than I can. But I think when you're in love, mostly you want the other person to be happy, to be around them, be with them, keep them safe. Protect them from harm." He paused. "And it's different when you're young, Lyra, truly it is. You're in love with love, and scared to death of it. I don't mean to patronize you. But it's all new and exciting and frightening, and—you're in love with Trent, aren't you?"

"Sadrao, shhhh!" she yelped, stealing a glance over her shoulder. Trent was far out of earshot, making an intricate cat's-cradle between his fingers with a string while his gelding plodded stolidly onward. "I don't know. I've never been before. Not really."

She was blushing furiously. Sadrao shook his head, as if he did not know whether to be amused or not. "Jacyl was right," he muttered. Lyra's ears burned, and she stared at her saddlehorn, mortified.

"I won't tell anyone," he promised. "Just don't let Sinai know," added the dog-soldier with a sigh. "Otherwise she might drag him to Knaxos herself. In chains, if need be." He looked down at a glum Lyra. "Hey, now. Cheer up. I'll tell you about the last time I was in love."

She perked up immediately. "Okay."

Sadrao's eyes glazed over slightly with memory. "Well. Her name was Maja...and she was beautiful. She had fur like red gold and eyes like honey." He grinned at thin air. "She was funny, and clever, and she had a hell of a temper. She had a black spot over one eye—sort of like mine, but on her it looked like a pirate's eyepatch."

"And you loved her," said Lyra eagerly.

"Hmm? Oh, yes. We were friends first, and then she came into her heat and I fought in the circle for her—all the young dog-soldiers do—and Maja took me as her lover." He laughed. "I still have the scars from that fight. I'm rather glad they haven't faded, in truth."

Lyra absently fingered the fern-leaf bracer on her arm, and the long, healed scar under it.

"You'll do better next time," said Sadrao, as if following her thoughts.

"I could hardly do much worse," said Lyra darkly.

"Nonsense. You're alive. Can't do much better than that." The dog-soldier swished his tail absently, making a path through the dust motes kicked up under the horses' hooves.

"I suppose I'll need the practice, if I ever want to go back to—to my House." Lyra almost said "home," then choked it off.

Even if she did go back, she didn't know if it would ever be home again.

"With the Kytha, it will be sooner than you think," said Sadrao evenly. "If you still want to go."

"I do."

Sadrao nodded, almost to himself. "Well," he said, "you may get your practice soon enough, in any case."

"Huh?"

Sadrao gestured to the trail ahead of them. "Look. Hoofprints. Since the last rain."

Lyra looked at the pocked road and scratched behind one ear. "Couldn't it be another group of travelers?"

"Look at the hoofprints," said Sadrao, pulling to a halt and sliding off. "Come on, get down and take a look."

Lyra knelt in the dirt next to the dog soldier and stared at the track. Despite her intense scrutiny, it still just looked like a half-moon indentation in the dirt, no different than one of Jegger's.

The grey mare dropped her head and whuffled down the back of Lyra's collar. Lyra shoved Jegger's nose absently away. Following her original line of thought, she looked down under Jegger's feet, then down the backtrail of hoofprints.

Then it hit her. "They're not wearing horseshoes?"

"Excellent! I'll make a warrior of you yet. Now, if they aren't wearing horseshoes...?"

"Umm. They can't afford it? No. They don't want horseshoes, because horseshoes slip on rocks, and they want the horses as surefooted in rock as possible because they spend a lot of time in the mountains, off the road. So they can set up ambushes, and hit travelers when they aren't expec—oh. Dear. That's not good."

"I told Sinai you were bright," said Sadrao proudly. "They're probably going to try to hit us down the road a bit, when they've got a good place to get down behind us."

"Won't they just shoot us?" asked Lyra numbly, climbing back on Jegger. The skin between her shoulderblades itched as if expecting to be feathered with arrows at any moment.

"No," said Sadrao. "We don't have enough gear to be a particularly rich haul. They'll want the horses, and at least you and Jacyl alive."

"Oh," said Lyra. "Lovely."

"That's what they're thinking, yes. Of course, they've been up in the mountains all winter, so Sinai and Trent might be starting to look good, too."

Lyra stared at her hands on the reins. "So they won't risk shooting just at you, for fear of hitting the horses and the rest of us."

"That's my guess." Sadrao shrugged. He looked remarkably unruffled. "I've fended off more bandits in my time than Jacyl has suitors."

"Yay," said Lyra, loosening up the binding on her sword.

As it turned out, Sadrao was exactly right. They had no sooner passed a slide of loose scree than a dozen men rode onto the path. Five of them came down the slide, their shaggy little mountain ponies surefooted on the slope, while the other seven appeared on the road before them.

They leapt off their ponies at once. Of course, there was no way mountain raiders would have battle-trained steeds. Lyra saw out of the corner of her eye that Sadrao had dropped from his plowhorse, pulling Mohenja. Sinai had also vaulted from the back of Jacyl's white stallion and looked fully willing to take on all twelve by herself.

Trent drew his sword and more or less fell off his gelding.

Lyra stayed on Jegger, set her feet in the stirrups and said, to no one in particular, "Oh dear."

Then things started happening very rapidly, and all at the same time.

Lyra heard Sadrao roar and Jacyl say something very unlady-like, and at least one man screamed, but the only thing she really saw was a short, surprisingly jovial-looking man grabbing Jegger's reins.

Lyra went for her sword. Her fingers actually closed on the hilt, and then she squawked and dropped it in favor of two hand-fuls of mane as Jegger went up on her hind legs.

Oh god oh god I'm going to fall oh god Mattress never did this oh god.

Ironshod forehooves came down on the man's head and shoulder. Jegger's grey hocks were suddenly liberally splashed with scarlet.

The mare came neatly back down, then danced fastidiously out of the way to avoid stepping on the dead man.

Lyra, her weight distributed completely wrong, slammed hard against the pommel of the saddle and tried very hard not to throw up.

She reached for her sword again. She was pretty sure that, provided she didn't kill herself or Jegger with it, having her sword out would be A Good Thing.

Once again, her fingers closed on the hilt, and then were unexpectedly mashed into it.

Lyra yelped, looked down, and saw that another man had caught her right hand in his much larger one and was pinning her fingers to the hilt, and the sword to its sheath.

Acting purely on instinct, she rammed her left elbow into his face. He grunted, but didn't let go. Lyra hit him again. She felt something crunch under her elbow.

The man blocked the third blow with his free hand. Blood was leaking from his nose. He got his hand around her arm and hauled.

Lyra shrieked. Her right foot, braced in the stirrups, was the only thing keeping her on Jegger, and she was losing her hold.

The bandit dropped her right hand—the one on the sword—and grabbed her shoulder. Hunched over as she was, Lyra couldn't draw her sword without gutting herself. She groped at her belt. Her fingers felt squashed.

Her honor knife, with the highly conspicuous sixteen-inch blade, was stashed in her pack. The knife on her belt was barely a third as long, but it made a very satisfactory wet *thunk* when she buried it in the man's arm.

Luck, or the Kytha, or the gods were with her. The blade skittered briefly over bone, skidded out of control, and then dropped between the long bones of the forearm. The man screamed. Lyra screamed back.

Jegger whirled. The mare's shoulder slammed into the injured man, and he dropped away, taking the knife with him.

Unfortunately, wrenched by the movement and by the drag on her arm, Lyra's already tenuous balance failed utterly. She overcompensated, had a moment when she might have regained her seat, and then Jegger twisted to avoid stepping on the first downed man. Lyra fell off.

She rolled, came up to her feet, and had her sword in her hand. Then she thought, *Whoa, how did I manage to do that?*

She didn't have time to analyze it. The man she'd stabbed was in front of her, and judging by the look in his eye, he was *not* planning on taking her alive anymore, Sadrao's analysis of the bandits' situation notwithstanding.

Lyra's heart was frozen in her chest. It was with absolute astonishment that she watched herself lunge to meet the bandit's charge, duck under his short bronze sword, and come up to one side of him, hip to hip, so close they were practically touching.

It was actually a very safe place to be. She couldn't use her sword effectively, but neither could he, and as long she stayed pinned to his side—

He moved. She moved with him, her left hand on his left shoulder, whirling like a dervish when he tried to spin and catch her. In the back of her mind she couldn't believe that it was working, but she seemed to have abandoned conscious control of her actions. There was a hot, dazzling feeling in her muscles, her vision shot with sparks.

It was the Kytha, of course.

As she recognized the feeling, she recognized the pose. Swallow Dance. It was the most natural thing in the world, from her current position, to sink her weight just a little into the hips, pull him toward her with the hand on his shoulder, and let him turn.

This time, she didn't turn with him. Her sword-hand went up into his face, in an arc like a swallow launching itself from the eaves, and he recoiled.

Cracking him across the face with the hilt of her sword was probably not good form for that particular Kytha, but by then he was so far off balance that she barely needed to follow through. He went down, clutching his face.

"Oh, very nice," said Sinai behind her.

Lyra whirled around, to find the elf-woman grinning at her. Her dark grey leathers were spattered with blood and dust.

Lyra stared at the elf, wild-eyed, the Kytha still itching in her feet and her palms and along the knobbed cord of her spine. She took several deep, ragged breaths.

Sinai strode past her. Lyra looked around, saw half the men down, the rest vanished into the mountains. Sadrao was moving toward her. Jacyl was stripping the bodies of valuables with a practiced efficiency that sat jarringly on such a compassionate, gentle woman.

Lyra turned around and came face to face with the grisly sight of Sinai cutting the bandit's throat. His blood was shockingly red on the elf's slim white hands. Lyra gasped, took a step backwards, turned, and heaved her guts up across the trail. The Kytha vanished under a flood of bile.

Jacyl and Sadrao converged on her. Two pairs of hands, one furry, one cool-skinned, held her. Jacyl smoothed Lyra's hair back with her fingers, while Sadrao held her shoulders and patted her gently on the back.

"Just like that?" Lyra asked, when she could talk again. She wiped her lips. "It's over? Just like that?"

"Just like that," said Sadrao. And then, when she looked up at him in dismay, "What, would you rather it went on a bit longer?"

"No," she said, hoarsely. "No." In the back of her mind, it was still going on, must always be going on. She shuddered.

"Your hand!" said Jacyl, startling her.

"I'll get the salve," rumbled Sadrao.

Lyra looked down at her right hand, which had been crushed against the sword hilt. Jacyl was holding it, making clucking sounds over the livid red marks left in the shape of the bandit's fingers. They were already starting to puff around the edges.

"Ow," said Lyra, more because it looked bad than because it was starting to hurt.

Sadrao, who returned with his herb-scented unguent, appeared to be unscathed. Jacyl, too, was uninjured, having stayed on her stallion for the entire fight. Lyra was surprised to see the good-natured white horse, always so polite when she was grooming him, standing with his hooves coated in gore and his delicate feathered hocks matted with blood.

Trent was patching up a shallow gash across his ribs. Lyra noticed somewhat sheepishly that no one was hovering around him.

"I'm fine," she said. "I'll be fine."

"Hmmmph," said Sadrao, taking her hand in one of his. His rough-padded fingers were gentle as he spread the cinnamon-scented balm across her hand. "This will keep the swelling down, but try not to bang it on anything."

Lyra nodded. Overhead, carrion crows were circling, sliding down out of the sky on ragged black wings. Their harsh calls echoed from the rocks.

By the time they rode away, the crows were already feasting.

Chapter Thirteen

Trent and Sinai were fighting.

Sadrao's tail was curled tightly against his haunches in distress. Jacyl was thin-lipped, her blue eyes hard. Lyra hunched her shoulders as a particularly loud invective came from behind the door.

The three of them were waiting outside Sinai and Jacyl's room, where Sinai had dragged Trent within twenty minutes of their arrival in Delta.

The privacy was nonexistent. Lyra winced as Sinai's voice carried clearly through the door.

"I know you worked magic on the road, boy! I felt it!"

"Yes," Trent snarled back, "and I'd do it again!"

Lyra flushed and turned blindly down the hall. She bolted to her room.

Sadrao followed and caught the edge of her door.

"You know something about this," he said quietly, jerking his head in the direction of the muffled voices.

Lyra dropped her face and mumbled something.

She remembered it quite vividly.

Three days out from Delta, exhausted from sword practice, she was making her way down to the stream for a bath. She was threading her way down the fern-encrusted slope when she heard a branch breaking behind her.

She looked up. Trent was standing at the top of the slope. He waved. She lifted a hand from where it was braced on a tree trunk to wave back.

It was as she was turning back downslope that her foot slid neatly into a rabbit hole and she went down.

Reflexes honed by the Kytha saved her from serious injury. She tucked her shoulder, rolled, and came up to her feet. Then she promptly sat down again, her left ankle buckling, the pain enough to wring a cry from her.

Trent came skittering and scrabbling down the slope, sticks and moss flying from under his feet.

"Are you okay?" he asked, sliding to an awkward halt next to her.

"Son of a bitch," she cursed, holding her ankle. "It's pretty bad," she admitted. Tears were welling in her eyes. "I don't think it's broken, but—*ahh!*"

He sat down next to her on the slope. She leaned forward over her ankle, breathing hard.

"It's ironic, you know," she said, blotting tears with her wrist, "I've been hit with swords, and it didn't hurt this bad. Not at first, anyway."

Trent caressed the back of her neck with his fingertips. At first, Lyra barely registered the touch, and then it seemed so wildly inappropriate to the circumstances that she stiffened.

Then a warm, numb feeling spread out from her spine. The pain vanished. Lyra, already drawing breath to demand an explanation, suddenly went up half an octave in surprise and squeaked, "WHA—*at?*"

Trent knelt at her feet and started unlacing her boot.

"You fixed it!" said Lyra in disbelief. "The pain's gone!"

"I didn't fix it," said the half-elf, working a knot out of her lace. "I just blocked the pain for a moment."

"But it's fine! I can walk!" She started to rise. Trent put one hand on her shoulder and shoved her firmly back down.

"No, you can't. You'll hurt yourself. Pain is a good thing, in moderation. Now let me get this boot off."

She subsided, watching with interest as Trent nimbly unworked the laces and slid the leather off her foot. He removed her sock and took her foot in both hands.

"Sprain," he said, after working the joint gently for a moment. "A bad one."

"Damn," she muttered. Even though the pain was gone, she knew from personal experience that a bad sprain could be worse than a break and keep her off her feet for a week. "Sinai's not going to be happy."

"Sinai's not going to know," said Trent, giving her a conspiratorial glance. "This is going to feel strange."

It did feel strange. Even though there was no pain, she was suddenly intensely aware of the way her foot was put together, the ropes of tendon braced around the cradled knot of bone. Her foot, already starting to swell, felt warm, then began to tingle, as if it had been asleep. Trent bent his head over her ankle, an expression of fierce concentration on his face.

"You have warm hands," she said dreamily, feeling slightly divorced from reality.

He looked up at her and raised an eyebrow. "Thanks," he said dryly.

"Mmm."

"This should be good," he said finally. He patted her knee and let her rise.

"Thank you," she said, testing it. It felt completely normal. Even the odd awareness of the bones began to fade. "You did a really good job."

Trent, quite unexpectedly, turned red. Lyra felt herself blushing in response, and turned away.

"Thanks," he said quietly. "I—nobody's told me my magic was any good since my father—"

Lyra blinked. She had thought of Vade as a great evil, but ultimately a faceless one. That he might praise his son for a job well done had never even occurred to her.

She turned back around, but Trent was already walking rapidly back toward camp, with his head down. Sinai's sharp voice drifted back to her.

She loved Sinai, but the elven woman had no kindness in her for her cousin's son. Lyra wondered at it, abruptly—to be torn between two people, a man who committed great evils, but who had raised you, and who had praised you, and perhaps even loved you, and a good woman whose sense of honor was grim and hard and without mercy.

She wondered if Trent ever missed his father.

The ankle was as good as new. Lyra walked back to camp on it, a sprain that would have doubled their time on the road to Delta, but Sinai had a nose for guilt like a bloodhound, and they had barely arrived in Delta before she had collared Trent and was berating him in the largely fictional privacy of one of the rooms.

"He healed my ankle," Lyra mumbled to Sadrao. "It wasn't—he didn't—Sinai's wrong!"

The dog-soldier sighed and rubbed at the base of his ears.

"I think so, too," he admitted.

Into the little silence between them came the slam of a door, and Sinai's voice, ragged with anger and what Lyra knew was fear, shouting, "Stay away from her, *ashtuk!*"

"I have to go," said Lyra thickly. "I can't take this." She pushed past Sadrao toward the door.

Jacyl blocked her briefly. "Be careful," said the elven woman. And, as she stepped aside, "Lyra, she doesn't mean to catch you in the middle."

"I know," said Lyra, shaking her head rapidly, like Jegger would fight against the reins. "I know. But it's not any easier."

"Lyra," said Sadrao firmly. "Here."

Lyra turned back toward the dog-soldier.

Something came, rapidly, at her head.

Lyra snapped up both hands and felt the polished wood of her staff slap against her palms with a hard *thwack!*

"No naked steel within city limits," said Sadrao pleasantly, "so take your staff."

Lyra nodded, not trusting herself entirely to speak, and bolted from the inn.

There were six of them.

There might as well have been sixty.

They descended on her in an alley three blocks from the inn. She practically plowed into one of them, walking as she was, rapidly with her head down.

When she jumped back, stammering an apology, she realized at once that the trio of men facing her were not friendly.

The scrape of boots on the ground behind her informed her that they were also not alone.

"I don't want any trouble," she said in a high voice. Water was gurgling around her feet, between the cobblestones. She could see the reflection of her face in the water practically at her assailant's feet, and was shocked at how pale she looked.

Oh, you fool. Sadrao told you to be careful, but he probably thought you'd have the sense to stay to the main streets. But you had to get angry and storm out of the inn, and right into the arms of...

Before she could adequately frame a good name for the men—*thugs* and *brigands* were the two top contenders—one of them stepped up and grabbed at the end of her staff.

Lyra stared dumbly at the hands on the end of her weapon. She almost couldn't believe her luck.

"Wait!" she said, with a sudden laugh, looking up into the face of the still-silent man. "I know this one!"

It was about the only complicated staff move that Sinai and Sadrao had succeeded in hammering into her. She stepped forward, using her right hand as the pivot of a lever, and shoved down with her left while swinging the far end up. The end of the staff cracked the man across the face, and he went over backwards with a grunt.

Lyra was so stunned that it actually worked that it took a moment for her to comprehend that five men had moved to encircle her.

They still didn't say anything. That ruled them out as mere robbers. They were carrying heavy clubs and cudgels, she saw, eyes flashing from one to the next, but no blades.

She would've bet gold coins to Jegger's hoof-parings that they didn't have rape on their minds. There was nothing lascivious about their expressions.

What could they possibly want?

She swung at one with the end of her staff. He stepped backwards easily.

Shit. Shit. What do I do? What do they want?

They closed on her.

This would be a damn good time for the Kytha to kick in, thank you very much! She kicked out at one and smacked another across the ribs, but she was no match for their numbers.

What do they want?

A hand grabbed her by the shoulder. She looked down at it. She could hear her heartbeat pounding in her ears.

The fingernails were ragged. There were fine black hairs across the back and a heavy scar jagged across the knuckles.

She had all the time in the world to see this, all the time in the world as the Kytha woke with sudden, hurricane intensity and the end of her staff came up under his jaw and into his throat with the sickening *crunch* of shattered cartilage. All the time in the world to watch him fall, and to turn, and to smash the other end into the gut of the man swinging a club at her head. She heard the snap of ribs under the iron cap of the staff.

What do they want?

There were too many of them, Kytha or no. Perhaps if she had been older in her power, perhaps if Sadrao had had more than a month to beat skill into her unresponsive muscles. Her staff was wrenched out of her hands. The Kytha deserted her as suddenly as it had come. She had a single instant to feel betrayed.

What do they want?

And then, it hit her.

Sweet goddess, she thought, in the last heartbeat before a cudgel descended on her head, *I'm being kidnapped!*

⁂

Her ankles were chained to the wall. That was the first thing that Lyra realized, waking with a throbbing skull. She stared blankly at the iron cuffs on her legs and tried to move them. The chains clinked softly. They were surprisingly heavy and would have hampered her even if they hadn't been attached to the wall.

She felt tentatively across her face. There was a spreading soreness across her left cheek and jaw, just short of the temple. It turned into a raw agony at her jaw.

Is my jaw broken? Oh, gods, don't let my jaw be broken.

Fighting sudden panic, she probed at her face with her fingers. Her cheekbone ached, but it wasn't broken. Her jaw felt like a horse had stepped on it. She ran a tentative tongue across her teeth and her eyes teared as she hit the exposed root of a broken molar.

Oh, great. My teeth start to go, and I'm not even twenty. It probably wouldn't be visible. Lyra fished the fragments out with a finger and had to stop and bite her knuckle with pain.

This is no time for vanity. It's not so bad. My jaw's not broken, thank you, gods. I don't think I'm too badly concussed.

Her head ached, but her vision was mostly clear. She could focus her eyes if she worked at it. Her captors evidently knew their business. She felt slightly queasy, but she didn't think she was going to be sick.

She was in a stable, grey and shadowed. Musty straw poked her through her clothes, and the dry, organic smell of ancient dung filled her nostrils. Moonlight filtered over the top of the horse stalls from a small barred window in the wall. She could hear, faintly, the sounds of other people's breathing, the clink of chains in other stalls.

Her first thought was that Vade had kidnapped her. The second was that that was ridiculous—incredibly powerful sorcerers hardly needed a group of thugs to whack her on the head, and certainly wouldn't leave her chained in an old stable.

Someone had kidnapped her. Lyra. Of all people.

It was totally beyond her experience. The whole notion was absurd. Lyra shook her head in disbelief, leaning back against the wall. *How incredibly bizarre.*

She fugued out for a moment. She realized that she had drifted when she tried to look at her feet and discovered that her eyes had crossed again, and she now had four boots on as many feet.

Lyra put a hand to her head and thought very carefully about breathing. *Okay, maybe I am a bit concussed. Kytha. There was a Kytha for concussion, wasn't there?*

Yes, of course there was. The Third Sword Kytha was a lovely bit of motion, and Sinai had mentioned, in one of those off-hand comments, that it could clear the problems of concussion for a few hours.

I can't do the Kytha chained to a bloody wall.

Lyra tried to come up to her knees and discovered rapidly that she'd woken up at least once before, and the reason she didn't feel sick was because there was no longer anything in her stomach. She wiped the hand that had landed in vomit on a clean hank of straw and recoiled as far as the chains would allow her.

Hell with it. Even if I could do it without falling over, I can't possibly get enough room to do it in these chains.

Shit.

Sinai always said the Kytha was in your mind. "Dance it in your mind, and the body follows." I always thought that was some kind of mystic claptrap.

Out of Sinai? Come on.

But I'm obviously not going anywhere anyway.

So, feeling slightly foolish, Lyra closed her eyes and tried to call up the image in her mind. The Third Sword Kytha—hands in front *so*, left foot forward, right under her, and facing slightly outward, *so*. Breathe in, and step, hands drawn down, left hand up, palm out, and step...

When she opened her eyes again, a few minutes later, her vision, and more importantly, her mind, was starkly clear.

Sweet Goddess of Everything, it worked!

Lyra didn't waste time gloating. She didn't know how long the effects would last, and she needed to take stock of the situation.

Fact one—there were other people in the stable, presumably brought by the same group. Fact two—nothing had indicated that the kidnappers knew anything about her specifically. They had probably just grabbed a lone woman on the street. She rather doubted that they would have chosen her as sailing material, which meant that she hadn't been shanghaied.

Which meant slavers.

Lyra allowed herself a shudder, and a moment to wonder if they'd sell her as menial labor or, gods forbid, a bed slave. Ugh. Wretched thought. Her father, assuming he had survived this far, would have died of outrage on the spot.

On the other hand, they probably wouldn't damage a bed-slave by cracking her across the face. Unless they cater to the types who don't mind their slaves bruised.

Oh, pleasant thought. Let's not borrow trouble, shall we?

Well. What would Sadrao do in this circumstance—assuming he wasn't one of the other people chained in another cell? Lyra smiled to herself.

He'd escape, of course.

The stable windows had bars across them, apparently new. First things first, though; she couldn't climb out the window with chains on her legs.

"Thank you, Sadrao," she murmured, pulling the locks on her shackles into the watery grey light from the window. The long afternoons on horseback fiddling with that damned padlock had not been wasted after all. No lockpick. Damn, she wouldn't forget to wear that again. Dagger? She checked in both boots and found them gone. Hmmm. Damn. Something long and fairly narrow.

Lyra rolled her sleeve back. The filtered moonlight gleamed dully off the iron filigree on her wrist. Trent's gift.

The last sweep of the bracer, curling up her forearm, ended in a rounded point, a little narrower than her smallest finger. Lyra pulled the bracer from her arm, wrenched her fingers raw bending the tip, and inserted the end into the padlock.

It was harder than the one Sadrao had giver her to practice on, but it was also larger and hence, gave her more room to work with. Half an hour later, with a soft *chink!* the cuff popped open.

The second one fell off even faster. As Lyra rubbed blood back into her feet, she felt a sudden, giddy rush of triumph. She'd done it herself. No one had helped her, not Sadrao, not *anyone.*

Ten minutes later, running her fingers over the bars of the window, she felt far less optimistic. The bars were new, and even if she began chipping at the stone around the window, it would take hours...maybe days.

She slumped back down in the stall, thinking. The others were almost certainly searching for her—the moon had moved enough to make her think that she'd been unconscious for several hours. In this warren of a city, however, even Sadrao couldn't track her scent. *Hmm.*

She had just begun to crawl out of the stall, intending to check the doors at the ends of the stable, when a shadow covered the barred window.

"Lyra?" whispered a deep voice.

"Trent?!" She reached up to the window. That familiar, startlingly strong grip closed over her hand.

"Lyra—thank the gods—I thought—" Moonlight gleamed off his glasses as he crouched down.

"How'd you find me?" Lyra hissed.

The hand on hers tightened. "I used a spell," he said hoarsely. "Sinai wouldn't let me—she said it was sorcery, unclean. She and Sadrao fought over it, Sadrao said he didn't care, we had to find you. I snuck out of my room. I know Jacyl saw me, but she didn't say anything. I cast a seeking—I figured it was probably slavers, and I was afraid they'd get you on a boat. I'm babbling, aren't I?"

"Doesn't matter," said Lyra, limp with sudden relief. "Can you do something about the bars...or...hmm...."

"In for a penny," said Trent, with a weak laugh. "Sinai can only kill me once. Get back from the bars."

Lyra wouldn't have believed it if she hadn't seen it. Trent stepped back from the window, then put his hands together and murmured a few words. At first, Lyra thought the moonlight had strengthened. Then she realized that the light was coming from Trent's hands—a soft, blue-grey glow running from fingers to elbow. The light flared eerily, lighting twin reflections in the lenses of his spectacles.

He reached out and grabbed the bars.

Iron hissed and smoked under his touch. Lyra's sore jaw dropped.

Trent held the bars for a moment, gripping the top and bottom of each one. Then he murmured another word and the light faded.

"Stand back from the window," he instructed. Lyra complied, expecting a spectacular explosion or—well, something bizarre and magical, anyway.

Instead, Trent took another step back and kicked. The weakened grate snapped under the impact and fell to the straw.

Distant shouts echoed through the stable, and one of the doors creaked open. Lyra said a word that Sadrao had used when his horse had stepped on his foot, but had later refused to translate.

Trent reached through the narrow space and grabbed her forearms, hauling her out of the stable by main force. She wriggled through the window, scraping her shoulders and hips on the stumps of the iron bars, and staggered into the street. Her cramped ankles protested the sudden activity.

"Come on!" the half-elf hissed in her ear. His strides were much longer than hers and she staggered. He jerked her

The light was coming from Trent's hands, a soft, blue-grey glow.

mercilessly upright, almost dragging her behind him. They ran pell-mell through the streets, fog curling around their legs. Their breath steamed in the cold air.

"Quick, in here!" Trent dove into an alley, flattening against the wall. Lyra crouched beside him. Cold air burned in her lungs. The sounds of running feet passed them in the fog, then faded into the distance.

They waited for a time, panting, but the slavers were evidently more concerned with keeping their current stock intact than in pursuing a runaway. Gradually, when the night revealed nothing more threatening than a stray cat prowling through the alley, the pair relaxed.

Trent turned his face toward her with an exhausted sigh. "They didn't hurt you, did they?"

"Not really," said Lyra, automatically, and then, remembering the concussion, broken tooth, and bruise already purpling across her jaw, "well, yeah, but I'll live." She realized that she was gripping Trent's hand with white-knuckled strength and released him. "You came after me," she said, surprised even as she said it. "You saved me."

"You'd have done the same for me," he demurred.

"No, really." She lifted her hand. "Your bracer. I used the end to pick the locks on my chains."

The brick wall was cold against her back. She wore only her thin linen shirt and leather pants, her tunic and cloak still back at the inn. She shivered, hugging herself, the weariness and fear she had been fighting back suddenly rising in the back of her throat.

"You're cold—here—" He let her go, swinging his cloak off his shoulders. Light from the mouth of the alley illuminated the edge of his face and winked from his spectacles.

Trent settled the cloak around her shoulders, fastening the catch in front. Lyra lifted her hands and caught one of his between them.

"Thank you," she said faintly, looking into his face.

"I couldn't let them take you," he rasped, and suddenly he was holding her so tightly that Lyra would have feared for her ribs, had she not been hugging back with all her strength. She clung to him, shaking with delayed terror, wanting nothing so much as to hold—and be held—so tightly that their very bones locked. His lean, wiry form was a solid foundation in a world much more dangerous than she had ever realized. Lyra was conscious of the heat of his body, a degree or two warmer than a human's, the warmth of wool across her back, and the soft weave of the linen shirt he wore. Her face pressed into his shoulder, she could feel the rapid beating of his heart.

They might have continued to cling together until daybreak, but Sadrao skidded to a halt at the mouth of the alley and threw his arms around them both.

"Thank the gods," said the dog-soldier hoarsely, lifting Lyra for a brief, bone-jarring hug. Lyra had never felt anything so welcome as the familiar soft-fur-over-hard-muscle of Sadrao's arms.

He set her down and turned to Trent, his eyes gleaming yellow in the darkness. "And you. You found her." He paused, for a moment, head tilted to one side, the great outswept ears pricked forward. "Brother, I would call you," he said, finally. He reached up to his ear and plucked out one of the gold rings, and offered it to Trent, who took it gravely and placed it in his own ear. Lyra realized, abruptly, where Sinai's gold earring must have come from.

As if the thought had summoned her, a boot scuffed the ground at the end of the alley. All three of them looked up. Lyra realized that the sound must have been deliberate, for Sinai, standing silhouetted against the light of the street, could have crept up on them without making a sound.

Her naked sword was in one hand. Sadrao moved, smoothly, placing himself between Trent and the elven women. His fingers curled, but he did not reach for Mohenja.

"You used sorcery," said Sinai flatly.

"I did." Trent stepped out from behind the dog-soldier. "I'd do it again. We had to find her."

"If Vade was looking, he would have sensed your spell. Every witch and moss-wife and half-baked herbalist in this town *did* sense it."

"There was no other choice," Trent said, as if explaining a chess move to a disapproving master. Light winked off the sliver of gold in his earlobe.

Mist curled around the elf. She stood for a long moment, poised, like the angel of judgment. Then, with a whisper of steel, she sheathed the blade.

"The tree has fallen," she said dryly. "Might as well carve it as cry over it. Will you go to Frieze, old wolf?"

"I don't see much choice," said Sadrao. "We can find passage there, certainly."

"Very well. Jacyl and I had planned to leave in the morning, but, since Trent's little display has no doubt alerted half the town, we'll go tonight. You should go as well, quickly. Don't wait for a boat. Go overland—it's more hazardous, but not as hazardous as staying here. Jacyl has the horses saddled at the inn."

"Just when I could have used a hot bath," muttered Lyra.

Farewells were brief. Jacyl hugged her tightly and pressed a silver ring into her fingers. "It's not much," she murmured in Lyra's ear, "but if you ever need aid, hold it and think of me, and maybe—well, who knows?"

"Is it magic?"

Jacyl trilled her laugh. "I'm no mage. But love is better than magic, sometimes." She hugged Trent, too, and whispered something that made him laugh.

There were four horses in the courtyard. Sinai emerged from the stable, leading an unfamiliar fifth. She tossed the horse's reins over its head, ground-tying it, and walked to the small knot of travelers.

Sadrao she only clasped hands with, in the way of old warriors who know that they will meet again. When she turned to Trent, she seemed to pull herself upright, her face as still and calm as a statue carved of moonlit marble.

"I still don't know about you," she said quietly.

Trent swallowed hard, several times.

There was a brief silence which Lyra hoped that one of them would break, but neither did. Finally, Sinai nodded once, sharply. And turned, at last, to Lyra.

"You have been a willing student," she said, tilting her head so that the moonlight sparked in her eyes like polished silver.

"Practice the Kytha. I have been fortunate—I think, perhaps in this, the student will surpass the teacher."

"You've given me such a gift," said Lyra, softly, realizing that the elven woman's instruction in the Kytha had been, in many ways, a turning point in her life.

A smile crossed Sinai's face, fleetingly, like clouds slipping over the moon. "It was within you already—I merely pointed the way. But I do have a gift for you. Take Jegger."

"What?" The words might have been spoken in Elvish for all Lyra understood them. "Your *horse?*"

"You've been riding her for days," said Sinai irritably. "We were never particularly well-suited, though I've come to respect her judgment. And," she looked almost embarrassed, "she likes you."

Lyra shut her mouth, which had been dangling open. "Ah, I... thank you. I'll, um, take good care of her." What was the proper etiquette for such a magnificent gift?

"She'll take care of you, more likely," said Sinai. Another smile passed her face, and stayed a little longer this time. Then she clapped her hands and spun on her heel, stalking toward her horse.

"That's it, then," said Jacyl, giving Sadrao a kiss on the nose—he snorted—and mounting up. The two elves turned their steeds and left the courtyard with a clatter of cobblestones. Jacyl waved. Sinai never looked back.

"Come on," said Sadrao, after they had gone. "We've got a long ride in front of us."

Jegger whuffled as Lyra clambered onto her back. The dark grey mare had a long, even stride. Lyra listened to her hoofbeats as they cantered out of Delta, each one carrying her farther into the darkness.

❧

"No," said Iyara.

The Archmage blinked at her. He had expected reproach again, that distant, disappointed flicker in her eyes. He had welcomed it, in fact, as a necessary flagellation of an already guilty soul.

He had not expected refusal.

"But the last man—you did well, Iyara, you found someone who deserved to die—"

Iyara shook her head, slowly, her jaws opening and closing in what the Archmage realized suddenly was disgust.

"He tried to kill you!" he said, disbelief sharpening his tone. Iyara—how dare she turn on him; she was a *dog-soldier*! Loyalty was their great fame!

"Because I made myself bait," she said tonelessly. "And if I had killed him then, it would have been justice. But there is no honor in this…this…trolling for desperate prey. If you must have a life, take mine. I cannot do this again."

The Archmage sat back and put his face in his hands.

After a moment, he dropped them again. Very well, then—he had pushed too far, too fast, and now he had to deal with the consequences of misjudging his servant.

"I'm sorry, Iyara. You're right, of course. You have been the voice of my conscience." He prided himself on the shame in his voice, and allowed a little frustration to slip through next. "It is only—I must defend the House of Diamond, and I do not know how to do it! I find myself grasping at any tool—but no. This is too much. I am ashamed that I have done this."

Her face shown with naked relief. He wondered that he had ever thought the dog-soldier hard to read. Perhaps he'd never bothered to look.

"I will find another way, Iyara. Thank you."

She bowed to him, her ears almost flattened with gratitude, and left the room.

He would have to send Ralthas for the next proxy. The House of Diamond had stood for a thousand years, and he would not be the Archmage whose name was written next to the account of its fall.

Chapter Fourteen

Between Delta and Frieze there was a peninsula. It was this long neck of land that added a week's travel time by sea, but even so, more people took passage from Delta, and not only because Frieze was a hotbed of the notoriously prickly Church of the Sacrificed God.

No, the real reason was the swamp.

Half a day's travel north of Delta the ground turned to muck. Fed by one of the final tributaries of the Tanglelore, a massive bog stretched in all directions, turning into a salty marsh on the peninsula, eventually breaking into tropical jungle several hundred miles to the northeast.

The passage between Frieze and Delta was actually at one of the narrowest points of the bog, but it was still several days' ride. Not that anyone rode. On good ground, Sadrao said, the distance might have been easily ridden in a day. The bog added a three day slog.

Sadrao called a halt on the edge of the swamp, and they made an uneasy camp. They had ridden for the rest of the night since Lyra's escape, and the world had slowly turned from black to grey, from grey to the muted shades of predawn, and then finally the sun broke over the trees with disgusting glory. They made camp at midmorning.

Lyra's adrenaline high of the night before had petered out before dawn, and she was swaying in the saddle before they called a halt. Her head ached abominably, even though Sinai had assured her that the Kytha would keep her from permanent injury there. Her broken tooth also ached, a sharp stab of agony. The Kytha evidently didn't do teeth. She was barely able to give Jegger a perfunctory grooming before collapsing into her sleeping roll.

She mumbled an apology to Sadrao as the dog-soldier set water on to boil.

"Never fear," he said, patting her shoulder with a blunt-clawed hand. "You get hit over the head and still manage to pick your locks, you get out of the chores for a morning. I'm proud of you, Lyra. And you, Trent—" the dog-soldier raised his voice, "stop playing the martyr and go to bed. I know what spellcasting takes out of a sorcerer, and I am perfectly capable of making camp by myself for once, so lay down before you *fall* down."

"Good god, now I know where Sinai learned it," said the half-elf weakly, but he, too, crawled for his bedroll, leaving Sadrao sitting like a large, furry stone besides the fire.

They didn't wake until mid-afternoon. Sadrao lay curled in his usual neat ball, and only flicked an ear when Lyra rose. "I'll be up shortly, child," he said, without opening his eyes. "Build up the fire a little, if you would."

Trent was already gone from his side of the fire. Lyra fed twigs to the blaze, then rose in search of more wood. Her head felt better. Her tooth did not, but that was another matter. She met Trent on the edge of the trees, carrying an armful of branches.

"Poor Sadrao," he murmured, keeping his voice low. "He was more worried about you than he'll admit, and I know he stayed up for hours after you and I. There's a pond over that way—I thought we could catch some fish and save him having to hunt dinner."

"Good thought." Lyra twisted to look at the large-eared form wrapped in his blanket by the fire. "He's saved my life—probably more times than I even know. He really is extraordinary, and without him, the gods only know how we'd manage."

Trent nodded, shoving his glasses higher up on his nose. Brown hair fell into his eyes and he pushed it away impatiently. "Let's hope we never have to find out."

⚜

The swamp was horrible. It stank of decay and stagnant water, buzzed with the thin whine of mosquitoes, and rang with the calls of frogs and other, less wholesome beasts. Pallid plants clawed out of the thick murk among the gnarled roots of twisted, moss-drenched trees.

The path was all but invisible, but somehow Sadrao picked their way through. Lyra had no real idea what criteria he used, wading knee deep through the muck, leading his massive, placid horse behind him. Lyra spent more time leading Jegger than riding her, but the mare, mud spattered clear to her belly, followed her with matter-of-fact acceptance.

Trent's horse, on the other hand, shied at every strange sound and eventually had to be blindfolded and led, shivering, through the muck.

Lyra missed her staff desperately, wishing she had something to feel through the muddy ground in front of her. She hoped the slavers had sold it and gotten cheated miserably on the bargain. Reduced to steel, she had strapped her sword to Jegger rather than drag the weapon through the mud and water. Trent's blade was slung crosswise across his shoulders, like Sadrao's, but Lyra was fairly certain that she'd lose an ear if she tried to draw from that position.

When evening fell, strange lights flickered through the swamp, foxfire, corpse-candles, will-o'-the-wisps. Sadrao liked the strange lights no more than Lyra did and called a halt at a wide patch in the path, hardly more than a tussock of dry grass above the squelching mud.

Their camp was cold that night. They lit a fire for only a few minutes, and then put it out, not liking the way that eyes gathered in the darkness around them. Sadrao prowled around the small perimeter like a caged tiger while true night fell. The strange lights still flickered, far off in the swamp, and Sadrao, muttering in his own language, seemed to come to a decision.

"Trent," he said finally, "can you put up a...circle? A ward?"

Trent ran his tongue over dry lips. "Yes," he said finally. "I can. It will attract things, though—it will keep things out, but there may be things pressing around the edges that we would rather not see."

Sadrao sighed. "I would rather see things and know they can't get me than not see them and wonder where they were."

Trent nodded. "Bring the horses in as close as you can," he instructed, fishing a small bag from his pack. Sadrao complied, leading them close, until the trio was huddled practically under their legs. He hobbled Trent's skittish mount but left Jegger and the draft horse unfettered.

Meanwhile, Trent had already gashed his arm with quick, surgical precision. Lyra was a little surprised at how quickly she'd become used to the sight. He opened the bag and poured a measured quantity of fine white sand into his red-stained palm. Moving slowly around the hummock, he traced an irregular circle with the sand, chanting softly in a tongue that Lyra did not recognize.

When he closed the circle, with himself inside, he murmured a final phrase, then dusted his hands off and turned around. The circle was less than a dozen paces across. "Don't leave the circle," he warned. "And whatever you may see, or think you see, ignore it. We should blindfold the horses, just in case, but whatever you do, don't leave the circle, and don't listen to anything that anything out there might promise." He was looking at Lyra as he said it. She flushed, feeling like a child being lectured and resenting it. She knew full well that she was the weak link in the chain.

"I've been through here before," said Sadrao over a cold dinner of ration bars. The nervous edge of a growl sharpened his voice. "Alone, even. It was never like this."

"You've never traveled here with me before," said Trent, bleakly. "They can taste my magic. It attracts them like moths to a flame..." He rubbed the bridge of his nose wearily and pulled his cloak around him. He looked thoroughly wretched, his long legs folded up, for all the world like a bedraggled stork. Lyra laid a hand sympathetically on his shoulder and he gave her a faint smile that didn't reach his eyes.

They slept huddled together, as much for security as warmth. Sadrao and Trent faced outward, Lyra wedged between them with her back pressed against Trent's, and her face against Sadrao's shoulder. The dog-soldier's long brown and black fur tickled her nose when he moved. His hand lay on Mohenja's hilt, the naked blade beside him like a lover.

Lyra didn't sleep well. That was probably an understatement. She would start to doze off, then a particularly loud splash, or gurgle, or weird, echoing cry would jerk her back to wakefulness. She settled into an uneasy half-sleep, laying on her belly with her head pillowed on one arm.

It must have been nearly midnight when something brought her fully awake. Lyra's eyes snapped open, focusing on a tuft of reeds several inches from her nose. There was nothing obviously wrong, but the marsh had gone terribly quiet.

Hair lifted on the back of her neck. Her first instinct was to lay totally still, and she went limp, unable to shake the feeling that Something was looming over her.

Gradually, she realized that her companions were also awake, sleepless on either side of her. Sadrao sighed like a restless hound, the heavy muscles of his arms bunching as he took a tighter grip on Mohenja's hilt. When Lyra tilted her head to one side, she saw Trent lying on his back, staring wide-eyed and unfocused into the darkness. At the slight sound of her movement, he looked over at her, the murky light making grey-green shadows under the too-delicate elven cheekbones.

She rolled over on her back with a wriggle—and screamed.

Tried to scream.

Trent's hand slammed over her mouth, and only a muffled squeak trickled out between his fingers.

"They've been there for almost an hour," he said softly, as Sadrao's ears flicked back toward them and Jegger stamped uneasily. "Yelling won't drive them away, and the gods only know what it might attract."

Lyra swallowed, repeatedly, as Trent moved his hand away, resting it a few inches away from her face.

Hanging in midair, two man-heights above her head, seemingly flattened against an invisible barrier, was a grimacing, mud-colored creature. It was about the size of a cat, with a gaping maw full of broken, discolored fangs. Batlike wings splayed over the surface of the invisible wall.

Nor was there only one. On all sides, their wings curled and overlapped, a dome of ugly, grey-green beasts covered every inch of the barrier. The wall ran from several feet above the edges of Trent's circle to a point just above the horses' heads, visible only by the hideous patchwork of bat-like beasts pressed against it. As Lyra watched in horror, the one above her extended a long, spotted tongue and ran it over the invisible surface, giggling like a maddened monkey.

"What...what are they?" whispered Lyra.

"Damned if I know," said Trent. "Sadrao?"

The dog-soldier rolled on his back as well, his long legs drawn up. "No," he said. "They don't *smell* like anything, though, and they aren't giving off any heat."

"Illusions," said Trent. "I thought it might be—I can see them perfectly well without my glasses, and I couldn't tell you if Jegger was a horse or a camel at this distance. And the horses don't seem bothered by the noises at all."

"Why send illusions at us?" asked Lyra, more than a little disgusted by the creatures.

"I doubt it's a conscious effort," said Trent thoughtfully. "More likely some creature has evolved that particular illusion as a defense—something to frighten off predators, perhaps—and was attracted to our fire. It's responding to our thoughts and perceptions, not to any intelligent direction."

"Nasty little things," muttered Lyra, rolling over. "Even if they are all in my head." She yanked the blanket over her head.

A few minutes later, snores emerged from under the blanket. Sadrao and Trent exchanged amused glances.

"First Law of Childhood," whispered Trent. "As long as absolutely no flesh is exposed, the monsters can't get at you."

Sadrao laughed softly at that, but his fingers did not leave the hilt of his sword.

⚜

The creatures vanished an hour or so before dawn. Sadrao roused the humans almost as soon as the bat-like beasts melted away, and the three ate a hurried—and cold—breakfast, then saddled the horses in the gloomy light of predawn. Jegger stamped and blew under Lyra's ministrations, but seemed as eager to leave as her rider.

The trio stood in the center of Trent's circle for a moment. Sadrao cocked his head, earrings gleaming dully in his ears. "Trent? Is there any procedure to follow?"

Trent shook his head, pushing his glasses farther up on his nose. "I grounded it as soon as it got light. We just go."

Sadrao shrugged and strode out, leading the massive black horse behind him. Lyra and Trent mounted and followed.

The second day was more of the same, as was the night that followed. The bat-like creatures did not come back, and Sadrao found a wider patch, almost a clearing, to make camp, so they had a little more space to sleep. Sadrao made up a small plug of shredded tobacco and herbs and wedged it (with much grimacing on Lyra's part) into Lyra's broken tooth. It made her mouth taste like an ashpit, but she had to admit it did kill the pain nicely.

Halfway through the third day, almost between one stride and the next, the swamp turned into a shallow, stagnant lake. Great mats of reeds and rotting plant life drifted by, like anchorless islands. The path vanished completely.

Somehow, Sadrao was able to determine which of the tangles of grass and reed were only floating vegetation and which were small hills thrusting out of the water. He led them, splashing through knee-deep water, from copse to copse, still somehow moving north.

"This is the worst season to travel the swamp," remarked the dog-soldier, picking duckweed out of his fur. "During the rest of the year this is all mud flat, and if you stay out of the quicksand it isn't bad."

"If you stay out of the quicksand—!" muttered Lyra to Trent in disbelief. The half-elf laughed, shortly, but none of them had any breath to spare for talking.

It was early evening by the time they pulled out of the lake. Sadrao called a halt as soon as he found the path. Lyra was so exhausted that she slumped onto a dead log and put her face in her hands.

"Lyra," said Trent in a voice that compounded concern, amusement, and disgust, "don't open your eyes."

"Huhn?" she said, opening her eyes, and then, "Yecccchh!"

When they reached the lake, Lyra and Trent had rolled up their leggings and taken off their boots. In the haze of walking, Lyra hadn't looked down for hours, and she was now repelled to discover a half-dozen fat-bodied grey leeches clinging to her calves and feet.

"Ah—agh—Sadrao, *get them off me!*" She did a frantic little dance, unwilling to touch them, feeling physically ill at the thought of the slimy things drinking her blood.

"Sit," commanded Sadrao. She sat. Sadrao built up a fire and methodically burnt off the leeches while Lyra's skin crawled.

"Goddess help me," she said, watching Sadrao burn the second-to-last of the leeches off, a particularly fat one clinging to her big toe, "I am not cut out for adventure."

"No one is," said Sadrao, sitting back on his heels, "but you learn to deal with it eventually. You're young. In the meantime—" he handed her a twig glowing crimson at the tip, "You saw how I did it. You can do the last one."

Lyra gritted her teeth and burned the last leech off her right ankle. It left a red ring that oozed clear fluid. "I feel unclean," she muttered.

"Sadrao's school for young adventurers," said Trent with a grin. "By the time he's done with you, you'll be as bad as he is."

The dog-soldier chuckled, his tail thumping agreeably as he lifted his horse's hooves and rubbed a dry cloth down the animal's leg. "Jacyl was worse than you are when I found her, believe it or not. You at least had the sense to get out of there—I rode into her village and pulled her out of a burning building." His nose wrinkled at the memory. "She was trying to save her wardrobe, I believe."

They all laughed at that, then sat around the fire in companionable silence while the shadows deepened. Finally, Trent rose to cast the circle around them, while Sadrao tended to the horses, paying particular care to hooves and hocks that had been soaking in water all day. Lyra stretched and ran through the Serpent Dance, first and quickest of the Kytha routines. Sinking rapidly into the clear dazzle of the Kytha trance, she rejoiced at the energy flowing through her, from the very air itself. When she came out again, bowing to the four quarters, it was fully dark.

They sat around the fire, letting it die away to embers, eating the first hot food in several days. Lyra wrapped her hands around her mug of tea and was taking a sip when a light flared suddenly through the trees.

It was a harsh, actinic white light that left them all dazzled with after-images, suddenly night-blind. In the darkness that followed, Lyra heard Sadrao scrabbling and the cold steel hiss of Mohenja. The horses, blindfolded for the night, stomped nervously.

A cold wind whipped up and blew through them, smelling of damp earth and deep things uprooted. It swirled around them, then fled, leaving an unnatural stillness behind.

"Lyra," said Sadrao evenly, "put out the fire."

Blinking away tears, a huge, rainbow-edged spot burned in the center of her retinas, Lyra kicked sand over the fire and saw, in her peripheral vision, Sadrao standing a few feet away, Mohenja drawn.

There was movement behind her. She started, then felt Trent's hand on her shoulder.

"If anything happens," Sadrao said, still in that clipped, even voice, "take Jegger and run. She'll see you safe out of the swamp if anyone can."

"I'm not leaving you and Trent," she snapped. It sounded like bravery, but in actuality, Lyra could not bear the thought of a run through the damp, listening darkness, hunched over Jegger's back while moss slid over her face like wet lace, and *things* wriggled after them in the ooze. Especially alone.

Trent squeezed her shoulder. "I agree with her," he said. "None of us should leave the circle."

A light was moving through the trees. Lyra watched it, a soft, sickly, corpse light that slid through the swamp without illuminating anything.

Sadrao moved, two long strides, and put himself between the two humans and the light.

It was a noble, futile gesture. Another light appeared, twin to the first, then a third, a fourth. Dozens of lights surrounded them, in quick succession, like the torches of a distant army.

"*This* isn't good," said Lyra, and immediately wished she hadn't. Fortunately, both her companions ignored her.

The lights moved closer, pressing the edges of the circle like the bat-winged illusions had. Lyra stared at one of the lights, certain that there was something in the heart of it, something like a small, beautiful face —

The will-o'-the-wisp's face turned rotten in an instant, lips shriveling back from long teeth, flesh flaking off the bone. Lyra recoiled in horror as the tiny, demonic light pressed closer.

"They're pushing the circle in," Trent observed, as if commenting on the weather. "We should load up the horses and pull them together as close as we can."

"Can you hold them off?" Sadrao had sheathed Mohenja and was packing at a furious rate.

"I can't." Trent looked surprised. "This isn't...I can't get a grip on them at all. They're too small...too many...it's like fighting gnats..." He put his hand to his head, grimacing. "There's something else out there, driving them. They wouldn't act like this on their own." The half-elf drew a few drops of blood with the edge of his blade in an absent gesture, still staring into the middle distance.

Lyra joined Sadrao, throwing gear into packs and onto the horses with a fine disregard for breakables. The lights were swirling closer now, circling several feet within the original boundaries of the circle.

Trent swayed on his feet as Lyra threw the saddle on Jegger's back and pulled the cinch tight in one quick, frantic motion. He hadn't lost more than a thimbleful of blood—not enough to make him faint. She turned, and saw his skin, already pale in the sickly yellow light, turn absolutely white as he fell.

She caught most of his weight, staggering under it, and held him upright while Sadrao saddled the other two horses with impossible speed.

"I can see it!" whispered Trent abruptly, with a queer, frightened exultation. He was still laying limply against her, utterly oblivious. "The thing...*the mind*..."

Sadrao crowded the horses forward as the lights nipped close to their rumps. "Never mind that!" growled the dog-soldier. "Can you stop it?"

Lyra was holding Trent up by sheer force now, her knees already buckling as he lay across her shoulders. For someone who didn't have an ounce of spare flesh on his bones, he was astonishingly heavy. His face twisted at Sadrao's question. "I don't know... it must have a weakness..."

Sadrao had packs on two of the horses now and was rapidly piling a third onto the restive Jegger.

"What are you afraid of?" asked Trent, in Lyra's ear, but the question, she sensed, was not directed at her. He stiffened, straightening up. "That? Ahhh...the child of light..."

Lyra grunted as Trent suddenly stood on his own feet. She rubbed at her aching shoulder as the half-elf took a stride forward, staring at something only he could see. His lips moved, formed a question, then something woke in his eyes.

He turned on her, abruptly, grabbing her arms with a vise-like grip. "Lyra! The Kytha—*the Kytha*—do you know, did Sinai teach you the Phoenix Dance? Did she?"

"Yes. No." said Lyra hoarsely. Trent's grey eyes were wide and not sane. "She showed me once. Just once."

Trent threw his arms around her and laughed, oblivious to the evil lights dancing barely an armslength away. "Remember—remember when I said that there must be a Kytha for summoning demons?"

"Yes, but—"

"*Demons?*" roared Sadrao, clutching the horses' reins tightly under their chins. "Trent, have you gone mad?!"

"Not demons—a phoenix! There's one out there, Lyra—I can't explain it, but there is one, I can feel it! It's like—like fire, feathers, air, it can't be anything else. Dance! I'll do the rest—just do the dance! We don't have much time!"

"Phoenixes," said Sadrao, with the total calm of a man who has just taken a mortal wound, "have been extinct for well over a century."

Trent shoved wet hair out of his eyes. Even in desperate danger he found a wan sarcasm. "I didn't, you know, say it was alive. Lyra," his voice was low and urgent, "you've got to do it now."

Lyra stepped away from him. There was a space, barely three paces across, where she could move without running into either the horses or the seething wall of lights.

Phoenix Dance. Sure. Simple. She took the opening stance for all the forms, feet apart, knees a little bent. *Saw it done once. Great. We're all going to die. Why couldn't it be the goddamn Heron Dance, or even just one of the ones I've actually done before?*

But the essence of the Kytha is concentration. She moved into the first form as she had remembered Sinai doing, lifting her arms like giant wings, turning, leaping. She came down on one foot, landed badly, corrected, and pushed off again, turning, motions that could have been a dance or a battle.

Trent was chanting, his hands lifted over his head, but Lyra didn't hear him. Inside her mind the door had opened, and power, hot and fiery, flowed up her spine. She moved faster, one move following the next. She was no longer following Sinai's half-remembered example, but following the path that the Kytha laid out before her, her eyes closed, the power flowing with sweet, burning ecstasy.

Sadrao would have stepped back, if there were any room. Trent's gelding reared his head back, but the dog-soldier held him tightly. He didn't blame the animal. Not one bit.

Fire was flowing off Lyra's body, a shadowy second skin that flickered around her, magnificently golden against the unhealthy foxfire glow. It swirled, following her movements, forming long wings of flame, a fiery tail and crest. The corpselights milled agitatedly about, so close that Sadrao imagined he could hear tiny, mocking voices.

"Not enough!" Trent's voice was frantic, breaking into the chanting of his own spell. "God help me, not enough!" The young mage looked around wildly, knife in hand. Lyra's skin was starting to turn angry red under the blaze of shadowy fire.

The half-elf lunged at Sadrao. Sadrao's eyebrows went up, and he recoiled with an involuntary snarl, but Trent went right past him, ducked under the reins he held, and buried his dagger deeply into the neck of his own gelding.

The horse screamed and bucked, nearly wrenching Sadrao's arm from the socket. Trent snapped out an incomprehensible phrase, sounding less mystical and more harried, dropped his knife, and did something that looked to Sadrao as if he'd grabbed something in thin air and *yanked.*

The gelding's scream became a throttled squawk, and it fell over. Sadrao caught a hoof across the thigh and grunted. Lyra was still dancing, faster and faster, but the odor of burning hair was beginning to drift across the clearing.

Trent took two steps toward her, shouting the last words of his spell, and plunged both bloody hands into the heart of the blaze.

An explosion rent the air above them. It knocked both Trent and Lyra flat and threw Sadrao backwards into the horses. The animals neighed and staggered, and it was only luck, Jegger's training, and Sadrao's death-grip on their reins that kept them together as Sadrao's draft horse tried to bolt.

White light, pure as milk, streamed from a shape hovering overhead. Lyra, half-pinned under Trent's body, looked up and saw a form that was more living flame than bird, like molten silver. Its massive wings spread wide, the feathers rippling in an unseen wind.

Trent pushed himself up on one elbow, shielding Lyra with his body. "Sweet goddess," he said hoarsely.

It was a phoenix. It looked down on them with an eye that flared blue-white as a star. Its beak parted, and a voice emerged, sweet and brazen like shattering bells.

"*AT LAST....!*"

The light of its body ignited the tiny corpselights and swallowed them with pure, cleansing flame. It spun in the air, dancing, a glory to which Lyra's dance had been only a pale echo. "FREE!" it cried, rising higher, the echoes of its voice singing from the trees.

The flames of its tail brushed the faces of the beings lying under it, but did not burn. Tears streamed down Lyra's face at the beauty of it, left dusty tracks on Trent's face, and long black trails in Sadrao's fur.

"Free," whispered the phoenix. "Ahh...so long, so cold. Trapped. You've freed me...I will repay you, little friends—little mage, little dancer. Brave warrior."

It circled higher, above the level of the trees now, its voice a dirge for mirthful suns, glorious beyond sorrow. "Safe passage, I grant you," it cried. "The one who bound me is broken. It was an old thing. Like me. My time is past as well."

It swept in a circle, rose higher. From its throat came no longer speech but a song of impossible beauty, something that Lyra could never have described, like a dream that vanishes on waking. Trent held her, weeping softly, and she clung back, as moved as he.

The phoenix rose higher as the flames consumed it, growing smaller, until it was one with the stars and the dark velvet sky between them. Its voice faded away, but in the three who listened the music remained, never quite silenced. Would always remain.

The little voice in the back of Lyra's mind said *What the hell just happened?!* but she had sense enough not to say anything. Even if she could have forced words out through the tears in her throat.

The last phoenix faded into the night, and its kind was never seen again in that age of the world.

Chapter Fifteen

In Lyra's pack, in a narrow rosewood box that also held an elf-woman's ring and the honor dagger of the house of Volfrieds, lay a single feather. It was silver and glowed with its own faint light. Trent had found it lying on the ground while preparing to break camp the following morning.

He offered it to her gravely, and as gravely, she had accepted. "It was an old evil," said Trent, stroking the silver primary across her palm. "And an old glory to fight it. There was nothing left of them but the memory anyway. If we die tomorrow, we have done a good in the world, at least." He closed her fingers over the feather. Argent light strayed across her palm. They did not speak of it again.

That was later, however—after the swamps, after Frieze, after Lyra regained consciousness.

They had left the swamps behind the following day. Lyra was not aware of it. Perhaps the Phoenix's gift of safe passage held true, because the path stayed dry and straight clear to the edge of the marsh. Lyra was not aware of that, either. She was face-down across Jegger's neck, tied into the saddle with rope, dead utterly to the world.

Sadrao, checking every half-hour to make sure that she was breathing, thought that it was probably best she was unconscious. Massive blisters had formed on her fingertips and in stripes across the backs of her arms and legs, as if she had been exposed to intense but focused heat. He would not have moved her, but the middle of a swamp was arguably the worst place possible to recover, particularly since the task was going to involve lancing, which was practically begging for infection. Trent could barely stand up himself, let alone muster the strength for healing, and was staggering along, clinging to the saddle of Sadrao's plowhorse. Sadrao had been meaning to say something about the dead gelding, but he'd found the semi-conscious Trent weeping quiet apologies over it, and he'd decided to let the matter drop. So the dog-soldier tied Lyra to the saddle, and winced when the ropes rubbed the blisters and broke them, even though Jegger stepped along as daintily as a ballet dancer under her.

They made for Frieze. Sadrao hated Frieze, but it was a town, and it would have inns and a bed and a chance to dry out.

The city of Frieze was unpleasant.

Everything in it was hard—hard stone, hard streets, rock-hard beliefs. There were street preachers on every corner, and people stared at Sadrao as if they had never seen a non-human before. Around every throat was the tiny human-figure-in-a-circle symbol of the Church. It took five tries to find an inn that would take them, and Sadrao knew with glum certainty that they were paying an exorbitant rate for the smallest and meanest room in the building, shoved up under the eaves so tightly that his ears hit the ceiling when he stood.

It was another day before Lyra regained consciousness. Trent reassured Sadrao that she wasn't dead, nor particularly injured, just exhausted.

"What did she do?" the dog-soldier asked, one black paw curled loosely around her wrist. There was one bed. There had been no discussion about who got it.

Trent shook his head. "I don't really know. I don't even really know what I did. It was the Kytha, and blood magic, together, but the Kytha drove it. I don't know if it could be done again." He sighed. "If that is what it feels like to be a Kythar, I wouldn't want to be one."

Sadrao nodded. He had lanced the blisters and salved them to the best of his ability, while Lyra mumbled and whimpered in her sleep. He had already known, from long years of friendship with Sinai, that Kythar were not to be envied. At several points during the evening, while lancing the blisters with a hopefully sterile needle and sponging clear, nasty fluid out of the resulting coin-sized holes in the backs of Lyra's arms, he thought glumly that their friends weren't particularly to be envied either.

Trent had taken one look and opted for the dour company of the common room instead of staying. If anybody had noticed that his face was too thin, and his ears a little too pointed, he hadn't said, and Sadrao, heating his needle over a small, guttering lamp, hadn't asked.

Lyra woke up the next morning, tried to roll over onto her back, and yowled like a doused cat. Sadrao took this as a good sign, and clung to hope grimly when she lapsed into a low fever later that day and lay sweating and pale and grumbling in the low room under the eaves. He sent Trent out for herbs. The half-elf was no haggler, so what he brought back wasn't much and cost an absurd amount, but in xenophobic Frieze half the merchants wouldn't talk to Sadrao for any amount of money, so the dog-soldier was forced to make do.

Lyra was confined to bed for three days, fever wandering in and out, so that she alternately boiled under the threadbare blanket and froze. Her teeth chattered constantly. "I hate this," she said, dicing the words out between clicks. "I mean, I really, really hate this."

"It's the Kytha," said Sadrao, "and infection. You asked a great deal, and it took it out of you."

"*Trent* isn't sick," said Lyra sulkily, aware that she was whining and not really able to stop herself.

"Trent's magic is blood magic. The gelding he killed for it would probably gladly trade places with you."

She subsided, chastened.

Eventually the fever broke, the blisters healed, and Sadrao pronounced her well enough to get out of bed, which she did with great enthusiasm. Even half-sick, she was twice the haggler that Trent was, and the price of their stay in Knaxos dropped significantly. They found a cheaper place to stable Jegger and the plow-horse, they replenished their supplies, and after a morning spent scouring the docks, Lyra found them passage out to Knaxos.

None of them were sorry to see the wharf fade behind them.

⹀⹀⹀

"I thought we were going to the House of Diamond."

"We are," said Sadrao.

The House of Diamond, the dog-soldier explained, was both a place and a grouping. The sprawling library complex, from which the Isle of Books took its name, was known as the House of Diamond. It housed not only books and archives but also quarters for the army of librarians, guards, servants, and scholars that kept the library functioning. Headed by a magician called an Archmage, the House was a nearly autonomous nation unto itself.

The House of Diamond also referred to the strange kinship of which all the librarians and many of the scholars took part. Two clans, tracing their lineage back to the founding of Knaxos, provided the core of the House.

"Different species," said Sadrao absently, leaning against the railing of the ship with Lyra beside him. The white marble of the House shone against the slate-grey sky like an egg against a hen's belly as the ship circled toward Knaxos's main port. "Hereditary albinos. One human clan, one Ferran."

"The Ferran are interesting," said Trent, coming up beside them. He wiped salt spray from his glasses. "Albinism is more common in them than in us, of course—" Lyra was unsure whether he meant elves or humans, "—but the clan is weasel-like, and true albinos, not like the ermine types, who get a white winter coat half the year. Most other Ferran resemble badgers, or otters— I've heard rumors of wolverine-types farther north—"

"They're true," rumbled Sadrao. "Larger than humans. Almost the equal of a dog-soldier in a fight." He spoke with unconscious pride.

"Albinos only?" asked Lyra, staring down at the grey-green water and feeling a faint nausea. She squelched it.

"No, there's an adoptive process," said Trent. "Those who join from outside undergo a bleaching process. Magic—dyes, for those with fur—to give them the white coat. And some who are born albino seek Knaxos out anyway, for acceptance."

"There is a white dog-soldier there," offered Sadrao. "I don't know her name, but I heard of her from a clan-sister some years ago. I am not surprised she went—white-furred ones are often sensitive to sunlight. The desert is hard on them."

"Maybe you'll get a chance to meet her," said Lyra, waggling her eyebrows suggestively. "Sounds...exotic."

"Mmm." Sadrao licked his lips and gave her an exaggerated leer. "We'll be there for a few days, at least, while they poke around in Trent's head—"

"Oh, thanks," said Trent darkly.

"—and once they realize he's the honorable young man we know and love, we can head back to Anu'tintavel," finished Sadrao, unruffled. "I don't know how long these things take. Trent?"

"I don't know," said Trent. "I've never been interrogated by mages who specialize in the mind before. The elven council took only a day to examine me, and they felt quite...thorough." He shivered. "But they have the facilities here, so it could take hardly any time, or a great deal longer."

Lyra patted his shoulder sympathetically. "There'll be books," she said, consolingly. "I'm sure they'll let you read while you're there, and then we can go back."

He nodded. "If this is what it takes so that the council will let me help them with their war, then so be it. Bring on the Archmage."

✦✦✦

When they entered the House of Diamond and explained their business, a pair of white-clad guards immediately showed them to an audience chamber. Lyra had only a glimpse of high, vaulting ceilings, many stories overhead, and a plunging central chamber cutting down through floor after floor of bookcases, like a mineshaft sunk in some bizarre literary strata, before they were hustled across the gleaming floor to an unobtrusive rosewood door. Yet another guard went to summon the Archmage at once, while the original pair flanked the door.

The chamber was small, with a golden marble floor and elegant, uncomfortable wooden furniture. None of them sat. Sadrao prowled briefly around the room, then settled with his arms folded in a militant parade rest.

Lyra didn't like having guards by the door. She didn't like the fact that they'd checked their weapons at the entrance to the library. She missed her sword, and she missed Sadrao having Mohenja even more.

The House of Diamond was a book-lover's dream.

But.

But something. There's something I don't like here.

Even glimpsing the vast bookshelves towering high above her head, more volumes than any one being could hope to read in a lifetime—even that could not assuage Lyra's growing tension. The library guards were a little too well armed. There was armor under the drape of their white cloaks. They had swords.

"Do you get many dangerous bibliophiles?" she asked of one of the guards, nodding at the sword.

"We get enough of them," he said, without cracking a smile.

She might have continued to bait him, but the door opened again. Lyra took a step back in surprise, as one of the white wolverines Trent had mentioned came through the door. He was as tall as Lyra, but nearly twice as broad across the shoulders. Heavy lower canines protruded like tusks on either side of his muzzle, worked with elaborate silver scrimshaw. Lyra lifted both her eyebrows.

The Archmage?

No. The wolverine, though clad in more elaborate armor than the other guards, had stepped aside to allow in the figure that could only be the Archmage.

He was an older human man, as tall as Trent, but his stooped shoulders and defensive air made him seem shorter. He was pleasant, and genial, and Lyra mistrusted him immediately.

His hair was white-blonde and curly, but starting to recede, giving him a slightly frayed look. A true albino, he had watery pink eyes that flicked over Trent and Lyra, dismissed them, and settled on Sadrao. He reached toward the dog-soldier with hands that were stained with ink and callused by the pen instead of the sword.

"My friends!" said the Archmage. He clasped the hand of a startled Lyra, clapped Trent on the shoulder, then turned and swept a bow to Sadrao. "My lord dog-soldier! They tell me you come as a servant of the elven council."

Sadrao's ears eased ever so slightly back at the word "servant," but he answered civilly enough. "A messenger of the council, yes." He proffered the sealed message tube.

The Archmage took out a jewel-hilted knife and worked the blade under the seal. "Half a moment," he muttered. "Just got to get this here..."

Lyra feigned scratching her cheek to hide her smile from the Archmage. When Sinai had handed Sadrao the tube, in that long ago tavern in Jeppeth, the dog-soldier had removed a thin-bladed instrument from his pack, heated it at the table lamp, and promptly inserted it under the wax seal. While the elven woman looked on in amusement, he had read the letter, then nodded, re-folded the letter along the original creases, and re-sealed the tube with a skill better suited to a forger than a warrior.

She tried to trade an amused glance with Trent. Unfortunately, Trent was doing his best to fade into the woodwork, which was not easy for someone in excess of six feet tall.

"Ah, yes," murmured the Archmage, his eyes flicking across the parchment. "Hmm, yes." His smile slowly faded, and he chewed on his lower lip. "Ah, hmm. Yes."

Sadrao did not quite roll his eyes, but the tip of his brushy tail was twitching in a suspicious fashion.

That suggestion of a wag died the instant the Archmage looked up, his eyes bloody red and hard as rubies.

"This is him," said the Archmage flatly. "This is the half-elf." He tapped the parchment with an ink-stained hand, his gaze riveted on Trent.

"This is Trent," said Sadrao quietly.

The Archmage looked at the dog-soldier for a moment, his eyes oddly expressionless, and then he smiled suddenly. "Of course. Most excellent. Thank you for bringing him."

One of the guards opened the door.

Sadrao's eyebrow spots rose. Trent blinked owlishly behind his glasses.

"We will, of course, contact the elves with our findings," said the Archmage. He moved smoothly forward, toward Sadrao, obviously intending to make the dog-soldier step back politely, toward the door. Sadrao did no such thing. Lyra raised an eyebrow, wondering if the albino would simply walk into Sadrao's chest and bounce off or if he would stop.

He stopped. Lyra felt slightly disappointed.

"That's good," said Sadrao pleasantly. "Meanwhile…?"

The Archmage put an arm out, laid it on the air somewhere near Sadrao's shoulder, and attempted again to move the dog-soldier toward the door. Sadrao might as well have been a statue of garnet and ebony.

Lyra was rather interested to see if the Archmage would try actually touching Sadrao next, but instead another door opened in the room, and several more white-clad figures emerged.

"Meanwhile, feel free to avail yourselves of the library for the duration of your visit," said the Archmage pleasantly.

Trent did his best, but he was simply not made of the same stuff as Sadrao. Two more albinos herded him from the room, like white sheepdogs. He cast a slightly bewildered glance over his shoulder at Lyra and Sadrao, and the door closed behind them.

The Archmage seemed, almost imperceptibly, to relax. "Thank you again. Now, if you'll excuse me, very busy—"

"When will you be finished?" rumbled Sadrao.

"Hard to say," said the Archmage, "hard to say."

"I will be coming to check on my friend tomorrow, then," said Sadrao, and the rumble had an edge to it, the merest shadow of the possibility of a growl.

"Doubtless you will," said the Archmage, leaving the room.

They stood there and stared at the door. After a long moment Sadrao exhaled and said, "Well."

"I don't like this," said Lyra nervously.

Sadrao turned on his heel. The silvered guards at the door watched him with impassive pink eyes. Lyra hurried after him, listening to the click of claws on tile and wondering just what had happened.

⁂

Iyara saw the other dog-soldier in the great central hall of the House of Diamond.

He was three stories down, striding across the white stone tiles of the main floor, and Iyara, passing along the balcony, recoiled immediately into the shadows of the stacks. The sight was like a blow, like a blast of heat, as if she had stepped from darkness into the blazing desert sun. Her head ached with it.

She inched forward, just a little, half-hidden behind one of the pillars, and watched. Foreshortened by the angle, she could see the top of his head, the twitching ears, the stiff, upright mane, the empty scabbard of the curved sword across his back.

One of the two humans he was with said something, and he laughed, a barking, breathy sound that drove her back into the stacks again.

She thought, *Oh, ancestors, mothers of my mothers, what have I done?*

All the rationalizations she had so carefully made, all the constructions in her head, fell apart in the presence of another dog-soldier. She thought of trying to explain what she had done—the sacrifice she had procured and her silence as others were brought—to another of her kind, and a whine started deep in her throat. She choked it down with iron pride. She was vaguely surprised that she had any left at all, but it seemed that this, too, she had remembered.

Iyara knew immediately, bleakly, that no matter what she had told herself, even in the service of her ostensible pack leader, she had done terrible things.

If I hide—if I don't talk to him, he won't know—

Her own contempt withered her. She was a dog-soldier. Even if she barely deserved the name, even if her mothers and uncles would have curled their lips back to see her now, she was still a dog-soldier. Dog-soldiers were not perfect, no one was, but they did not cower away from their own mistakes. She had done wrong. Very well. Hiding from it would not change that fact.

She took a deep, hissing breath, then another. Her hackles settled, and the spiked fur along the nape of her neck smoothed down. The white dog-soldier turned into the bookcases and walked away, her ears held high.

⊰⊱

Trent was standing in another room connected by a short hall to the one Sadrao and Lyra had just left and was trying to make conversation with two pink-eyed men who were not saying anything.

"So, err, what happens next?"

They continued not saying anything.

"I'm just wondering…"

They were very good at it.

The door opened. Two guards in silver armor came in, one human, one the massive-bodied white wolverine with scrimshawed fangs. The Archmage followed.

Trent smiled, a little nervously. "Ah, perhaps you could tell me—"

The Archmage made a quick gesture with one hand.

"Hey!" yelped Trent, startled, as the white-clad guards moved smoothly forward and caught his upper arms. "What?"

"Take him," snapped the Archmage.

Trent was trying to shake off their pale hands. "I haven't *done* anything!" he protested angrily.

"I highly doubt that," said the Archmage. "Take him to the Silent Walk," he ordered the guards.

"But—"

Light came glittery-flittery around the Archmage's hands, a sparkling, twinkling sort of effervescence that looked like the footsteps of fairies and felt like a mule-kick when it landed squarely on Trent's skull. The world went glittery blue, then blood red, and finally familiar black.

Sadrao and Lyra went back the next day and asked to see Trent. The wolverine with the scrimshawed fangs told them the half-elf was busy.

They went back the third day and asked to see Trent, or the Archmage. They were both busy.

The fourth day, Sadrao lowered his muzzle until he was on eye level with the broad skull of the wolverine, gold eyes facing impassive pink, and said, "How long are they likely to be busy?"

"The foreseeable future," said the wolverine, unimpressed.

The fifth day, there was a note from the Archmage. It said, in a thin, spidery hand, that Trent was presumed dangerous and was being held for observation, and it ordered Sadrao to take this information back to the elves. Sadrao read it, several times, and looked up to stare into the grim pink eyes of the wolverine. Lyra took the letter from his fingers, read it, and stammered "But—but—but—"

Wolverine and dog-soldier ignored her.

"What if I try to go through you?" asked Sadrao pleasantly.

"I'd like that," said the wolverine, and drew his lips back in an elegant scrimshaw smile.

"If I had my sword," said Sadrao, still very calm, "I believe I would."

"I have no doubt you'd try."

Lyra interrupted this discussion by saying, "You have to let us in!" and grabbing the wolverine's shoulder.

The wolverine stiffened and aimed a slap at her head. His claws were longer than her fingers and would have laid her face open to the bone, but Sadrao's foot had somehow gotten tangled up in hers, and she landed with a squawk on the marble floor while the claws whizzed harmlessly over her head.

"Don't do that," said Sadrao, displaying his own interlocking ivory grin. He picked Lyra up with one hand. The wolverine's smile, if anything, got even wider. Sadrao studied him, the door, the vast labyrinth of corridors and bookshelves, and said, "We'll be back."

"I'm sure you will," said the wolverine.

And then, for lack of anything better to do, they left.

⁂

"But what are we going to *doooo?*" whined Lyra, fully aware that she was whining and not yet ready to stop.

"Simple," said Sadrao, striding down the main street of downtown Knaxos. They had reclaimed their weapons and left the House of Diamond. The sun had moved barely a handbreadth in the sky, and their whole journey was suddenly turned on its ear.

Lyra had to hurry to keep up with the dog-soldier's long legs.

"You have a plan?" She felt a sudden, overwhelming relief. Sadrao would figure something out. He wouldn't let them keep

Trent, when they obviously thought he was some kind of dangerous criminal.

"Yes," said Sadrao, turning suddenly and ducking into a tavern. As Lyra followed, the dog-soldier shoved his way to a table, sat down, and said "We're going to get very drunk."

Lyra found herself utterly without words and stared at Sadrao with open mouth.

Sadrao ordered something from the bar. She didn't notice. She was trying not to get hysterical.

"Drink up," said Sadrao, plopping a glass down in front of her.

"This is not going to help Trent," she said, hearing her voice spiraling higher and trying to clamp down on it.

"No, it won't," said the dog-soldier, tossing back half of his drink, "but it'll help me, and that's all to the good."

Lyra stared into the anonymous amber liquid and felt ill. "Sinai couldn't have meant for them to just—just—"

"No, she couldn't have." Sadrao slammed the other half and ordered another.

"So someone must have—"

The dog-soldier waved a clawed finger at her. "No more questions, speculations, or complaints until you take a drink." And then, a little more kindly, "Child, we'll think of something. But we can't do anything tonight, and trust me, this will take the edge off."

Lyra took a tentative sip. It was like drinking raw fire, with a touch of lemon. She spluttered, set the cup down, and coughed furiously.

"No, no. A lot, all at once, it numbs the throat."

"Can't hunt," he added under his breath, in his own language. "Can't fight, can't ride. Can't drink. What are they *teaching* girls these days?"

"I know four languages," said Lyra acerbically, in surprisingly fluent dog-soldier, "not including what I've picked up of yours, and Elvish. I can run the books of a merchant house, and I can read and write, unlike most of the people in this bar. I dance badly and my embroidery—" she had to drop back into tradetongue, since Sadrao's tongue had no words for embroidery,

"—is definitely substandard. And I *cannot* cook. But those are the things they taught me."

Sadrao laughed aloud, a barking sound, and swallowed most of his drink. "I stand corrected. Forgive me, Lyra. I spoke badly. You've learned a great deal, especially of my language. Drink up."

Lyra curled her upper lip, aware that Sadrao was watching her with a faintly challenging air, and slammed a good two-thirds of the contents of the glass. She gulped air—it was raw on the back of her throat—but she would rather have slit her wrists than cough.

Sadrao slapped her on the back and ordered another.

There was a method to the dog-soldier's madness. While Trent's plight turned itself over in the back of his brain, Lyra was well and truly distracted, and before the hour was up, too drunk to care if her firstborn child was being held prisoner, let alone a half-elf she was merely somewhat in love with.

Which was another worry entirely, and not one Sadrao was going to waste time on. Honor demanded he free Sinai's cous-in-son. The elven woman would have been the first to break in, sword in hand: no one treated one of Sinai's clan like that, even a dishonored half-breed. He'd read the letter she sent. The mind-mages of the house were to deliver their findings to him, and their recommendations, which, along with Trent—if he passed—the dog-soldier would have delivered to the council in Anu'tintavel. They were not to drag Trent off like a criminal into the bowels of the library and provide a single, terse note.

He frowned into the amber liquid. Suppose that they were right. Suppose that Trent was, indeed, a tool of Vade. There was at least a chance of that, a good chance even, or they would not have sent him to Knaxos at all. And he must have hidden it very well indeed, or the elves themselves would have found out, not sent him halfway across the continent to Knaxos and the mindmages.

And yet…and yet…

He didn't believe it. He was fallible, certainly, but the only rat he smelled right now was a pink-eyed one sitting in the House of Diamond. And if Sinai were—

Sinai would have been calling for blood.

He took another drink, to quell the growl growing in his throat.

⟫

The Silent Walk was a chamber four feet wide and thirty feet long, with a door at one end. The door was thick stone, uncarved on the inside, and it fitted into the lintel so closely that one of Sadrao's whiskers would not have fit into the crack.

It was completely silent.

Trent had been awake for nearly a minute before he realized it because he could not hear his own breathing. His hands scrabbled at the stone, their nails scraping across the hewn granite, and made less sound than a mouse running across thick carpet.

He was a prisoner.

He rose and went to the door. It was locked. There was no handle on this side.

There were no windows. It was dark as pitch.

Panic engulfed him and he threw himself at the door like an animal in a trap.

His body struck noiselessly. His fists made no sound.

He screamed.

Nothing.

Am I deaf?

He threw himself at the door again.

That bastard Archmage!

"Let me out!" he shouted, again and again, screaming threats and promises, begging with no pride at all. Only silence came out. His throat was raw from the volume, and yet there was nothing, nothing at all.

What is going on?!

Oh god, even the Council never locked me up like this…

Claustrophobic memories threw iron bands across his chest. His head swam.

There were cells under Ironspine, hewn out of the rock, rooms so dark that you no longer believed in light. Rooms full of things that Vade had not summoned, but which were drawn to the echoes of power and pain that his magic created, things that had crawled under the earth and up from the ground to feed.

Things old and powerful, and bound by rules and rituals that no one remembered anymore.

Trent knew those rooms intimately, as prisoner and jailer both.

I can't go back. I can't let them take me back.

Oh, by all the gods—and Lyra's Goddess! Don't let Vade find me, now that we've stopped moving! At least let that bastard Archmage do that much!

He slumped to the floor again and put his head in his hands. His heart pounded in his ears.

His heart pounded in his ears.

He could hear that.

Trent closed his eyes and listened, hard, to that one sound, inside him. After a few moments, as he rested, it grew slower and quieter, but he could still hear it.

There was a very soft whisper at the bottom of each exhalation, too, the sound inside his lungs.

On a sudden hunch, he pinched his nostrils shut and exhaled, forcing the pressure in his ears to equalize with a *pop!*

He could hear all the sounds inside of him, but every sound that entered the air vanished, sucked into the walls, deadened so that not even a suggestion of them remained.

It was bizarre.

It was terribly unnerving.

Trent had never stopped to think about how much noise a person made. Moving. Clothes rustling. Muttering to oneself. But this deadly silence swallowed all of that, negating the sound of his existence.

You could go mad in a room like this.

Why? Why put me in here?

He paced up and down the thirty-foot walk a few times, then stopped. The not-sound of his footsteps was too much.

Does he think I'm one of those sorcerers who has to make sounds to make magic?

He was wary of magic now, but the Archmage's magic *should* keep Vade from noticing any small spell of Trent's—and to be honest, he couldn't bear not knowing. If his magic worked, he knew, he'd try to break out.

What would Sinai say if I ran from the House of Diamond? he asked himself ruefully, imagining his aunt's response.

She wouldn't say anything. She'd take it as confirmation, and let her sword do the talking.

Oh, well. In for a penny… He summoned light.

It didn't come.

He tried again, thinking about it very carefully, now, mentally etching each sigil of power in red on the inside of his eyes. Not a big light. Just a little amber glow around the fingers, the sort that came when you tried most of the more powerful magics anyway, as power bled off into the ether.

Nothing.

Sorcery was learned, he had told Lyra, and that was true. You learned to understand and visualize an entire language of sigils and forms—not so much symbols of power as conduits through which power was channeled to assume any number of forms, as simple as warming one's hands or complex enough to heal, or destroy, an entire forest.

Light was one of the simplest. One rune to channel the power and one to give it form, both of them basic, geometric, easy.

I could make light when I was nine. I could make light half-dead, half-sick, bound and gagged, with bugs crawling on me and somebody's knife in my ribs. I could make light without calling on more power than is contained in my smallest toe. I haven't had to shed blood for a spell that small in twelve years.

Inexplicably, the room stayed dark.

Trent curled up in a ball, his back to the wall, and listened to the sound of his own heart.

Within an hour, Lyra was, true to form, drunker than an acolyte on stolen wine. Sadrao's eyes were suspiciously bright. His charge was crooning the old, filthy song about the milkmaid and the virtuous wolverine, off-key. He kept time with his tail and one claw.

"…For I've an itch I cannae scratch," Lyra warbled, into her drink, "and your claws I ken no man can match…"

Sadrao flicked his ears, and wondered where the hell a human as sheltered as Lyra had picked up a drinking song like that.

"...Me claws be not the only part/ no human man ca' match, dear heart..."

Sadrao winced in anticipation of the next line.

It did not arrive.

With a shrill yell, like a saw blade over metal, something lithe and white landed in the middle of the table. Empty glasses scattered under it. Sadrao started and reached for his sword.

Lyra shoved back from the table, her reflexes absolutely shot, and her chair went over backwards. She was on the way to the floor when an enormous, furry hand, larger than her head, with blunt, inch-long claws, caught the back of the chair and set her neatly upright.

"Sadrao, you old dog," said the owner of the hand in a volcanic rumble, octaves lower than either Sadrao's or Trent's baritone. "Still herding children around like a mother duck, I see."

"Not even a proper furred one, this time," said the slender white form on the table, looking at Lyra.

Lyra stared at it—her—

She was a Ferran, one of the slim, delicate ermine-women, her fur snow white, her eyes blood-black and bright. She was barely three feet tall, her tail a good two feet long with an elegant black tip.

Her teeth were small and white and as sharp as the narrow rapier that hung from a belt at her low waist. Like Sadrao, she was not overly concerned with human notions of modesty—her black leather vest and fringed belt were strictly adornment over bare fur. Slightly thinner fur along her belly showed pale skin in two lines down her chest, dotted with small white mammaries. Her whiskers were several inches long, framing a small, twitching black nose.

Her companion, his hand still on the back of Lyra's chair, was a Slothan. The floorboards groaned when he moved. He stood over seven feet tall, towering over Sadrao (who, despite his lean, rangy musculature, was *not* a small creature) and was built more like a small mountain than anything else.

Lyra had seen—once—a massive ground sloth from which the Slothan race claimed distant descent. They stood over ten feet tall at the shoulder and weighed as much as three large horses. They were placid, docile animals, despite their massive claws, preferring lumbering flight to confrontation.

This creature was significantly smaller, probably no more than six hundred pounds, covered in thick, shaggy brown fur. The armor strapped across his body was primarily shoulder and joint protection, but gave a chilling testament that this sloth, unlike his cousin, was ready and willing for battle. Lyra couldn't imagine a sword penetrating the long fur, thick hide, and heavy layer of fat with any kind of skill. It would take a very determined swordsman—no wonder the ornate armor was mostly over vulnerable areas.

"Gunnar," said Sadrao in disbelief, rising. "Spite." A grin broke across his features, and he rushed to the Slothan and flung his arms around him. "The gods have their ears up," he said into the shag of the Sloth's fur, sounding deeply relieved.

"Good to see you, too," rumbled Gunnar, hugging the dog-soldier carefully. His wrists were as thick as Lyra's thigh, and he could have crushed Sadrao's spine in an instant. "Heard a dog-soldier arrived in Knaxos. Figured it might be you."

Spite was bobbing her head back and forth like a rattlesnake as she studied Lyra. Lyra had read about Ferran, even if she'd never had much contact with them. Her father hadn't invited many non-humans home, for some reason. She subjected Spite to the same thoughtful scrutiny, careful not to make direct eye contact, and kept her lips over her teeth when she smiled.

Abruptly, the Ferran put her nose practically against Lyra's and sniffed. Lyra stifled a recoil—she was too drunk to have reflexes any more, even if the Ferran's presence was sobering her rapidly—and sniffed back. The ermine smelled like sea air and salt, with a faint, but distinct, undertone of musk. It was not entirely unpleasant, but Lyra wouldn't have wanted to be in a closet with her for a very long time.

"I like this one," said Spite, sitting up. "Smells like booze and books. Try not to get her killed, Sadrao." Her voice was high and harsh, like a blue jay's scream.

Sadrao released Gunnar and offered Spite a grave hand. The ermine eyed it suspiciously, then launched herself at the dog-soldier, flowing in a white stream up his arm and around his shoulders. She poked her face up between his ears—which were as large as her head—and flicked her tail across his eyes.

"It's been a while," she said cheerfully, as the dog-soldier batted playfully at her tail. "You've gotten slow."

"I'm a bit drunk," said Sadrao honestly.

"Mmm. That explains it, then." She gathered herself like a cat on his shoulder, then sprang to Gunnar, who stood with the patience of a large dog being climbed on by small children.

"So what brings you to Knaxos?" asked Gunnar, lowering himself to the floor. There were no chairs to fit his giant frame, but even sitting on his haunches he was eye-level to Sadrao. Spite perched on his broad shoulder and groomed her tail with her tongue.

"Elves," said Sadrao. "Sinai."

"Trouble," rumbled Gunnar.

"Sinai? Your infamous elven friend?" asked Spite. "Gunnar's told me about her."

"Indeed." Sadrao rubbed his forehead. "It starts with her cousin-son."

He briefly outlined the situation. Lyra set her whiskey aside and confined herself to cider.

She almost protested the detail that Sadrao was going into, which included Vade and the dire situation of the elven nation—not that she didn't trust Sadrao's friends, but this was hardly a private location. She closed her mouth, however, when she realized that Sadrao was speaking in the more obscure dialect of High Trader, common to the south of Lyra's home, but almost entirely displaced by trade-tongue this far north of the Tanglelore Hills. While it was possible that someone in this bar spoke High Trader, it wasn't likely. It was even less likely that it was their first language, and with Sadrao's peculiar growling accent, they would have had to listen very carefully to make sense of the speech, laced as it was with words from dog-soldier and Elvish.

For their part, Spite and Gunnar listened intently. Gunnar's small black eyes flicked occasionally from Sadrao to Lyra and back. Lyra could not shake the feeling of being studied by an interested iron mountain.

Spite continued to groom herself, demonstrating all the flexibility—and shamelessness—of a cat. Lyra was almost taken in by the Ferran's apparent indifference, but then she noticed that the small pink ears were always rotated to catch Sadrao's voice, no matter what contortions the ermine was engaged in.

"So," said Gunnar when Sadrao had finished, "it sounds like you need our help."

Sadrao lifted the tan patches of fur that doubled as eyebrows. "Yes. But you heard what I said. There's sorcery involved, and a war. I don't know how much profit there is in it."

"Doesn't matter," mumbled Spite, worrying at the fur between her toes with her teeth. Her spine made an impossible S-curve from ears to the tip of her tail. "Owe you one from the Redwing campaign. Pulled me out of the wreck before the Tchang fire sank her to the waterline." Her fur spiked briefly, and she began to soothe it irritably with her tongue. "Haven't forgotten that," she added through a mouthful of belly fur.

"Nor have I," added Gunnar. "The elves can pay us, if there's a war to be fought. First, though, we have to rescue your boy."

"Mmm. Yes. I don't know how to proceed. Perhaps we should try to find someone who knows the inside of the House of Diamond."

Gunnar smiled slightly, and shifted his gaze innocently to the rafters. "Hmmm. Yes."

Sadrao eyed him warily.

Spite abandoned her grooming and propped her chin up on her elbows, in between Gunnar's ears. "Might know," she purred. "Might just know someone like that."

Lyra covered her hand with her mouth to hide her grin.

"Spite," said Sadrao, obviously amused, "you didn't."

"Wasn't on Knaxos by accident," said Spite with a high-pitched chuckle. "Got a job. Needed to copy an old map for a friend. Thing is, whitecoats got it locked up tight."

"So you went in to get it," said Sadrao, amused. "Posing as a librarian?"

"Only briefly," said Gunnar, rolling his eyes up to his companion. "She's not good at intellectual debate, I'm afraid."

Spite bit his ear lightly. "Got in," she said. "Got thrown out again, but I found the vents." She leveled a claw at Sadrao. "Vents everywhere. Old style stonework. They go everywhere in the building. You get in them, go everywhere."

"*You* can go everywhere," said Sadrao. "I'd hardly fit."

"She would," said Spite, jerking her chin at Lyra. Lyra looked up, startled. "Get her in the vents, go find your elf-boy. You distract whitecoats. We'll keep a boat ready. Time it with the tide, get in, get out again. Go myself, but I'm not welcome in there anymore."

"You got your map copied?" asked Sadrao, amused.

"Copied. Sent by pigeon. Small thing." She made a gesture with two claws held slightly apart. "Come. I draw a map, show you where to get into vents."

She leapt down on the table and traced a claw through the stickiness of spilled ale.

Lyra and Sadrao bent over the table.

⸎

Trent must have slept, because the sudden spill of light from the doorway caught him by surprise. His eyes watered as he squinted toward the door, holding up a hand to block the brightness.

The figure silhouetted in the doorway made an imperious beckoning gesture with one hand.

Trent lifted an eyebrow.

A dark hand reached in, plucked him off the floor, and hauled him out.

Sound returned so abruptly that his ears popped painfully, yet so welcome that even his guard's truncated curse sounded like an aria. Trent scuffed his foot along the floor and laughed out loud in relief to hear the sound, and then again, in surprise, at his own laughter.

He could have done a spell, or three, or four. Even when the guard cuffed his hands in front of him and shoved him forward with a hand between his shoulderblades he could have done one. But he didn't. If this was all some horrible mistake—and surely it must be—killing a guard would not make resolving it any easier. If he could just speak to the Archmage this could be straightened out.

Trent squared his shoulders and went forth to be reasonable and conciliatory.

Trent was propelled headlong into the Archmage's spell chambers and fell to his knees on the stone floor. He looked up, shaking his head dizzily, his ears still singing with completely inappropriate joy at hearing sound again—even the sounds of cursing and struggling coming from another quarter of the room.

The Archmage shut the door behind them. Trent sat up as the Archmage crossed the room behind him.

"Let's talk about this," the half-elf said hoarsely. "There's been some mistake. Surely we can…"

He stopped.

There was a woman in the room with them, bound and on her knees, but not gagged. When she heard Trent speak she started yelling in earnest.

Trent had a sudden horrible feeling that if any mistake had been made, he'd been the one to make it.

The Archmage backhanded her casually. She fell to the floor. Trent could see her face under a fall of short, dark hair—an angry, young face, a few years younger than Trent himself, with furious, intelligent eyes, a Roman nose and strong jaw, and a voice like an enraged alley cat.

"*You sonofabitch, I don't care if you are the Archmage, untie me or I'll shove my knife so far up your ass you'll be spitting out iron filings!*"

Trent, despite the terribly dire circumstances, felt a pang of amusement.

The Archmage rolled her out of the way with one white-slippered foot, something he could do because she was trussed up like a turkey. She jackknifed in place and tried to bite his foot. Trent gave her points for stubbornness.

"Why are you doing this?" he asked the Archmage angrily. "What did *she* do—keep a book out on loan too long?"

The Archmage ignored them both and picked up a wand from a nearby table. The spell chamber was mostly bare except for a rack containing various magical accoutrements and a few low tables. The floor was marked with runes. Trent, his head still throbbing, sneered a little at the wand. Such talismans were generally the tools of younger wizards, little better than magical security blankets.

"You touch me with that thing," said the dark-haired captive furiously, "and I'll rip your lungs out!" She writhed against the ropes, succeeding only in drumming her heels on the stone floor.

Gesturing with the wand, the Archmage began to chant. Trent frowned, trying to get the energy to stand...and then the import of the syllables began to imprint themselves on his mind.

His eyes went wide. Behind them, he could see the runes starting to form, could see the sigil that meant *proxy,* and the dark, elegantly efficient figure that meant *Vade.*

Why is the Archmage summoning Vade's proxy?

Unless—

No. Surely not.

The Archmage finished a particularly long passage and looked down at Trent with a sinister smile. His mild, scholarly features were particularly ill-suited to the expression. He looked like a white rat.

"Why are you doing this?" asked Trent hoarsely, staring into those watery pink eyes.

"Vade will be most interested to see that I have you," said the Archmage thoughtfully. "I should receive quite a reward for you..." He tapped his wand against the palm of his hand.

Oh, by Lyra's Goddess.

He's sold out the elves.

Bizarrely, Trent's foremost feeling at that moment was not fear, or anger, but sorrow...sorrow for Sinai, of all people, who had hoped that the House of Diamond might unlock the secrets of Trent's mind...who did not deserve to be betrayed again.

"What is he offering you?" croaked Trent. "Money? Power? What made you betray the elves? Treasure?"

The Archmage looked slightly offended. "Of course not," he said. "Such things are merely temporary. The Lord of Ironspine gives me knowledge, great secrets of the ages."

Trent nodded slowly at that. The Archmage gave him an appraising look and began chanting again.

Knowledge. Of course. The only worthy coin for mages. Already on his knees, he sank down onto his elbows. *For knowledge he betrays the elves, sells me back to my sire, and kills this girl.*

For what? The names of every star? The Word that sets the tree spirits free to dance? The recipe for that spicy sauce that they make down in Dhena, with the pine nuts and the cilantro?

Oh, very funny. He's going to kill this girl—that's knowledge enough for you, I think.

Trent looked up at the struggling woman.

If he could have killed her, he would have. It would have been mercy, but the spell that had bound him was still filling his bones with lead. He could not reach her in time to strangle her, and the magic—

He didn't dare try magic. Did he?

Oh gods, if I have the power, I should, and risk be damned. She's barely older than Lyra. She doesn't deserve to get burned to a husk by Vade's mind, no one deserves that—

He caught her eyes. He could feel the runes starting to form, bubbles rising from the depths of his mind and breaking on the surface, in elegant scripted lines and curves.

Her eyes were dark brown, totally unmagical. There wasn't a drop of magecraft in her soul, not even the deep, half-animistic power of Lyra's Kytha. All she had was rage and stubbornness, and the grace that young women, regardless of magic, usually have. Trent ached for her.

The spell in his head was a killing spell. It was nothing so crude as stopping the heart—it would cause a single, massive brain hemorrhage that would kill her instantly and painlessly. Trent filled in the lines of the sigils as quickly as he could and knew as he worked that it would not be quick enough.

And because there was nothing else he could think of to say, he said "I'm sorry. I won't forget you."

She stared at him, her mouth open, and said, "Who in the Thirty-Seven Hells of the Burnt Man are *you?*"

He shook his head. "Doesn't matter," he said, feeling the magic building in the Archmage's voice, in the very stones of the room. The runes in his head were not keeping pace. He was too tired, too battered, too slow.

Oh goddess, I'm sorry, girl. I'm not going to be able to do this in time.

If he could have chanted aloud, without attracting the Archmage's attention, he might have been able to do it...but no.

He could feel the magic pressing down around them, pressure inside his skull like being too far below sea level.

"You're going to die in a moment," he said quietly. "Your mind's going to be taken over by a mage, and I can't stop it. I'm sorry."

Brown eyes went wide and white at the rims. "No. You're insane."

"I'm sorry," he said again. "If you tell me your name, I'll try to—I'll see that someone remembers. It's all I can do."

"Hester," she said, obviously still stunned. "And who are... *So, Archmage, you've summoned my attention...*"

The voice was Vade's. The girl had convulsed twice, her throat working, and suddenly that deep, silky voice was issuing from her throat. Trent let out of a low moan of sorrow and recognition. That voice was enough to smash Trent flat, like the paw of an enormous beast on his spine. The half-elf shuddered.

The power in the room suddenly flared up, and the Archmage stopped speaking. Trent fought the urge to cower down and hide behind his hands.

It's not really Vade, it's not really Vade, it's just an imprint, just a proxy, not really Vade.

"What do you want, Archmage?" flowed Vade's voice from the girl's throat.

"I've captured the boy," said the Archmage. "The one you wanted." His voice was cringing and subservient.

Fool, thought Trent, *to think that you can serve the tiger, and not be eaten.*

The girl, Hester, was looking at Trent. Tendons stood out like whipcords in her throat, and something fought like a mad animal in her eyes. In Trent's mind the sigils were almost complete.

"I—I—" The girl's voice choked high up on the scale.

The power flashed. Her voice broke, and her pupils expanded to thin her irises down to a ring of brown, and Trent knew, quite clearly, that the girl named Hester was gone.

As simply as that. As easily as that, Vade snuffs out a life.

"Did I do well, master?" asked the Archmage. "Will you give me the knowledge you promised?"

Vade's proxy ignored him. "Trent?!" The voice was surprised...and then amused. "How—"

Trent said nothing. The sigils were falling into place in his head, and he opened his mouth to speak the word.

" —not supposed to be there—"

"NO!" shouted Trent, not wanting to hear what the voice said, the terrible possibility that maybe he wasn't acting on his own at all, maybe Vade had allowed him to escape, maybe the elves were right, maybe *Sinai* was right, and he didn't know it, and—

He spoke the final word.

The proxy died at once. Vade could have stopped him, but this was not really Vade, only an imprint of him. Somewhere, staring into a pool of magma, the real Vade would have seen his proxy convulse. Blood was leaking from Hester's nose and ears. Her head struck the floor with a hollow wet sound.

Trent dropped his head back to the floor with a moan. The power that had briefly flowed had been dredged up from resources he barely had. He groaned.

When the Archmage, in a fury of thwarted frustration, began kicking him, Trent could only curl up into a ball and pray for the kindness of unconsciousness.

⤞

He roused briefly when the guards took him out of the room, hanging limply between them. He did not seem to be too badly injured, merely exhausted from the magic he should not have had to cast. He struggled to raise his head.

For a moment he thought exhaustion and despair had made him hallucinate, for there was a dog soldier in the hall.

She was the color of sunlight on ice, more slender than Sadrao, lithe instead of lean. Her fur caught the light with a glitter like snow. She looked like an angel, or a ghost.

Trent did not stop to think that her white fur meant she was a member of the House of Diamond, and thus served the Archmage. He did not think much of anything, except that this was a dog-soldier, and salvation.

His sudden lunge caught his captors off guard, and he broke free. Not far—he couldn't have moved far in any case—but he managed a stumbling run down the hall and caught the startled dog-soldier's forearm, falling to his knees literally at her feet.

Her fur glittered like snow. She looked like an angel, or a ghost.

"Help me," he begged, looking up, into blue eyes so pale they were almost white themselves. "Please—you're a dog-soldier—you have to help me. The Archmage just killed a girl—"

His guards descended and yanked him away. The dog-soldier's face was cool, watching without expression as they dragged him backwards down the hall.

If his eyes had not been fastened on hers, if he had not traveled with Sadrao for long enough to read the subtlest signs, he would not have seen the briefest flicker across her face, the stricken look of grief and overwhelming guilt. He sagged and watched the white figure recede into the distance, as remote and unhelpful as a star.

Chapter Sixteen

In the next two days Lyra had ample time to reflect on the bizarre nature of planning.

Particularly planning a covert mission.

It seemed to be based on nothing so much as a series of assumptions, all of them stacked inside each other like nested egg-cups, assumption after assumption.

Gunnar and Spite would have a boat ready to sail with the night tide. Lyra was under the assumption that the captain was the "friend" that had been so interested in certain maps. She asked Spite, half-serious, if they were treasure maps.

For weighing less than seventy pounds, the ermine woman could roar with laughter with the best of them.

"Nah, nah," she gasped, her tail spasming like a hysterical serpent. "Sailing maps. Rocks. Safe passage down the Whipcrack Coast, instead of paying those blood-sucking lemurian pilots." She wiped at her small black eyes. "Treasure, yah, yah. What kind of pirate buries treasure? Big X, yo ho ho, and a dead weasel's bones."

The boat was taken care of.

Everything else was assumption.

Assume that they could find Spite's vents and get in without being seen. Assume that Trent was being held in a ventilated area. *Don't* assume that his cell had a vent panel—assume Lyra would have to get out and get into the chamber.

Assume that there would be at least one guard.

And at this point, in Lyra's opinion, the assumptions broke down completely, because Sadrao told her flatly that she would have to deal with the guard.

"Don't try more than one," he said. "Don't forget you don't have a sword or a staff. And if you can, come up behind him, or lead him on a chase." He paused and gave her a drop-muzzled grin. "Don't underestimate the value of being small and female for making men underestimate *you*."

"Oh. Joy," said Lyra heavily, while the bottom dropped out of her stomach. "The last time I fought someone it didn't go so well."

"The last time, you fought *six* men," said Sadrao dryly. "The time before that, you did quite well."

"The time before that, I was on Jegger." Lyra scratched at her chin. "We *are* going through Frieze to get the horses afterwards, aren't we?"

"Yes," said Sadrao. "Don't change the subject."

"Jegger wouldn't fit in the vents anyway."

The dog-soldier's tail wagged briefly, even though he rolled his eyes. "To continue," he said. "Do NOT allow him to raise the alarm." His bronze eyes held hers, no trace of humor in them now. "Kill him if you must."

Lyra blanched. "*Kill* him? But—"

Sadrao tilted his head, candlelight gleaming on the gold rings in his ears.

"I am not saying you should murder him," the dog-soldier said quietly. "Forgive me if I say this ungently, but we have no time to be gentle. There is something bad going on here, something with sorcery in it. I smell it. I feel it in my claws, and my stomach, and the tip of my tail." He paused. "The elven nation may be in terrible danger. Trent *is* in terrible danger. Is a man's life worth that?"

Lyra stared at him, with a lump in her throat.

"You may not have to," said Sadrao calmly. "Try not to, in fact. But if you must kill him, can you do it?"

Trent. For Trent.

She tried to call up the image of Trent, his face, the way his hands felt. The weight of his body when he had fallen across her to shield her from the furnace blast of the Phoenix. Trent expounding at great length on some obscure bit of knowledge that they both, out of all the people on the continent, found fascinating.

Trent.

All she could see was Lisette, lying in a pool of dried black, killed in a conflict that had nothing to do with her, that wasn't her fault.

"I don't know," she said honestly, to Sadrao. "If I have to, maybe. But I don't know."

Sadrao gripped her shoulder briefly. "I *do* know," said the dog-soldier. "You're stronger than you know."

And then they plunged back into planning, too quickly for Lyra to really internalize the notion of killing a man deliberately. Assumption after assumption. Assume that she found Trent, that they managed to get him back in the vents. Assume that they could get back to their entry point. Assume that Sadrao met them there, assume that they could get out of the building, assume that Sadrao would be able to come up with some kind of distraction. Assume that they could get to the boat before the tide, before the alarm was raised.

Assume that the Archmage would not be able to stop them with a single flick of magical power.

Assumption after assumption after assumption. The only hard facts were that the House of Diamond loomed impregnable, with Trent somewhere behind its walls, that he had been gone for two days.

It would have been romantic, Lyra thought, to have dreadful nightmares of his captivity, but she was so exhausted from hours of arguing ridiculous possibilities and options, and from Spite's impromptu vent-crawling lessons ("Follow your whiskers! Follow your—oh, wait, never mind.") that she slept like the most somnolent of logs.

And then it was two days gone, and the boat was ready in a sheltered cove, and she and Sadrao were walking with falsely confident strides up to the doors of the House of Diamond.

"But what are *you* going to be doing?" Lyra asked plaintively, keeping an eye out for white-clad librarians.

"Simple," grunted Sadrao, the heavy cords of his arms standing out as he muscled the iron cover from the vent. "Planning for catastrophe." He set the grille down and gave her a wolfish grin.

Lyra opened her mouth in dismay, and shut it again. The vent was barely two feet on a side—large enough for Lyra to crawl through, but impossible for Sadrao's broad shoulders. "Oh, crap."

"Lovely *and* articulate," said Sadrao, settling the grate quietly to the floor. He reached under his cloak and slid a hand up under his tunic to the small of his back. Lyra lifted an eyebrow as the dog-soldier made a contortionist's wriggle, then pulled a long-knife from where he had concealed it against his back. He handed it to her, hilt first. "Take this with you. In tight places, one should never go unarmed."

Lyra swallowed hard and slid the knife through her belt. "Where will you be?" she asked dismally, as Sadrao made a stir-rup with his hands. She set her foot into the tough black palms.

He tossed her into the vent as if she weighed considerably less. "I," he said, looking up to meet her eyes, "will be somewhere very visible, arranging a cover story if you get caught."

Lyra, fear settling like lead in her belly, leaned down and dropped a kiss between Sadrao's eyes. "It's been fun," she said, with forced levity. "See you in a few hours."

"Be careful, Lyra," said Sadrao gravely. "If something goes wrong, find Gunnar and Spite at the dock and get away from here." He stretched up a fur-backed hand and ruffled her hair. "I am proud to have had the honor of teaching you."

"Shut up," said Lyra, her voice shaking. "I'll see you in a few hours, and you're buying the drinks."

He grinned at her, eyes citrine bright in the shadows. "Don't I always?"

She turned around because there were tears in her eyes, and she had some shred of pride left, at least. The stone was cool and dusty under her hands as she began crawling on all fours through the vent. She heard Sadrao slide the grate back into place behind her, and she tried not to feel as if the jaws of a trap were closing around her.

The light faded around her. For a moment, as her eyes strug-gled against the dark, she wondered if she should have brought a lamp, and then reflected that, while the sounds of a large rat in the wall would attract no attention, a rat carrying a lantern would undoubtedly bring white-clad guards running.

She began crawling again, fingers brushing against the stone. A passage opened on her left. Lyra paused with her fingers groping in the empty darkness, feeling like a worm struggling blind through the tunnels of the earth. Should she take the passage? How was she to know?

Sadrao trusted her to find the way. Sadrao trusted her, so it was obviously within her capabilities.

Lyra held her breath, listening, trying to feel the air currents swirling around her. *Feel with your whiskers. Gods, if only I had whiskers!*

The Cat Kytha won't even work in here—there's not enough light. Pity there's not a Bat Kytha.

Well, there probably is, but Sinai didn't know it.

Are you going to sit here talking to yourself, or are you going to listen?

Lyra shut off her internal dialogue and listened carefully in the dark.

She heard nothing at first, and tried not to imagine silent, shadowy beasts creeping up on her from the dark, open hole on her left.

Unconsciously, she found herself pressed against the right wall, inching past the dark opening. Air going to the rare-book libraries must come from the ground floor below, filtered by stone and grates to prevent any kind of weathering to the precious tomes. By the same token, air to the basement level below would also come filtered through the ground floor first, so that the delicate contents of the workrooms and magic storehouses would not be disturbed by the moist sea air. Heating was more of a concern in cold Knaxos than cooling, so large air intakes would not be scattered all over the building. At least if anything she'd read about architecture had been accurate. Not that she'd read a great deal about it—that and mathematics had been what she slogged through when she'd exhausted everything else in the library. But the theory ought to be sound.

"Therefore," said Lyra inaudibly, beginning to crawl down the corridor, "I just have to find where the air is coming from, and then where it's going. Easy as falling off a log." Her palms were damp against the stone.

A faint breeze cooled her face, tugging at her hair. Her foot brushed the open space of the left turning, catching slightly on the corner. The hair on the back of her neck rose as she crawled, leaving the empty opening behind her. If something came at her, she would be unable even to turn around in the narrow confines of the tunnel.

Nothing's there. Spite was here just a week ago.

Claustrophobia was beginning to gnaw at her in earnest, the massive weight of the House of Diamond pressing down on her, tons of rock and long centuries, each meticulously recorded in the books that would bury her under their crushing weight. She could not breathe in the incense-clogged vents, her throat closing, gagging on spice and sandalwood and terror.

It was—gods, it was *just* like being in the linen closet with the raiders in the house, too cramped to move. Was it only two months ago? Surely not. She tallied the weeks to distract herself. Two months, and a week or so in change.

Gods, even she couldn't believe the difference.

I am not the scared girl I was then. No. Absolutely not. I am a Kythar, and a friend of elves. I am in love. I think.

Sadrao is proud of me.

That got her moving again, a few more feet. From a little library mouse Sadrao and Sinai had molded the possibility of a warrior, however unlikely. Ironically, it was books, once her only escape, that were now likely to be the death of her.

Lyra had grown up loving books, but she felt suddenly, irrationally afraid of those around her, of thousands of volumes that weighted down the stones over her head. She would be drowned in dusty, yellowed paper and unread words. White-clad librarians would record her death in more books and shake their heads over the bloodstains she had left on irreplaceable volumes.

"Couldn't trust her," they would say, in their dry, papery voices. "Controlled by a sorcerer, no doubt. Pity."

She hung her head in the dark confines of the vent, breathing heavily. Sadrao was counting on her. He wouldn't let something as trivial as a thousand tons of stone stop him. Lyra started moving again.

Another passage opened, on her right this time. She moved doggedly past it, and the next one. On the fourth passage, to the left this time, she paused. A breeze was blowing from it, smelling faintly—so faintly—of salt, fresh and sharp against the heaviness of incense. She turned, scraping her fingers on the stone, and began crawling again.

Empty space opened under her outstretched hand. She froze, and a shudder slid down her spine. Stretching out her hand, she could not find the far end of the pit.

Blind. *Hmm.* She laid down flat and extended her arm into space. Air was coming from below. She had found the vent down. *Thank the gods.*

Her fingers felt nothing. She clamped her teeth on a whimper. Trent was depending on her, even more than Sadrao. She loved Trent. Didn't she?

Well, of course I do, and this is a really *crummy place for second thoughts.*

Did she love him more than she feared the dark closed space around her?

It doesn't matter, she decided, stretching over the vent and aware of the rank smell of her own fear. Whether or not she loved him, he was her friend and she would have crawled down here for Sinai or Jacyl or dear, gallant Sadrao as well.

"You better appreciate this," she muttered to an absent Trent, and dragged herself forward with her free hand and scrabbling feet. Her face and neck extended over the pit, and then her groping fingers found the far edge.

Quickly, so she wouldn't have time to think about it, she grabbed the stone lip and swung her hips forward, suspending herself in the vent by a hand on each side, legs dangling down into the shaft. Her heart raced as she leaned far back, shoulders and neck pressed against the wall, wedged her feet on either side, and began shinnying down the vent like a rock climber in a narrow crack.

Her descent was terrifying. It was too fast to be well controlled, her angle growing steeper and steeper, and she could feel skin flaying off her hands as they scrabbled against the rock. Trying to stop—even to slow—would have been a death sentence. She skittered down the vent, perilously close to losing control of her descent, and wondered if she would have any skin left on her hands when she hit bottom.

Light blossomed under her. A dark opening yawned suddenly in front of Lyra and her feet shot into empty space. She caught her legs in the side-passage, and would probably have begun falling headfirst to her death, but a huge iron intake grate appeared opposite the passage. Lyra threw out both hands in a desperate scrabble and hooked her fingers in the metal grille. With a jerk that threatened to tear her arms from the sockets, she stopped.

She thought her arms—and fingers—would be wrenched apart. Something gave inside her left hand with a sharp, popping pain—probably one of those tiny little bones. *Thank the gods it was my left hand,* she thought grimly, then bit her lips on a shriek as a similar pain shot through her right.

For a few seconds she could only hang on, determined not to scream, her legs caught several feet above her head while something warm and sticky trickled over her hands.

The cold, scholarly part of her mind noticed that her blood was dripping over a representation of Slath-Orn, the Goddess of the Wind, done in an elaborate wrought-iron style popular during the previous century. *Of course. What other goddess would you put on a ventilation system?*

The air in her face smelled like the sea. She was on the first level. *Down one more. Just one more.* The longer she waited, the worse it would be.

She pulled herself closer to the grate, praying that no one standing outside would notice the bloody fingertips hooked over the metal, and dragged her legs out of the opposite shaft.

Her intent was to cling to the grille long enough to wedge herself back into the rock-climber's descent. Lyra had realized that it would hurt, but she had not even guessed at how much it would hurt.

Ah—ah—owwww!

Fingers, already sorely abused, held her full weight for half a heartbeat, then gave way, leaving a smear of blood and at least one fingernail behind. Lyra twisted, kicked out hard, and failed utterly to catch herself.

Sinai might have been able to do it, but Sinai was ice and iron and Lyra only flesh and blood. Two months—even two months under Sadrao and the warrior Kythar—had made her more athletic than she had dreamed possible, but could not prepare her for this kind of challenge. Her head cracked against the wall, and bright grey flashes drifted across her vision.

Had the shaft continued straight down to the lowest level, she would have been killed, or crippled. At the very least she would have overshot her mark considerably. But a kind fortune, and an ancient architect, intervened.

Lyra landed in a sprawling crouch across a hard, damp surface. The impact knocked the wind out of her. A dark rectangle loomed before her, while the cool sea air slid past her aching body. Sobbing with effort, she clawed her way forward, got a full body-length into the passage, and collapsed.

She had landed across the heavy metal grate that filtered moisture from the air before passing it to the dry storerooms below. Condensation formed on the cold metal and dripped into a dozen narrow troughs under the grille. The troughs angled down to the wall, funneling the small amount of water away, out of sight. Wavering torchlight stabbed through the grate, making a hundred spearpoints in the darkness.

For a long time she waited, taking breath after shuddering breath. The sound of flesh hitting metal had seemed impossibly loud to her, but minutes dragged by and no one came to investigate.

She was cold. Her hands throbbed, and she curled around them in fetal position, cradling them against her body. The calluses of sword and quill had been shredded like parchment. Lyra wondered if she would ever hold either again. She stifled a whimper.

At that moment, lying wounded in the vents of the House of Diamond, Lyra was utterly beaten. She wanted to scream for Trent, Sadrao, Sinai, *anyone—!*

Had Vade Kingbreaker himself appeared and offered to set her a thousand miles away, she would have abandoned Trent and wept with gratitude at her salvation. She would have traded her immortal soul to be three feet below where she was, in the air and the light of the open corridor, instead of imprisoned in damp stone.

No one came to investigate the noise. No one magically appeared and offered rescue. Gradually her heart slowed, and Lyra took a deep breath without catching it in a silent sob.

It didn't matter that her hands hurt. Sadrao was elsewhere, risking his life to buy her time, and he couldn't help her. He could not save her life this time, or every time—he had done the best he could, and it was all up to her now. It didn't matter that her skin was clammy with shock and terror. Others were relying on her to do this thing.

I tried my best! she thought, self-pityingly, and then squelched the thought ruthlessly. That didn't matter either. If she tried and failed, others suffered. She had to succeed.

She thought of the Kytha. Snake Dance, fluid and slinking, gliding like oil, like blood. Sinai had said that it was good for slowing bleeding. She closed her eyes and summoned the images of the dance—the slow, boneless movements of the limbs, the flowing, sinuous curves of spine. Then, as Sinai had tried to teach her, she drew the power up from her body and sent it flowing into her hands.

Her hands seemed warmer, steadier. Lyra opened her eyes in the darkness and envisioned the Cat Kytha, electric-eyed, the prowler of dark spaces, unafraid. She took strength into her, and grace, then rolled to her hands and knees.

If I fail, someone else might pick up the slack—Sadrao, or Sinai, or someone I've never met—but then again, someone might not. Sadrao can't fight my battles for me. Sooner or later, I'll have to face Jasen, myself. Alone.

And even if Trent loves me, and stays with me, eventually it comes down to this. Being alone, in dark places, with yourself. In the end, it always comes to this.

Lyra crouched on her haunches and ripped a strip of cloth from the hem of her shirt with one aching hand and her teeth. It parted with a rip that sounded like thunder in her ears. She wound it carefully around the sticky pain of her palm, leaving the battered fingers free, then repeated the process on her other hand with another sacrificed strip of shirt.

She was the only person that she would be with for the rest of her life, for all her lives to come. Her friends might lend her strength, and knowledge, but ultimately, she must be able to go alone.

She must know that she was strong enough. She squared her shoulders and set her hands to the floor. They did not hurt as badly as she had feared. She gritted her teeth and began crawling through the vents, quick and sure and quiet. When a passage loomed to her left, dim grey in the blackness, she took it without hesitation.

She moved quickly through the ductwork, peering cautiously out through grates, forming a careful mental map of the area.

Under one of the grates she saw the warm shadows of lantern light, and cast across the floor like a black spearhead, the shadow of a guard.

She knew at once that the cell was nearby. She moved back down the tunnel—an unpleasant business, backing through the darkness, unable to turn until she reached the cross-vent—and went down it to the next vent. The rooms with vents were evenly spaced—storage rooms, libraries, archives. A sorcerer's workroom, to judge by the symbols etched across the floor. And after it—a break. She crawled forward, until she should have reached another vent. If her sense of distance was accurate, she knelt opposite the grate which had revealed the guard's shadow. She crawled another length forward and found another grille, this one to an unlighted room that smelled of must. In between the two there was a room without a vent.

A room where ventilation is less important than keeping someone from getting in or out. A cell, for example.

Guarded.

Hmm....

Unwilling to make a rash decision, she spent almost an hour slithering through the ducts, searching for another possibility. One corner of the building was not vented at all, but if memory served, that was the laboratory complex, which had its own separate system to prevent gases or corrosive fumes from pervading the building. Otherwise, the most likely candidate was the room beneath her—a narrow, surprisingly long room, like a hallway that went nowhere at all.

Well, maybe it's two cells back to back.

A guard. She truly didn't want to kill him—even assuming that she *could*, it would hardly improve matters to add murder to aiding the escape of a prisoner.

Sadrao says I can do it if I have to.

I'd really rather not have to.

Hmmm.

Invisibility was impossible, even had she been a Kythar of Sinai's quality. At best, she might go unnoticed, unremarked in plain sight, and the moment that she opened a door or did something to call attention to herself, she would be discouragingly visible. That was assuming she could even go unnoticed in the first place.

And let's be honest, that's highly unlikely. Can't even do the Hare Kytha for more than ten steps, never mind the Clouded Moon Kytha, or whatever the hell it is.

At last she settled on the vent into the unlit room next to Trent's cell. Pray the gods that it was Trent's cell, anyway. The grille was secured by metal screws threaded into the plaster from outside. The grille, however was not completely flush with the plaster—a narrow fraction of space remained.

Lyra drew her boot-knife, wedged the blade into the crack and began levering at the space. White dust filtered down into the room below. Hoping that no one would decide to use the room any time soon, she settled down to work.

⋘

Sadrao had waited until the barely audible rustle of Lyra's movements faded into the ventilation, then waited a few more minutes for good measure. After her scent had been buried under the potent incense he heaved a sigh, then forced a smile and strolled jauntily out into the House of Diamond.

He received directions from a thin, bespectacled young man whose pink eyes had Trent's myopic mildness, with none of the steel behind them. His stark white hair made him appear prematurely old, but he was eager to give Sadrao directions—*probably starved for an unfamiliar face*, thought the dog-soldier pityingly.

Following those directions led him in an ambling, roundabout path to one of the third floor libraries. He paused outside of several vents and listened, but Lyra appeared to be moving quietly indeed. He nodded, proud of the girl. She'd do well.

At last, he scented his quarry, and an involuntary grin spread across his canine features. Rounding a corner, he spotted her tall, pale form at the end of the row of shelves.

He opened his mouth to speak as she turned the far corner, her tail a white sweep behind her.

Sadrao broke into a jog, his claws clicking on the marble floor, and reached the corner just in time to see her turning down yet *another* corridor, only the tip of her flowing tail visible as it whisked away.

Sadrao muttered an obscenity and quickened his stride.

He reached the turn just as she was preparing to enter the stacks of shelves, where he might conceivably lose her for hours.

He howled.

It was not exactly a greeting—it was in fact the sort of yell that hunters use to let one another know where they are during the chase, or when traveling at night or in thick fog. Echoes shattered against the rows of leather spines. Sadrao could envision white heads popping up out of books in shock.

The white dog-soldier stopped dead in her tracks. She turned, already dropped into a defensive crouch and stared at him.

Sadrao strolled forward, holding up his hands in as non-threatening a gesture as he could conceive of, and said "Excuse me…"

There was a rather awkward moment when she remained crouched, almost at his feet, her eyes moving over him with a kind of blank amazement. It was a little embarrassing. He wasn't sure if he should drop to her level, or if she would then stand up, and he'd stand up, and then they'd be bobbing up and down like a pair of sandpipers.

Over seventy years old, he thought, a bit drolly, *and still beautiful women turn me into an idiot!*

She solved the problem by rising to her full height and stepping back. "Can I help you?" Her tone was not forbidding, but not exactly welcoming either.

"I certainly hope so," said Sadrao pleasantly, admiring the sight. Her fur was glacially white, the dark brindle of their race's markings transformed to cloudy whorls of pale grey. Her eyes were magnificently blue, a color rarely seen in dog-soldiers, and almost never without total blindness. Two plain silver rings gleamed in her ears, like ice among snow.

Almost without conscious thought, Sadrao dropped his shoulders slightly, posture loosening, letting his tall ears flatten a little.

It put them a little closer in height, and he could see her respond involuntarily to his friendly stance.

"Sadrao Majiid," he said, in his native tongue, "of the Sandblood Pack. Vayloor, the Dog-with-His-Back-to-the-Desert, stood as my sponsor."

An observer would have heard only curiously melodic whining. Even Lyra, with her halting knowledge of his language, could not have picked up a quarter of the nuance in that rich, musical speech.

"Iyara Salishi," she replied in the same tongue. "I was born to the Icemountain Pack. Kygra of the Nine Claws was my mother."

It was a standard courtesy, as normal as a human saying, "Good morning," and yet the smell that hit his nostrils had the acrid tang of intense distress.

Baffled, he bowed elegantly, even deeper than usual, spine arching, and straightened. She bowed solemnly in turn.

"Thank you, Sandblood," she said with a weak laugh. "I have not spoken my own language with someone for years. I had forgotten how it feels."

"Call me Sadrao," he said graciously. "And I would love to speak more with you at leisure, but there is a matter that weighs on my mind, and I had hoped that we might speak of it."

The distress scent roiled around her, her fur spiking, and he could see the quiver running through her hackles, the tremble in the furred fringe of her ears.

It took him a moment to recognize the signals as he blinked stupidly into her dilated blue eyes. In his defense, it was not something he had ever expected to see in another dog-soldier.

She was terrified of him.

He broke all courtesy and grabbed her forearm. She did not flinch away. She did not fear physical violence at his hands, then — it was something else. Something that roiled off her in great waves that stank of guilt and fear and shame.

It was Iyara that broke their tableau, as they stood staring at each other, both at a loss for how to proceed. She straightened up, and her ears swept forward, and with great effort she soothed her hackles down. "I suspect that I already know something of what weighs on your mind," she said, "and you may be able to explain more of what weighs upon mine."

Sometime later Sadrao was leaning back against a roughly plastered white wall in a small niche that, while not terribly comfortable, was also set so that it was nearly impossible for anyone to overhear a conversation. This was useful, because at least twice white-clad guards had walked by, eyeing them warily, even if none of them understood his native tongue.

His mind was a dreadful whirl.

Someone—and Sadrao was getting a sinking feeling that he knew who, even though he told himself there were many powerful men in the world, and there was no reason at all that the Lord of Ironspine should be involved—had been blackmailing Frieze. Frieze, in response, had been blackmailing the Archmage. The Archmage, desperate, had been engaging in a particularly vile form of blood magic to aid his efforts to negotiate with the shadowy figure behind it all, and Iyara had helped to secure the victims he needed.

"He said that he would stop," she said tonelessly, staring past him. "I told him there was no honor in it, and he said he had stopped. But I saw your friend, the half-elf, and he said the Archmage killed a girl. It must have been for another proxy. He has been securing others. Perhaps innocents."

She put her arms over her head, as if to shut out a world where such things might happen. One pale blue eye peered out at him through a cocoon of white fur. "I don't know why he wants the half-elf. The one blackmailing Frieze—and us—must want him for something."

Sadrao groaned. "It's Vade, or someone who knows Vade. It doesn't even really matter at this point, more's the pity. We have to get Trent out before the Archmage hands him over."

"I imagine your protégé is well on her way to doing so," said Iyara, a bit dryly. Sadrao blinked at her. She spread her hands, looking suddenly wry, a flash of the dog-soldier she must have been before guilt and shame had ground her down. "You would hardly have been so careful not to say where she was if she were not planning something nefarious."

"Hah! Yes, well…"

He did not want to push her. A dog-soldier's loyalties, even ones that had been so dreadfully abused, were not to be taken lightly, or broken at will.

"I will help you," she said, before he asked. "There are many guards, and many doors, between the cells and the outside." She sighed heavily and flicked her ears, and yet her scent was lighter, touched with purpose. "I can no longer trust the Archmage, after all, and I smell no evil on you."

"Thank you," said Sadrao Majiid.

⋘

Three stories below, Lyra was exploring cracks. She had worked two screws loose, dulling her knife considerably, and was almost finished with the third. White powder caked with dried blood on her hands to form an unpleasant pinkish grime.

The third screw yielded. She pushed down on the grate, feeling it pull away from the ceiling, and prayed that the last screw would hold the grate as she wriggled by it. Otherwise, her career as a cat-burglar would have a very quick, white-clad end as the clatter of fifty pounds of steel would bring the guards running.

Lyra pressed her feet against the edge of the grille and, suspending most of her weight on her much-abused hands, slid her feet over the edge and into empty space. Her calves followed, the leather protecting her (thank the gods) from the sharp edge of the grate, then knees and hips. The grate creaked dangerously.

Now came the tricky part. Sucking her breath in, and praying to any gods that might be in a good mood, she scooted her hands in front of her, hung dangerously unbalanced for a moment, and slithered into the crack. The metal creaked, groaned...(Lyra held her breath)...and held.

The grill swung on the single screw and pinched her fingers against the stone edge. She gritted her teeth and yanked her hands loose.

She fell only two or three feet, but her knees buckled on impact. Instinct—or the Kytha that Sinai had woken in her—took over and she rolled as she hit, slapping the ground, coming up in a crouch.

Reality exerted itself a moment later and she staggered and sat down hard.

Bodies are amazing things, really, Lyra reflected, staring up into the darkness while blood-rainbows danced before her eyes. Her hands throbbed painfully. *Trust them, and they'll carry you through almost anything. Try to second-guess matters, and you find out that you can't stand up.*

A few seconds slid by, and she sat up. *Well. That wasn't so bad.*

Bullshit, she thought dryly. *That was bloody awful.*

The room, she discovered, poking around cautiously, was, as she had thought, some type of storeroom. She lifted the lid on one chest and groped through it by feel. Fabric. Spools of thread. Thimbles. And—*ow! Damn!* Needles. She yanked her hand free, almost sucked the wounded finger, then remembered the bloody plaster dust coating her hands and refrained.

Sewing supplies. Hmmm.

Between Lyra and Trent was a guard. Hopefully he had the key—well, if he didn't, she'd cross that bridge when she came to it. She had to render him unconscious or distract him. Distraction seemed risky. Trying to knock him out was probably even worse. She gnawed on her lower lip.

What she needed, ideally, was both at once—a distraction that averted his notice long enough for her to slip out of the storeroom and sneak up and throttle him into unconsciousness.

And while we're at it, let's wish for a pet dragon to eat the guard right now, and a flying carpet to fly us out of here.

She turned her ring absently on her finger. Once. The pain made her subvocalize a number of words that Sadrao would have found hysterically funny. Swearing did not particularly help, but when she finished, she felt marginally better.

She moved quietly to the door. Listening for several minutes and hearing only the faint, unselfconscious fidgeting of the guard, she slipped a hand over the doorknob and turned it, very quietly. It was unlocked.

It occurred to her, somewhat belatedly, that she should probably have picked a vent several rooms away and tried to sneak through the corridors, so that the telltale opening of a door would not betray her. It was probably going to come down to a fight, and one slender girl was not going to—

Hmmmm…

Lyra looked down at herself thoughtfully. She was not at all an imposing presence. Not the sort that anyone would fear. If the guard was a man she might be able to fake her way in close—if it was a woman, she was going to have a more difficult time. Gods, if only she was an albino, or even just a blonde, to fit the dead-white pallor of the servants of the House of Diamond.

Well, she looked young and worse for wear, anyway. She pulled several lengths of fabric from the chest, setting aside what appeared to be a robe. Clumsy in the dark, she re-wrapped her fingers and straightened her clothing. Boatloads of scholars arrived from the mainland every day, some of them young students and their tutors. There was no use trying to pretend to be a member of the House, but she might pass for a young (and foolish) scholar.

She slid Sadrao's knife into her pants, feeling the leather sheath skidding against her thigh, which was clammy from exertion. In her right hand, she held one of the silk scarves Jacyl had given her, twisted into a loose cord.

Lyra took a deep breath and leaned her forehead against the cool stone. And she prayed, silently, to any god that had ever had mercy on lovers and lost causes. It was mostly incoherent, but it was heartfelt.

Let this work.

She shoved the door open, making no attempt at silence, and staggered out into the hallway.

Twenty feet away, the guard whirled. He was a burly man, clad in the mandatory white robes, with a cudgel hanging at his side. He looked surprised, but she saw no recognition in his eyes.

"Please, sair," she said, affecting the heavy accent of the Blue Havens, "y've got t' help me."

Suspicion clouded his face. She slumped against the wall, then forced herself away from it and took a few steps. The lantern light was so bright after total darkness that tears streamed from her eyes. All to the good—it made the act look better. She squeezed out several more tears and the beginning of a sob.

"M' teacher," she snuffled, limping closer. "He—he—oh, goddess, sair, it were turrible—"

The guard took a step forward, squinting at her. "Your teacher what, girl?"

Heavens, what did he do? "He—he—(sniff)—made m' get in the crawlspace, sair." Inspiration struck. "Th—the librarians wouldn't let him use some of the books, on account've 'em bein' too fragile an all, and he got mad, and he's got a turrible temper, sair, and he said I had to go find the books and take 'em, but I didn't want to, sair, and he told m' if I didn't get in th' hole and find 'im the books, and bring 'em back he'd beat me, and it was dark, sair, and I fell and cut m' hands, and I don't know where I'm at, and—and—he's goin' to kill me—!"

She drew the last words out in a quiet wail and fell practically at the guard's feet. There was a moment when she could feel the whole thing hanging in the balance, and gritted her teeth, desperately looking as fragile and helpless as she could.

C'mon, sucker, she thought, *just a little closer—*

"There, there, girl," said the guard gently, patting her shoulder. "It's okay."

"Don't make me go back t' the hole, sair!" she whimpered, flinching away from his hands. *Gods, I should go on stage with this—*

"No one will put you back in the hole," he said firmly, picking her up and setting her on her feet. She felt sorry for him. He seemed like a nice guy—fatherly type, kids of his own.

"He'll kill me," she mumbled, and flung herself forward. The guard tensed for a moment, then relaxed and patted her awkwardly as she sobbed piteously on his shoulder.

"There, there," he said. "I've got a girl almost your age." *Suspicion confirmed.* "Who is this master of yours?"

She had her arms around his neck at this point. With a sick dread, she lifted her head and leaned forward to murmur in his ear, drawing her left hand—silk cord held taut, down, across his collarbone. "His name is—" She choked out a last sob.

Then, heart pounding, she wrenched the twisted scarf tight and yanked, throwing her body around the side of the guard. He gagged and reached for her, but she skittered behind him, reacting before even conscious thought, dodging the clumsy swipes of his hand.

He continued to choke, clutching for the scarf. Panic lent unnatural strength to her slender frame as she wrapped the silk around her hands, one knee planted between his shoulder blades, and pulled.

He was no fool. He didn't waste time yanking at the cord. He reached back for her, obviously intending to flip her over his back and onto the ground in front of him.

Oh, shit, what do I do?

She had barely framed the thought when, with a prickly, indescribable feeling, an almost querulous mutter in the back of her mind—the Kytha woke.

In a heartbeat she had the cord wrapped around only one hand, her knee still braced against the back of his neck, driving him down onto the floor. Her free hand snaked around and caught his chin.

This looks like the Broken Branch Kytha, she thought almost dreamily. Her hand tightened on his jaw.

Then she realized what the next part of the motion was.

"No!" she gasped, and tried to pull her hand away before the Kytha gave a quick twist and snapped his neck.

It was hard. It wasn't like not being in control of her body—it was like not *wanting* to take her hand away. Why did she want to move her hand away? It felt so right where it was, so right to put pressure *here,* to move forward, to twist—

"It won't do anything you wouldn't do," Jacyl had said.

She squawked and dropped her hand. The man inhaled as her grip slackened, drawing breath to roar an alarm.

She yanked back, panicking. He was turning purple. The Kytha lingered in her blood, seeking to regain control, finish the move. She set her teeth and fought it back, wondering even as she did so if this was a dangerous thing to begin.

The strangling cord cut off the blood to her fingers as surely as it cut off the blood to his brain. When he finally slumped, she dropped to her knees beside him, hands cradled to her chest, wondering seriously if she would ever hold a sword—or write a word—again. Blood roared back into them, the pricking bringing tears to her eyes.

When she could see without the blurring of tears, she reached out and felt for a pulse.

The guard was alive.

Lyra's breath went out of her like a dying gasp, and she leaned against the wall, panting. She hadn't killed him. *Thank the gods. Spite will probably be disappointed — the vicious little weasel —* she thought wryly, but she had no desire to make an orphan of the man's daughter.

When she caught her breath a little — or rather, when the pain in her hands began to overwhelm her so that she had to focus on something else — she turned to the door set into the wall.

Carvings flickered and seemed to move in the torchlight, a relief of three entwining dragons, their scales inlaid with delicate runes. Lyra's eyes swam as she tried to focus, seeing the slender bodies writhe and move along the stone.

In the curve of one's tail there was a keyhole. Lyra set her teeth and rolled the guard over. She had to get her shoulder under his body and brace one foot on the floor, the other on the wall. Her boots left a print squarely in one of the dragons' open mouths.

There was — the Goddess was being kind — a ring of keys on the man's belt. Lyra picked it up with clumsy fingers, beginning to sympathize with creatures who lacked hands. *How do horses manage?*

Sorting keys with, alternately, her teeth and the crook of her left arm, she finally found a slim, dragon-handled key set with a small white chip of stone. She shoved it into the keyhole, said a brief prayer, and turned the key awkwardly with her elbow.

Something clicked. Nearly weeping with relief, she set her shoulder to the door and shoved it open.

The room was lit by a single candle. Torchlight spilled into the room from behind her, illuminating walls that extended far back into darkness. Rising to his feet, the candle flame making small yellow splashes in the lenses of his glasses, was Trent.

He stared at her with total incomprehension. Lyra slumped against the door frame, stone dragons cool beneath her cheek, and held up the key ring.

"Hey," she said hoarsely, feeling the energy draining out of her like water from a cracked cup, "you busy?"

Her feeble attempt at humor seemed to wake Trent from his trance. "Lyra," he mouthed silently, taking a step forward. Strong fingers closed over her arm.

Lyra didn't bother trying to come up with another clever comment. The wall was holding her upright—that and Trent's grip on her arm. It seemed impossible that she'd actually found him. She seemed to be watching the room from a vast distance.

Shock, she thought clinically, the scholar coolly cataloguing her symptoms. *Pulse weak. Hyperventilating. Body temperature lowering. Not a particularly good sign. Shouldn't be leaning on cold stone, in damp hallways, but you can't always choose the circumstances.*

Trent shoved an arm around her waist and tugged her out of the cell. Color seemed to return to his face as he passed the threshold, and he sank down on one knee, taking in deep breaths like a drowning man.

"Mage-sealed," he said, in answer to her unasked question. "I couldn't do anything—I'd see the patterns, but nothing happened." He reached out and caught her hands. "I can't believe you're really here."

Pain blotted out the rest on his words. Lyra swayed, the pressure on her hands excruciating. "Careful—" she hissed, unnecessarily. Trent was staring at her fingers with a horrified expression. "Had to—*ah!*—crawl through the vents. Banged myself up pretty good."

Trent's mouth worked, but it took a moment for sound to come out. "You. Crawled. Through. The. Vents."

"From the second floor," she said wryly. "Sadrao's making some kind of distraction, but I don't know how much time we have."

"Time enough for this," said Trent tightly. He took her hands as gently as if they had been made of glass, unwrapped the bloody strips of cloth, and set her fingers between his palms. His hands were so large compared to hers that he could hold them both at once.

He closed his eyes. Lyra felt the cool prickle of magic touch her, wrapping around her hands, curiously warm.

There were twin, elastic pains where the small bones had given way. They died away, then, to a vague queasy discomfort. The sharp, digging pains in her hands faded as well, melting into the itch of half-healed cuts and the ache of strained tendon. More than that, new energy seemed to flow into her, restoring reserves spent in endless, labyrinthine ductwork, straightening her stance and soothing the trembling in her muscles.

When the half-elf opened his eyes, she could see weariness reflected in them.

"I can't believe you came," he said, still holding her hands in his. "I didn't think—I never expected—"

"Can't get rid of me that easily," she mumbled, looking down. *I love you, and I don't know what the hell to do about it*, did not seem quite appropriate as a follow-up, so she didn't say anything.

He cupped her face in both hands, shaking his head in disbelief. "You and Sadrao. You've saved me. The Archmage is Vade's tool—he was going to give me to him, tonight or tomorrow, I think."

The cold part of her mind digested that and found it frightening. The less-cold part, which seemed to be in charge of her voice, stared fixedly at a pulse in the hollow of his throat and said, "Ah. Hmmm. Damn."

She was spared the burden of a more articulate response when Trent tipped her chin up, met her gaze with the eyes of a man who may regret what he is about to do, and kissed her.

How odd, thought Lyra distantly, *I nearly killed a man before I ever kissed one. My priorities are not what they could be...*

Lacking anything to compare it to, Lyra couldn't say for certain, but it seemed quite a passionate kiss. A bit wetter than she'd anticipated. She didn't feel her insides melt, like they said in the sagas, but she did get a startling jolt from the pit of her stomach.

Am I going to be sick? That'd be humiliating.

No, it's good. Um. I feel like my chest is full of feathers.

This is a really stupid time to be kissing.

When they broke apart, they looked at each other blankly.

"This is a really stupid time for this," said Lyra, because it was true, and then mentally kicked herself.

"Very true," said Trent gravely. "I think I'm going to do it again."

"Good," said Lyra.

"Absolutely a stupid time for this," she said a moment later, when they broke off again. She was aware that Trent had a vague, silly smile on his face, and wondered if she had one too.

"Yes," he said. He had an arm draped over her shoulders and was rubbing the back of his neck with his free hand, probably because he was a head taller than she was and bending down for a prolonged period of time was painful. "We really should get going."

Lyra gnawed on her lower lip. "Sadrao and I had thought to go back through the vents," she said, "but they're really not big enough for you. And there's a really big drop-off on the main shaft, and no way to climb it."

"So it's the hallways, then?"

"Yeah. I found some white robes, but we're obviously not albinos."

"Mmph."

"Can you conjure some illusions? Something to get us out of here?"

"I'm really not that kind of mage," said Trent.

She blinked at him.

"I can level cities," said Trent dryly. "Creating them or making them look like something else requires a different sort of touch. What I can do without a circle, and runes, and elaborate preparations, is fairly limited."

"You turned yourself into a deer—"

"It took me two months of preparation in secret. I need tools... runes...*time*..."

"Well," said Lyra testily, "what *can* you do?"

"I can stop a heart. Once. I can do some very minor healing. I could destroy a limited amount of metal, a little more of stone. Maybe a door's worth of wood."

"The walls between here and outside?"

"Not a chance."

They sat in glum silence. Lyra's elation at finding Trent was rapidly being crushed under the weight of a hundred thousand books, a stone keep, and a number of armed librarians.

"I can summon lightning," he offered. "Practically anybody can summon lightning."

"Oh, that's *real* useful."

"Sorry. The complexity of a sorcery is in direct proportion to the complexity of its preparation."

"So you could make illusions if you had the time?"

"No, but I could probably summon a demon who could."

"Is that all sorcery is?" Lyra ask irritably. "Calling up demons to do whatever you can't do yourself?"

"In a nutshell, yes."

Give me the Kytha over sorcery any day. It might not work half the time, but at least it's versatile. And fast. Not like all this blood and runes and fire and—

"Trent? Can you start fires?"

"I hope you're not suggesting we burn the books," said Trent stiffly.

"No, of course not." Lyra felt mildly hurt he'd even suggest such a thing. "But if we torched the storerooms, they'll have to contain the fire, and we might be able to slip out."

"Mmmm. Half a moment."

Lyra waited for him to call fire from the air.

Trent pulled a very unmagical fire-starter from a pocket of his robe, flicked the little pyrite wheel several times, and coaxed the sleeve of a discarded robe in flame.

"Knife." She handed him Sadrao's belt knife. He nicked his forearm, dripped three precise drops of blood around the fledgling fire, and cupped his hands over it. His face paled slightly.

"Okay, that should spread nicely. Let's move."

They stepped out the door. "Which way?" asked Trent.

The storeroom ignited with a *whoosh!* behind them. Trent said, "Oops."

"Shit!" They pelted down the hall.

Some minutes later, the white-clad librarians found smoke billowing from the storerooms. In the ensuing panic, as they battled the blaze, no one noticed two more shabby figures in white robes.

Soon thereafter Lyra was pounding down a corridor, trying to look librarianish, when a dark figure stepped out of the stacks and caught her around the waist. She yelped. Trent skidded to a halt, lifted a hand to do something explosive, and saw that it was Sadrao.

"We—we got—he's—Vade—" She started to laugh in sheer relief, tried to choke it back, and hiccupped loudly into the dog-soldier's face.

He put her down with a chuckle.

Trent was less amused. He caught at Sadrao's sleeve. "My cell was right by the fire. They'll see I'm gone any minute now!"

A loud, brazen warning bell clanged somewhere on the upper levels.

"Is that the fire bell, or the prisoner-escaping bell?" Lyra wondered out loud.

"Either," said Iyara Salishi, gliding out from behind a bookcase. Lyra yelped again.

"If that fire spreads, Sandblood, I shall be most irate," said the white dog-soldier serenely.

"It won't," Trent assured her. "It won't burn paper. I made sure. You could smother it with books, in fact."

Iyara raised a grey-whorled eyebrow. "Thank you," she said. And to Sadrao: "The west corridor. Take a left, then two rights. The blue door leads to the docks. I suggest you hurry."

Sadrao bowed, deeply, then leaned over and swiped her cheek with his tongue. He grinned rakishly at her, then followed Trent and Lyra around the corner.

Iyara silently cursed the white skin and nearly transparent fur that made her blush so immediately visible.

A pair of guards appeared. "We're looking for—"

"I know." Iyara cut them off. "Someone already told me. They'll have to get past me to get to the docks. I'd cover the main doors, if I were you."

"Now there's a dangerous woman," said Sadrao admiringly, as they loped out of earshot. "Pity we couldn't stay."

"Pity," agreed Trent ironically, as they burst through the door and down the steps to the docks. Spite waved wildly from the deck of a sloop.

As the ship skimmed out of the harbor, Lyra looked back. Rising wisps of smoke made great white wings over the House of Diamond, but the sea air held no scent of burning.

They gathered in the main cabin of the ship, a motley crew stationed around the single table. Gunnar sat on the floor and Spite sat on Gunnar. Lyra wedged herself in next to Trent and his hand clasped hers under the table.

Sadrao listened to the half-elf's tale of the Archmage's treachery with a grim expression, hackles up and ears back. When Trent had finished, the dog-soldier leaned back in his chair and gave a long sigh.

"Well," he said, after a few moments had passed in which the slap of waves against the hull were the only sound. "This is not good news."

"If the House of Diamond is working for Vade—they've been advisors and allies of the elves for a long time, and they've got to know everything, which means he's got to know everything..." Trent's voice was unsteady. "Plans, communications, codes—it's no wonder the elves haven't been able to mount a resistance. Vade must know everything."

"If he doesn't, he will soon," rumbled Gunnar. And when everybody looked at him, "Your Archmage sounds like he's been playing both sides, but now that the game's up, he's got no choice but to throw in with Vade, and feed him what information he's got left a piece at a time."

"Gunnar is correct," said Sadrao. "And that we cannot stop. But we can stop the elves from being further betrayed. We must get to Anu'tintavel, as quickly as we can."

"Vade knows at least approximately where I am," said Trent quietly. "He will be watching this entire area. I don't dare use magic of any kind, until we're well away." Under the table, his fingers squeezed Lyra's tightly.

"Will the Archmage come after us?" asked Lyra.

"Undoubtedly," said Sadrao. "His only chance is to stop us before we can inform the elves. So we must make the greatest speed possible, and try not to be captured—by either side—along the way."

Epilogue

The dog-soldier is listening.

She crouches on the cold stone floor in a line with her fellow acolytes, while the man who rules them stalks back and forth, hurling invectives. The stone is black beneath her palms, a stark contrast to the mottled white and grey fur on the backs of her hands.

The dog-soldier is afraid.

Iyara is not a warrior, not like the handsome Sandblood who came through the library today, nor like her fierce mother Kygra. She is a librarian. She is afraid of the Archmage, as a dog-soldier should not be afraid of anyone. When the Archmage stops in front of her, she fights to keep her ears erect. The pale fur on the back of her neck is already standing up in spikes.

"Iyara," he says pleasantly. He always mispronounces her name—not enough roll to the "R". Her hackles lift as he speaks.

"You spoke with that dog-soldier today," he says quietly. "One of your own kind. What was his name, again?"

"Sadrao of Sandblood pack," she says, almost inaudibly, and hates herself for it.

The dog-soldier is ashamed.

"The young mage escaped," says the Archmage, his voice growing cold and hard as adamant. "The dog-soldier broke him out of here, out of the House of Diamond! We were charged to keep that young man contained. He is a dangerous fugitive, an incredible prize, and *we let him go!*"

Crouching on the floor, last in the line of hunched and cringing librarians, Iyara thinks that it is not outrage in the Archmage's voice so much as thwarted ambition, some personal hurt that has nothing to do with a service to the elven nation. She thinks of the people who died to serve the Archmage's magic—two she knows of, and how many she does not?

"I'm only going to ask you this once," says the Archmage, and reaching out, he catches Iyara's crest and drags her skull back so that his pink eyes bore into her shocked blue ones. "Did you help the dog-soldier escape?"

The dog-soldier remembers.

Iyara remembers the soft growl of the Sandblood's voice as he explained the honorless way in which his friend had been taken by the Archmage. She remembers the name "Vade," and the curl of lips over fang that accompanied it. And she sees the Archmage, acting not like a jailor who has lost his captive, but like a man cheated of a prize.

She is not a warrior, but neither is she a fool. There is more at stake than keeping a promise to the elves.

She has faith in the honor of the Sandblood pack. Faith enough that when she had joined the search for the fugitives, she herself took the corridors where Sadrao's scent still hung in the air and searched them no more quickly or thoroughly than necessary.

A dog-soldier's honor over a human's ambitions is no choice at all.

The dog-soldier lies.

Iyara looks up into pale, fuming pink eyes and whispers, "No. I tried to find them. I swear."

He looks at her for a long moment, then, evidently satisfied, drops her. Her scalp smarts where his fingers dug into it. She looks at the floor.

Honor does not always lie in the straightforward path, as dog-soldier women have known for generations.

"We'll go after them," says the Archmage abruptly. "We'll send a group. Hasaan, Electri, Moss..." He pauses, then says, "Iyara, you'll go with them."

She bows until her forehead touches the floor, deeply enough to hide her smile. It is all teeth, and there is neither humor nor obedience in it.

Follow Lyra and her friends in their journey from the House of Diamond to Anu'tintavel and witness Lyra's final confrontation with Vade in BLACK DOGS—PART TWO: THE MOUNTAIN OF IRON, *the second and final volume in this series.*

About the Author

URSULA VERNON has built a career as an acclaimed storyteller, whether using illustration, words, or unique combinations of both. *Digger*, her epic fantasy webcomic about a wombat out of her element, has won several Web Cartoonists' Choice Awards and a Broken Frontier Award, and it led to her nomination for the 2006 Will Eisner Comic Industry Award in the category "Talent Deserving of Wider Recognition". *Nurk: The Strange, Surprising Adventures of a (Somewhat) Brave Shrew*, her first illustrated story book intended specifically for young readers, is currently on Oprah's Reading List for kids 10 to 12 years old, and has been adapted into a full-cast audiobook. Her *Dragonbreath* series uses a unique combination of prose and comic panels to recount the fantastic exploits of a young dragon named Danny and his nerdy friend Wendell, and has consistently received starred reviews from Kirkus Reviews, including two entries in their 2010 Best Children's Books list. Both *Nurk* and the *Dragonbreath* series have been Junior Library Guild Selections.

Black Dogs is Ursula's first novel, written prior to her successes with *Digger*, *Nurk*, or *Dragonbreath*. Although still in her teens at the time, the creativity and wry sense of humor that have won her fans world-wide were already well developed.

Ursula currently lives in Pittsboro, North Carolina, where she works full-time as an artist, writer, and creator of oddities. She lives with her boyfriend, his beagle, a small collection of cats, and a large collection of Indonesian masks, all of which mostly contrive to keep her out of trouble. You can learn more about all of her creative exploits at www.ursulavernon.com.